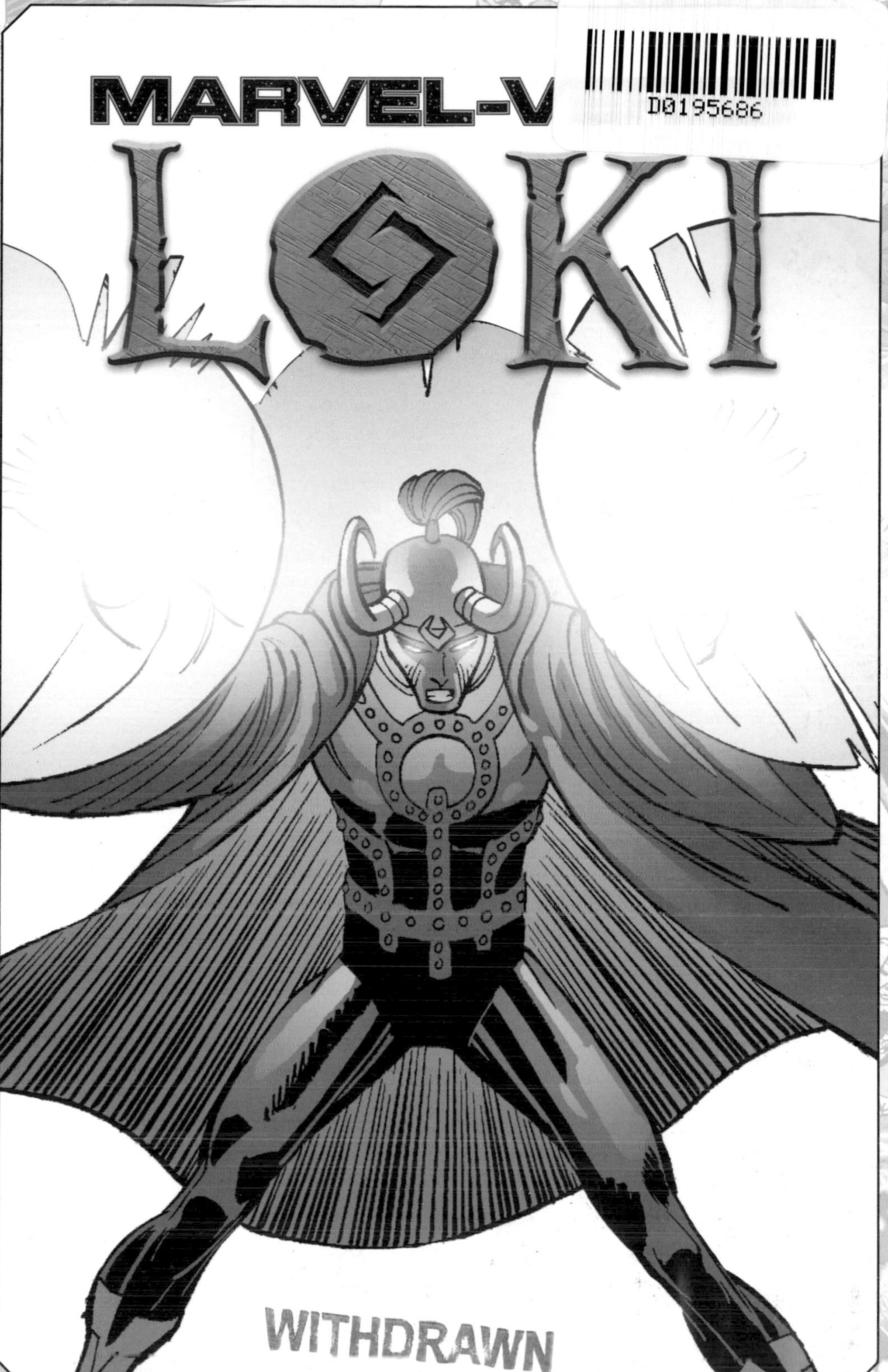
MARVEL-V
LOKI

MARVEL-VERSE
LOKI

SILVER SURFER #4

WRITER & EDITOR: **STAN LEE**
PENCILER: **JOHN BUSCEMA**
INKER: **SAL BUSCEMA**
LETTERER: **ARTIE SIMEK**

AVENGERS #300

WRITER: **RALPH MACCHIO**
ARTIST: **WALTER SIMONSON**
COLORIST: **GREGORY WRIGHT**
LETTERER: **JOHN WORKMAN**
EDITOR: **MARK GRUENWALD**

AMAZING SPIDER-MAN #503-504

CO-PLOTTER: **J. MICHAEL STRACZYNSKI**

CO-PLOTTER & SCRIPTER: **FIONA AVERY**

PENCILER: **JOHN ROMITA JR.**

INKER: **SCOTT HANNA**

COLORIST: **MATT MILLA**

LETTERER: **VC'S CORY PETIT**

ASSISTANT EDITOR: **WARREN SIMONS**

EDITOR: **AXEL ALONSO**

JOURNEY INTO MYSTERY #626.1

WRITER: **ROB RODI**

ARTIST: **PASQUAL FERRY**

COLORIST: **FRANK D'ARMATA**

LETTERER: **VC'S CLAYTON COWLES**

ASSISTANT EDITOR: **JOHN DENNING**

SENIOR EDITOR: **RALPH MACCHIO**

LOKI CREATED BY **STAN LEE**, **LARRY LIEBER** & **JACK KIRBY**

COLLECTION EDITOR: **JENNIFER GRÜNWALD** ASSISTANT EDITOR: **DANIEL KIRCHHOFFER**
ASSISTANT MANAGING EDITOR: **MAIA LOY** ASSISTANT MANAGING EDITOR: **LISA MONTALBANO**
ASSOCIATE MANAGER, DIGITAL ASSETS: **JOE HOCHSTEIN** MASTERWORKS EDITOR: **CORY SEDLMEIER**
VP PRODUCTION & SPECIAL PROJECTS: **JEFF YOUNGQUIST** RESEARCH: **JESS HARROLD**
BOOK DESIGNERS: **STACIE ZUCKER & ADAM DEL RE** WITH **JAY BOWEN**
SVP PRINT, SALES & MARKETING: **DAVID GABRIEL** EDITOR IN CHIEF **C.B. CEBULSKI**

MARVEL-VERSE: LOKI. Contains material originally published in magazine form as AMAZING SPIDER-MAN (1999) #503-504, JOURNEY INTO MYSTERY (2011) #626.1, AVENGERS (1963) #300 and SILVER SURFER (1968) #4. Third printing 2021. ISBN 978-1-302-93082-0. Published by MARVEL WORLDWIDE, INC., a subsidiary of MARVEL ENTERTAINMENT, LLC. OFFICE OF PUBLICATION: 1290 Avenue of the Americas, New York, NY 10104. © 2021 MARVEL No similarity between any of the names, characters, persons, and/or institutions in this book with those of any living or dead person or institution is intended, and any such similarity which may exist is purely coincidental. **Printed in Canada.** KEVIN FEIGE, Chief Creative Officer; DAN BUCKLEY, President, Marvel Entertainment; JOE QUESADA, EVP & Creative Director; DAVID BOGART, Associate Publisher & SVP of Talent Affairs; TOM BREVOORT, VP, Executive Editor; NICK LOWE, Executive Editor, VP of Content, Digital Publishing; DAVID GABRIEL, VP of Print & Digital Publishing; JEFF YOUNGQUIST, VP of Production & Special Projects; ALEX MORALES, Director of Publishing Operations; DAN EDINGTON, Managing Editor; RICKEY PURDIN, Director of Talent Relations; JENNIFER GRÜNWALD, Senior Editor, Special Projects; SUSAN CRESPI, Production Manager; STAN LEE, Chairman Emeritus. For information regarding advertising in Marvel Comics or on Marvel.com, please contact Vit DeBellis, Custom Solutions & Integrated Advertising Manager, at vdebellis@marvel.com. For Marvel subscription inquiries, please call 888-511-5480. **Manufactured between 10/22/2021 and 11/23/2021 by SOLISCO PRINTERS, SCOTT, QC, CANADA.**

10 9 8 7 6 5 4 3

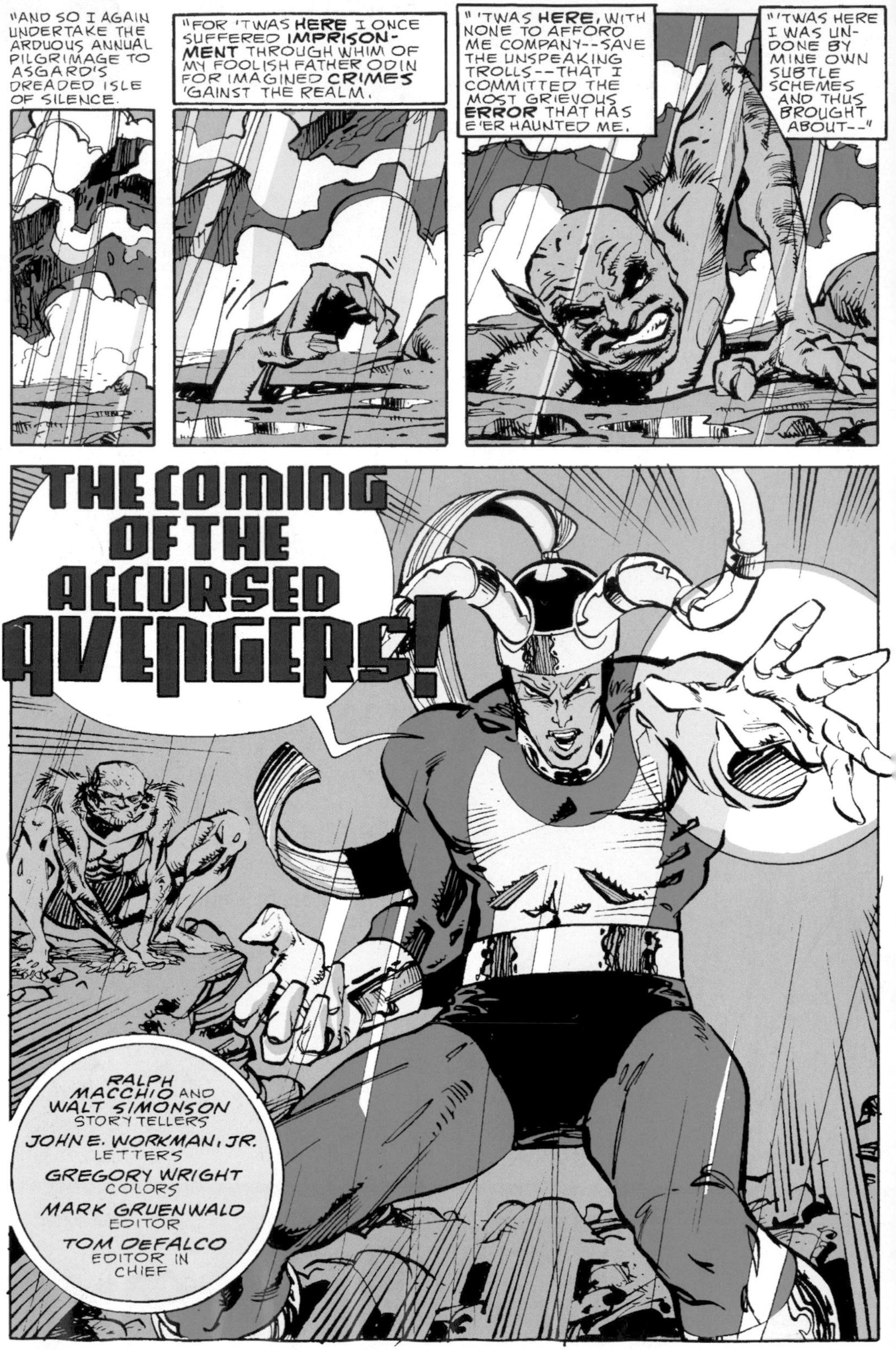
"AND SO I AGAIN UNDERTAKE THE ARDUOUS ANNUAL PILGRIMAGE TO ASGARD'S DREADED ISLE OF SILENCE.
"FOR 'TWAS HERE I ONCE SUFFERED IMPRISONMENT THROUGH WHIM OF MY FOOLISH FATHER ODIN FOR IMAGINED CRIMES 'GAINST THE REALM.
"'TWAS HERE, WITH NONE TO AFFORD ME COMPANY--SAVE THE UNSPEAKING TROLLS--THAT I COMMITTED THE MOST GRIEVOUS ERROR THAT HAS E'ER HAUNTED ME.
"'TWAS HERE I WAS UNDONE BY MINE OWN SUBTLE SCHEMES AND THUS BROUGHT ABOUT--"
THE COMING OF THE ACCURSED AVENGERS!
RALPH MACCHIO AND WALT SIMONSON STORY TELLERS
JOHN E. WORKMAN, JR. LETTERS
GREGORY WRIGHT COLORS
MARK GRUENWALD EDITOR
TOM DEFALCO EDITOR IN CHIEF

AVENGERS #300

IT'S A NEW SPIN ON THE CLASSIC FORMING OF THE AVENGERS AS ONLY LOKI COULD TELL!

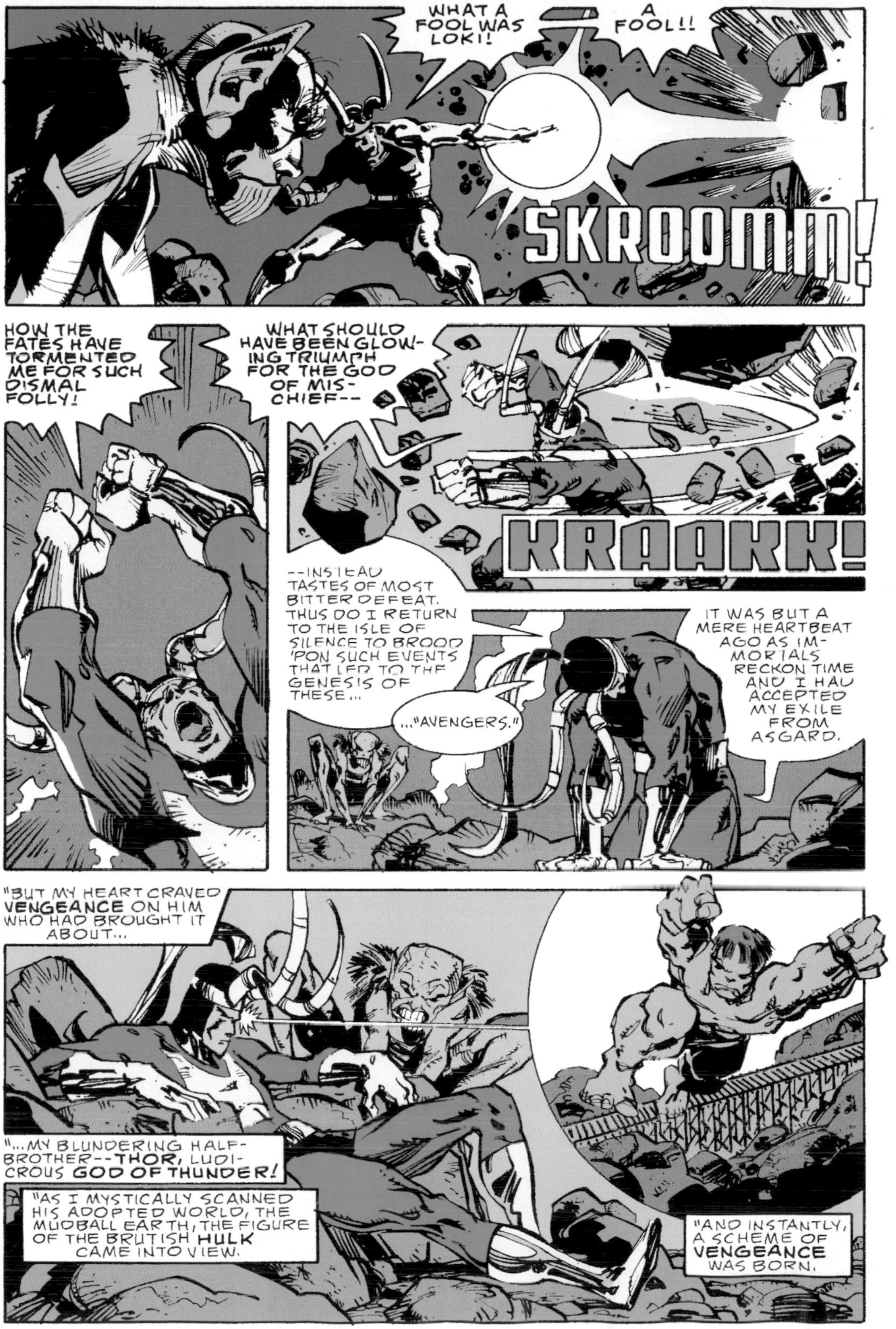
WHAT A FOOL WAS LOKI!
A FOOL!!
SKROOMM!
HOW THE FATES HAVE TORMENTED ME FOR SUCH DISMAL FOLLY!
WHAT SHOULD HAVE BEEN GLOWING TRIUMPH FOR THE GOD OF MISCHIEF--
KRAAKK!
--INSTEAD TASTES OF MOST BITTER DEFEAT. THUS DO I RETURN TO THE ISLE OF SILENCE TO BROOD 'PON SUCH EVENTS THAT LED TO THE GENESIS OF THESE...
..."AVENGERS."
IT WAS BUT A MERE HEARTBEAT AGO AS IMMORTALS RECKON TIME AND I HAD ACCEPTED MY EXILE FROM ASGARD.
"BUT MY HEART CRAVED VENGEANCE ON HIM WHO HAD BROUGHT IT ABOUT...
"...MY BLUNDERING HALF-BROTHER--THOR, LUDICROUS GOD OF THUNDER!
"AS I MYSTICALLY SCANNED HIS ADOPTED WORLD, THE MUDBALL EARTH, THE FIGURE OF THE BRUTISH HULK CAME INTO VIEW.
"AND INSTANTLY, A SCHEME OF VENGEANCE WAS BORN.

"I PROJECTED A **MENTAL IMAGE** 'PON NEARBY RAILROAD TRACKS.

"THE DIM-WITTED HULK SPOTTED IT AS I KNEW HE WOULD.

"HE HEARD THE APPROACH OF AN ONCOMING TRAIN AND ATTEMPTED TO SNUFF THE DYNAMITE BEFORE IT COULD EXPLODE.

"HIS PLUNGE DAMAGED THE TRESTLE AND THE MULTI-WHEELED CONVEYANCE HEADED FOR ALMOST CERTAIN DOOM,"

LOOK! THAT HEAD JUTTING THROUGH THE TRACKS!

IT'S THE HULK! HE DID THIS!

HE'S TRYING TO KILL US ALL! I-I CAN'T STOP IN TIME!

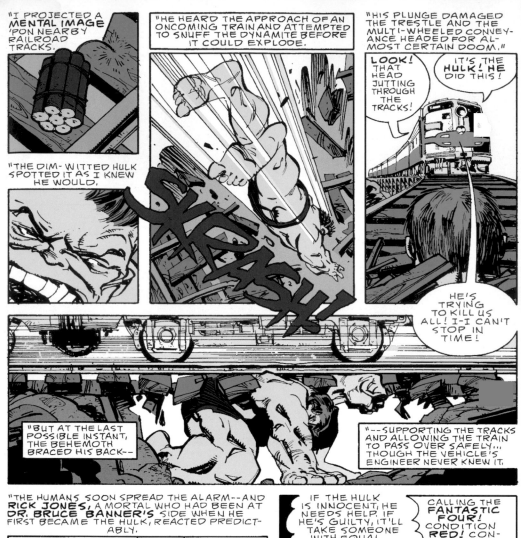

"BUT AT THE LAST POSSIBLE INSTANT, THE BEHEMOTH BRACED HIS BACK--

"--SUPPORTING THE TRACKS AND ALLOWING THE TRAIN TO PASS OVER SAFELY... THOUGH THE VEHICLE'S ENGINEER NEVER KNEW IT.

"THE HUMANS SOON SPREAD THE ALARM--AND **RICK JONES**, A MORTAL WHO HAD BEEN AT **DR. BRUCE BANNER'S** SIDE WHEN HE FIRST BECAME THE HULK, REACTED PREDICTABLY.

IT CAN'T BE!

HULK!

IF THE HULK IS INNOCENT, HE NEEDS HELP. IF HE'S GUILTY, IT'LL TAKE SOMEONE WITH EQUAL POWERS--LIKE THE **FANTASTIC FOUR** TO STOP HIM!

CALLING THE **FANTASTIC FOUR!** CONDITION **RED!** CONTACT THE **TEEN BRIGADE!** HULK MUST BE FOUND!! DO YOU READ ME?

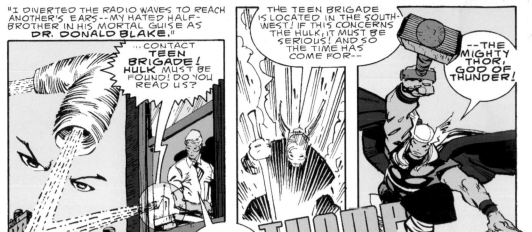

"I DIVERTED THE RADIO WAVES TO REACH ANOTHER'S EARS--MY HATED HALF-BROTHER IN HIS MORTAL GUISE AS **DR. DONALD BLAKE.**"

...CONTACT **TEEN BRIGADE!** HULK MUST BE FOUND! DO YOU READ US?

SOUNDS LIKE A CALL FOR THOR!

THE TEEN BRIGADE IS LOCATED IN THE SOUTH-WEST! IF THIS CONCERNS THE HULK, IT MUST BE SERIOUS! AND SO THE TIME HAS COME FOR--

--THE MIGHTY THOR, GOD OF THUNDER!

THOMP

"OTHER SUPER-POWERED BUFFOONS ANSWERED THE SUMMONS, AS WELL."

WOWEE! IT'S THOR!

IT WOULD SEEM THE GANG'S ALL HERE, EH, LADS?

WHY ART THOU SUR-PRISED? THOU DID SEND FOR ME!

"THE OTHERS' ARRIVAL COM-PLICATED AFFAIRS FOR ME! I NEEDED TO SEPARATE THOR FROM THE REST!"

"A SIMPLE ILLUSION CAST OF THE HULK! NO NEED TO DISTURB THE OTHERS!"

IMPOSSIBLE! MY HAMMER--IT WENT RIGHT **THROUGH** HIM!

'TWAS MERELY A MENTAL IMAGE!

ONLY **LOKI** IS CAP-ABLE OF SUCH WIZARDRY! HE WAS WARNED NE'ER TO MEDDLE IN EARTHLY AFFAIRS!

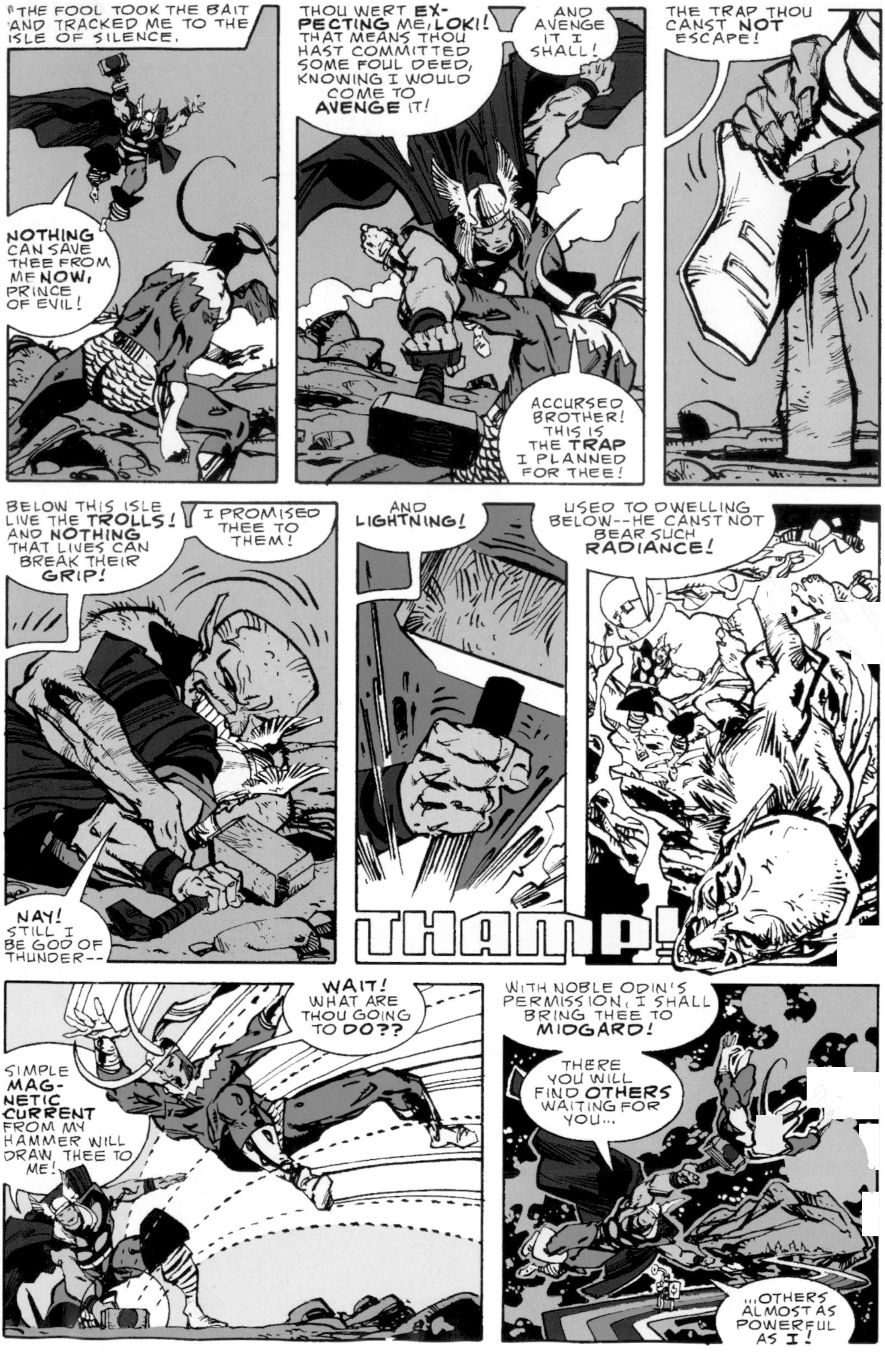
"THE FOOL TOOK THE BAIT AND TRACKED ME TO THE ISLE OF SILENCE.
NOTHING CAN SAVE THEE FROM ME NOW, PRINCE OF EVIL!
THOU WERT EXPECTING ME, LOKI! THAT MEANS THOU HAST COMMITTED SOME FOUL DEED, KNOWING I WOULD COME TO AVENGE IT!
AND AVENGE IT I SHALL!
ACCURSED BROTHER! THIS IS THE TRAP I PLANNED FOR THEE!
THE TRAP THOU CANST NOT ESCAPE!
BELOW THIS ISLE LIVE THE TROLLS! AND NOTHING THAT LIVES CAN BREAK THEIR GRIP!
I PROMISED THEE TO THEM!
NAY! STILL I BE GOD OF THUNDER--
AND LIGHTNING!
THAMP!
USED TO DWELLING BELOW--HE CANST NOT BEAR SUCH RADIANCE!
SIMPLE MAGNETIC CURRENT FROM MY HAMMER WILL DRAW THEE TO ME!
WAIT! WHAT ARE THOU GOING TO DO??
WITH NOBLE ODIN'S PERMISSION, I SHALL BRING THEE TO MIDGARD!
THERE YOU WILL FIND OTHERS WAITING FOR YOU...
...OTHERS ALMOST AS POWERFUL AS I!

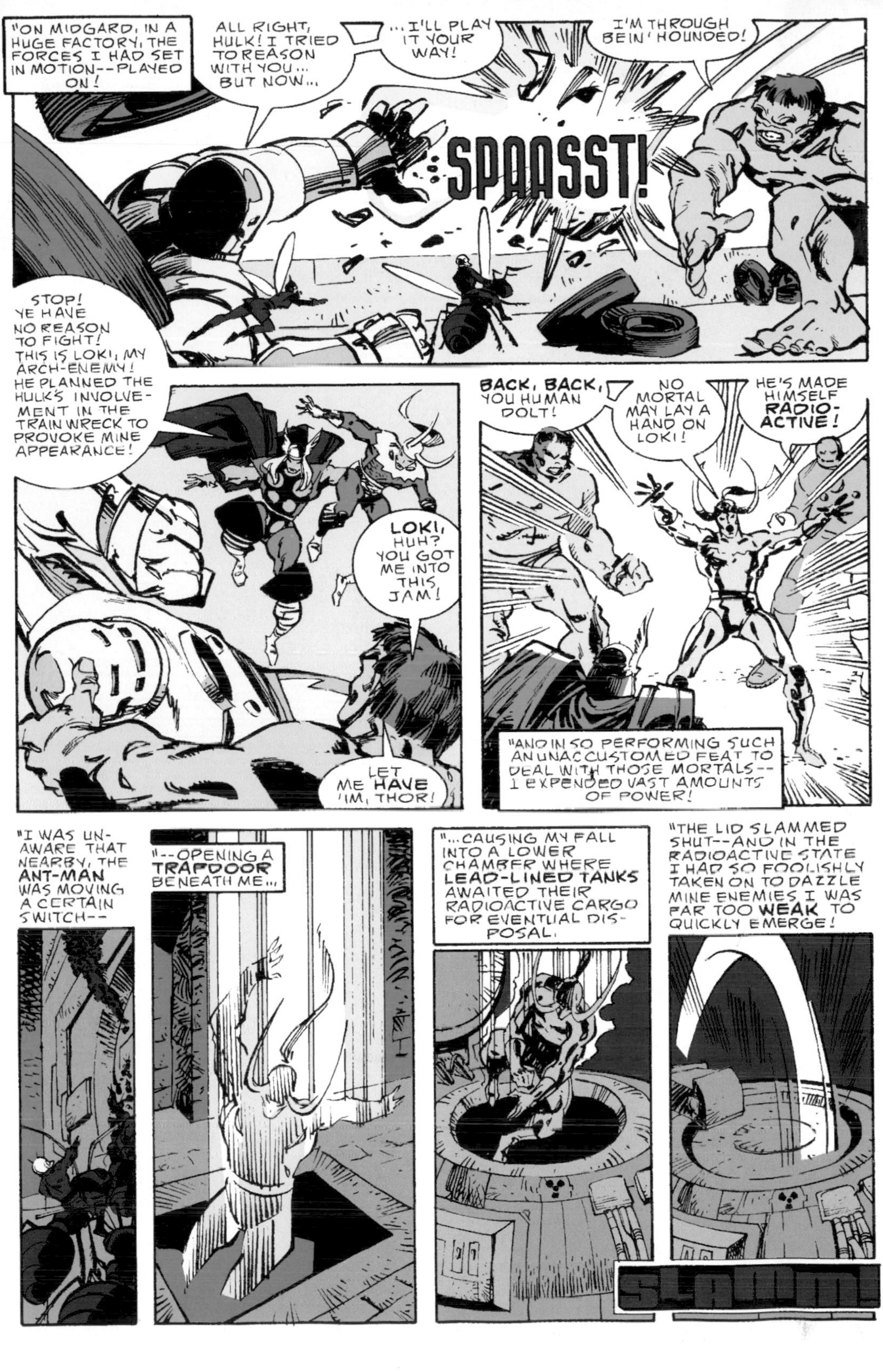
"ON MIDGARD, IN A HUGE FACTORY, THE FORCES I HAD SET IN MOTION--PLAYED ON!
ALL RIGHT, HULK! I TRIED TO REASON WITH YOU... BUT NOW...
...I'LL PLAY IT YOUR WAY!
I'M THROUGH BEIN' HOUNDED!
SPAASST!
STOP! YE HAVE NO REASON TO FIGHT! THIS IS LOKI, MY ARCH-ENEMY! HE PLANNED THE HULK'S INVOLVEMENT IN THE TRAIN WRECK TO PROVOKE MINE APPEARANCE!
LOKI, HUH? YOU GOT ME INTO THIS JAM!
LET ME HAVE 'IM, THOR!
BACK, BACK, YOU HUMAN DOLT!
NO MORTAL MAY LAY A HAND ON LOKI!
HE'S MADE HIMSELF RADIO-ACTIVE!
"AND IN SO PERFORMING SUCH AN UNACCUSTOMED FEAT TO DEAL WITH THOSE MORTALS--I EXPENDED VAST AMOUNTS OF POWER!
"I WAS UNAWARE THAT NEARBY, THE ANT-MAN WAS MOVING A CERTAIN SWITCH--
"--OPENING A TRAPDOOR BENEATH ME...
"...CAUSING MY FALL INTO A LOWER CHAMBER WHERE LEAD-LINED TANKS AWAITED THEIR RADIOACTIVE CARGO FOR EVENTUAL DISPOSAL.
"THE LID SLAMMED SHUT--AND IN THE RADIOACTIVE STATE I HAD SO FOOLISHLY TAKEN ON TO DAZZLE MINE ENEMIES I WAS FAR TOO WEAK TO QUICKLY EMERGE!
SLAMM!

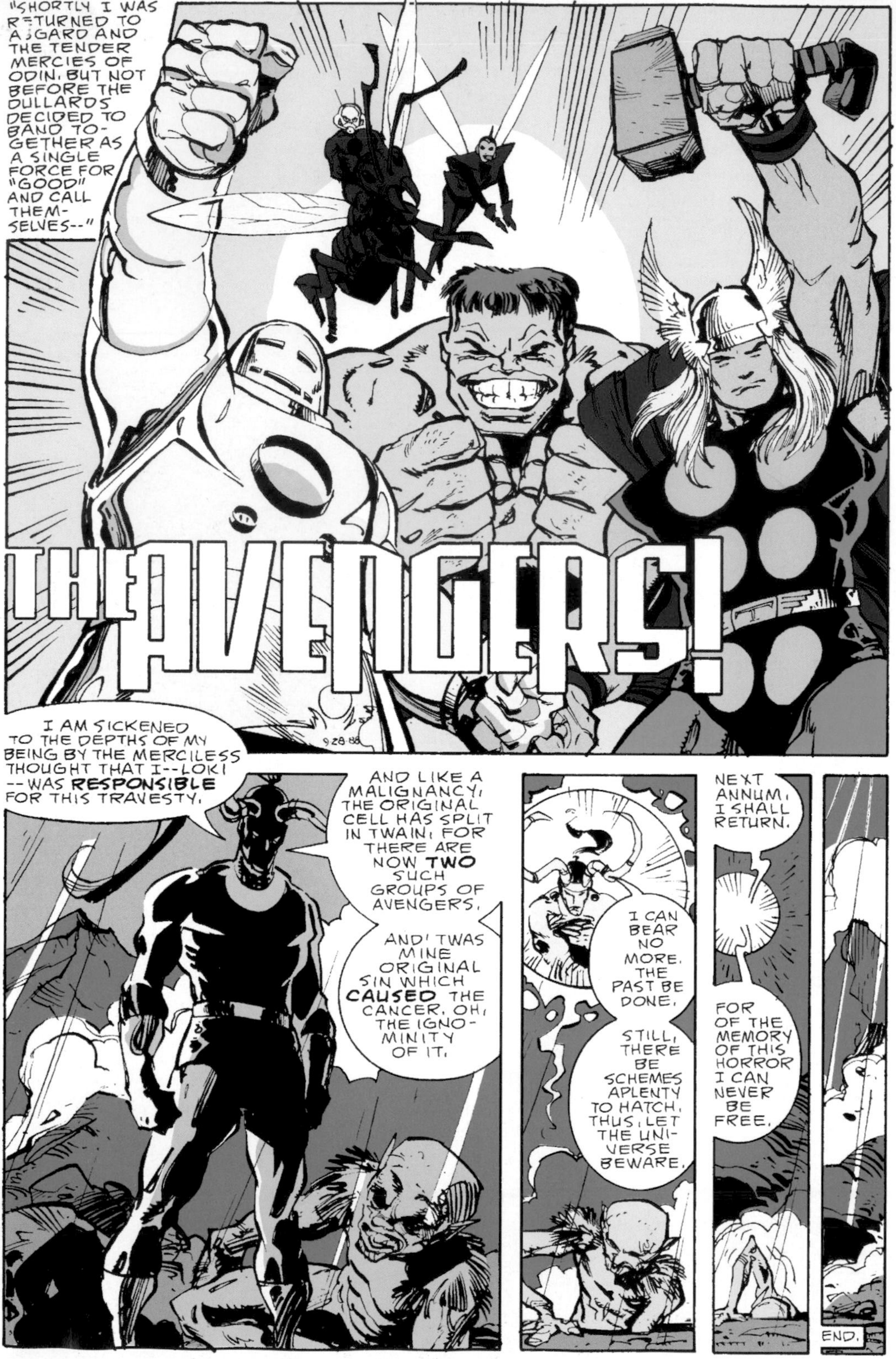
"SHORTLY I WAS RETURNED TO ASGARD AND THE TENDER MERCIES OF ODIN, BUT NOT BEFORE THE DULLARDS DECIDED TO BAND TO-GETHER AS A SINGLE FORCE FOR "GOOD" AND CALL THEM-SELVES--"
THE AVENGERS!
I AM SICKENED TO THE DEPTHS OF MY BEING BY THE MERCILESS THOUGHT THAT I--LOKI --WAS RESPONSIBLE FOR THIS TRAVESTY.
AND LIKE A MALIGNANCY, THE ORIGINAL CELL HAS SPLIT IN TWAIN, FOR THERE ARE NOW TWO SUCH GROUPS OF AVENGERS.
AND 'TWAS MINE ORIGINAL SIN WHICH CAUSED THE CANCER. OH, THE IGNO-MINITY OF IT.
I CAN BEAR NO MORE. THE PAST BE DONE.
STILL, THERE BE SCHEMES APLENTY TO HATCH. THUS, LET THE UNI-VERSE BEWARE.
NEXT ANNUM, I SHALL RETURN.
FOR OF THE MEMORY OF THIS HORROR I CAN NEVER BE FREE.
END.

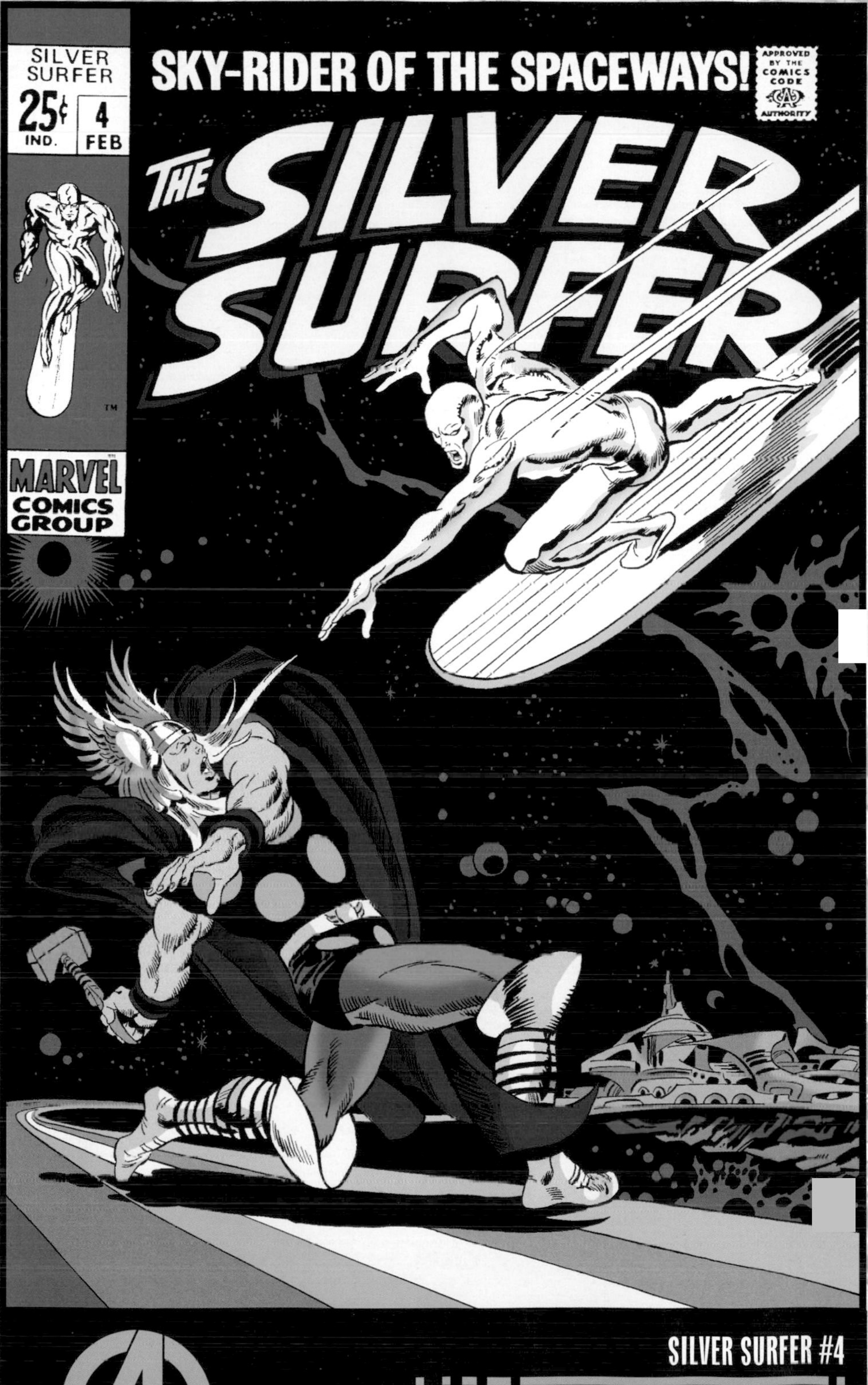
SILVER SURFER
25¢
IND.
4
FEB
SKY-RIDER OF THE SPACEWAYS!
APPROVED BY THE COMICS CODE AUTHORITY
THE SILVER SURFER
MARVEL COMICS GROUP

SILVER SURFER #4

LOKI IS UP TO HIS OLD TRICKS WHEN HE CONVINCES THE SILVER SURFER TO BATTLE HIS BROTHER, THE MIGHTY THOR!

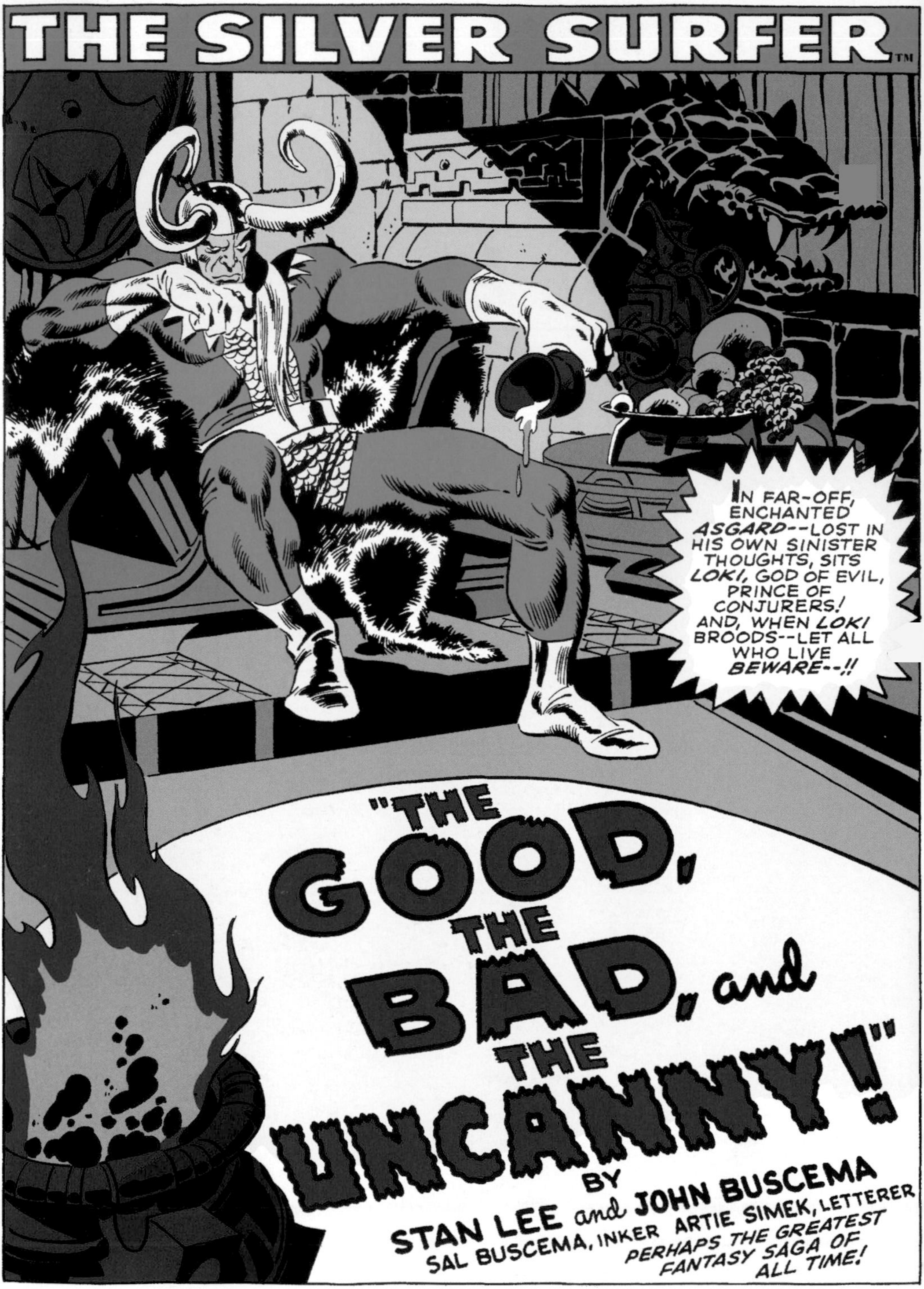
THE SILVER SURFER™
IN FAR-OFF, ENCHANTED ASGARD--LOST IN HIS OWN SINISTER THOUGHTS, SITS LOKI, GOD OF EVIL, PRINCE OF CONJURERS! AND, WHEN LOKI BROODS--LET ALL WHO LIVE BEWARE--!!
"THE GOOD, THE BAD, and THE UNCANNY!"
BY STAN LEE and JOHN BUSCEMA
SAL BUSCEMA, INKER ARTIE SIMEK, LETTERER
PERHAPS THE GREATEST FANTASY SAGA OF ALL TIME!

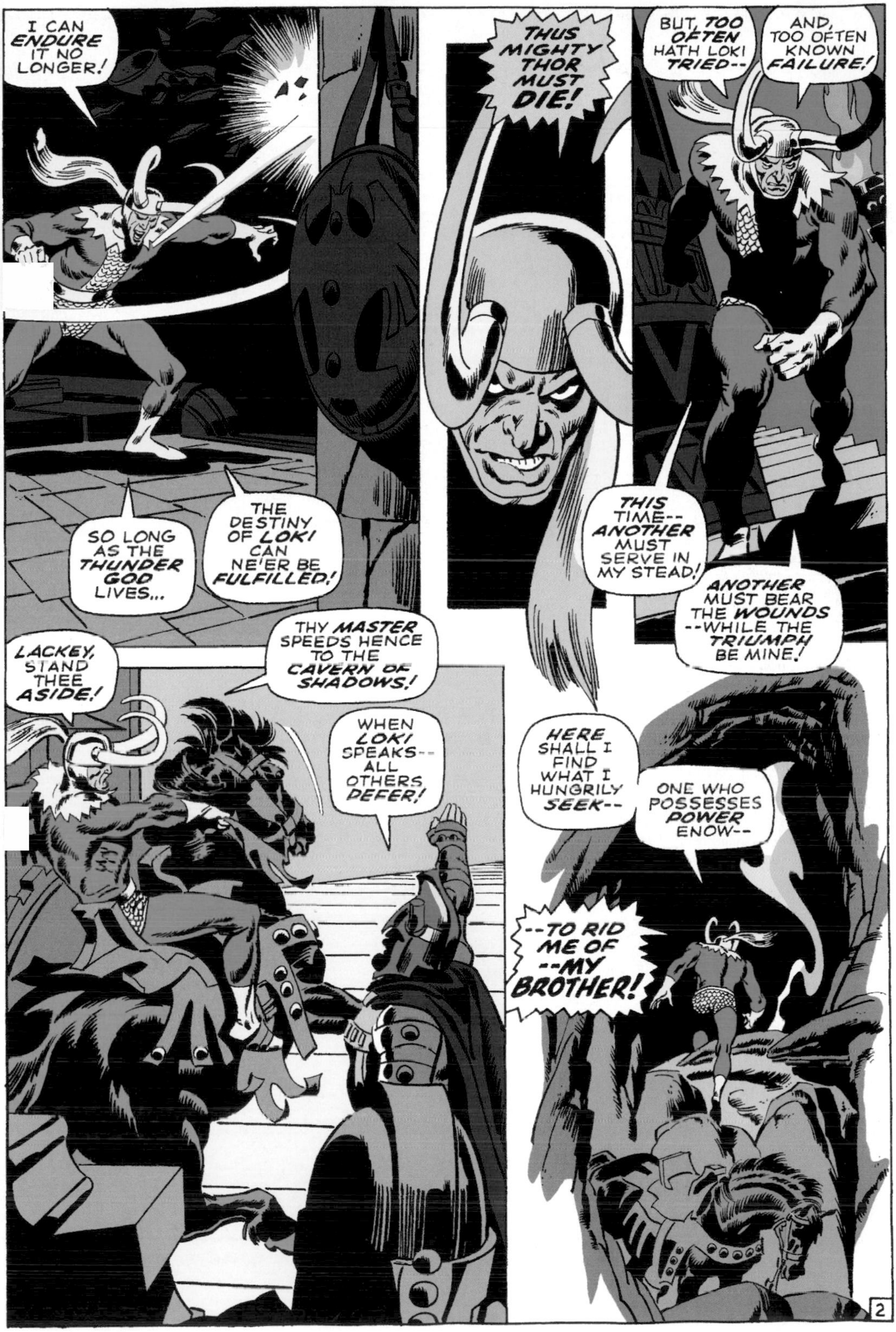
I CAN ENDURE IT NO LONGER!
SO LONG AS THE THUNDER GOD LIVES...
THE DESTINY OF LOKI CAN NE'ER BE FULFILLED!
THUS MIGHTY THOR MUST DIE!
THIS TIME-- ANOTHER MUST SERVE IN MY STEAD!
BUT, TOO OFTEN HATH LOKI TRIED--
AND, TOO OFTEN KNOWN FAILURE!
ANOTHER MUST BEAR THE WOUNDS --WHILE THE TRIUMPH BE MINE!
LACKEY, STAND THEE ASIDE!
THY MASTER SPEEDS HENCE TO THE CAVERN OF SHADOWS!
WHEN LOKI SPEAKS-- ALL OTHERS DEFER!
HERE SHALL I FIND WHAT I HUNGRILY SEEK--
ONE WHO POSSESSES POWER ENOW--
--TO RID ME OF --MY BROTHER!
2

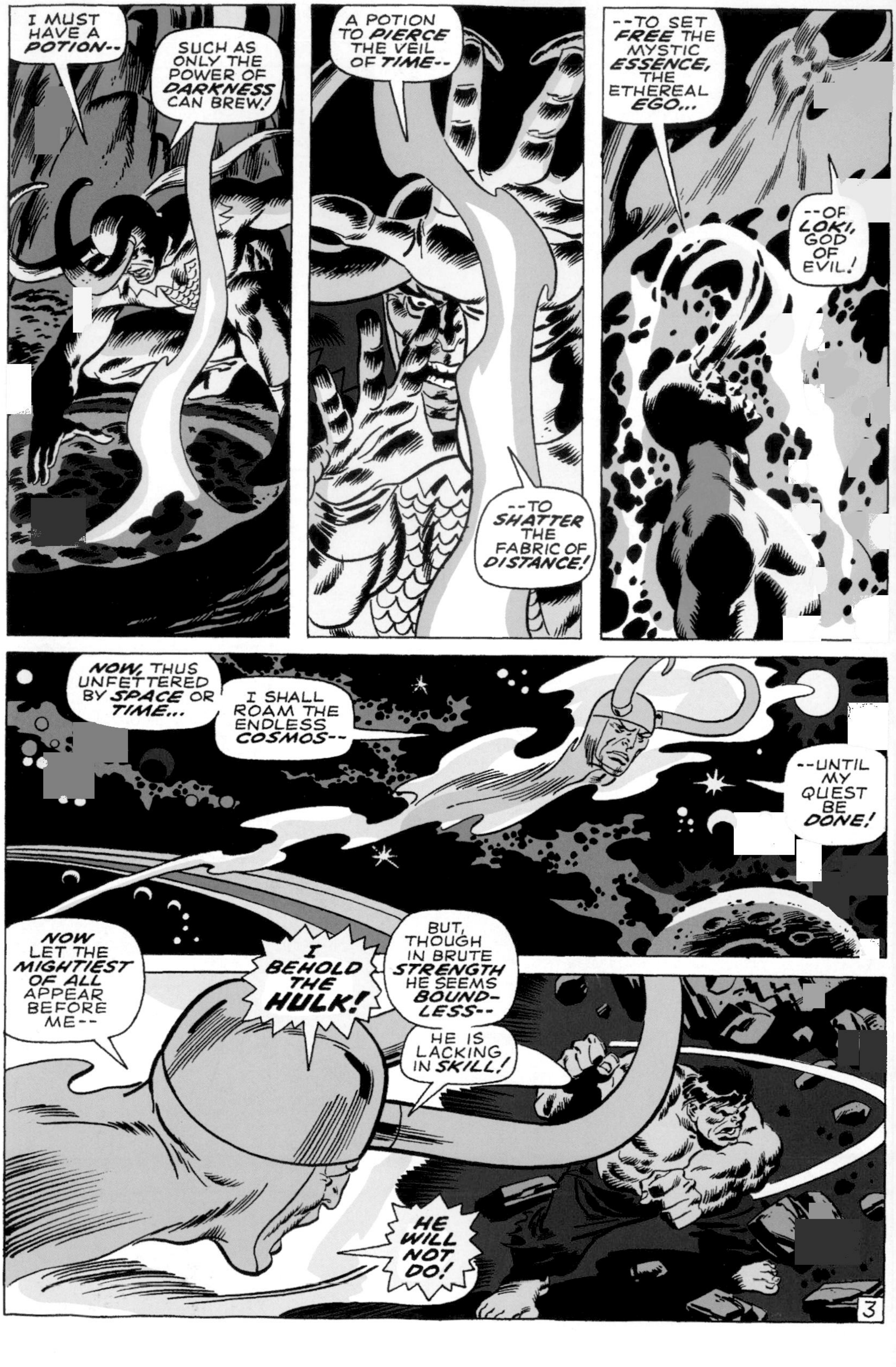
I MUST HAVE A POTION--
SUCH AS ONLY THE POWER OF DARKNESS CAN BREW!
A POTION TO PIERCE THE VEIL OF TIME--
--TO SHATTER THE FABRIC OF DISTANCE!
--TO SET FREE THE MYSTIC ESSENCE, THE ETHEREAL EGO...
--OF LOKI, GOD OF EVIL!
NOW, THUS UNFETTERED BY SPACE OR TIME...
I SHALL ROAM THE ENDLESS COSMOS--
--UNTIL MY QUEST BE DONE!
NOW LET THE MIGHTIEST OF ALL APPEAR BEFORE ME--
I BEHOLD THE HULK!
BUT, THOUGH IN BRUTE STRENGTH HE SEEMS BOUNDLESS--
HE IS LACKING IN SKILL!
HE WILL NOT DO!
3

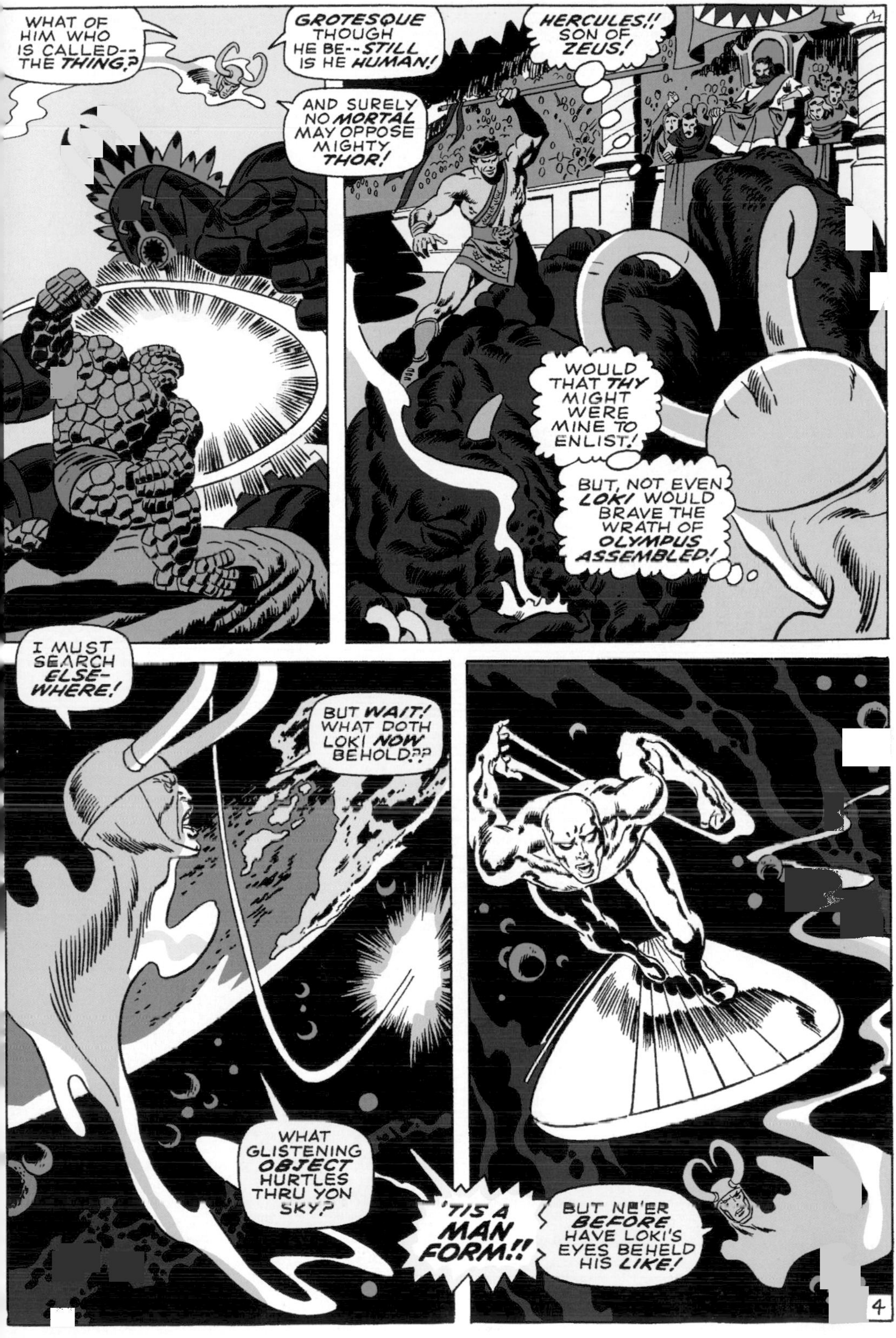
WHAT OF HIM WHO IS CALLED-- THE THING?
GROTESQUE THOUGH HE BE--STILL IS HE HUMAN!
AND SURELY NO MORTAL MAY OPPOSE MIGHTY THOR!
HERCULES!! SON OF ZEUS!
WOULD THAT THY MIGHT WERE MINE TO ENLIST!
BUT, NOT EVEN LOKI WOULD BRAVE THE WRATH OF OLYMPUS ASSEMBLED!
I MUST SEARCH ELSE-WHERE!
BUT WAIT! WHAT DOTH LOKI NOW BEHOLD??
WHAT GLISTENING OBJECT HURTLES THRU YON SKY?
'TIS A MAN FORM!!
BUT NE'ER BEFORE HAVE LOKI'S EYES BEHELD HIS LIKE!

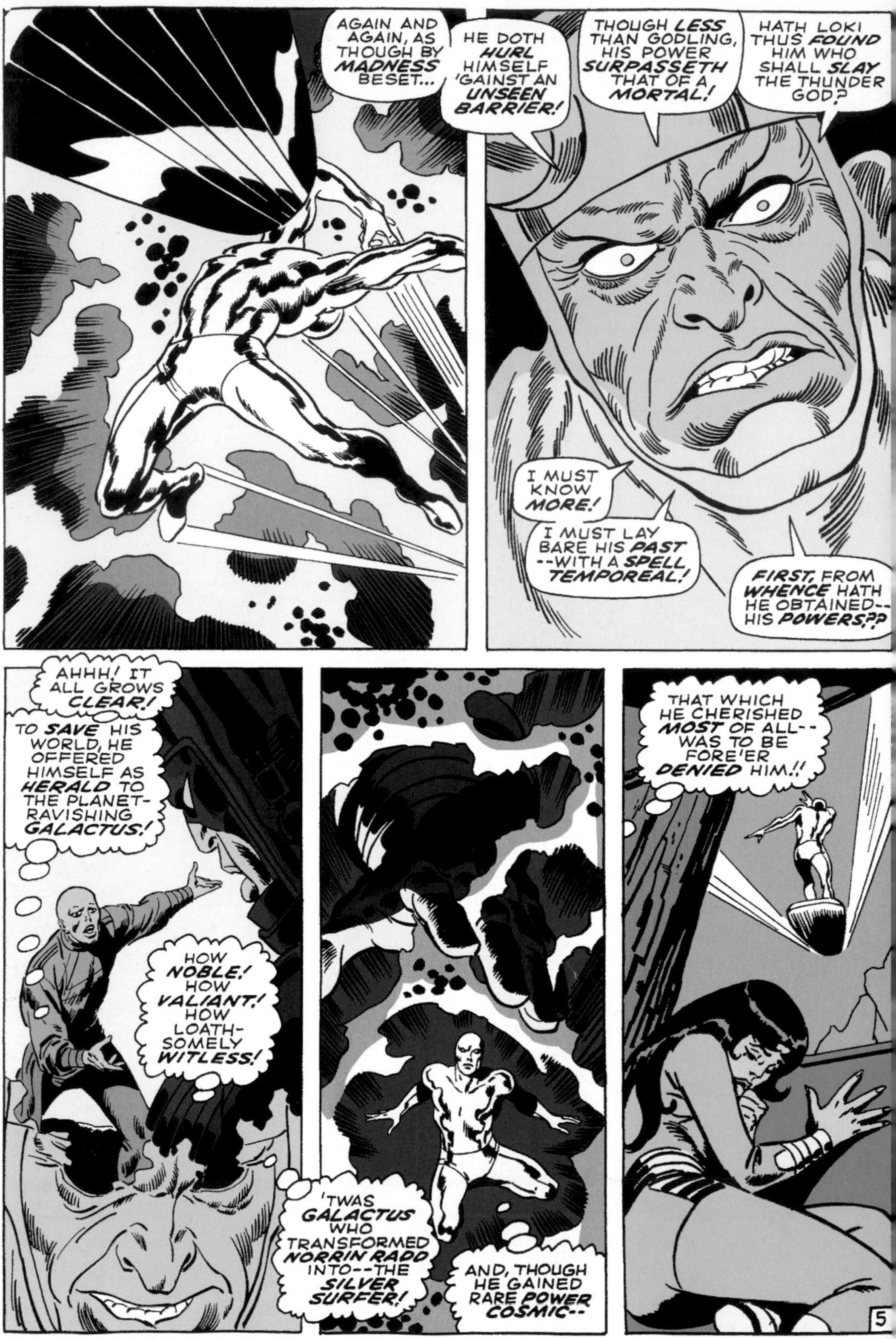
AGAIN AND AGAIN, AS THOUGH BY MADNESS BESET...
HE DOTH HURL HIMSELF 'GAINST AN UNSEEN BARRIER!
THOUGH LESS THAN GODLING, HIS POWER SURPASSETH THAT OF A MORTAL!
HATH LOKI THUS FOUND HIM WHO SHALL SLAY THE THUNDER GOD?
I MUST KNOW MORE!
I MUST LAY BARE HIS PAST --WITH A SPELL TEMPOREAL!
FIRST, FROM WHENCE HATH HE OBTAINED-- HIS POWERS??
AHHH! IT ALL GROWS CLEAR!
TO SAVE HIS WORLD, HE OFFERED HIMSELF AS HERALD TO THE PLANET-RAVISHING GALACTUS!
HOW NOBLE! HOW VALIANT! HOW LOATH-SOMELY WITLESS!
'TWAS GALACTUS WHO TRANSFORMED NORRIN RADD INTO--THE SILVER SURFER!
AND, THOUGH HE GAINED RARE POWER COSMIC--
THAT WHICH HE CHERISHED MOST OF ALL-- WAS TO BE FORE'ER DENIED HIM!!
5

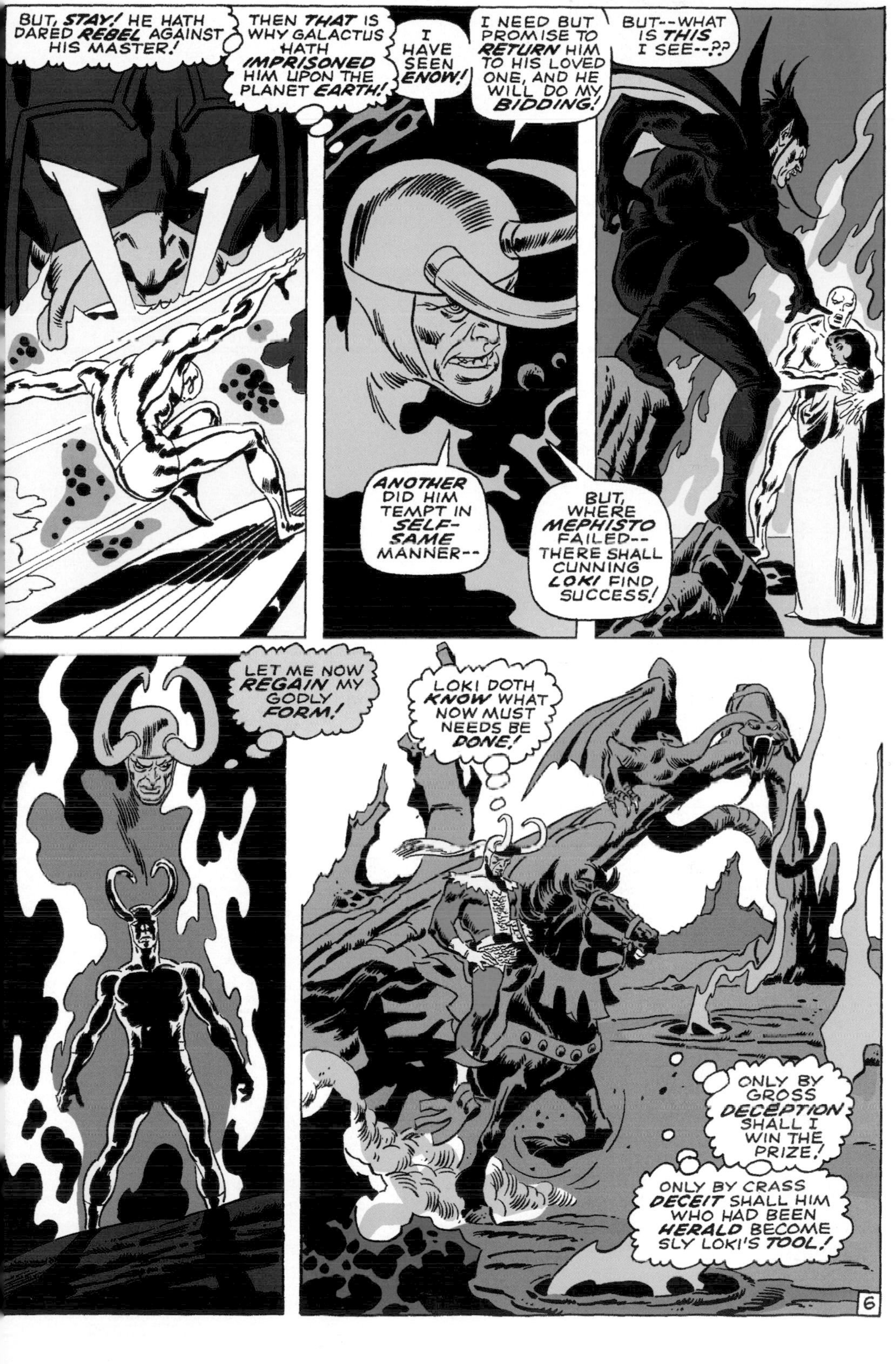
BUT, STAY! HE HATH DARED REBEL AGAINST HIS MASTER!
THEN THAT IS WHY GALACTUS HATH IMPRISONED HIM UPON THE PLANET EARTH!
I HAVE SEEN ENOW!
ANOTHER DID HIM TEMPT IN SELF-SAME MANNER--
I NEED BUT PROMISE TO RETURN HIM TO HIS LOVED ONE, AND HE WILL DO MY BIDDING!
BUT, WHERE MEPHISTO FAILED-- THERE SHALL CUNNING LOKI FIND SUCCESS!
BUT--WHAT IS THIS I SEE--??
LET ME NOW REGAIN MY GODLY FORM!
LOKI DOTH KNOW WHAT NOW MUST NEEDS BE DONE!
ONLY BY GROSS DECEPTION SHALL I WIN THE PRIZE!
ONLY BY CRASS DECEIT SHALL HIM WHO HAD BEEN HERALD BECOME SLY LOKI'S TOOL!
6

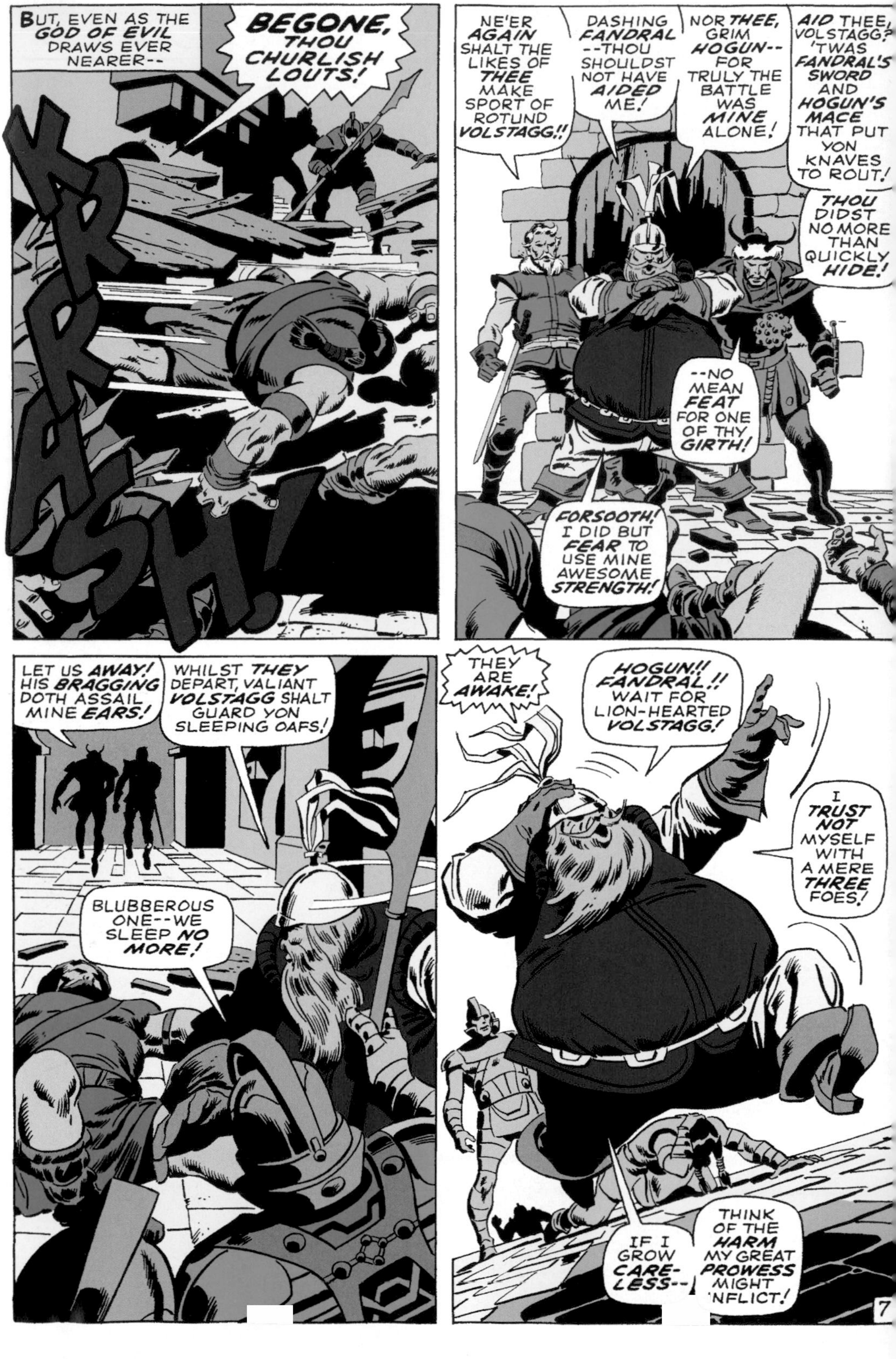

BUT, EVEN AS THE GOD OF EVIL DRAWS EVER NEARER--
BEGONE, THOU CHURLISH LOUTS!
KRRAASH!
NE'ER AGAIN SHALT THE LIKES OF THEE MAKE SPORT OF ROTUND VOLSTAGG!!
DASHING FANDRAL --THOU SHOULDST NOT HAVE AIDED ME!
NOR THEE, GRIM HOGUN-- FOR TRULY THE BATTLE WAS MINE ALONE!
AID THEE, VOLSTAGG? 'TWAS FANDRAL'S SWORD AND HOGUN'S MACE THAT PUT YON KNAVES TO ROUT!
THOU DIDST NO MORE THAN QUICKLY HIDE!
--NO MEAN FEAT FOR ONE OF THY GIRTH!
FORSOOTH! I DID BUT FEAR TO USE MINE AWESOME STRENGTH!
LET US AWAY! HIS BRAGGING DOTH ASSAIL MINE EARS!
WHILST THEY DEPART, VALIANT VOLSTAGG SHALT GUARD YON SLEEPING OAFS!
BLUBBEROUS ONE--WE SLEEP NO MORE!
THEY ARE AWAKE!
HOGUN!! FANDRAL!! WAIT FOR LION-HEARTED VOLSTAGG!
I TRUST NOT MYSELF WITH A MERE THREE FOES!
IF I GROW CARE- LESS--
THINK OF THE HARM MY GREAT PROWESS MIGHT INFLICT!

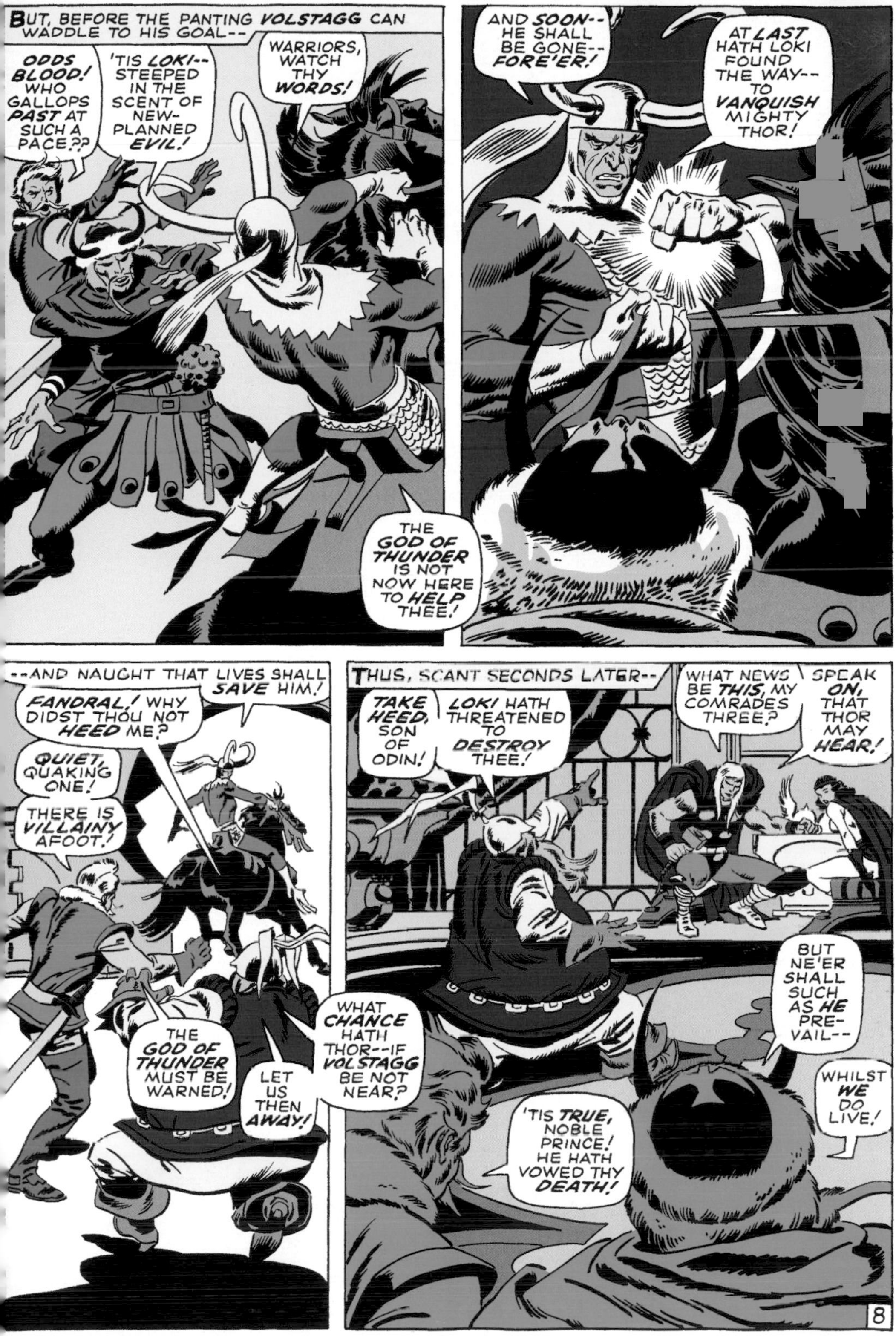
BUT, BEFORE THE PANTING VOLSTAGG CAN WADDLE TO HIS GOAL--
ODDS BLOOD! WHO GALLOPS PAST AT SUCH A PACE??
'TIS LOKI-- STEEPED IN THE SCENT OF NEW-PLANNED EVIL!
WARRIORS, WATCH THY WORDS!
AND SOON-- HE SHALL BE GONE-- FORE'ER!
AT LAST HATH LOKI FOUND THE WAY-- TO VANQUISH MIGHTY THOR!
THE GOD OF THUNDER IS NOT NOW HERE TO HELP THEE!
--AND NAUGHT THAT LIVES SHALL SAVE HIM!
FANDRAL! WHY DIDST THOU NOT HEED ME?
QUIET, QUAKING ONE!
THERE IS VILLAINY AFOOT!
THE GOD OF THUNDER MUST BE WARNED!
LET US THEN AWAY!
WHAT CHANCE HATH THOR--IF VOLSTAGG BE NOT NEAR?
THUS, SCANT SECONDS LATER--
TAKE HEED, SON OF ODIN!
LOKI HATH THREATENED TO DESTROY THEE!
WHAT NEWS BE THIS, MY COMRADES THREE?
SPEAK ON, THAT THOR MAY HEAR!
BUT NE'ER SHALL SUCH AS HE PRE-VAIL--
WHILST WE DO LIVE!
'TIS TRUE, NOBLE PRINCE! HE HATH VOWED THY DEATH!
8

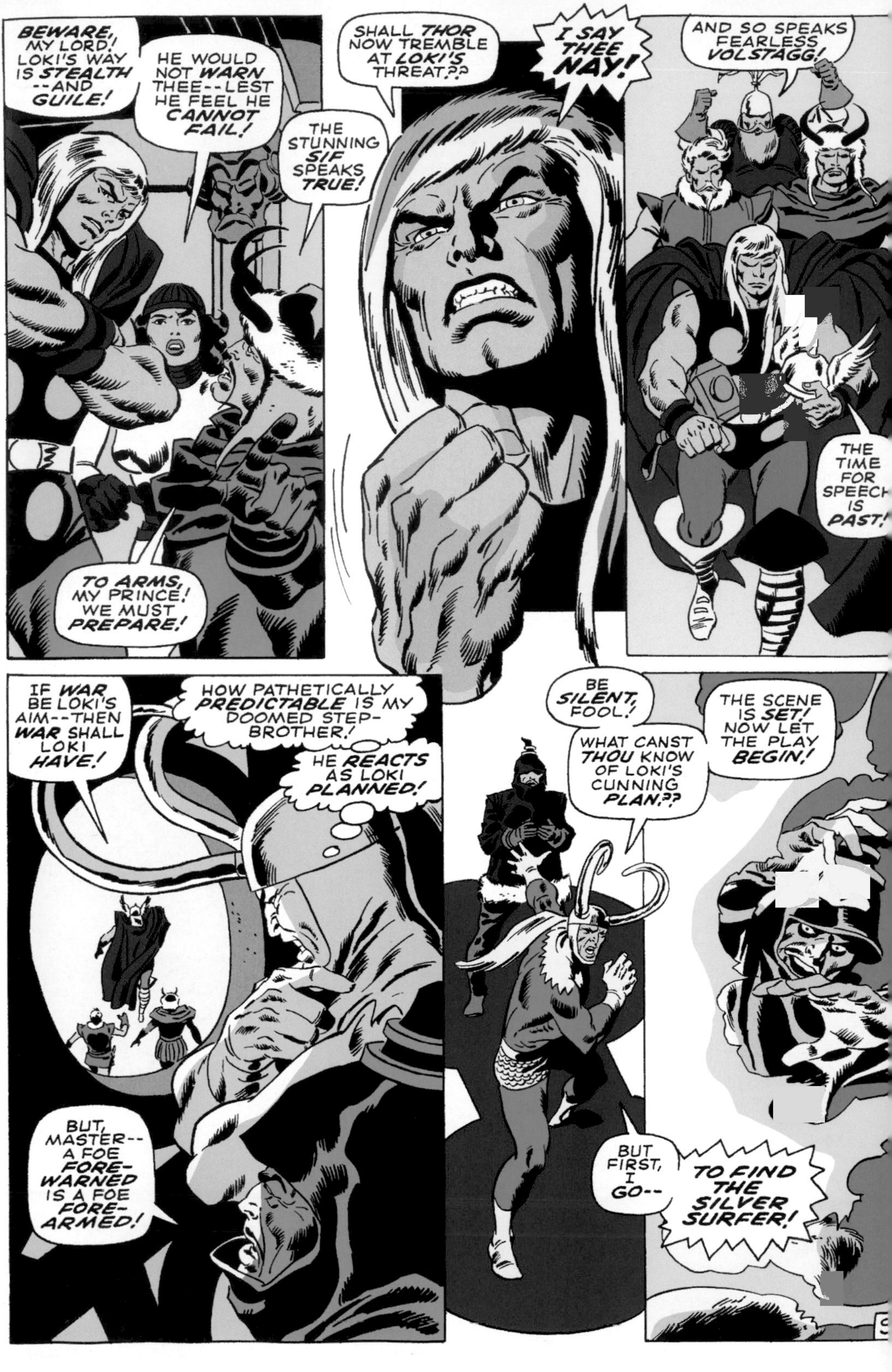
BEWARE, MY LORD! LOKI'S WAY IS STEALTH --AND GUILE!
HE WOULD NOT WARN THEE--LEST HE FEEL HE CANNOT FAIL!
THE STUNNING SIF SPEAKS TRUE!
TO ARMS, MY PRINCE! WE MUST PREPARE!
SHALL THOR NOW TREMBLE AT LOKI'S THREAT??
I SAY THEE NAY!
AND SO SPEAKS FEARLESS VOLSTAGG!
THE TIME FOR SPEECH IS PAST!
IF WAR BE LOKI'S AIM--THEN WAR SHALL LOKI HAVE!
HOW PATHETICALLY PREDICTABLE IS MY DOOMED STEP-BROTHER!
HE REACTS AS LOKI PLANNED!
BUT, MASTER--A FOE FORE-WARNED IS A FOE FORE-ARMED!
BE SILENT, FOOL!
WHAT CANST THOU KNOW OF LOKI'S CUNNING PLAN??
THE SCENE IS SET! NOW LET THE PLAY BEGIN!
BUT FIRST, I GO--
TO FIND THE SILVER SURFER!

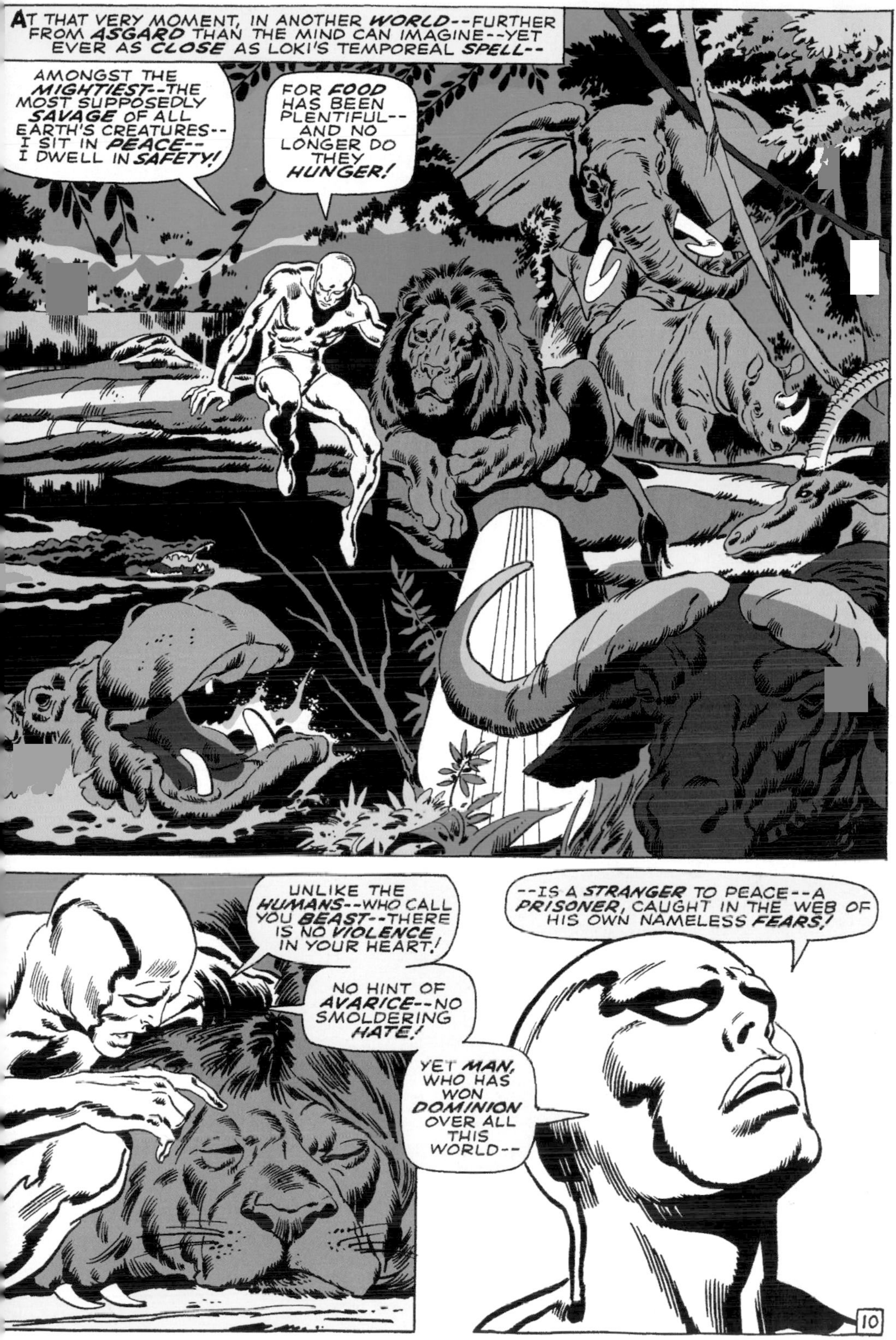
AT THAT VERY MOMENT, IN ANOTHER WORLD--FURTHER FROM ASGARD THAN THE MIND CAN IMAGINE--YET EVER AS CLOSE AS LOKI'S TEMPOREAL SPELL--
AMONGST THE MIGHTIEST--THE MOST SUPPOSEDLY SAVAGE OF ALL EARTH'S CREATURES--I SIT IN PEACE--I DWELL IN SAFETY!
FOR FOOD HAS BEEN PLENTIFUL--AND NO LONGER DO THEY HUNGER!
UNLIKE THE HUMANS--WHO CALL YOU BEAST--THERE IS NO VIOLENCE IN YOUR HEART!
NO HINT OF AVARICE--NO SMOLDERING HATE!
YET MAN, WHO HAS WON DOMINION OVER ALL THIS WORLD--
--IS A STRANGER TO PEACE--A PRISONER, CAUGHT IN THE WEB OF HIS OWN NAMELESS FEARS!
10

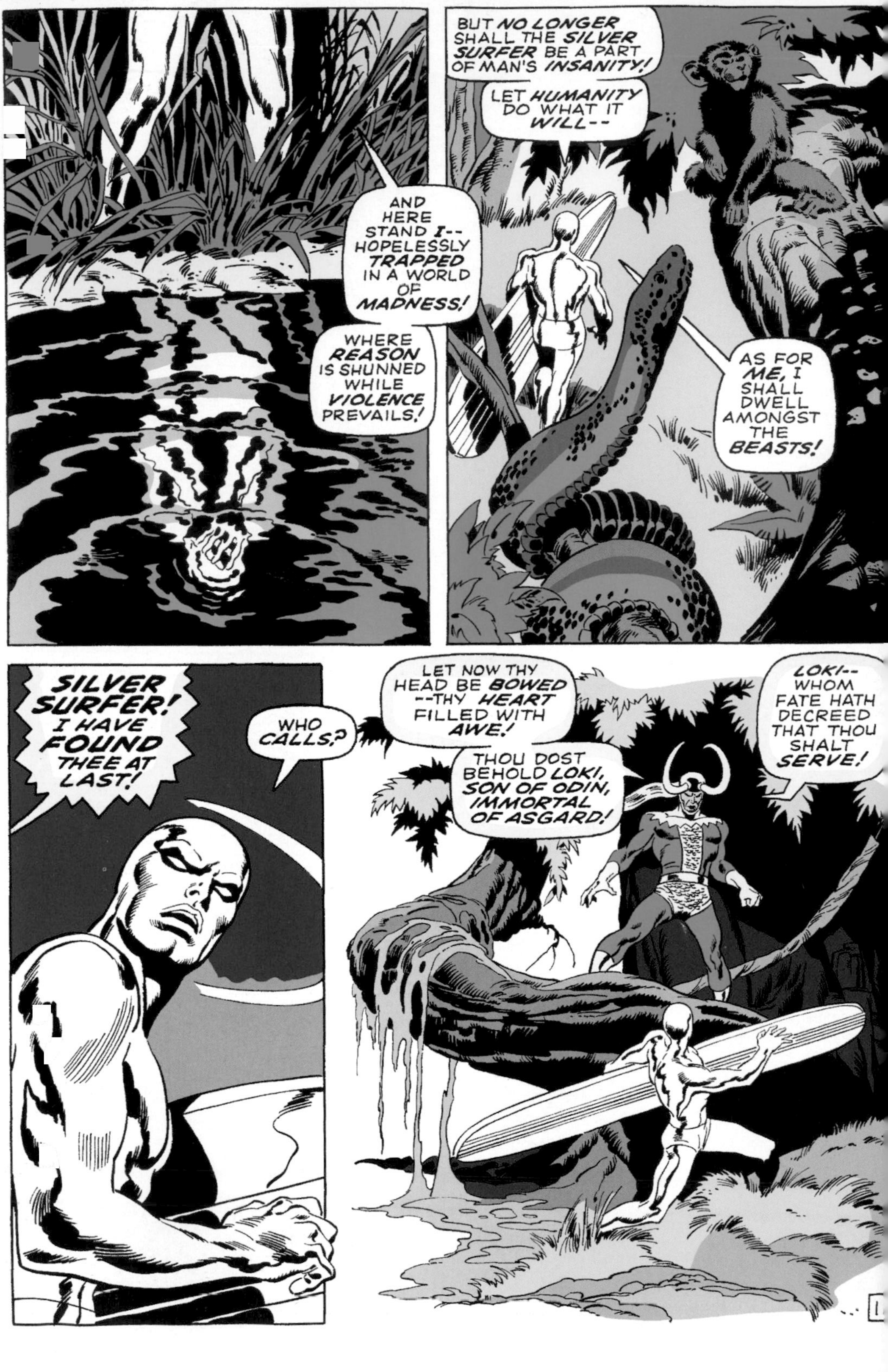
AND HERE STAND I-- HOPELESSLY TRAPPED IN A WORLD OF MADNESS!
WHERE REASON IS SHUNNED WHILE VIOLENCE PREVAILS!
BUT NO LONGER SHALL THE SILVER SURFER BE A PART OF MAN'S INSANITY!
LET HUMANITY DO WHAT IT WILL--
AS FOR ME, I SHALL DWELL AMONGST THE BEASTS!
SILVER SURFER! I HAVE FOUND THEE AT LAST!
WHO CALLS?
LET NOW THY HEAD BE BOWED --THY HEART FILLED WITH AWE!
THOU DOST BEHOLD LOKI, SON OF ODIN, IMMORTAL OF ASGARD!
LOKI-- WHOM FATE HATH DECREED THAT THOU SHALT SERVE!

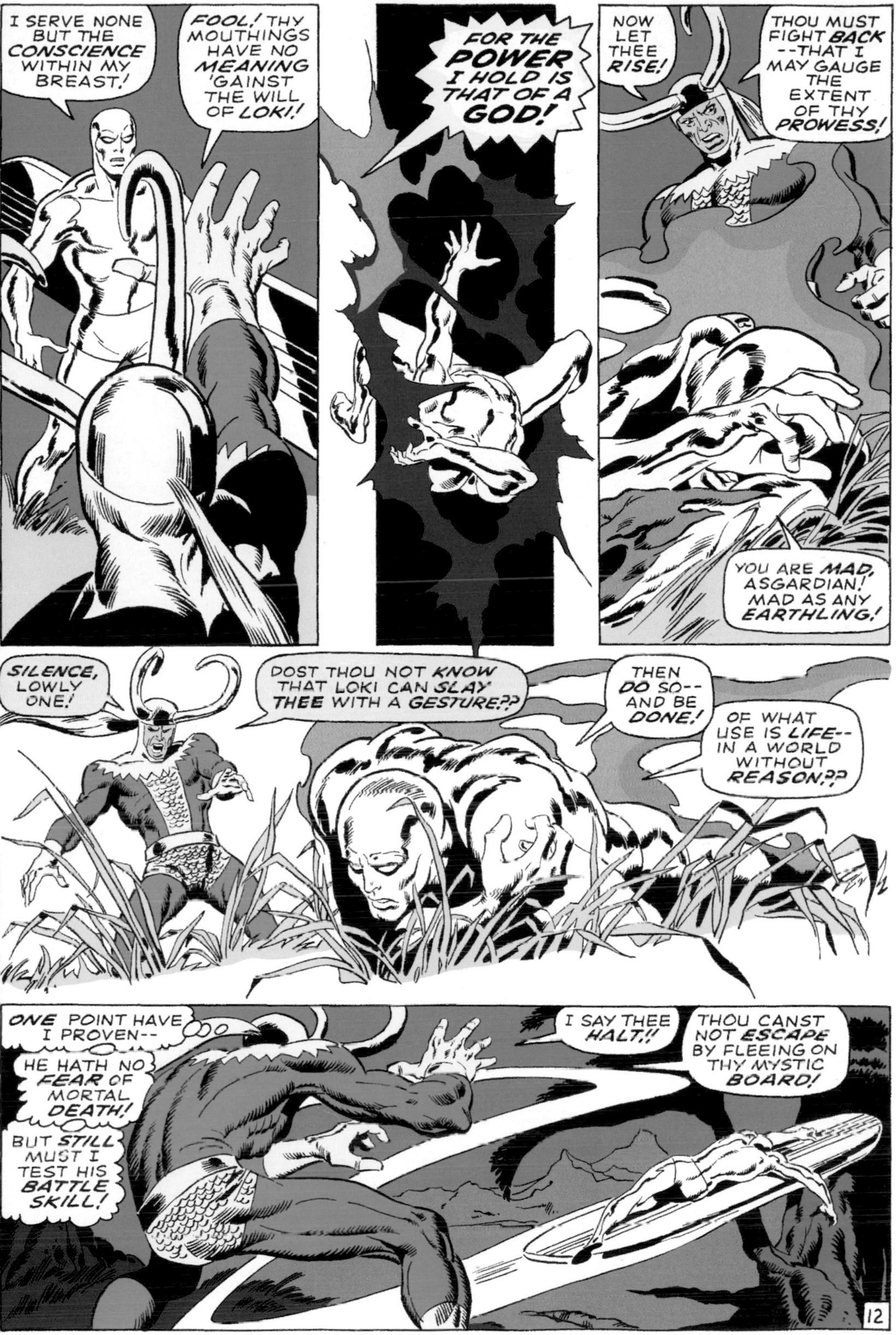
I SERVE NONE BUT THE CONSCIENCE WITHIN MY BREAST!
FOOL! THY MOUTHINGS HAVE NO MEANING 'GAINST THE WILL OF LOKI!
FOR THE POWER I HOLD IS THAT OF A GOD!
NOW LET THEE RISE!
THOU MUST FIGHT BACK --THAT I MAY GAUGE THE EXTENT OF THY PROWESS!
YOU ARE MAD, ASGARDIAN! MAD AS ANY EARTHLING!
SILENCE, LOWLY ONE!
DOST THOU NOT KNOW THAT LOKI CAN SLAY THEE WITH A GESTURE??
THEN DO SO-- AND BE DONE!
OF WHAT USE IS LIFE-- IN A WORLD WITHOUT REASON??
ONE POINT HAVE I PROVEN--
HE HATH NO FEAR OF MORTAL DEATH!
BUT STILL MUST I TEST HIS BATTLE SKILL!
I SAY THEE HALT!!
THOU CANST NOT ESCAPE BY FLEEING ON THY MYSTIC BOARD!
12

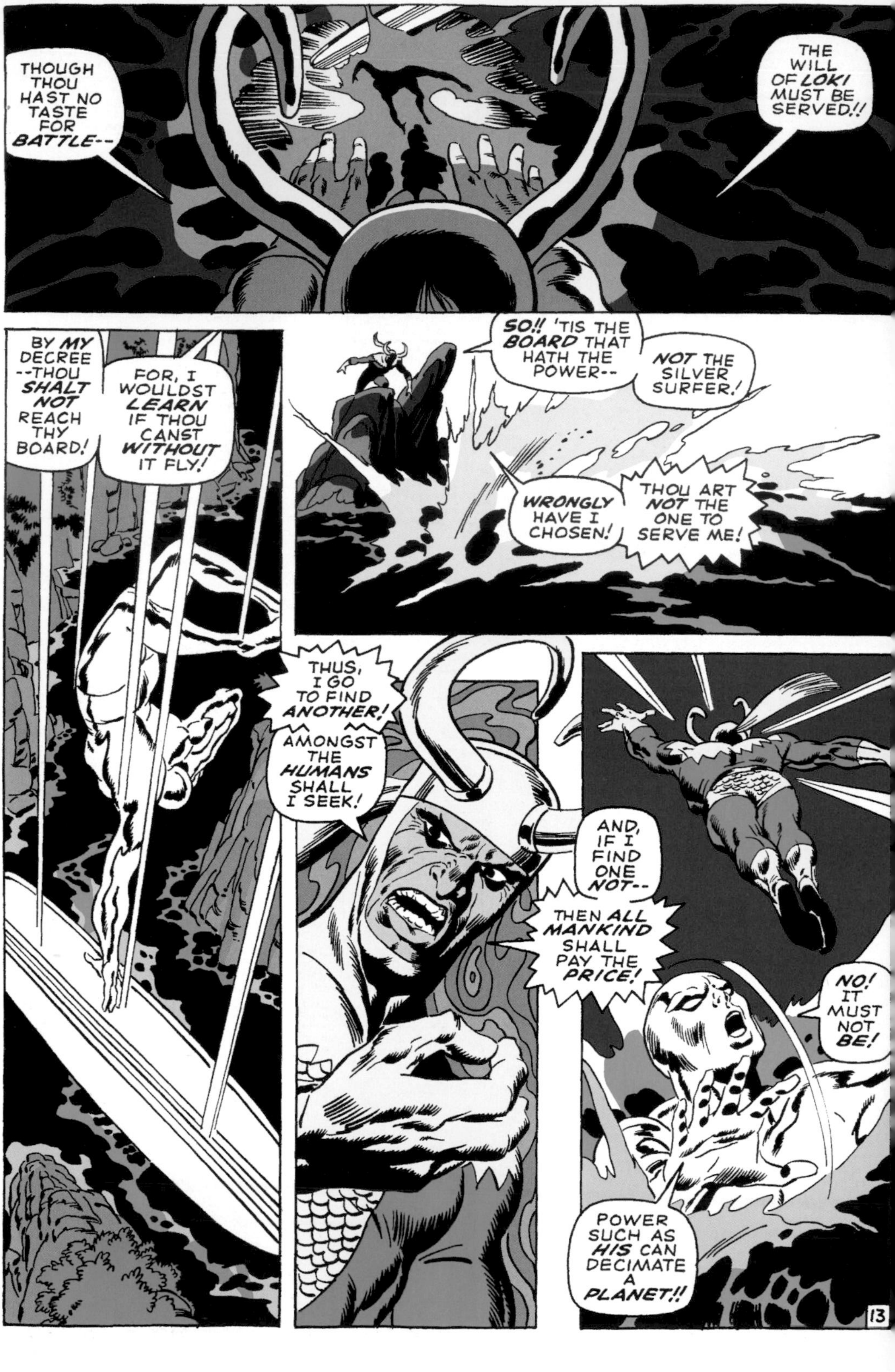
THOUGH THOU HAST NO TASTE FOR BATTLE--
THE WILL OF LOKI MUST BE SERVED!!
BY MY DECREE --THOU SHALT NOT REACH THY BOARD!
FOR, I WOULDST LEARN IF THOU CANST WITHOUT IT FLY!
SO!! 'TIS THE BOARD THAT HATH THE POWER--
NOT THE SILVER SURFER!
WRONGLY HAVE I CHOSEN!
THOU ART NOT THE ONE TO SERVE ME!
THUS, I GO TO FIND ANOTHER!
AMONGST THE HUMANS SHALL I SEEK!
AND, IF I FIND ONE NOT--
THEN ALL MANKIND SHALL PAY THE PRICE!
NO! IT MUST NOT BE!
POWER SUCH AS HIS CAN DECIMATE A PLANET!!
13

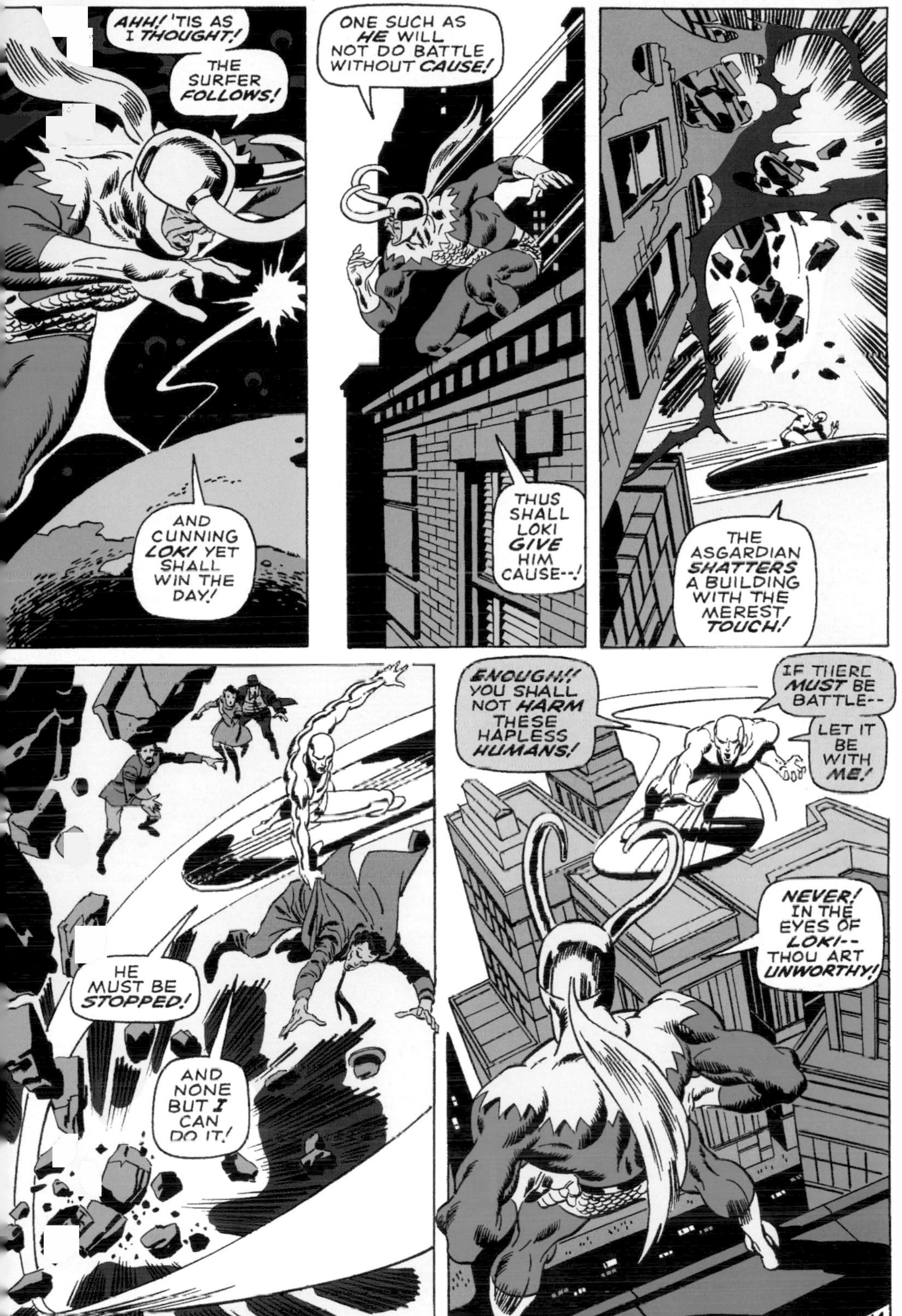
AHH! 'TIS AS I THOUGHT!
THE SURFER FOLLOWS!
AND CUNNING LOKI YET SHALL WIN THE DAY!
ONE SUCH AS HE WILL NOT DO BATTLE WITHOUT CAUSE!
THUS SHALL LOKI GIVE HIM CAUSE--!
THE ASGARDIAN SHATTERS A BUILDING WITH THE MEREST TOUCH!
HE MUST BE STOPPED!
AND NONE BUT I CAN DO IT!
ENOUGH!! YOU SHALL NOT HARM THESE HAPLESS HUMANS!
IF THERE MUST BE BATTLE--
LET IT BE WITH ME!
NEVER! IN THE EYES OF LOKI--THOU ART UNWORTHY!
14

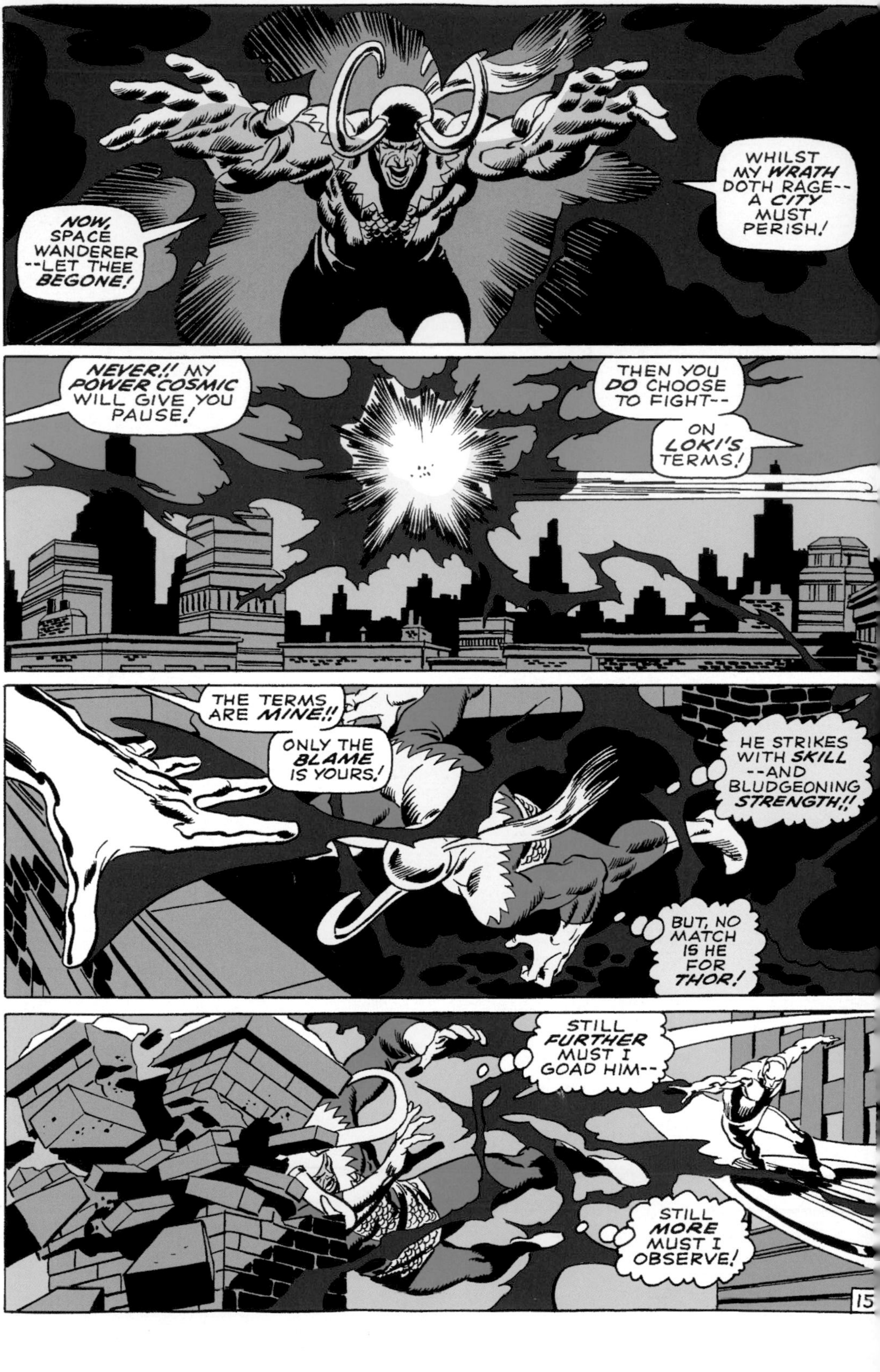
NOW, SPACE WANDERER --LET THEE BEGONE!
WHILST MY WRATH DOTH RAGE-- A CITY MUST PERISH!
NEVER!! MY POWER COSMIC WILL GIVE YOU PAUSE!
THEN YOU DO CHOOSE TO FIGHT--
ON LOKI'S TERMS!
THE TERMS ARE MINE!!
ONLY THE BLAME IS YOURS!
HE STRIKES WITH SKILL --AND BLUDGEONING STRENGTH!!
BUT, NO MATCH IS HE FOR THOR!
STILL FURTHER MUST I GOAD HIM--
STILL MORE MUST I OBSERVE!
15

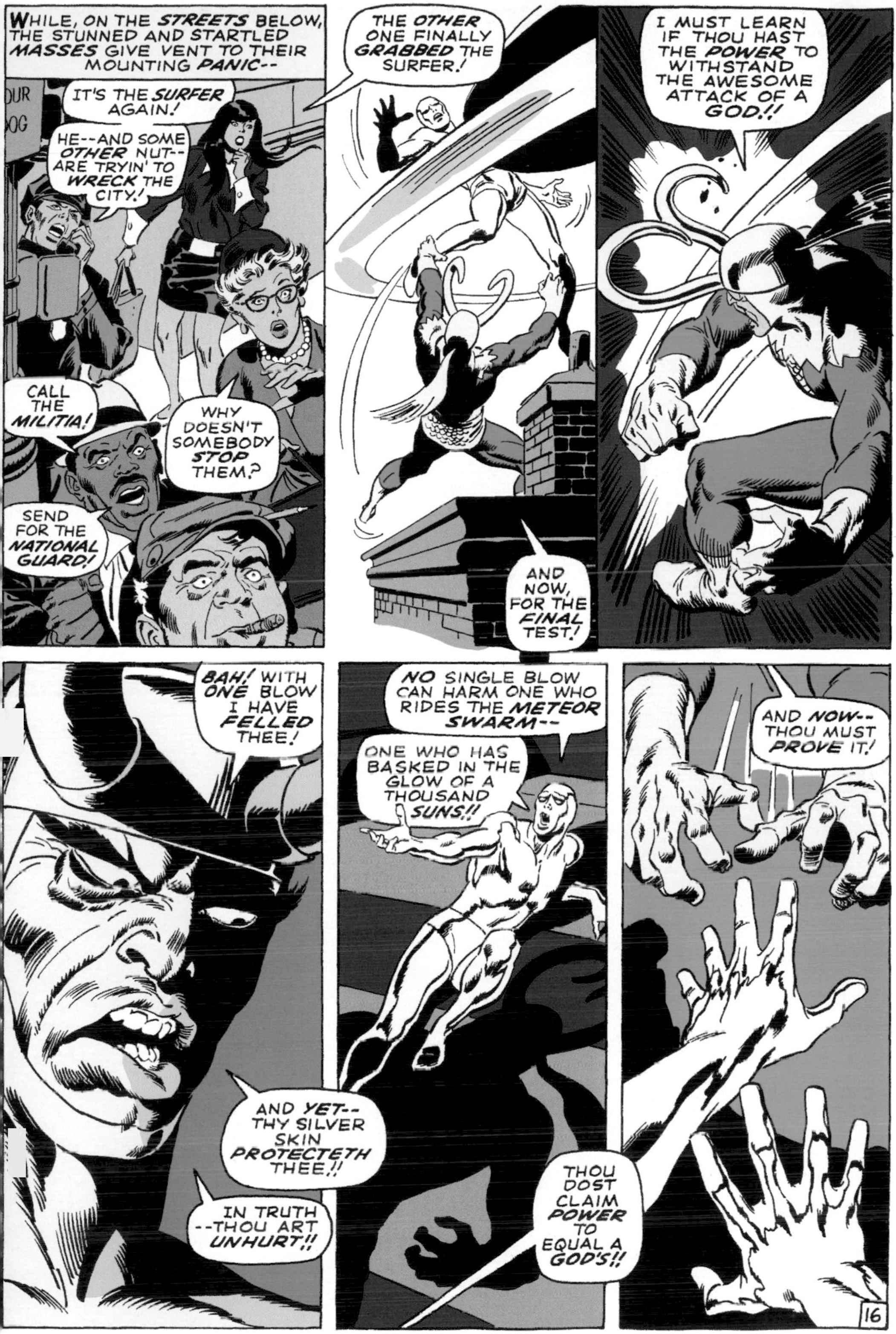

WHILE, ON THE STREETS BELOW, THE STUNNED AND STARTLED MASSES GIVE VENT TO THEIR MOUNTING PANIC--
IT'S THE SURFER AGAIN!
HE--AND SOME OTHER NUT--ARE TRYIN' TO WRECK THE CITY!
CALL THE MILITIA!
WHY DOESN'T SOMEBODY STOP THEM?
SEND FOR THE NATIONAL GUARD!
THE OTHER ONE FINALLY GRABBED THE SURFER!
AND NOW, FOR THE FINAL TEST!
I MUST LEARN IF THOU HAST THE POWER TO WITHSTAND THE AWESOME ATTACK OF A GOD!!
BAH! WITH ONE BLOW I HAVE FELLED THEE!
AND YET--THY SILVER SKIN PROTECTETH THEE!!
IN TRUTH --THOU ART UNHURT!!
NO SINGLE BLOW CAN HARM ONE WHO RIDES THE METEOR SWARM--
ONE WHO HAS BASKED IN THE GLOW OF A THOUSAND SUNS!!
THOU DOST CLAIM POWER TO EQUAL A GOD'S!!
AND NOW--THOU MUST PROVE IT!
16

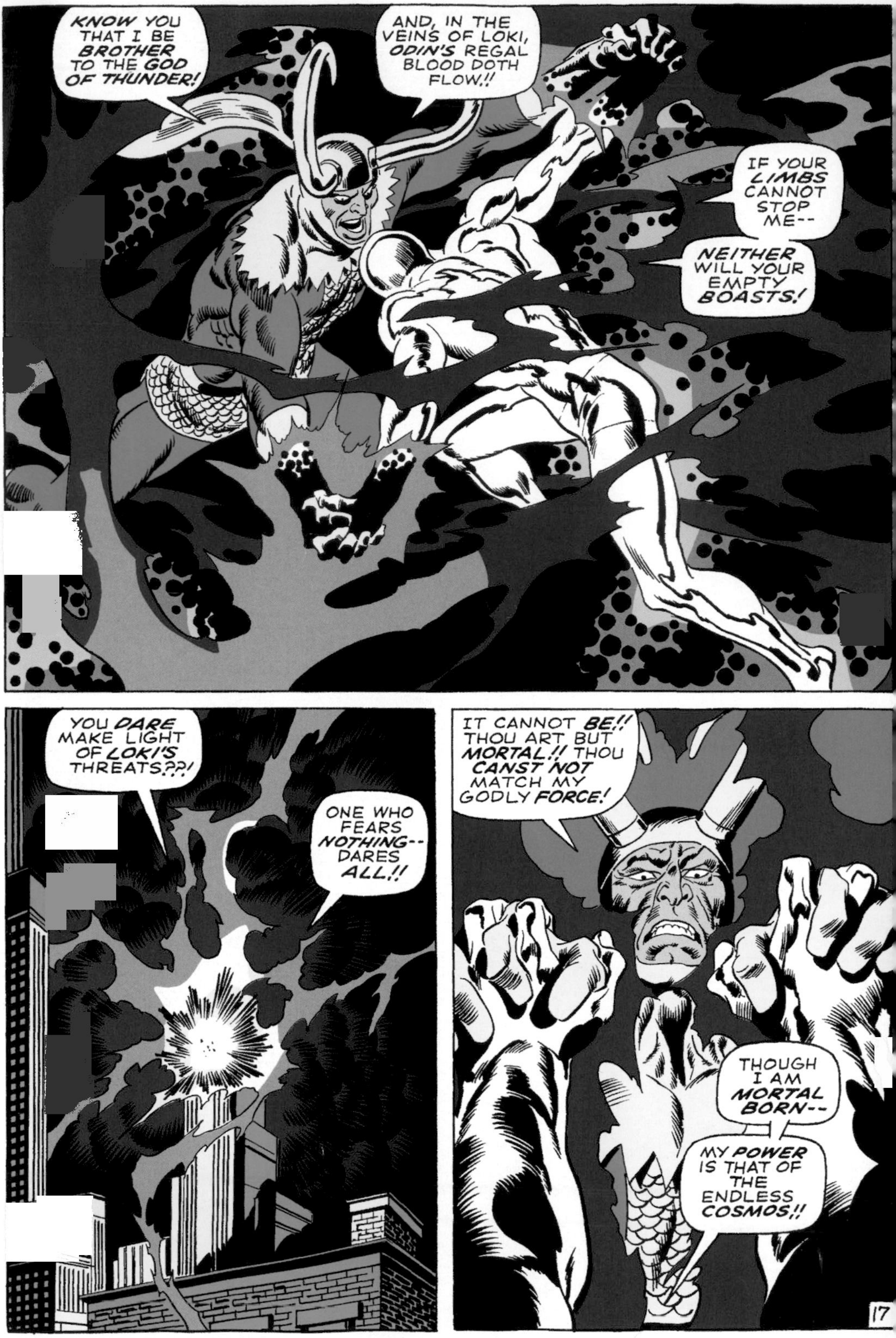
KNOW YOU THAT I BE BROTHER TO THE GOD OF THUNDER!
AND, IN THE VEINS OF LOKI, ODIN'S REGAL BLOOD DOTH FLOW!!
IF YOUR LIMBS CANNOT STOP ME--
NEITHER WILL YOUR EMPTY BOASTS!
YOU DARE MAKE LIGHT OF LOKI'S THREATS???!
ONE WHO FEARS NOTHING-- DARES ALL!!
IT CANNOT BE!! THOU ART BUT MORTAL!! THOU CANST NOT MATCH MY GODLY FORCE!
THOUGH I AM MORTAL BORN--
MY POWER IS THAT OF THE ENDLESS COSMOS!!

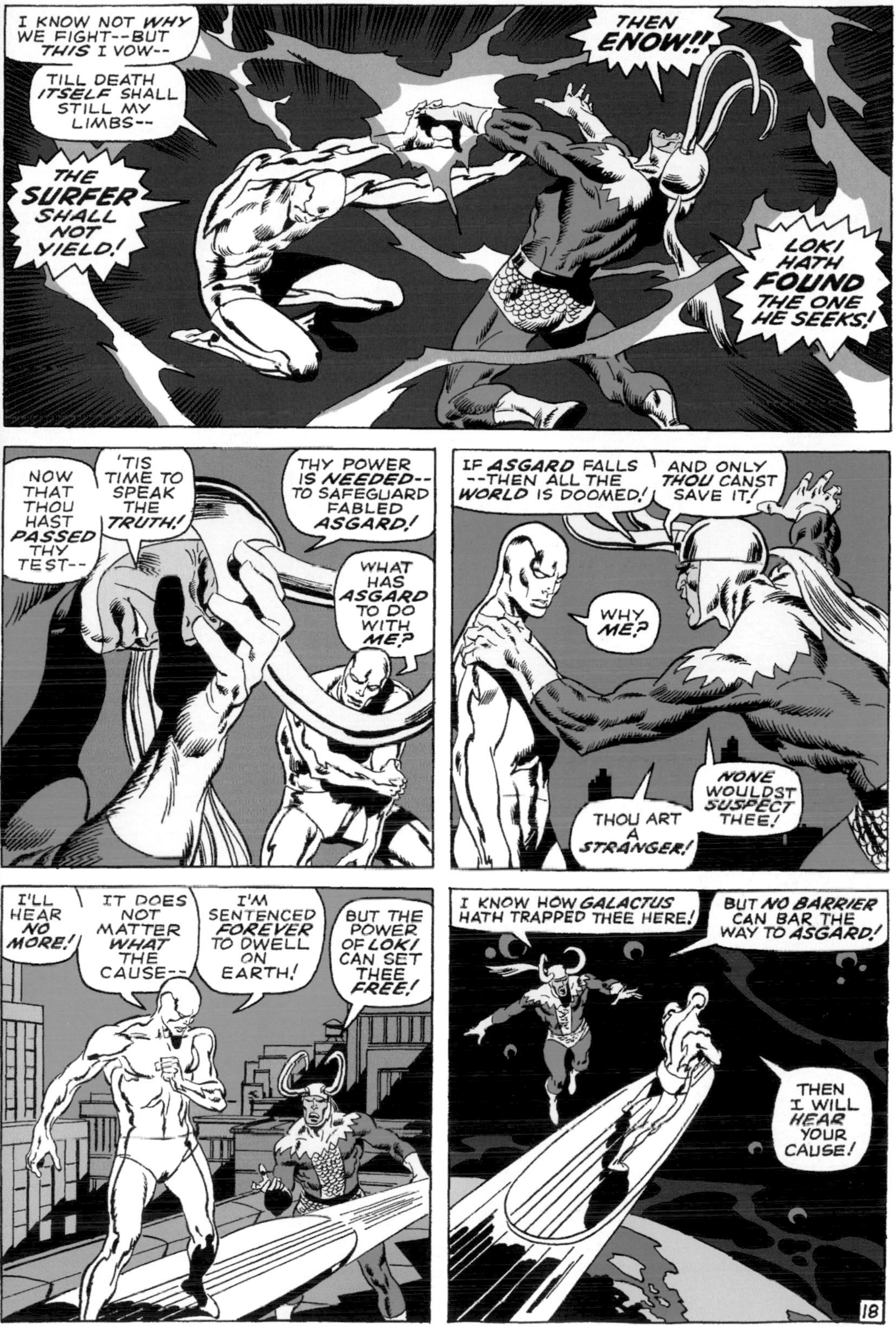
I KNOW NOT WHY WE FIGHT--BUT THIS I VOW--
TILL DEATH ITSELF SHALL STILL MY LIMBS--
THE SURFER SHALL NOT YIELD!
THEN ENOW!!
LOKI HATH FOUND THE ONE HE SEEKS!
NOW THAT THOU HAST PASSED THY TEST--
'TIS TIME TO SPEAK THE TRUTH!
THY POWER IS NEEDED--TO SAFEGUARD FABLED ASGARD!
WHAT HAS ASGARD TO DO WITH ME?
IF ASGARD FALLS--THEN ALL THE WORLD IS DOOMED!
AND ONLY THOU CANST SAVE IT!
WHY ME?
THOU ART A STRANGER!
NONE WOULDST SUSPECT THEE!
I'LL HEAR NO MORE!
IT DOES NOT MATTER WHAT THE CAUSE--
I'M SENTENCED FOREVER TO DWELL ON EARTH!
BUT THE POWER OF LOKI CAN SET THEE FREE!
I KNOW HOW GALACTUS HATH TRAPPED THEE HERE!
BUT NO BARRIER CAN BAR THE WAY TO ASGARD!
THEN I WILL HEAR YOUR CAUSE!
18

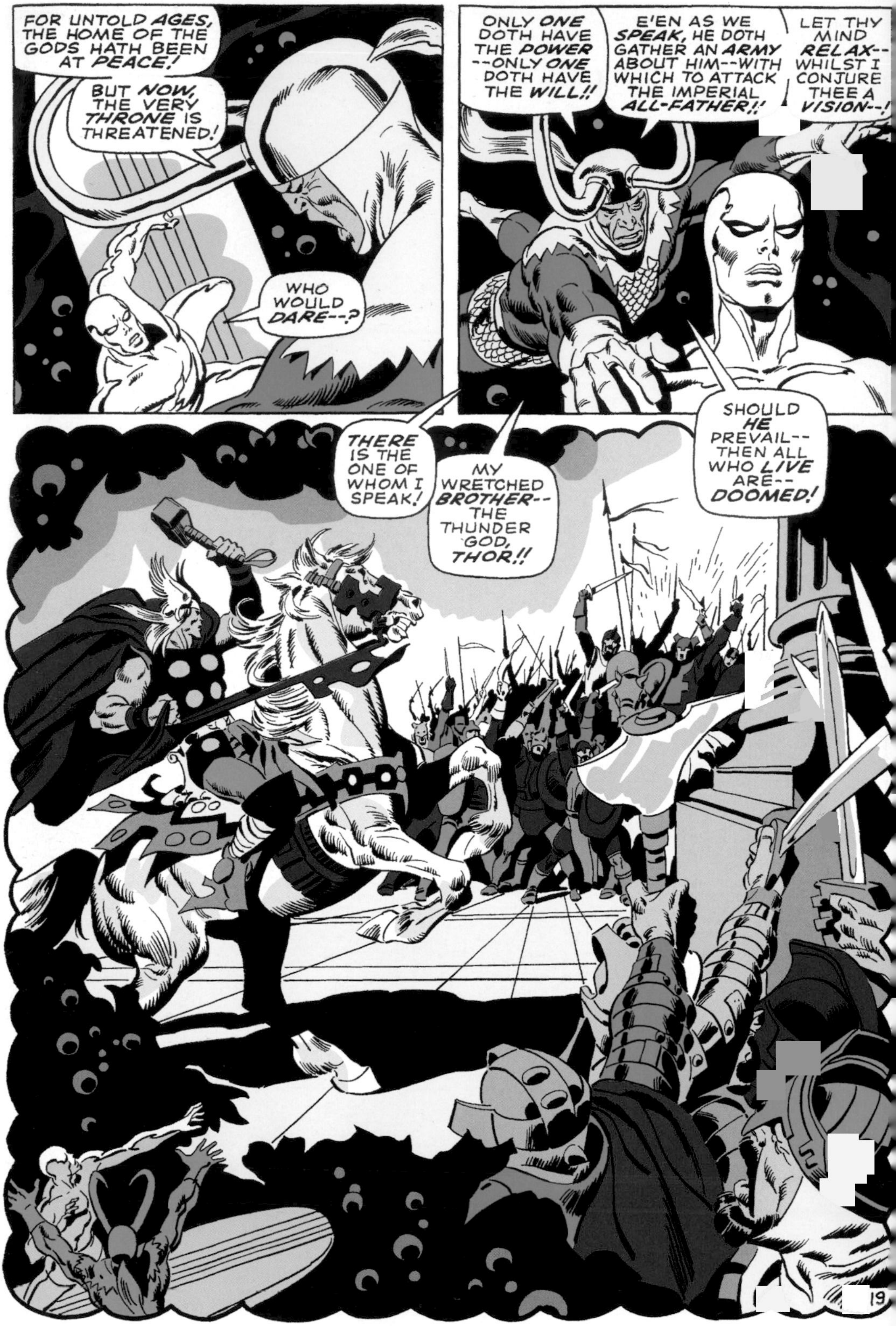

FOR UNTOLD AGES, THE HOME OF THE GODS HATH BEEN AT PEACE!
BUT NOW, THE VERY THRONE IS THREATENED!
WHO WOULD DARE--?
ONLY ONE DOTH HAVE THE POWER --ONLY ONE DOTH HAVE THE WILL!!
E'EN AS WE SPEAK, HE DOTH GATHER AN ARMY ABOUT HIM--WITH WHICH TO ATTACK THE IMPERIAL ALL-FATHER!!
LET THY MIND RELAX--WHILST I CONJURE THEE A VISION--!
THERE IS THE ONE OF WHOM I SPEAK!
MY WRETCHED BROTHER--THE THUNDER GOD, THOR!!
SHOULD HE PREVAIL--THEN ALL WHO LIVE ARE--DOOMED!

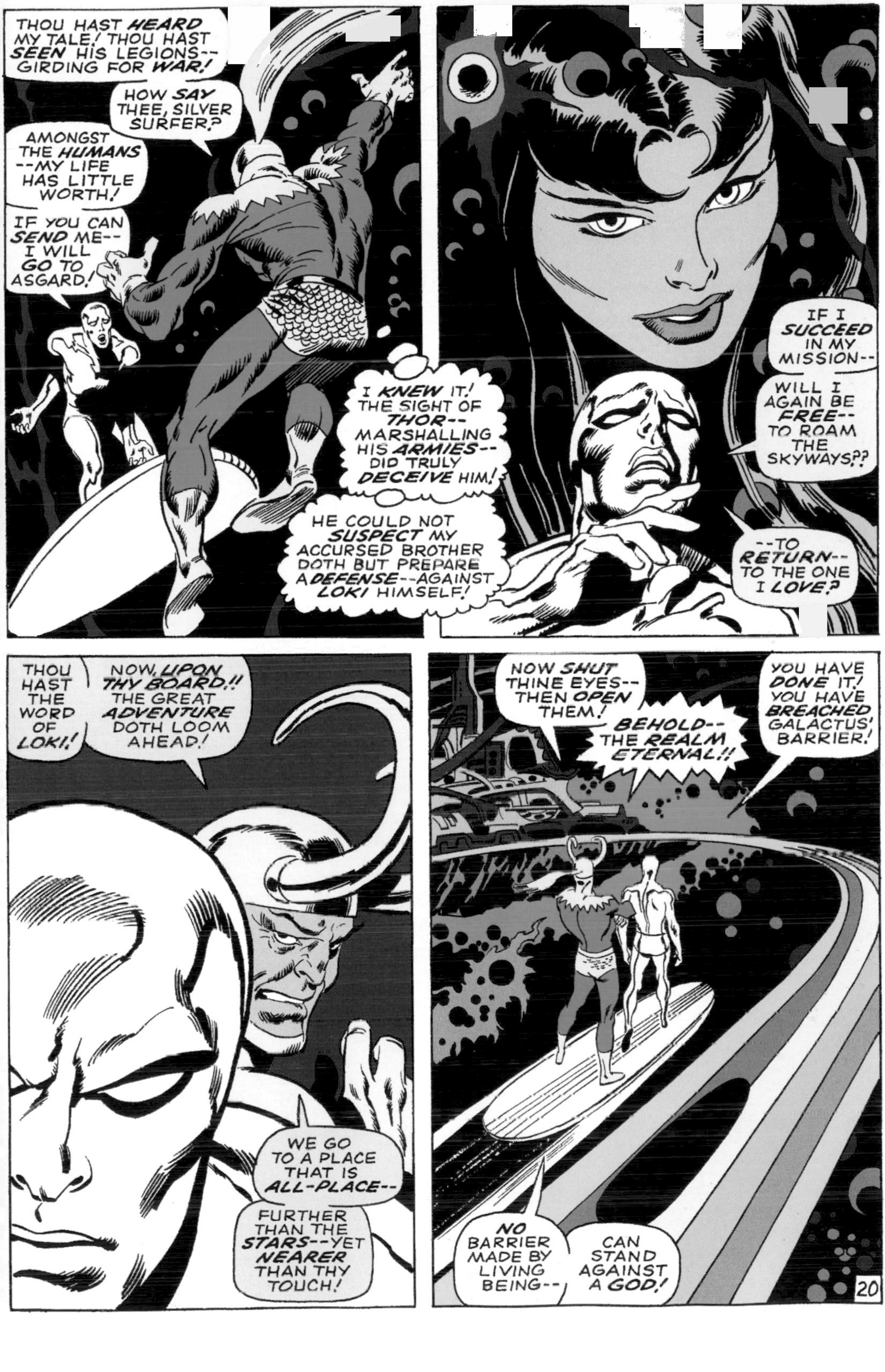
THOU HAST HEARD MY TALE! THOU HAST SEEN HIS LEGIONS--GIRDING FOR WAR!
HOW SAY THEE, SILVER SURFER?
AMONGST THE HUMANS--MY LIFE HAS LITTLE WORTH!
IF YOU CAN SEND ME--I WILL GO TO ASGARD!
I KNEW IT! THE SIGHT OF THOR--MARSHALLING HIS ARMIES--DID TRULY DECEIVE HIM!
HE COULD NOT SUSPECT MY ACCURSED BROTHER DOTH BUT PREPARE A DEFENSE--AGAINST LOKI HIMSELF!
IF I SUCCEED IN MY MISSION--
WILL I AGAIN BE FREE--TO ROAM THE SKYWAYS??
--TO RETURN--TO THE ONE I LOVE?
THOU HAST THE WORD OF LOKI!
NOW, UPON THY BOARD!! THE GREAT ADVENTURE DOTH LOOM AHEAD!
WE GO TO A PLACE THAT IS ALL-PLACE--
FURTHER THAN THE STARS--YET NEARER THAN THY TOUCH!
NOW SHUT THINE EYES--THEN OPEN THEM!
BEHOLD--THE REALM ETERNAL!!
YOU HAVE DONE IT! YOU HAVE BREACHED GALACTUS' BARRIER!
NO BARRIER MADE BY LIVING BEING--
CAN STAND AGAINST A GOD!

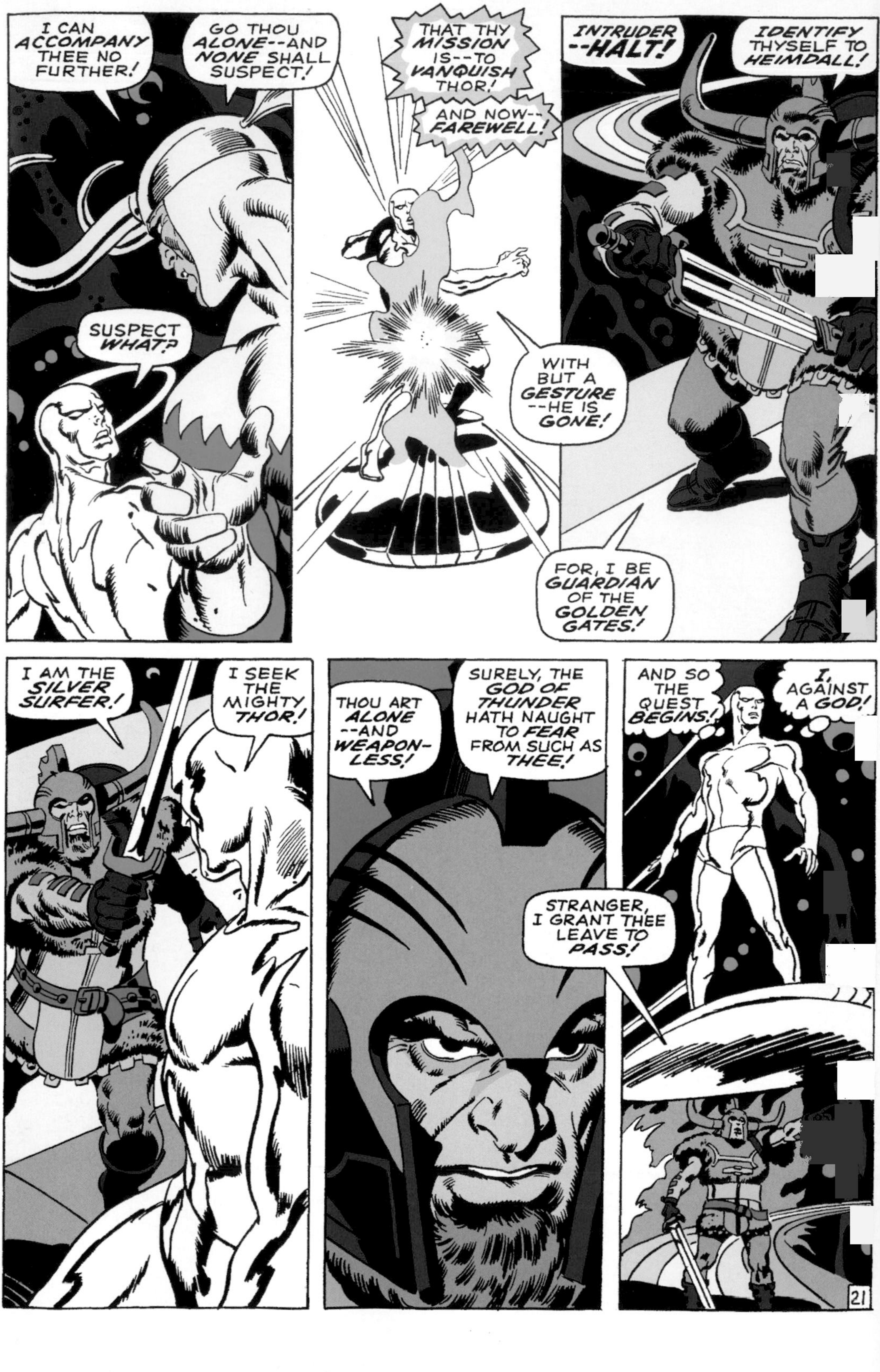
I CAN ACCOMPANY THEE NO FURTHER!
GO THOU ALONE--AND NONE SHALL SUSPECT!
SUSPECT WHAT?
THAT THY MISSION IS--TO VANQUISH THOR!
AND NOW--FAREWELL!
WITH BUT A GESTURE --HE IS GONE!
INTRUDER --HALT!
IDENTIFY THYSELF TO HEIMDALL!
FOR, I BE GUARDIAN OF THE GOLDEN GATES!
I AM THE SILVER SURFER!
I SEEK THE MIGHTY THOR!
THOU ART ALONE --AND WEAPON-LESS!
SURELY, THE GOD OF THUNDER HATH NAUGHT TO FEAR FROM SUCH AS THEE!
AND SO THE QUEST BEGINS!
I, AGAINST A GOD!
STRANGER, I GRANT THEE LEAVE TO PASS!
21

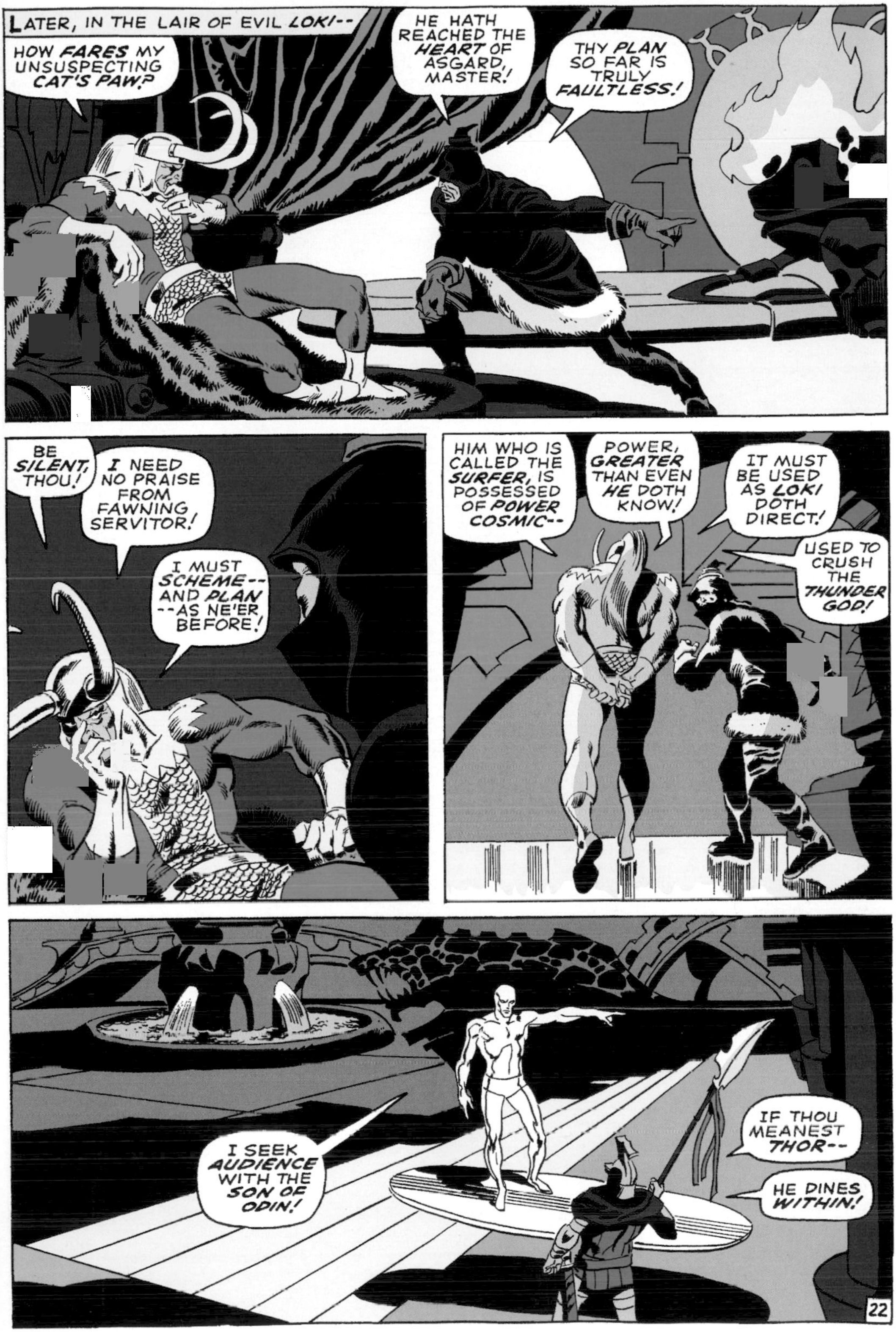
LATER, IN THE LAIR OF EVIL LOKI--
HOW FARES MY UNSUSPECTING CAT'S PAW?
HE HATH REACHED THE HEART OF ASGARD, MASTER!
THY PLAN SO FAR IS TRULY FAULTLESS!
BE SILENT, THOU!
I NEED NO PRAISE FROM FAWNING SERVITOR!
I MUST SCHEME-- AND PLAN --AS NE'ER BEFORE!
HIM WHO IS CALLED THE SURFER, IS POSSESSED OF POWER COSMIC--
POWER, GREATER THAN EVEN HE DOTH KNOW!
IT MUST BE USED AS LOKI DOTH DIRECT!
USED TO CRUSH THE THUNDER GOD!
I SEEK AUDIENCE WITH THE SON OF ODIN!
IF THOU MEANEST THOR--
HE DINES WITHIN!
22

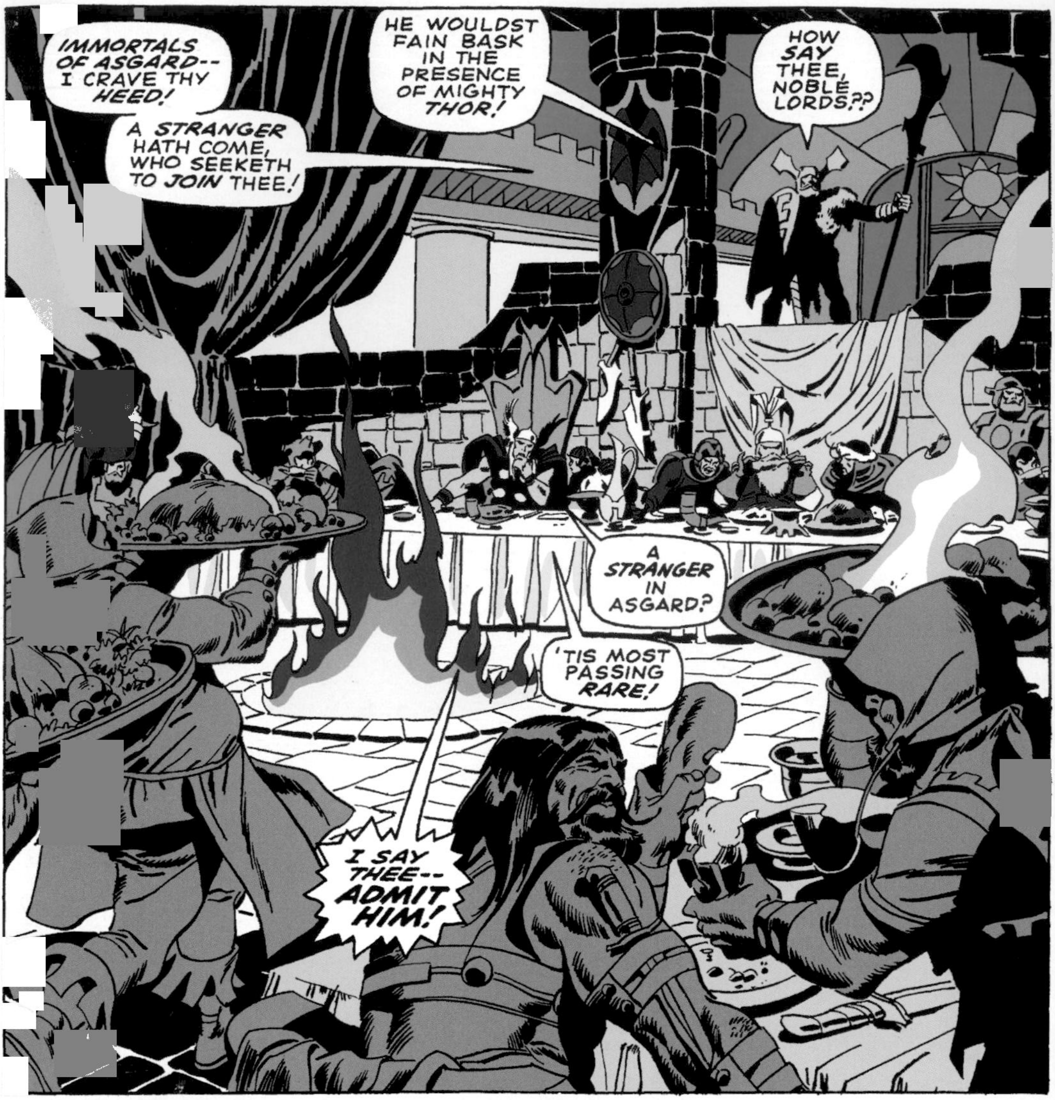
IMMORTALS OF ASGARD-- I CRAVE THY HEED!
A STRANGER HATH COME, WHO SEEKETH TO JOIN THEE!
HE WOULDST FAIN BASK IN THE PRESENCE OF MIGHTY THOR!
HOW SAY THEE, NOBLE LORDS??
A STRANGER IN ASGARD?
'TIS MOST PASSING RARE!
I SAY THEE-- ADMIT HIM!

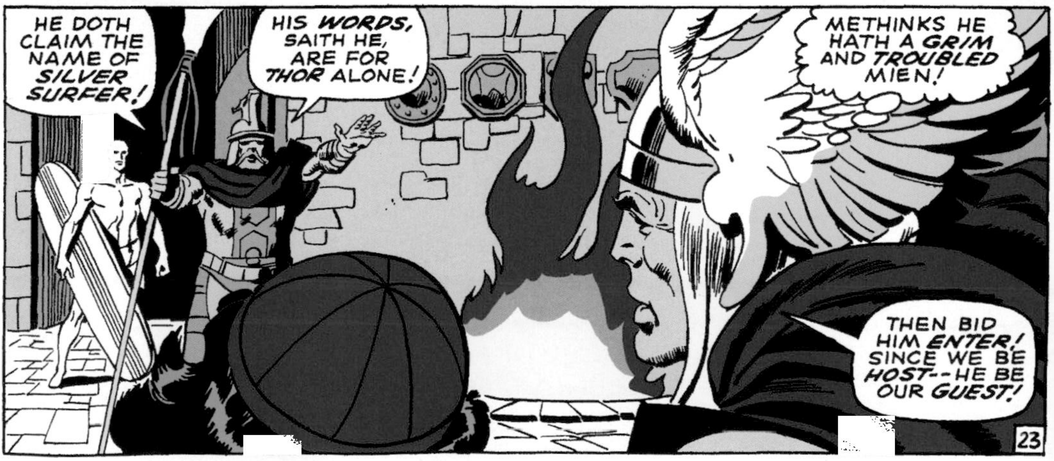
HE DOTH CLAIM THE NAME OF SILVER SURFER!
HIS WORDS, SAITH HE, ARE FOR THOR ALONE!
METHINKS HE HATH A GRIM AND TROUBLED MIEN!
THEN BID HIM ENTER! SINCE WE BE HOST--HE BE OUR GUEST!
23

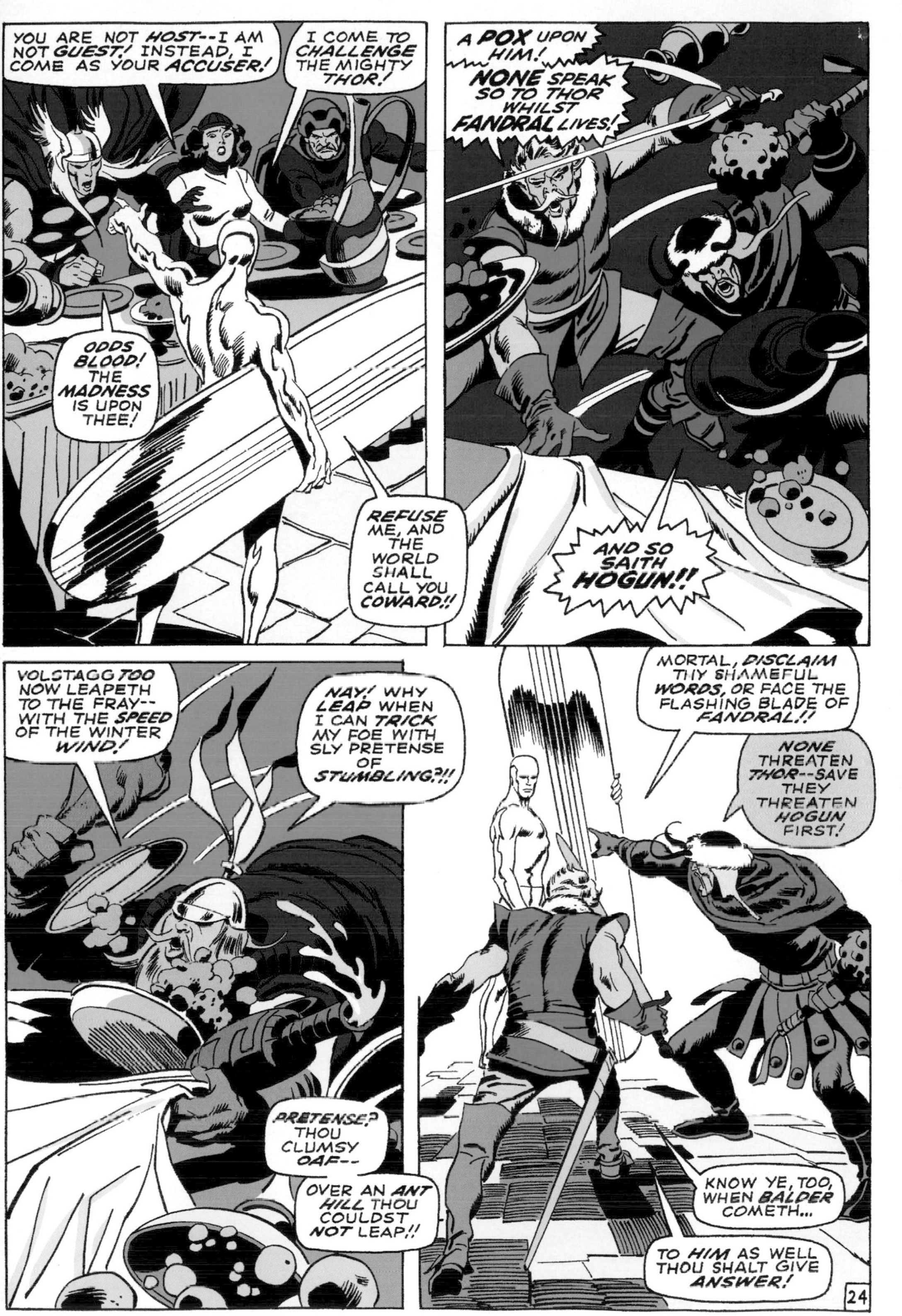
YOU ARE NOT HOST--I AM NOT GUEST! INSTEAD, I COME AS YOUR ACCUSER!
I COME TO CHALLENGE THE MIGHTY THOR!
ODDS BLOOD! THE MADNESS IS UPON THEE!
REFUSE ME, AND THE WORLD SHALL CALL YOU COWARD!!
A POX UPON HIM! NONE SPEAK SO TO THOR WHILST FANDRAL LIVES!
AND SO SAITH HOGUN!!
VOLSTAGG TOO NOW LEAPETH TO THE FRAY--WITH THE SPEED OF THE WINTER WIND!
NAY! WHY LEAP WHEN I CAN TRICK MY FOE WITH SLY PRETENSE OF STUMBLING?!!
PRETENSE? THOU CLUMSY OAF--
OVER AN ANT HILL THOU COULDST NOT LEAP!!
MORTAL, DISCLAIM THY SHAMEFUL WORDS, OR FACE THE FLASHING BLADE OF FANDRAL!!
NONE THREATEN THOR--SAVE THEY THREATEN HOGUN FIRST!
KNOW YE, TOO, WHEN BALDER COMETH...
TO HIM AS WELL THOU SHALT GIVE ANSWER!
24

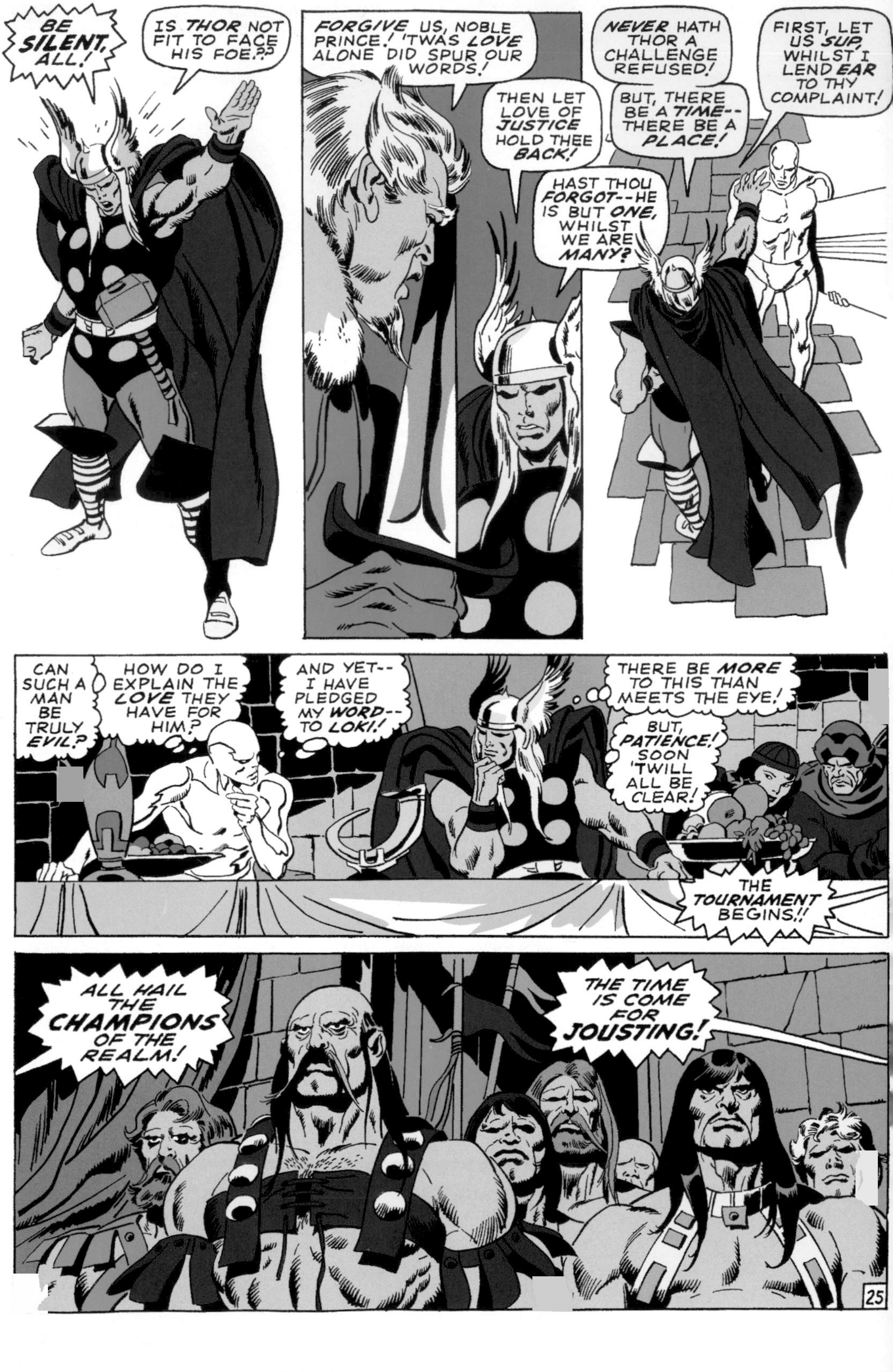
BE SILENT, ALL!
IS THOR NOT FIT TO FACE HIS FOE?!?
FORGIVE US, NOBLE PRINCE! 'TWAS LOVE ALONE DID SPUR OUR WORDS!
THEN LET LOVE OF JUSTICE HOLD THEE BACK!
HAST THOU FORGOT--HE IS BUT ONE, WHILST WE ARE MANY?
NEVER HATH THOR A CHALLENGE REFUSED!
BUT, THERE BE A TIME-- THERE BE A PLACE!
FIRST, LET US SUP, WHILST I LEND EAR TO THY COMPLAINT!
CAN SUCH A MAN BE TRULY EVIL?
HOW DO I EXPLAIN THE LOVE THEY HAVE FOR HIM?
AND YET-- I HAVE PLEDGED MY WORD-- TO LOKI!
THERE BE MORE TO THIS THAN MEETS THE EYE!
BUT, PATIENCE! SOON 'TWILL ALL BE CLEAR!
THE TOURNAMENT BEGINS!!
ALL HAIL THE CHAMPIONS OF THE REALM!
THE TIME IS COME FOR JOUSTING!

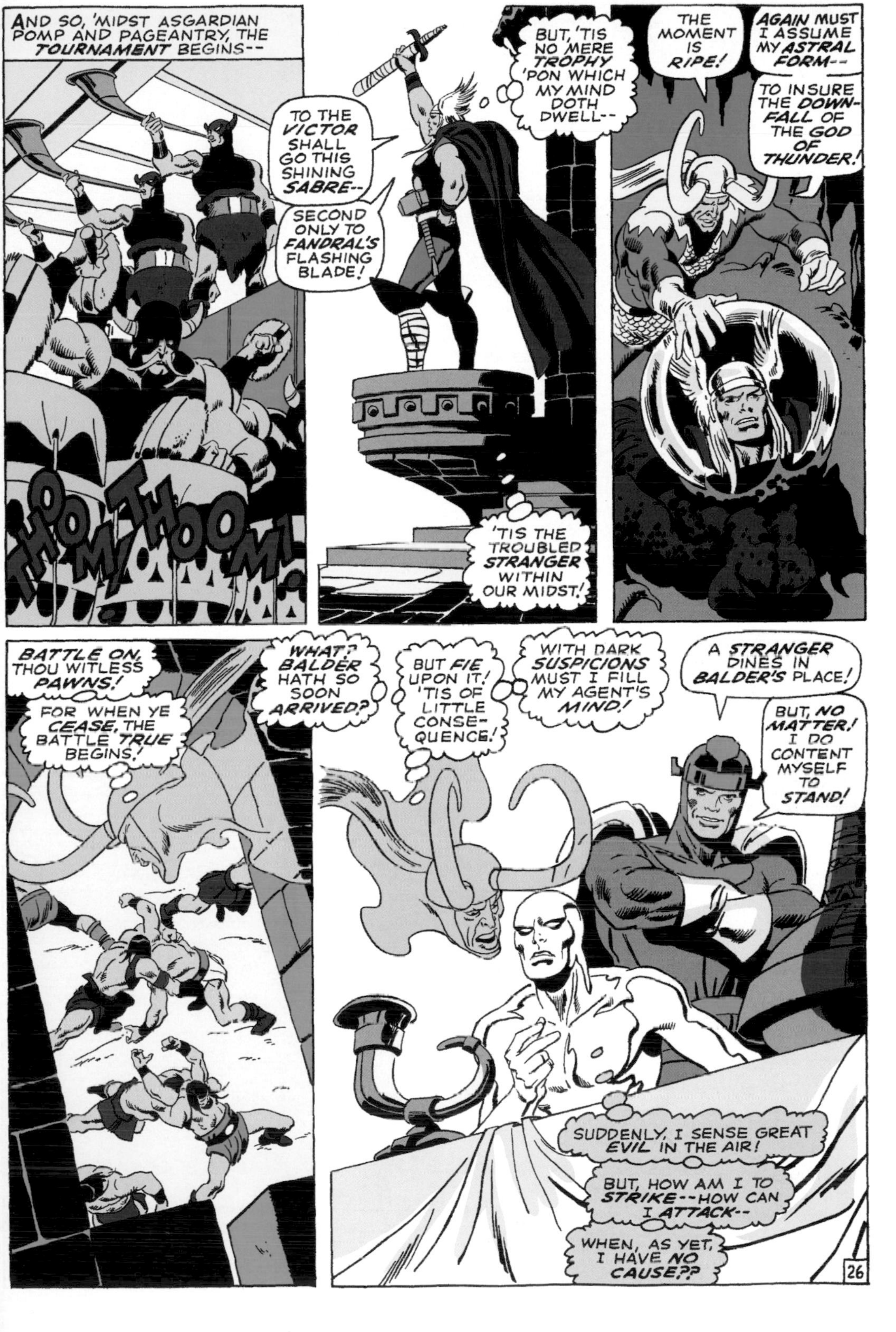
AND SO, 'MIDST ASGARDIAN POMP AND PAGEANTRY, THE TOURNAMENT BEGINS--
THOOM! THOOM!
TO THE VICTOR SHALL GO THIS SHINING SABRE--
SECOND ONLY TO FANDRAL'S FLASHING BLADE!
BUT, 'TIS NO MERE TROPHY 'PON WHICH MY MIND DOTH DWELL--
'TIS THE TROUBLED STRANGER WITHIN OUR MIDST!
THE MOMENT IS RIPE!
AGAIN MUST I ASSUME MY ASTRAL FORM--
TO INSURE THE DOWNFALL OF THE GOD OF THUNDER!
BATTLE ON, THOU WITLESS PAWNS!
FOR WHEN YE CEASE, THE BATTLE TRUE BEGINS!
WHAT? BALDER HATH SO SOON ARRIVED?
BUT FIE UPON IT! 'TIS OF LITTLE CONSEQUENCE!
WITH DARK SUSPICIONS MUST I FILL MY AGENT'S MIND!
A STRANGER DINES IN BALDER'S PLACE!
BUT, NO MATTER! I DO CONTENT MYSELF TO STAND!
SUDDENLY, I SENSE GREAT EVIL IN THE AIR!
BUT, HOW AM I TO STRIKE--HOW CAN I ATTACK--
WHEN, AS YET, I HAVE NO CAUSE??
26

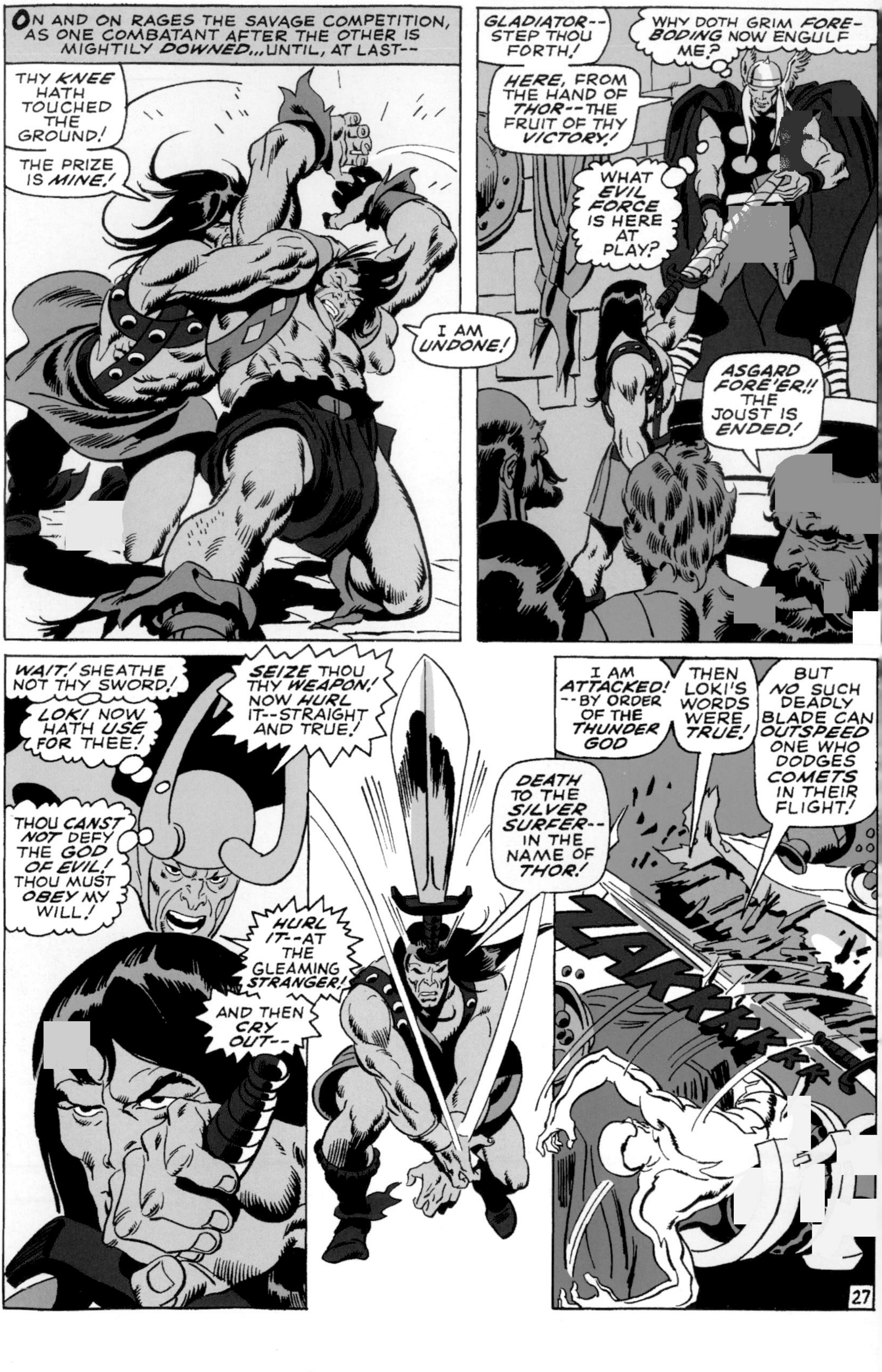
ON AND ON RAGES THE SAVAGE COMPETITION, AS ONE COMBATANT AFTER THE OTHER IS MIGHTILY DOWNED... UNTIL, AT LAST--
THY KNEE HATH TOUCHED THE GROUND!
THE PRIZE IS MINE!
I AM UNDONE!
GLADIATOR-- STEP THOU FORTH!
WHY DOTH GRIM FOREBODING NOW ENGULF ME?
HERE, FROM THE HAND OF THOR--THE FRUIT OF THY VICTORY!
WHAT EVIL FORCE IS HERE AT PLAY?
ASGARD FORE'ER!! THE JOUST IS ENDED!
WAIT! SHEATHE NOT THY SWORD!
LOKI NOW HATH USE FOR THEE!
SEIZE THOU THY WEAPON! NOW HURL IT--STRAIGHT AND TRUE!
THOU CANST NOT DEFY THE GOD OF EVIL! THOU MUST OBEY MY WILL!
HURL IT--AT THE GLEAMING STRANGER!
AND THEN CRY OUT--
DEATH TO THE SILVER SURFER-- IN THE NAME OF THOR!
I AM ATTACKED! --BY ORDER OF THE THUNDER GOD
THEN LOKI'S WORDS WERE TRUE!
BUT NO SUCH DEADLY BLADE CAN OUTSPEED ONE WHO DODGES COMETS IN THEIR FLIGHT!
ZAKKKKK

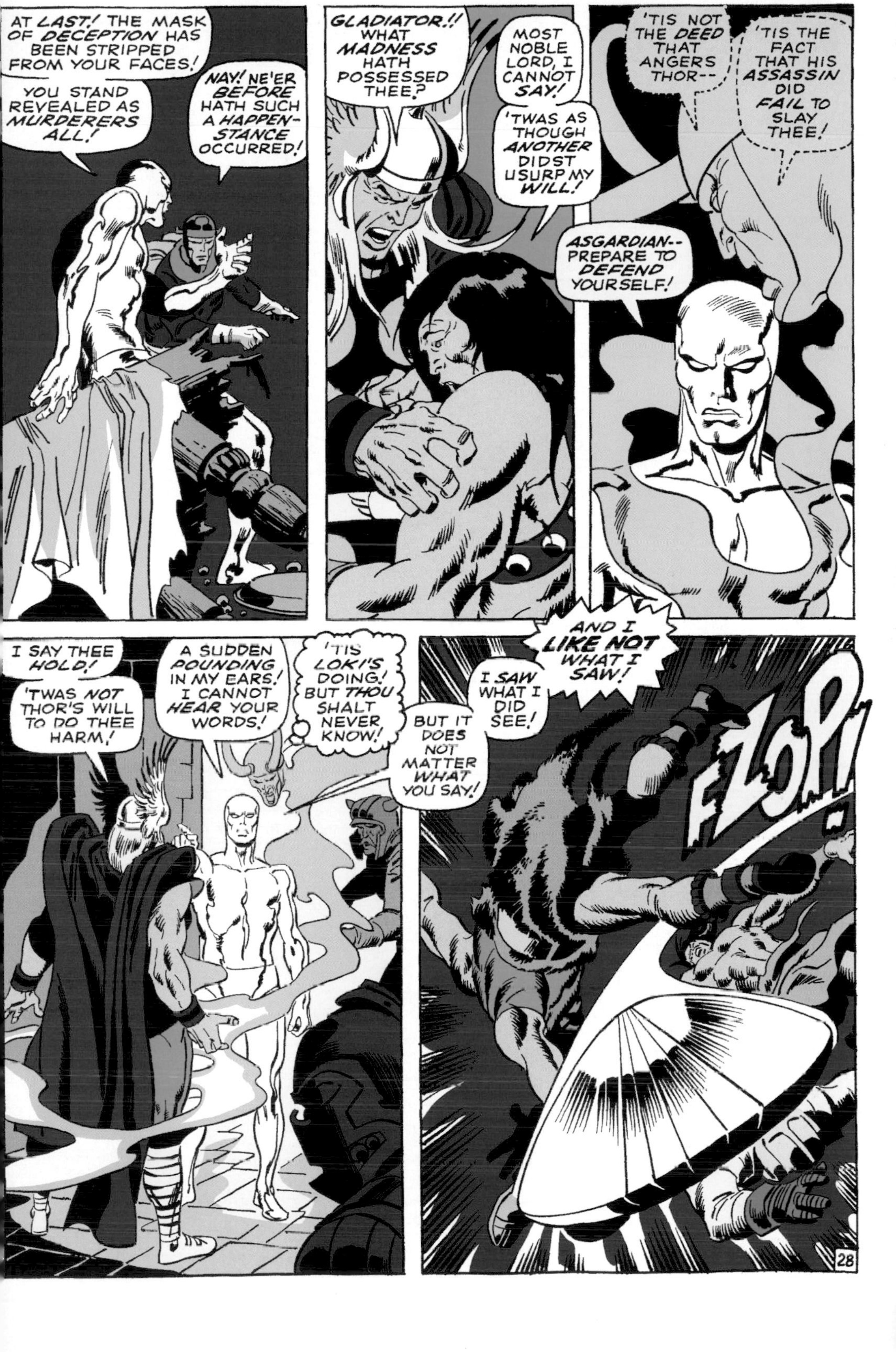

AT LAST! THE MASK OF DECEPTION HAS BEEN STRIPPED FROM YOUR FACES!
YOU STAND REVEALED AS MURDERERS ALL!
NAY! NE'ER BEFORE HATH SUCH A HAPPEN-STANCE OCCURRED!
GLADIATOR!! WHAT MADNESS HATH POSSESSED THEE?
MOST NOBLE LORD, I CANNOT SAY!
'TWAS AS THOUGH ANOTHER DIDST USURP MY WILL!
'TIS NOT THE DEED THAT ANGERS THOR--
'TIS THE FACT THAT HIS ASSASSIN DID FAIL TO SLAY THEE!
ASGARDIAN-- PREPARE TO DEFEND YOURSELF!
I SAY THEE HOLD!
'TWAS NOT THOR'S WILL TO DO THEE HARM!
A SUDDEN POUNDING IN MY EARS! I CANNOT HEAR YOUR WORDS!
'TIS LOKI'S DOING! BUT THOU SHALT NEVER KNOW!
BUT IT DOES NOT MATTER WHAT YOU SAY!
I SAW WHAT I DID SEE!
AND I LIKE NOT WHAT I SAW!
FZOP!

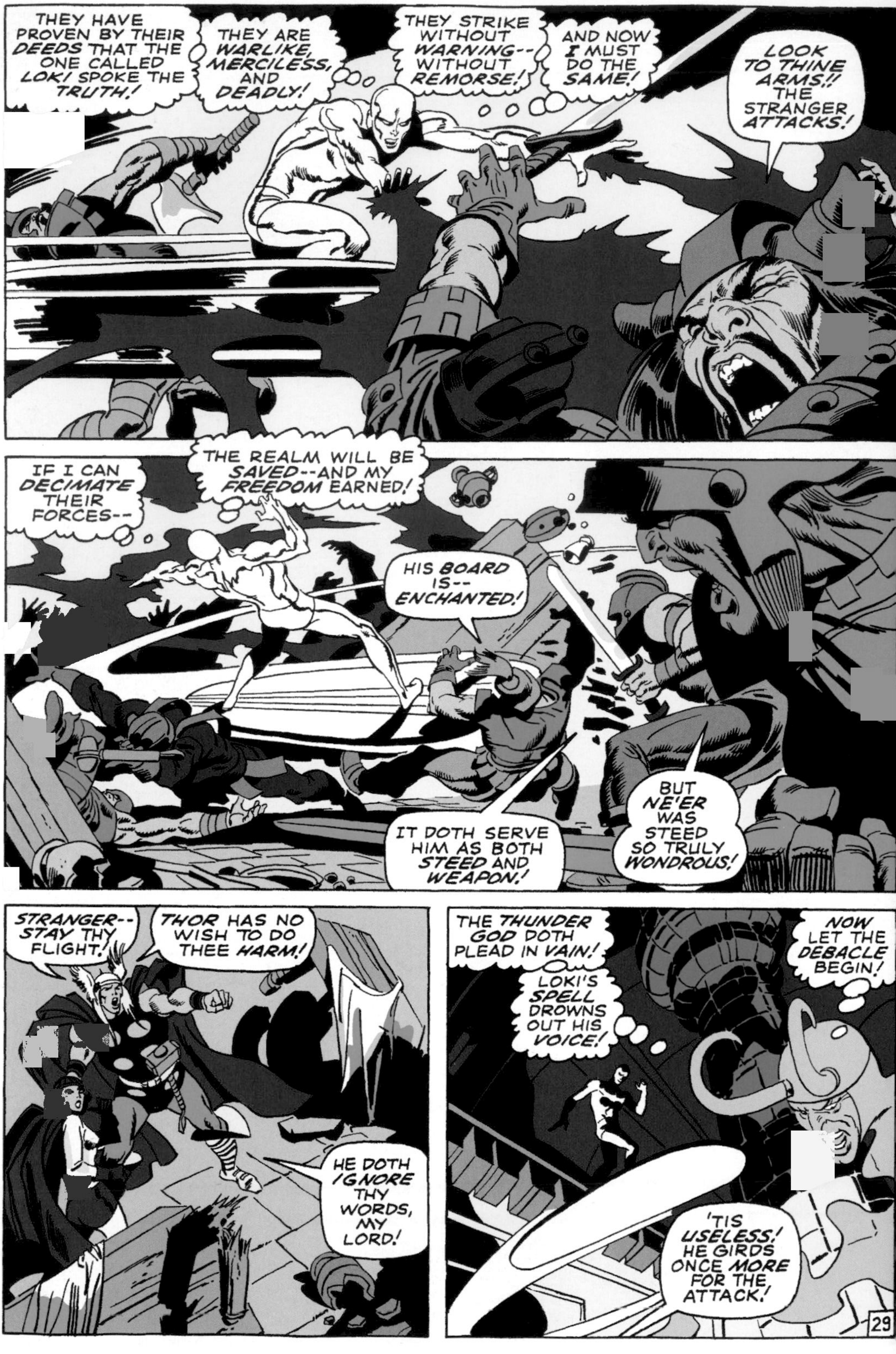
THEY HAVE PROVEN BY THEIR DEEDS THAT THE ONE CALLED LOKI SPOKE THE TRUTH!
THEY ARE WARLIKE, MERCILESS, AND DEADLY!
THEY STRIKE WITHOUT WARNING--WITHOUT REMORSE!
AND NOW I MUST DO THE SAME!
LOOK TO THINE ARMS!! THE STRANGER ATTACKS!
IF I CAN DECIMATE THEIR FORCES--
THE REALM WILL BE SAVED--AND MY FREEDOM EARNED!
HIS BOARD IS--ENCHANTED!
IT DOTH SERVE HIM AS BOTH STEED AND WEAPON!
BUT NE'ER WAS STEED SO TRULY WONDROUS!
STRANGER--STAY THY FLIGHT!
THOR HAS NO WISH TO DO THEE HARM!
HE DOTH IGNORE THY WORDS, MY LORD!
THE THUNDER GOD DOTH PLEAD IN VAIN!
LOKI'S SPELL DROWNS OUT HIS VOICE!
NOW LET THE DEBACLE BEGIN!
'TIS USELESS! HE GIRDS ONCE MORE FOR THE ATTACK!

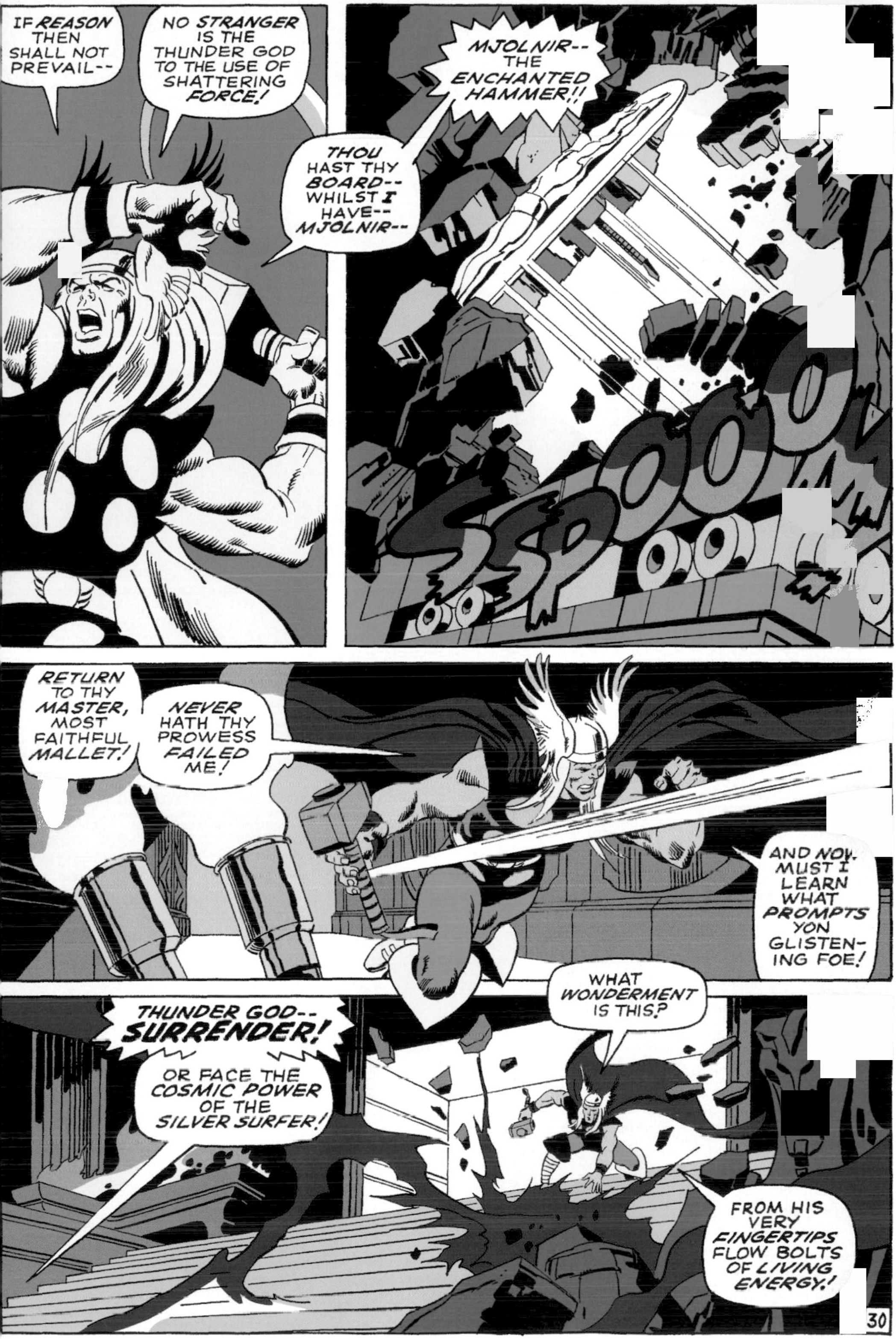
IF REASON THEN SHALL NOT PREVAIL--
NO STRANGER IS THE THUNDER GOD TO THE USE OF SHATTERING FORCE!
MJOLNIR-- THE ENCHANTED HAMMER!!
THOU HAST THY BOARD-- WHILST I HAVE-- MJOLNIR--
SSPOOOOM
RETURN TO THY MASTER, MOST FAITHFUL MALLET!
NEVER HATH THY PROWESS FAILED ME!
AND NOW MUST I LEARN WHAT PROMPTS YON GLISTEN-ING FOE!
THUNDER GOD-- SURRENDER!
OR FACE THE COSMIC POWER OF THE SILVER SURFER!
WHAT WONDERMENT IS THIS?
FROM HIS VERY FINGERTIPS FLOW BOLTS OF LIVING ENERGY!
30

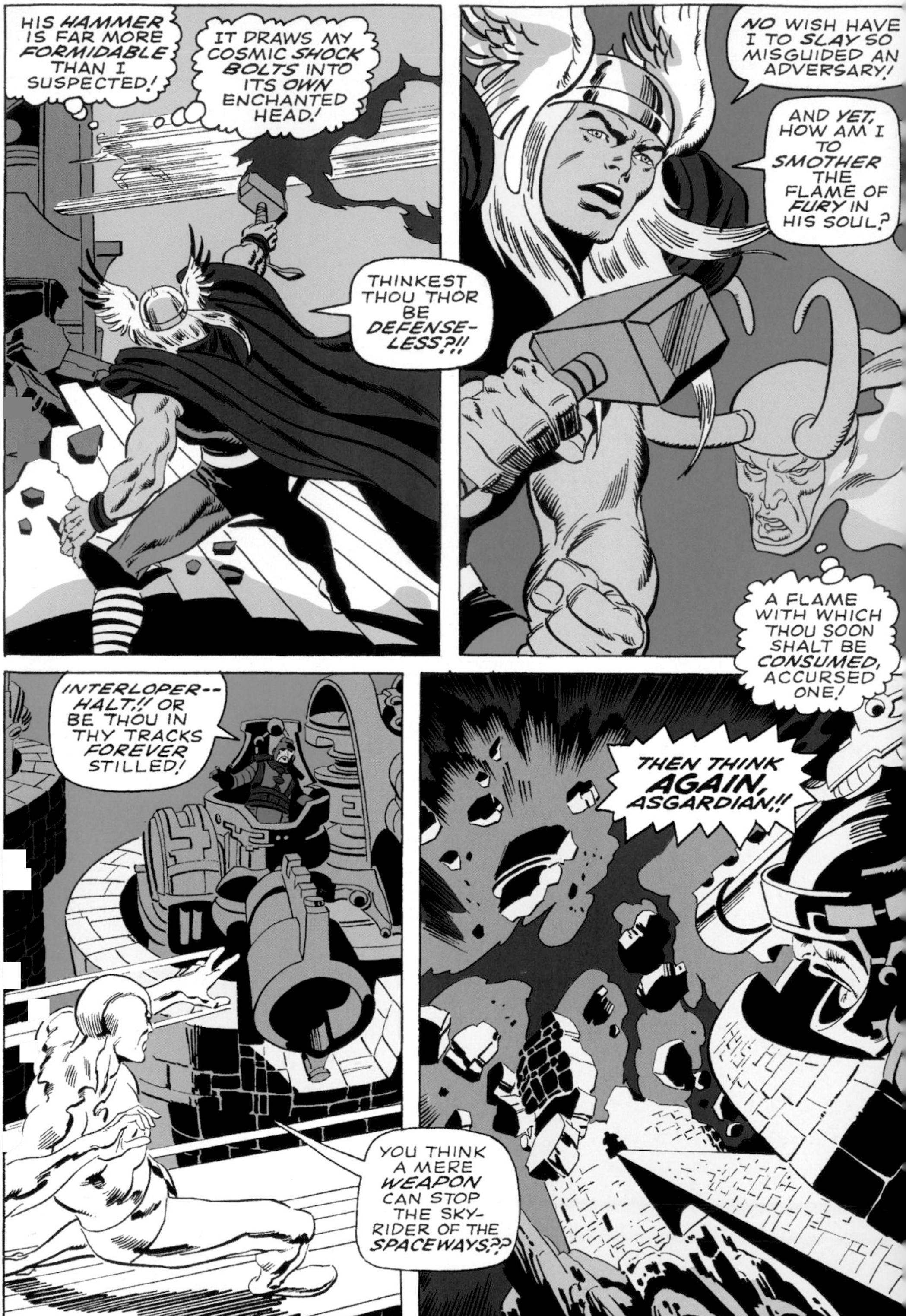
HIS HAMMER IS FAR MORE FORMIDABLE THAN I SUSPECTED!
IT DRAWS MY COSMIC SHOCK BOLTS INTO ITS OWN ENCHANTED HEAD!
THINKEST THOU THOR BE DEFENSE-LESS?!!
NO WISH HAVE I TO SLAY SO MISGUIDED AN ADVERSARY!
AND YET, HOW AM I TO SMOTHER THE FLAME OF FURY IN HIS SOUL?
A FLAME WITH WHICH THOU SOON SHALT BE CONSUMED, ACCURSED ONE!
INTERLOPER--HALT!! OR BE THOU IN THY TRACKS FOREVER STILLED!
YOU THINK A MERE WEAPON CAN STOP THE SKY-RIDER OF THE SPACEWAYS??
THEN THINK AGAIN, ASGARDIAN!!

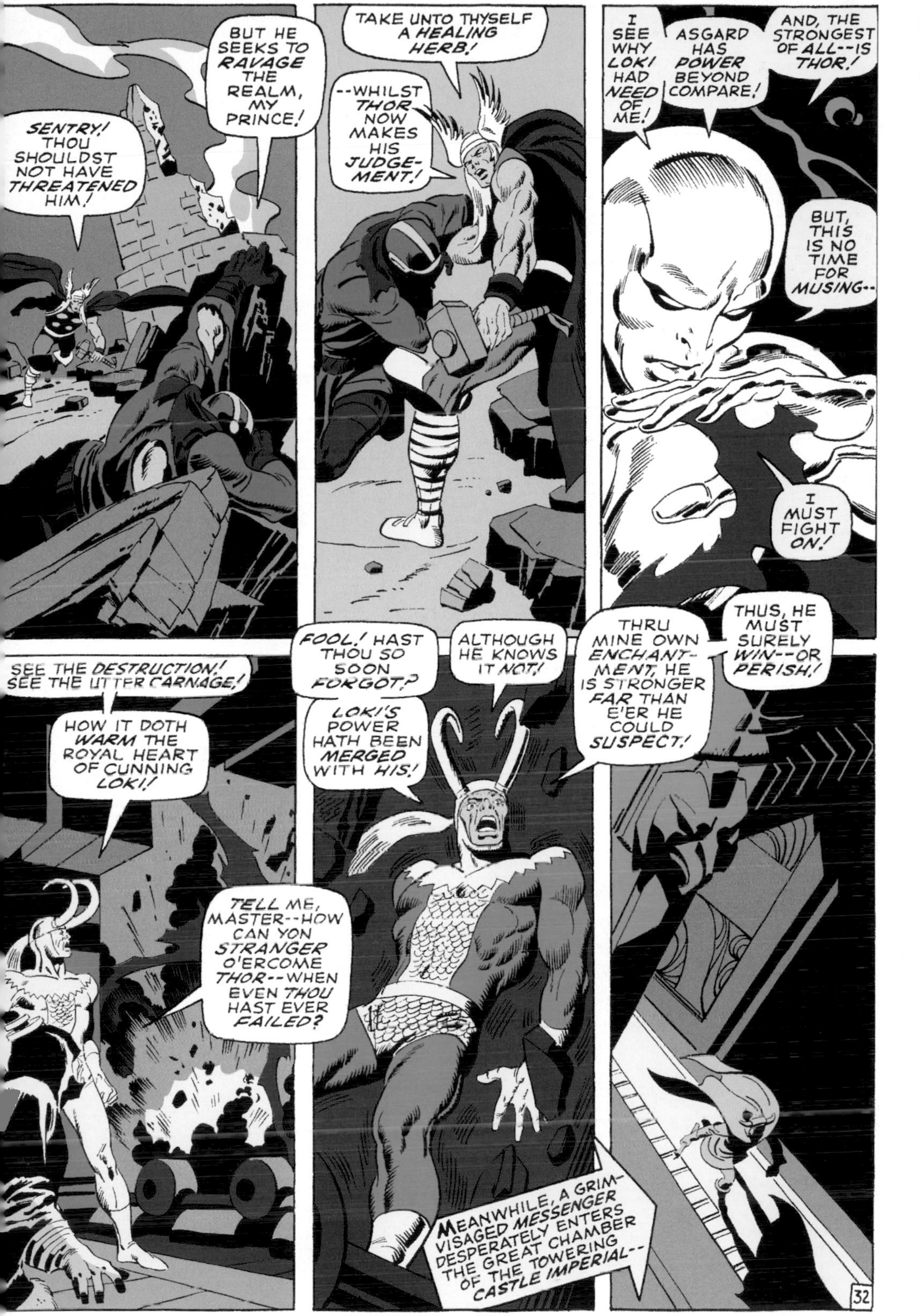

BUT HE SEEKS TO RAVAGE THE REALM, MY PRINCE!
SENTRY! THOU SHOULDST NOT HAVE THREATENED HIM!
TAKE UNTO THYSELF A HEALING HERB!
--WHILST THOR NOW MAKES HIS JUDGEMENT!
I SEE WHY LOKI HAD NEED OF ME!
ASGARD HAS POWER BEYOND COMPARE!
AND, THE STRONGEST OF ALL--IS THOR!
BUT, THIS IS NO TIME FOR MUSING--
I MUST FIGHT ON!
SEE THE DESTRUCTION! SEE THE UTTER CARNAGE!
HOW IT DOTH WARM THE ROYAL HEART OF CUNNING LOKI!
TELL ME, MASTER--HOW CAN YON STRANGER O'ERCOME THOR--WHEN EVEN THOU HAST EVER FAILED?
FOOL! HAST THOU SO SOON FORGOT?
LOKI'S POWER HATH BEEN MERGED WITH HIS!
ALTHOUGH HE KNOWS IT NOT!
THRU MINE OWN ENCHANTMENT, HE IS STRONGER FAR THAN E'ER HE COULD SUSPECT!
THUS, HE MUST SURELY WIN--OR PERISH!
MEANWHILE, A GRIM-VISAGED MESSENGER DESPERATELY ENTERS THE GREAT CHAMBER OF THE TOWERING CASTLE IMPERIAL--
32

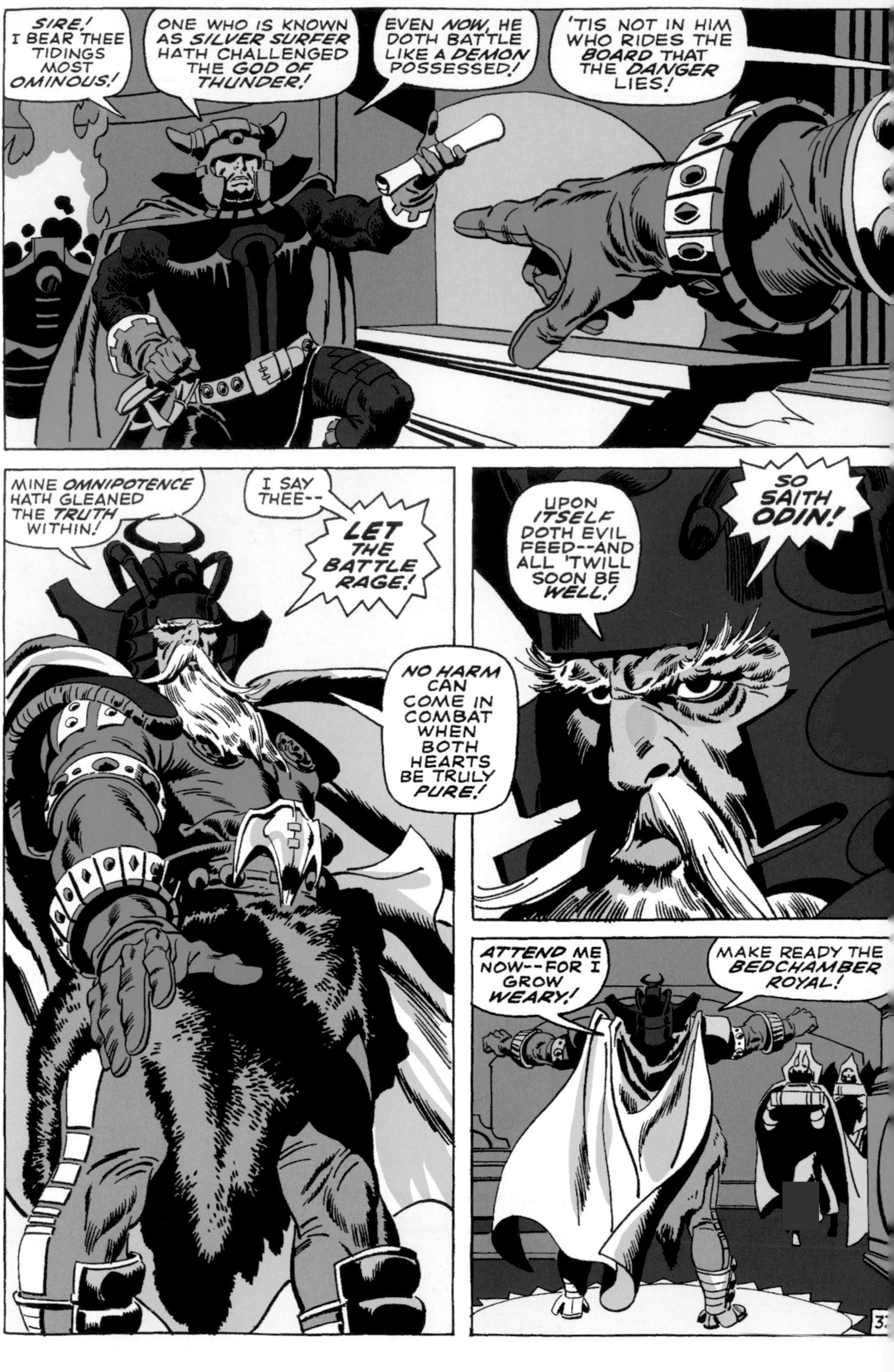
SIRE! I BEAR THEE TIDINGS MOST OMINOUS!
ONE WHO IS KNOWN AS SILVER SURFER HATH CHALLENGED THE GOD OF THUNDER!
EVEN NOW, HE DOTH BATTLE LIKE A DEMON POSSESSED!
'TIS NOT IN HIM WHO RIDES THE BOARD THAT THE DANGER LIES!
MINE OMNIPOTENCE HATH GLEANED THE TRUTH WITHIN!
I SAY THEE--
LET THE BATTLE RAGE!
NO HARM CAN COME IN COMBAT WHEN BOTH HEARTS BE TRULY PURE!
UPON ITSELF DOTH EVIL FEED--AND ALL 'TWILL SOON BE WELL!
SO SAITH ODIN!
ATTEND ME NOW--FOR I GROW WEARY!
MAKE READY THE BEDCHAMBER ROYAL!
31

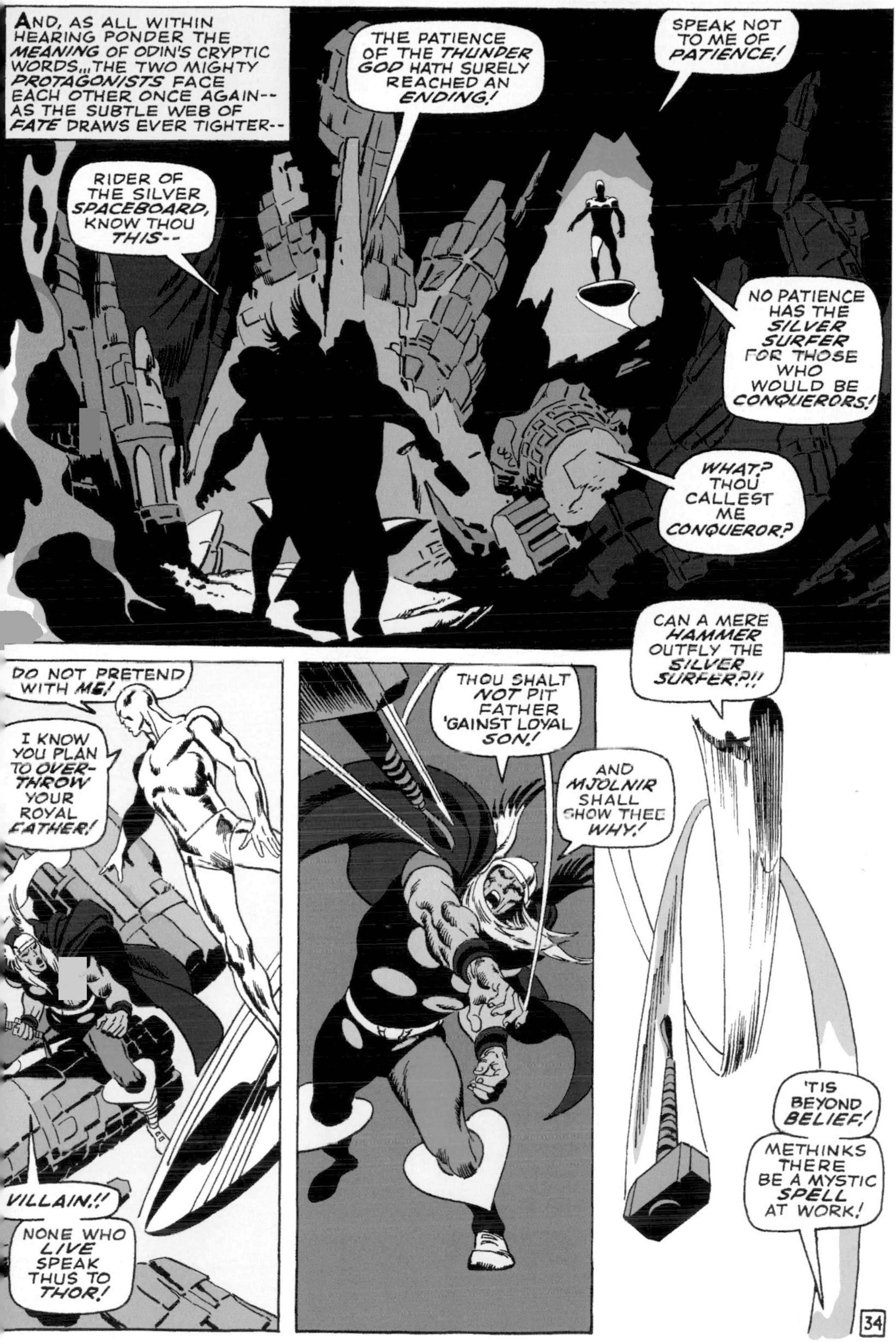
AND, AS ALL WITHIN HEARING PONDER THE MEANING OF ODIN'S CRYPTIC WORDS... THE TWO MIGHTY PROTAGONISTS FACE EACH OTHER ONCE AGAIN-- AS THE SUBTLE WEB OF FATE DRAWS EVER TIGHTER--
RIDER OF THE SILVER SPACEBOARD, KNOW THOU THIS--
THE PATIENCE OF THE THUNDER GOD HATH SURELY REACHED AN ENDING!
SPEAK NOT TO ME OF PATIENCE!
NO PATIENCE HAS THE SILVER SURFER FOR THOSE WHO WOULD BE CONQUERORS!
WHAT? THOU CALLEST ME CONQUEROR?
DO NOT PRETEND WITH ME!
I KNOW YOU PLAN TO OVER-THROW YOUR ROYAL FATHER!
VILLAIN!!
NONE WHO LIVE SPEAK THUS TO THOR!
THOU SHALT NOT PIT FATHER 'GAINST LOYAL SON!
AND MJOLNIR SHALL SHOW THEE WHY!
CAN A MERE HAMMER OUTFLY THE SILVER SURFER?!!
'TIS BEYOND BELIEF!
METHINKS THERE BE A MYSTIC SPELL AT WORK!

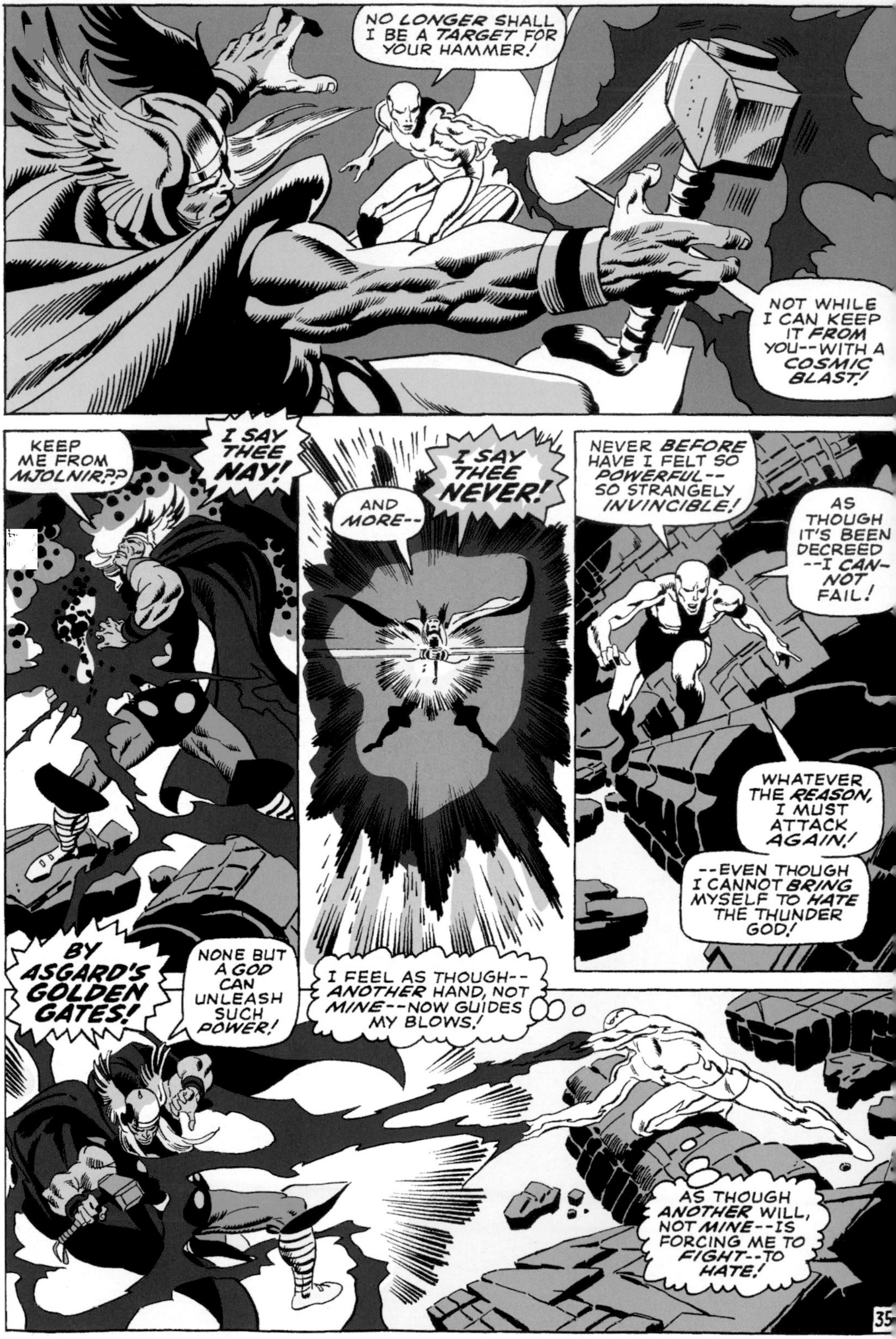

NO LONGER SHALL I BE A TARGET FOR YOUR HAMMER!
NOT WHILE I CAN KEEP IT FROM YOU--WITH A COSMIC BLAST!
KEEP ME FROM MJOLNIR??
I SAY THEE NAY!
AND MORE--
I SAY THEE NEVER!
NEVER BEFORE HAVE I FELT SO POWERFUL-- SO STRANGELY INVINCIBLE!
AS THOUGH IT'S BEEN DECREED --I CANNOT FAIL!
WHATEVER THE REASON, I MUST ATTACK AGAIN!
--EVEN THOUGH I CANNOT BRING MYSELF TO HATE THE THUNDER GOD!
BY ASGARD'S GOLDEN GATES!
NONE BUT A GOD CAN UNLEASH SUCH POWER!
I FEEL AS THOUGH-- ANOTHER HAND, NOT MINE--NOW GUIDES MY BLOWS.
AS THOUGH ANOTHER WILL, NOT MINE--IS FORCING ME TO FIGHT--TO HATE!
35

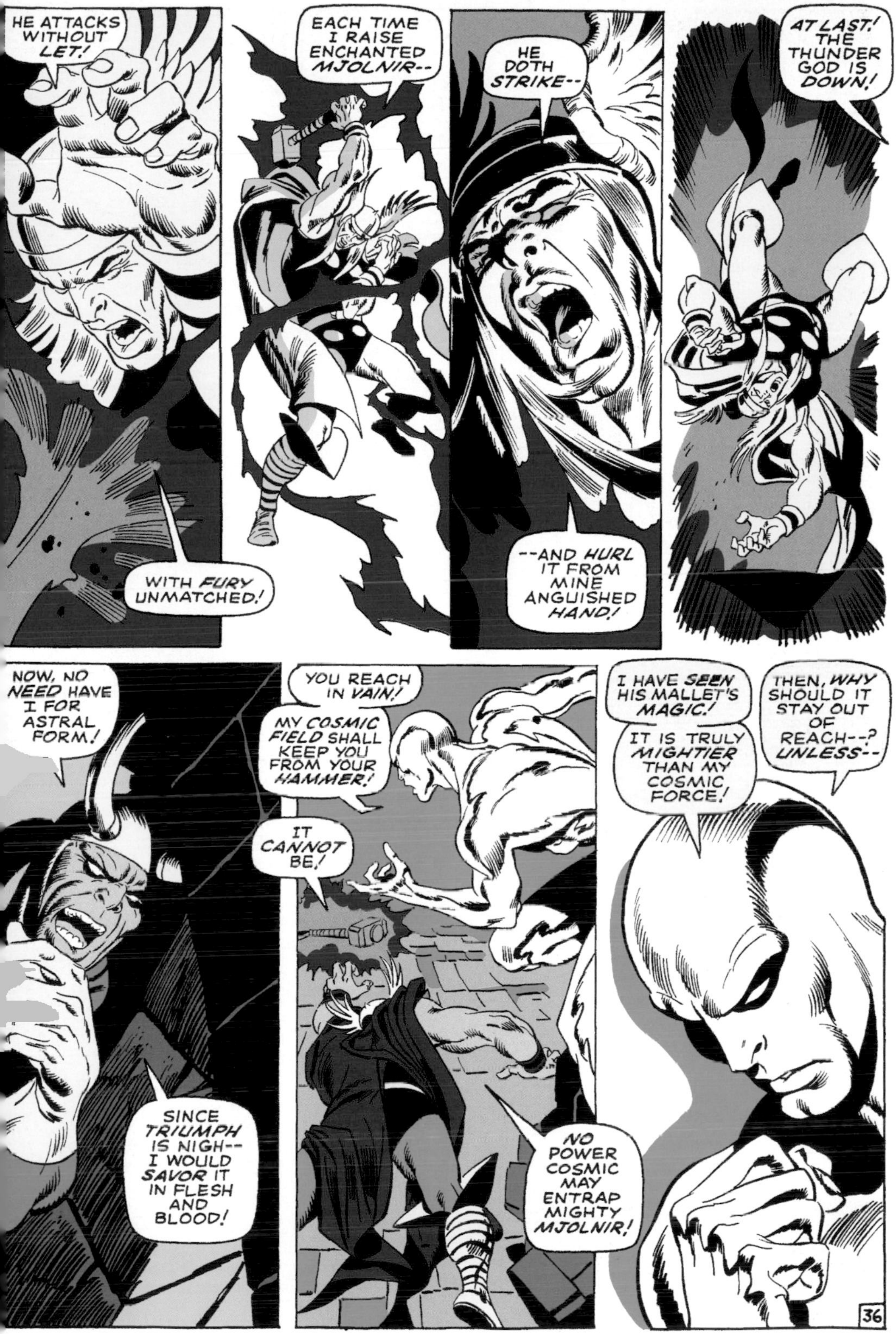
HE ATTACKS WITHOUT LET!
WITH FURY UNMATCHED!
EACH TIME I RAISE ENCHANTED MJOLNIR--
HE DOTH STRIKE--
--AND HURL IT FROM MINE ANGUISHED HAND!
AT LAST! THE THUNDER GOD IS DOWN!
NOW, NO NEED HAVE I FOR ASTRAL FORM!
SINCE TRIUMPH IS NIGH-- I WOULD SAVOR IT IN FLESH AND BLOOD!
YOU REACH IN VAIN!
MY COSMIC FIELD SHALL KEEP YOU FROM YOUR HAMMER!
IT CANNOT BE!
NO POWER COSMIC MAY ENTRAP MIGHTY MJOLNIR!
I HAVE SEEN HIS MALLET'S MAGIC!
IT IS TRULY MIGHTIER THAN MY COSMIC FORCE!
THEN, WHY SHOULD IT STAY OUT OF REACH--? UNLESS--
36

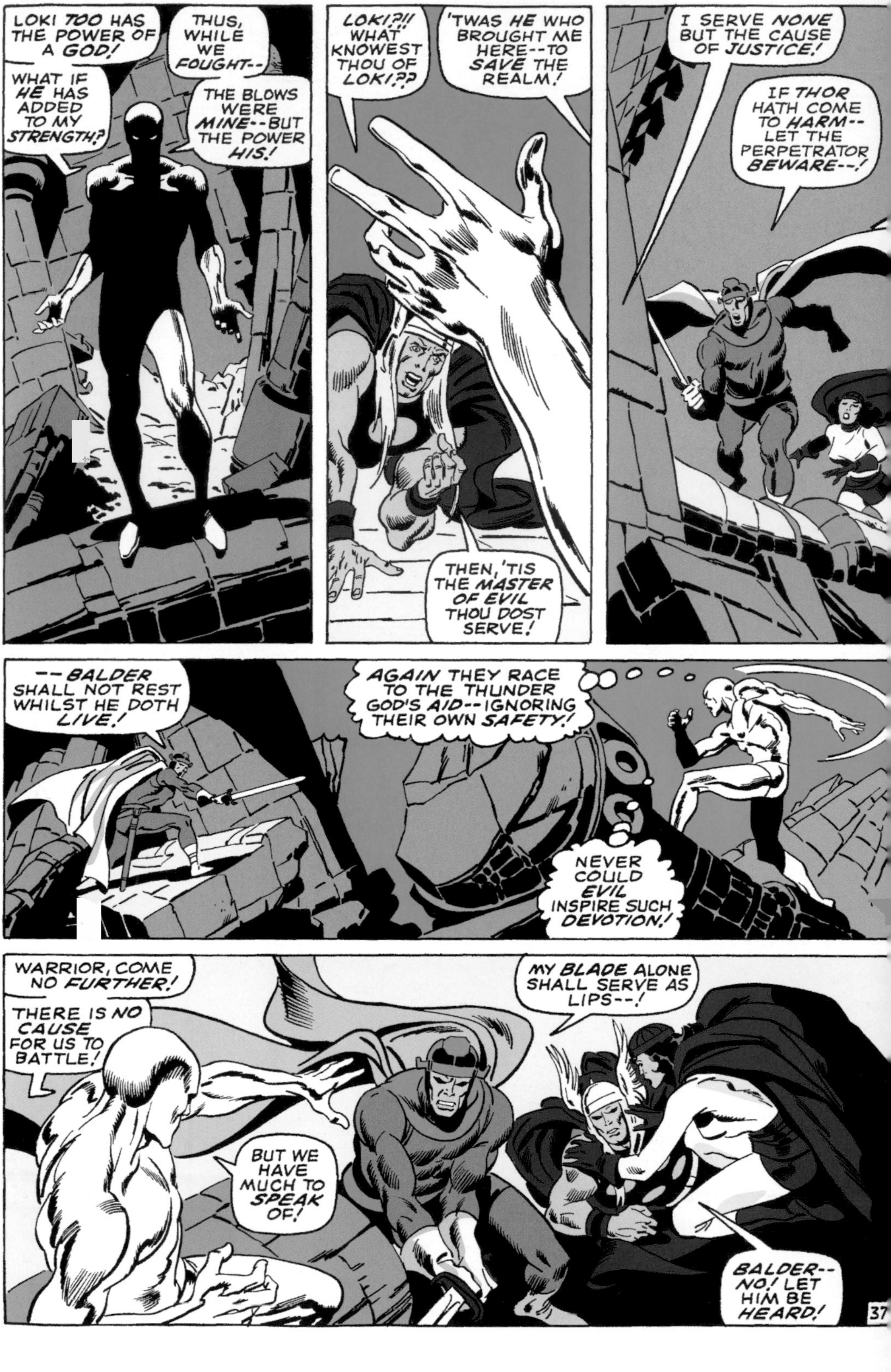
LOKI TOO HAS THE POWER OF A GOD!
WHAT IF HE HAS ADDED TO MY STRENGTH?
THUS, WHILE WE FOUGHT--
THE BLOWS WERE MINE--BUT THE POWER HIS!
LOKI?!! WHAT KNOWEST THOU OF LOKI??
'TWAS HE WHO BROUGHT ME HERE--TO SAVE THE REALM!
THEN, 'TIS THE MASTER OF EVIL THOU DOST SERVE!
I SERVE NONE BUT THE CAUSE OF JUSTICE!
IF THOR HATH COME TO HARM--LET THE PERPETRATOR BEWARE--!
--BALDER SHALL NOT REST WHILST HE DOTH LIVE!
AGAIN THEY RACE TO THE THUNDER GOD'S AID--IGNORING THEIR OWN SAFETY!
NEVER COULD EVIL INSPIRE SUCH DEVOTION!
WARRIOR, COME NO FURTHER!
THERE IS NO CAUSE FOR US TO BATTLE!
BUT WE HAVE MUCH TO SPEAK OF!
MY BLADE ALONE SHALL SERVE AS LIPS--!
BALDER--NO! LET HIM BE HEARD!

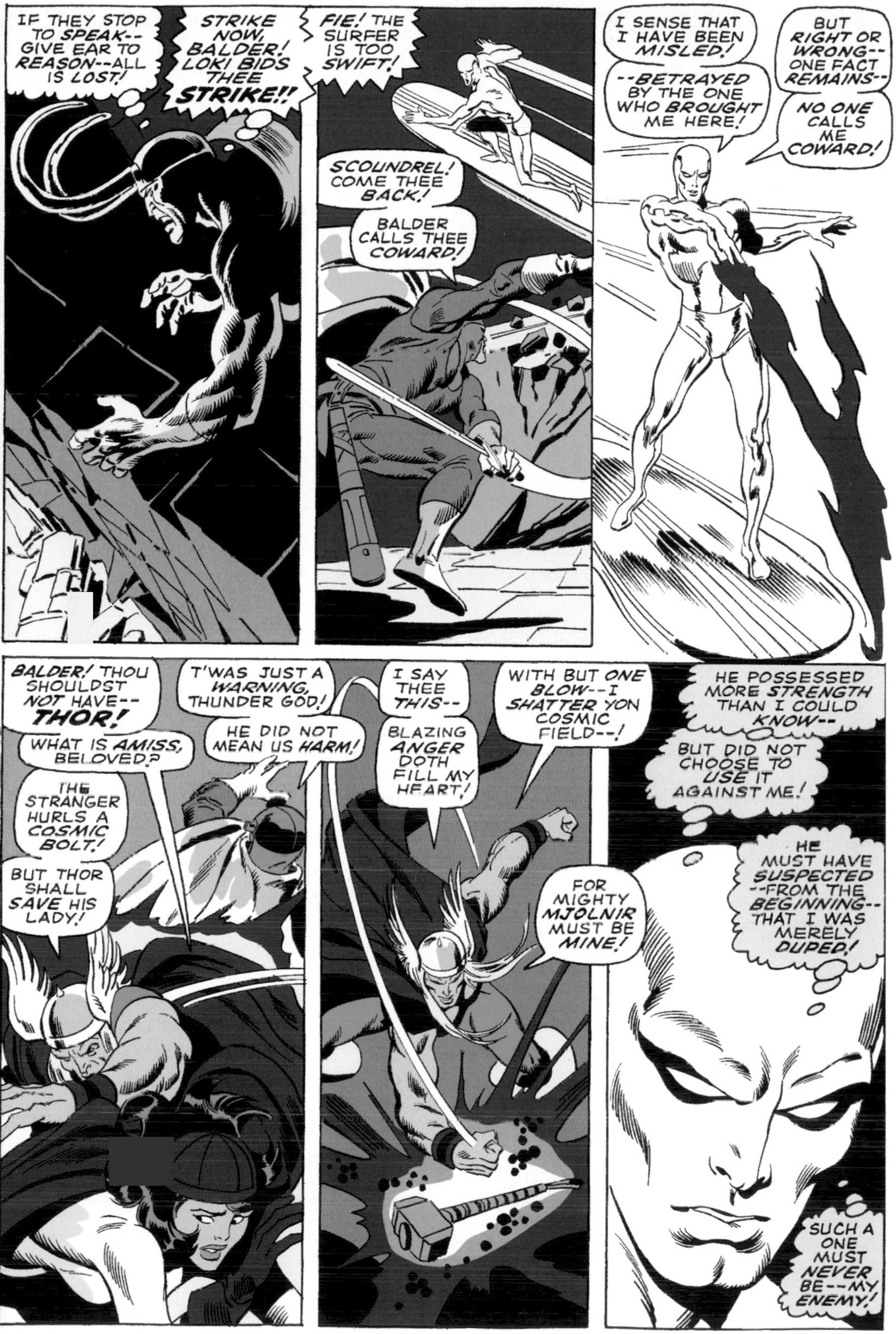

IF THEY STOP TO SPEAK--GIVE EAR TO REASON--ALL IS LOST!
STRIKE NOW, BALDER! LOKI BIDS THEE STRIKE!!
FIE! THE SURFER IS TOO SWIFT!
SCOUNDREL! COME THEE BACK!
BALDER CALLS THEE COWARD!
I SENSE THAT I HAVE BEEN MISLED!
--BETRAYED BY THE ONE WHO BROUGHT ME HERE!
BUT RIGHT OR WRONG--ONE FACT REMAINS--
NO ONE CALLS ME COWARD!
BALDER! THOU SHOULDST NOT HAVE--THOR!
WHAT IS AMISS, BELOVED?
THE STRANGER HURLS A COSMIC BOLT!
BUT THOR SHALL SAVE HIS LADY!
T'WAS JUST A WARNING, THUNDER GOD!
HE DID NOT MEAN US HARM!
I SAY THEE THIS--
BLAZING ANGER DOTH FILL MY HEART!
WITH BUT ONE BLOW--I SHATTER YON COSMIC FIELD--!
FOR MIGHTY MJOLNIR MUST BE MINE!
HE POSSESSED MORE STRENGTH THAN I COULD KNOW--
BUT DID NOT CHOOSE TO USE IT AGAINST ME!
HE MUST HAVE SUSPECTED--FROM THE BEGINNING--THAT I WAS MERELY DUPED!
SUCH A ONE MUST NEVER BE--MY ENEMY!

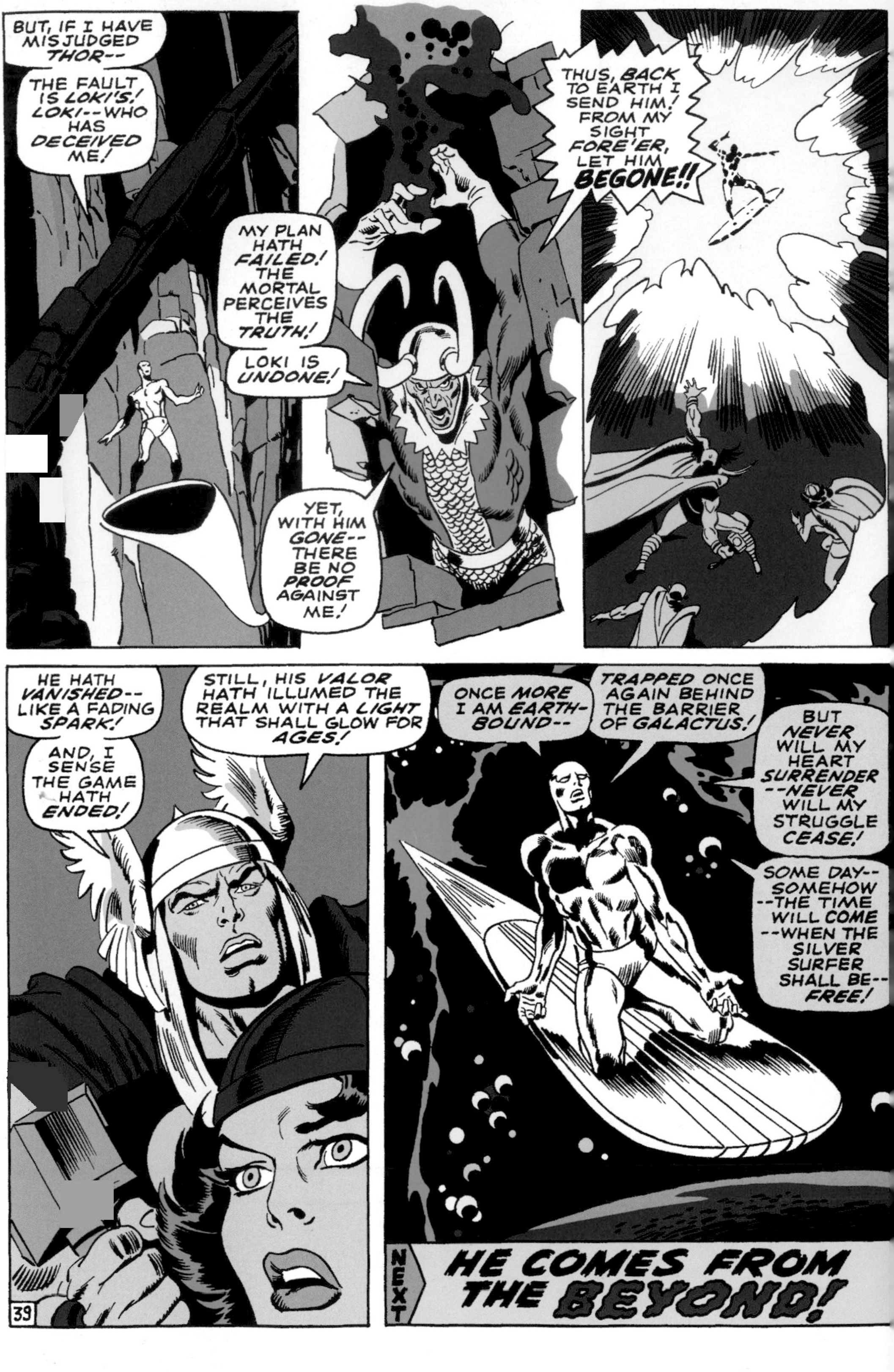
BUT, IF I HAVE MISJUDGED THOR--
THE FAULT IS LOKI'S! LOKI--WHO HAS DECEIVED ME!
MY PLAN HATH FAILED! THE MORTAL PERCEIVES THE TRUTH!
LOKI IS UNDONE!
YET, WITH HIM GONE--THERE BE NO PROOF AGAINST ME!
THUS, BACK TO EARTH I SEND HIM! FROM MY SIGHT FORE'ER, LET HIM BEGONE!!
HE HATH VANISHED--LIKE A FADING SPARK!
AND, I SENSE THE GAME HATH ENDED!
STILL, HIS VALOR HATH ILLUMED THE REALM WITH A LIGHT THAT SHALL GLOW FOR AGES!
ONCE MORE I AM EARTH-BOUND--
TRAPPED ONCE AGAIN BEHIND THE BARRIER OF GALACTUS!
BUT NEVER WILL MY HEART SURRENDER--NEVER WILL MY STRUGGLE CEASE!
SOME DAY--SOMEHOW--THE TIME WILL COME--WHEN THE SILVER SURFER SHALL BE--FREE!
NEXT
HE COMES FROM THE BEYOND!

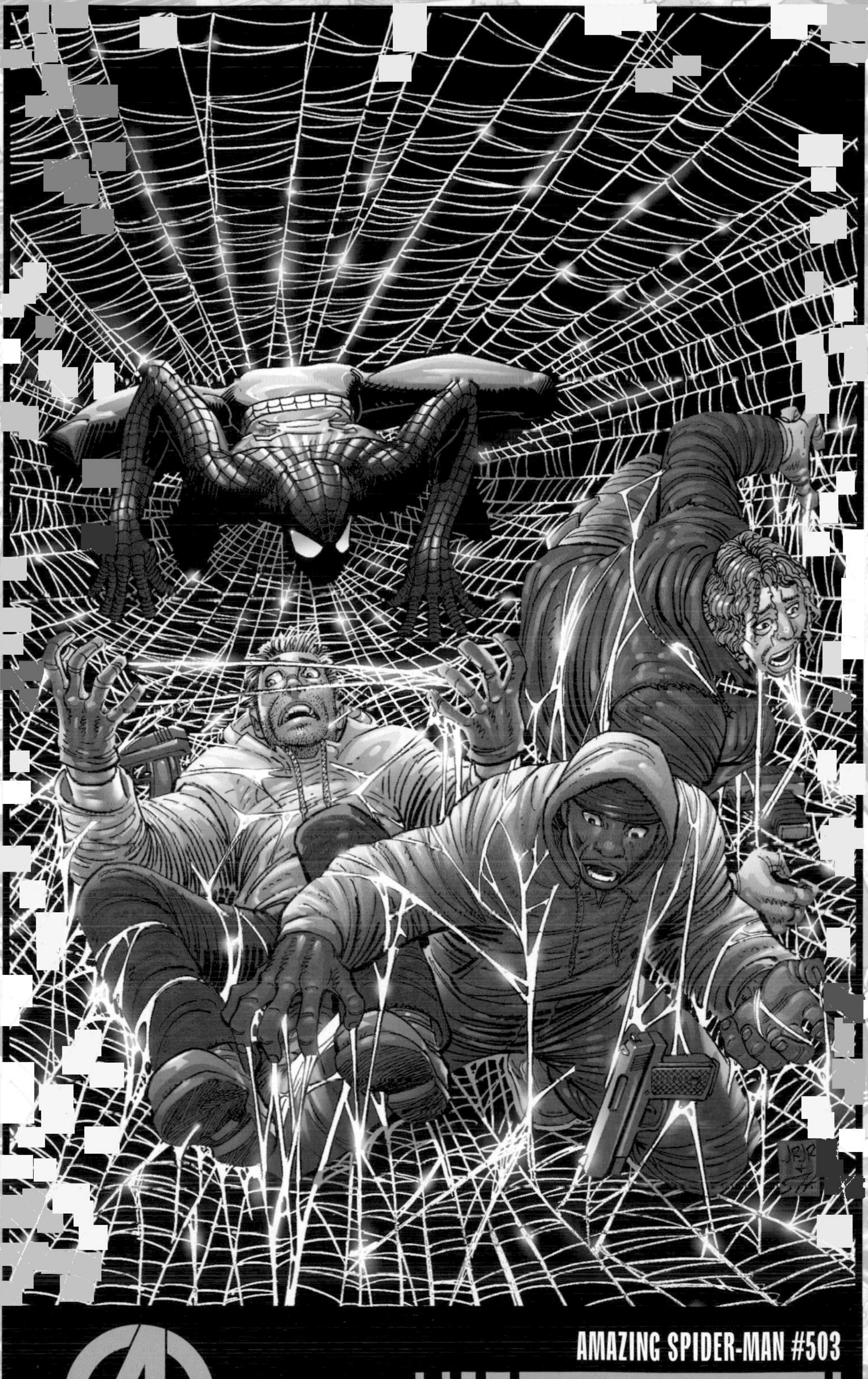

AMAZING SPIDER-MAN #503

THE SORCERESS MORWAN HAS BEEN SET FREE FROM YEARS OF CAPTIVITY AND EMBARKS ON A QUEST TO THANK THE ONE RESPONSIBLE FOR HER FREEDOM: SPIDER MAN! AND IF THINGS WEREN'T BAD ENOUGH, LOKI IS ON THEIR TRAIL.

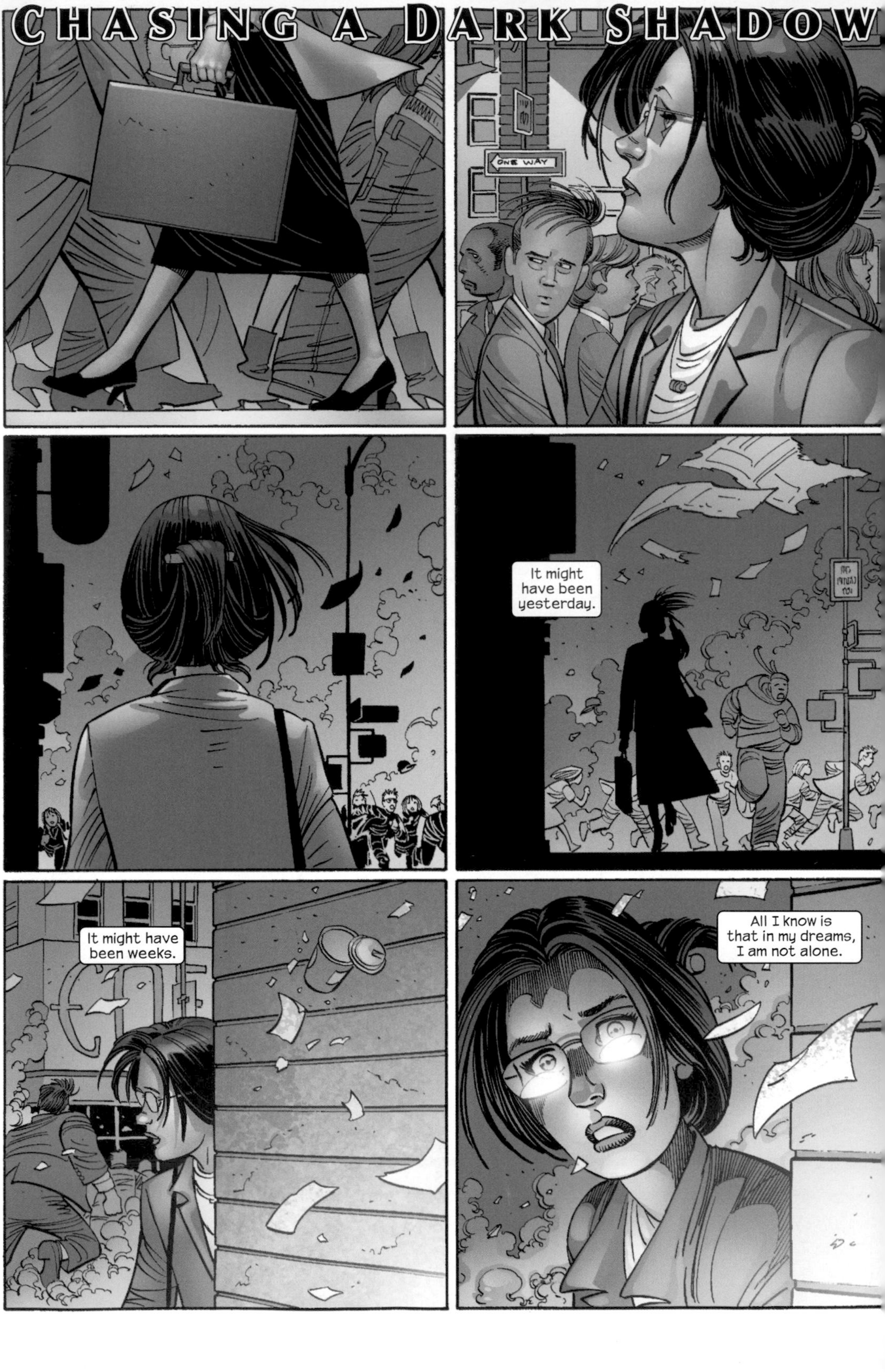
CHASING A DARK SHADOW
ONE WAY
It might have been yesterday.
It might have been weeks.
All I know is that in my dreams, I am not alone.

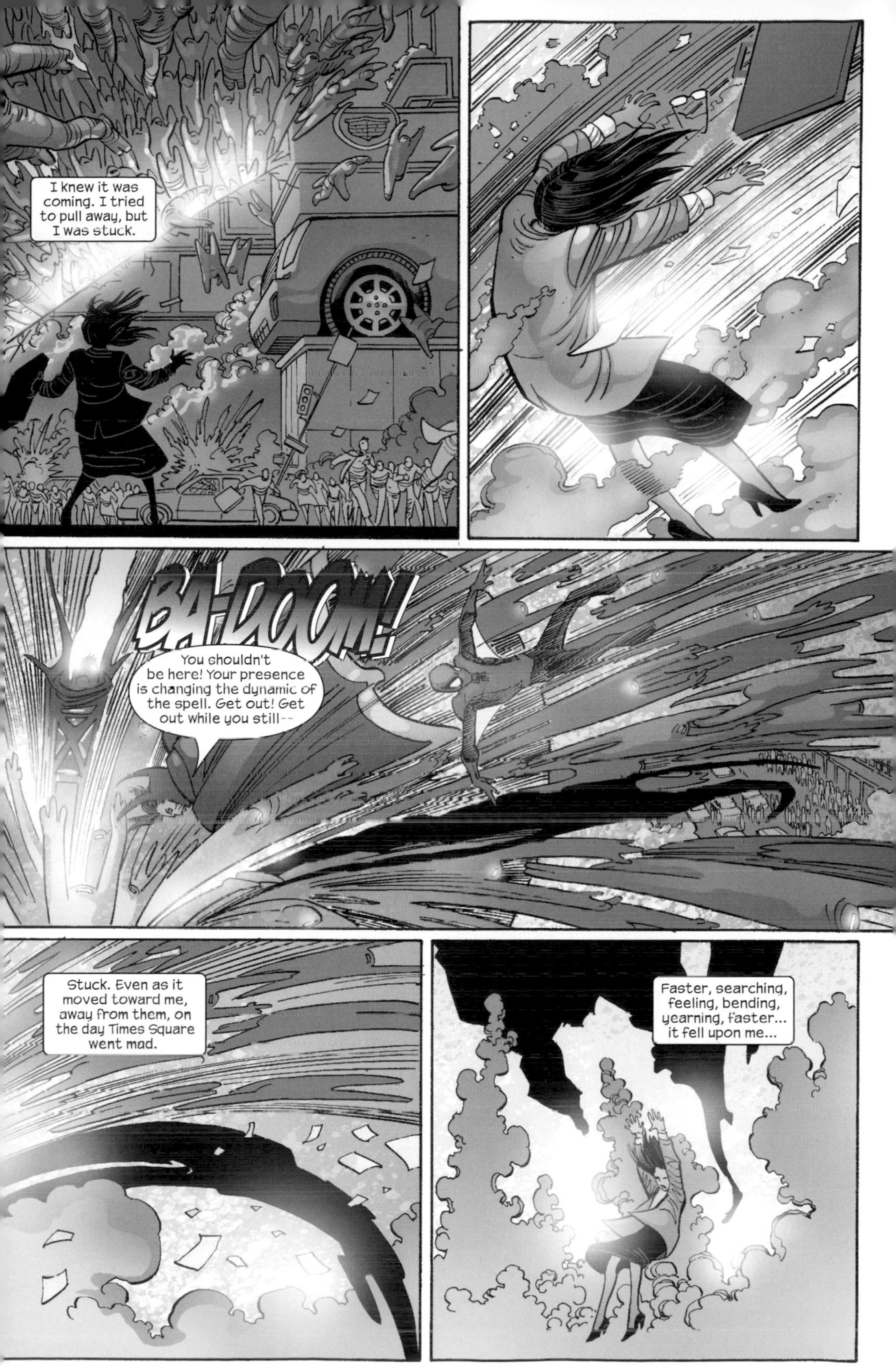
I knew it was coming. I tried to pull away, but I was stuck.
BA-DOOM!
You shouldn't be here! Your presence is changing the dynamic of the spell. Get out! Get out while you still--
Stuck. Even as it moved toward me, away from them, on the day Times Square went mad.
Faster, searching, feeling, bending, yearning, faster... it fell upon me...

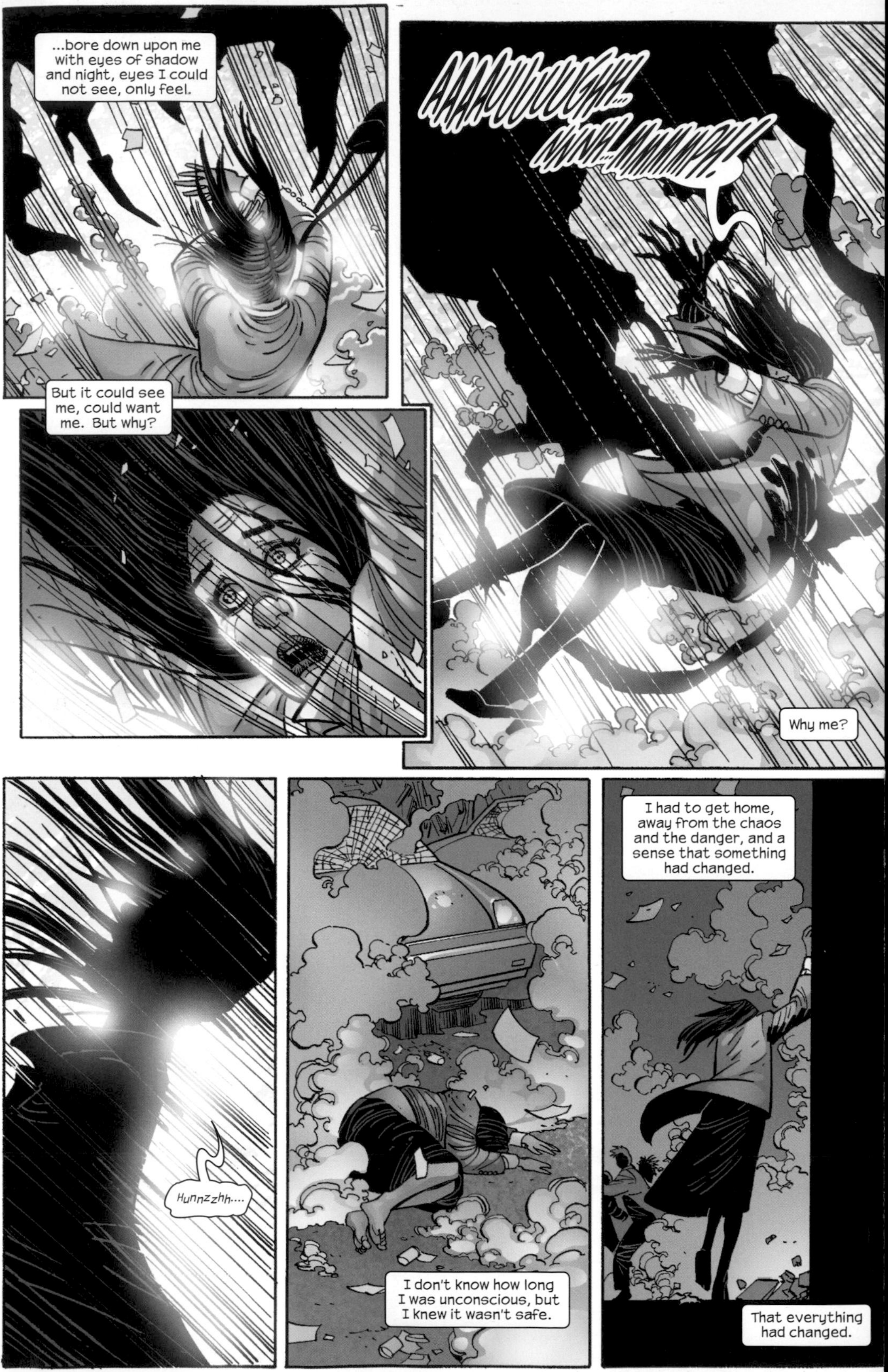
...bore down upon me with eyes of shadow and night, eyes I could not see, only feel.
But it could see me, could want me. But why?
Why me?
Hunnzzhh....
I don't know how long I was unconscious, but I knew it wasn't safe.
I had to get home, away from the chaos and the danger, and a sense that something had changed.
That everything had changed.

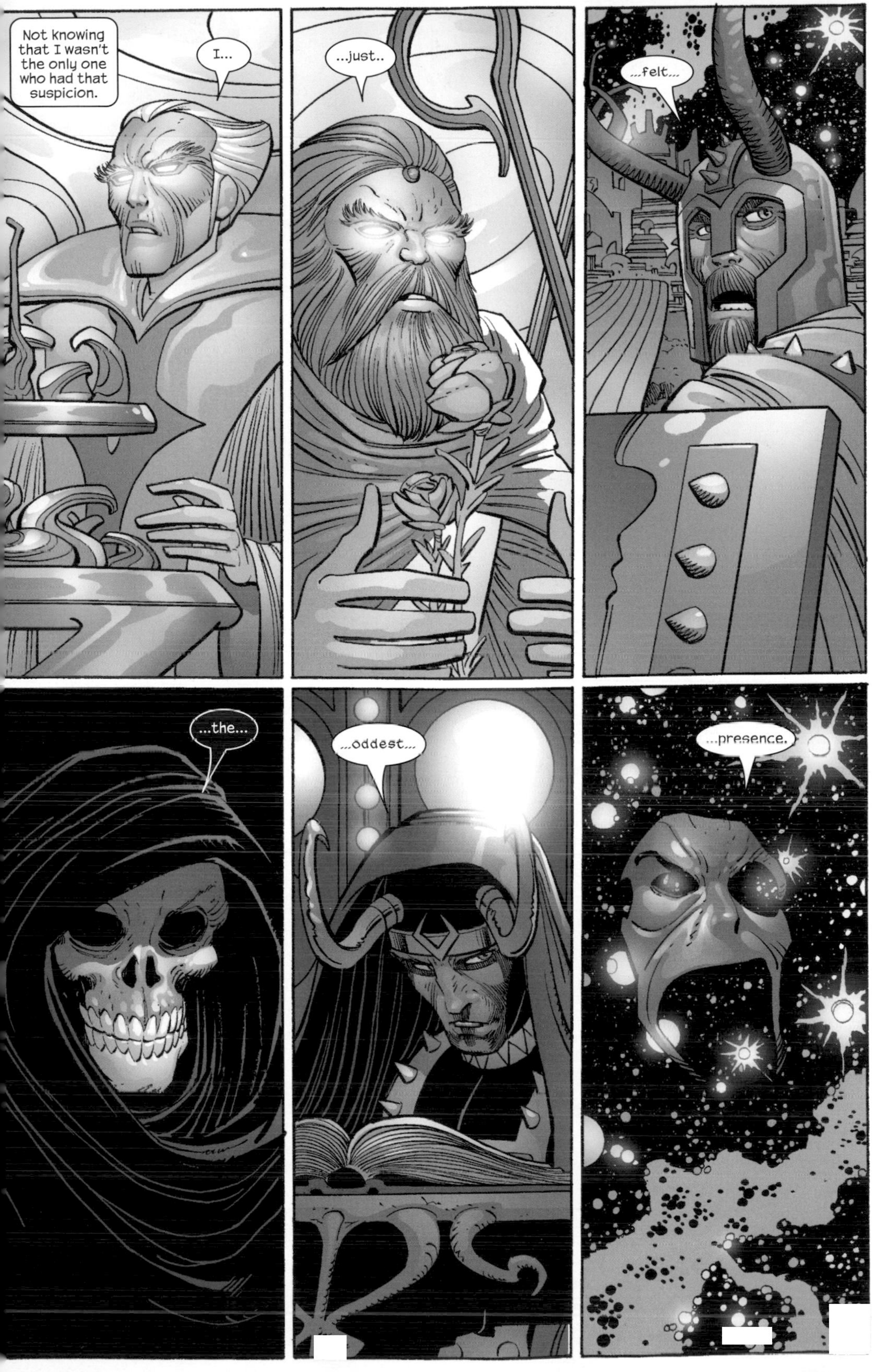
Not knowing that I wasn't the only one who had that suspicion.
I...
...just..
...felt...
...the...
...oddest...
...presence.

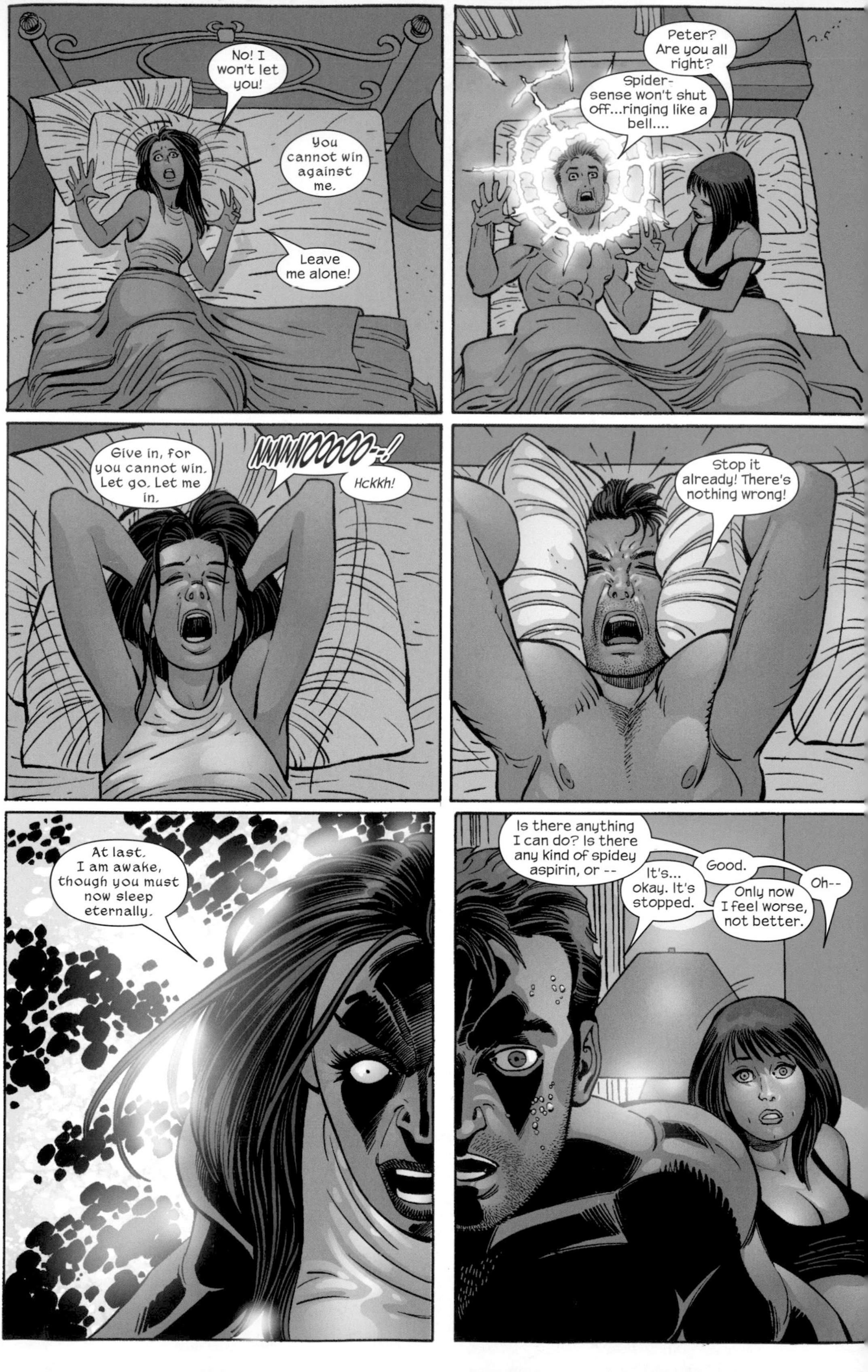
No! I won't let you!
You cannot win against me.
Leave me alone!
Peter? Are you all right?
Spider-sense won't shut off...ringing like a bell....
Give in, for you cannot win. Let go. Let me in.
NNNNOOOOO--!
Hckkh!
Stop it already! There's nothing wrong!
At last. I am awake, though you must now sleep eternally.
Is there anything I can do? Is there any kind of spidey aspirin, or --
It's... okay. It's stopped.
Good.
Oh--
Only now I feel worse, not better.

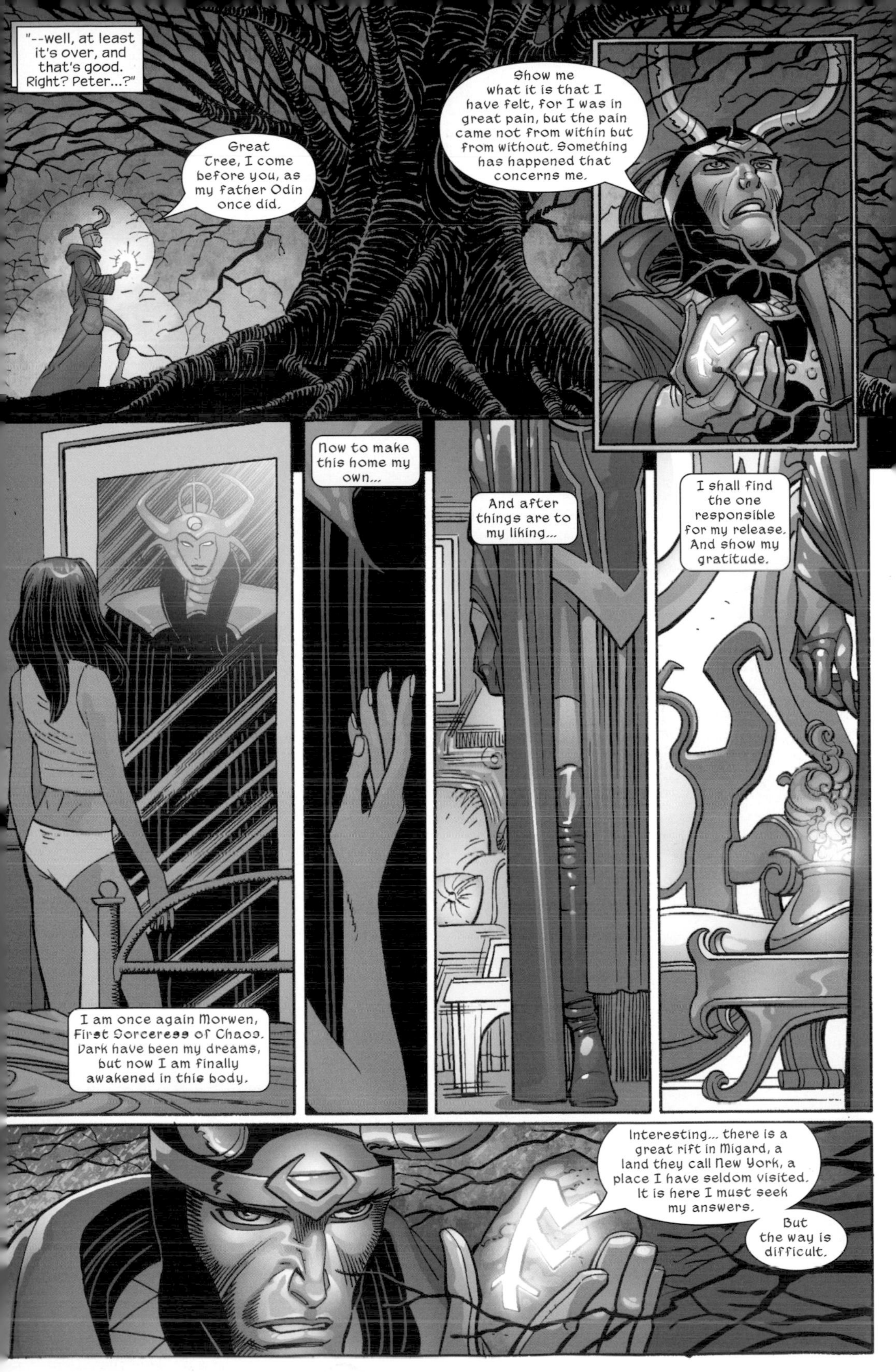
"--well, at least it's over, and that's good. Right? Peter...?"
Great Tree, I come before you, as my father Odin once did.
Show me what it is that I have felt, for I was in great pain, but the pain came not from within but from without. Something has happened that concerns me.
I am once again Morwen, First Sorceress of Chaos. Dark have been my dreams, but now I am finally awakened in this body.
Now to make this home my own...
And after things are to my liking...
I shall find the one responsible for my release. And show my gratitude.
Interesting... there is a great rift in Migard, a land they call New York, a place I have seldom visited. It is here I must seek my answers.
But the way is difficult.

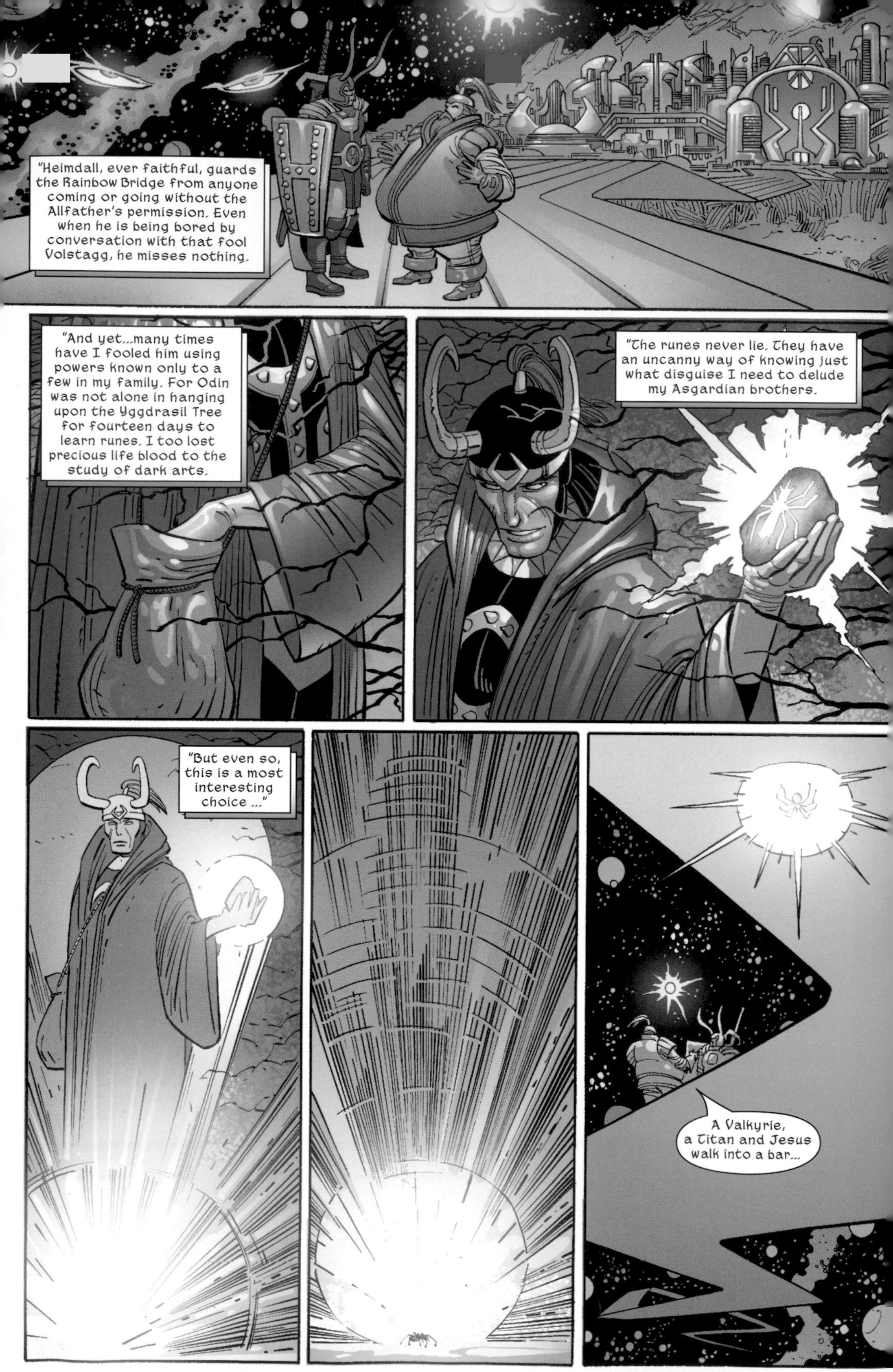
"Heimdall, ever faithful, guards the Rainbow Bridge from anyone coming or going without the Allfather's permission. Even when he is being bored by conversation with that fool Volstagg, he misses nothing.
"And yet...many times have I fooled him using powers known only to a few in my family. For Odin was not alone in hanging upon the Yggdrasil Tree for fourteen days to learn runes. I too lost precious life blood to the study of dark arts.
"The runes never lie. They have an uncanny way of knowing just what disguise I need to delude my Asgardian brothers.
"But even so, this is a most interesting choice ..."
A Valkyrie, a Titan and Jesus walk into a bar...

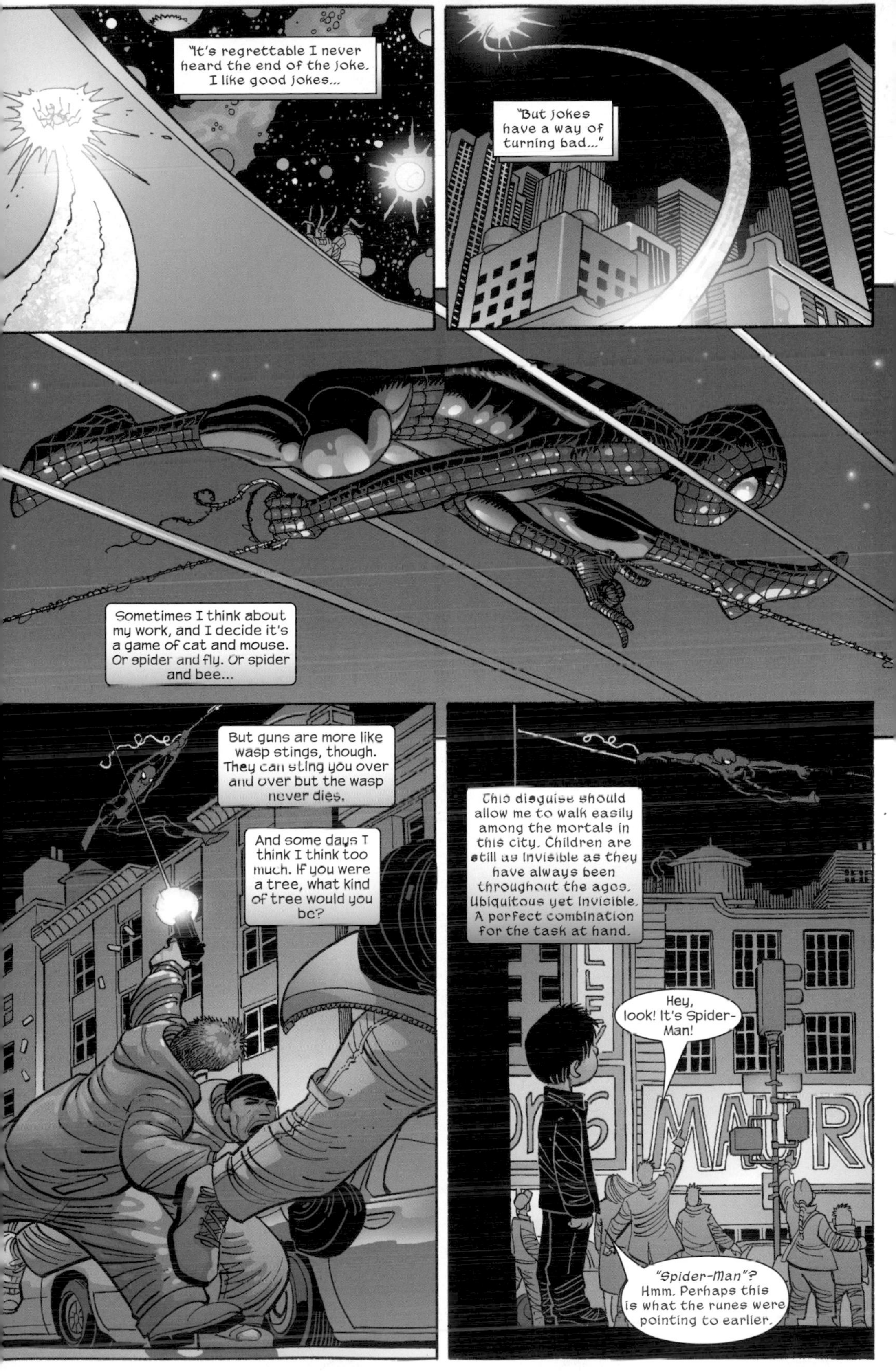
"It's regrettable I never heard the end of the joke. I like good jokes...
"But jokes have a way of turning bad..."
Sometimes I think about my work, and I decide it's a game of cat and mouse. Or spider and fly. Or spider and bee...
But guns are more like wasp stings, though. They can sting you over and over but the wasp never dies.
And some days I think I think too much. If you were a tree, what kind of tree would you be?
This disguise should allow me to walk easily among the mortals in this city. Children are still as invisible as they have always been throughout the ages. Ubiquitous yet invisible. A perfect combination for the task at hand.
Hey, look! It's Spider-Man!
"Spider-Man"? Hmm. Perhaps this is what the runes were pointing to earlier.

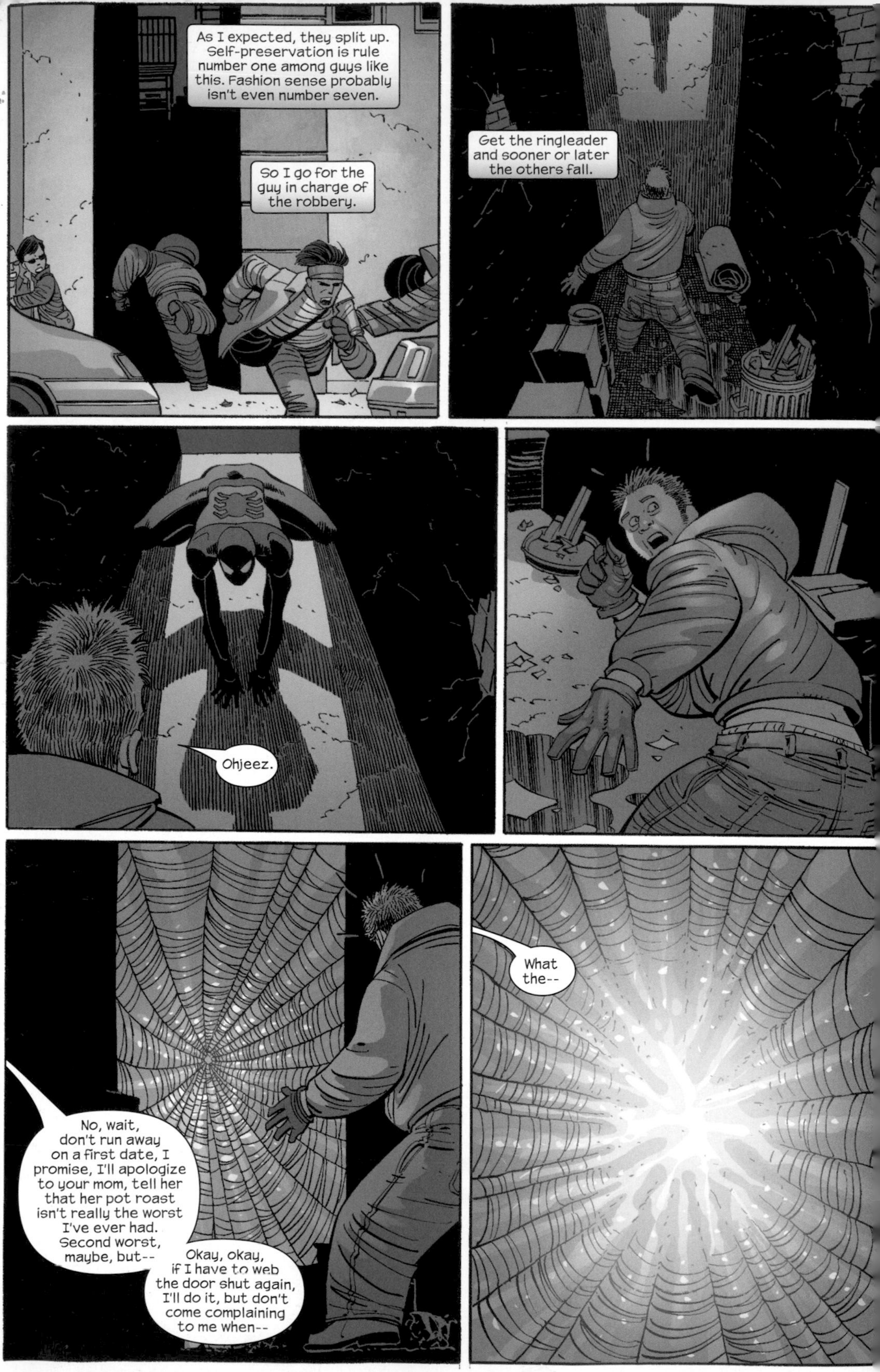
As I expected, they split up. Self-preservation is rule number one among guys like this. Fashion sense probably isn't even number seven.
So I go for the guy in charge of the robbery.
Get the ringleader and sooner or later the others fall.
Ohjeez.
What the--
No, wait, don't run away on a first date, I promise, I'll apologize to your mom, tell her that her pot roast isn't really the worst I've ever had. Second worst, maybe, but--
Okay, okay, if I have to web the door shut again, I'll do it, but don't come complaining to me when--

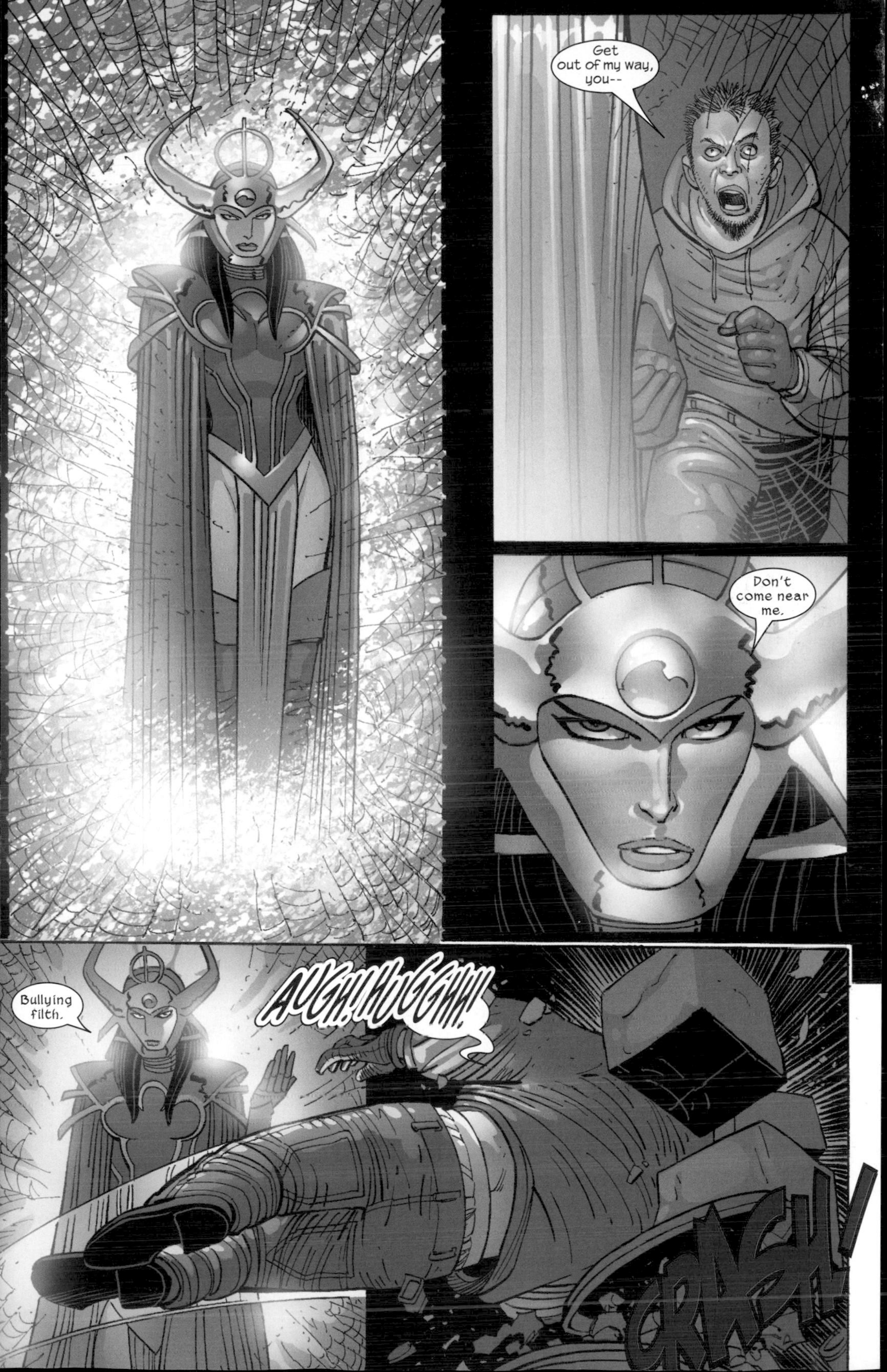

Get out of my way, you--
Don't come near me.
Bullying filth.
AUGH! HUGGHH!
CRASH!

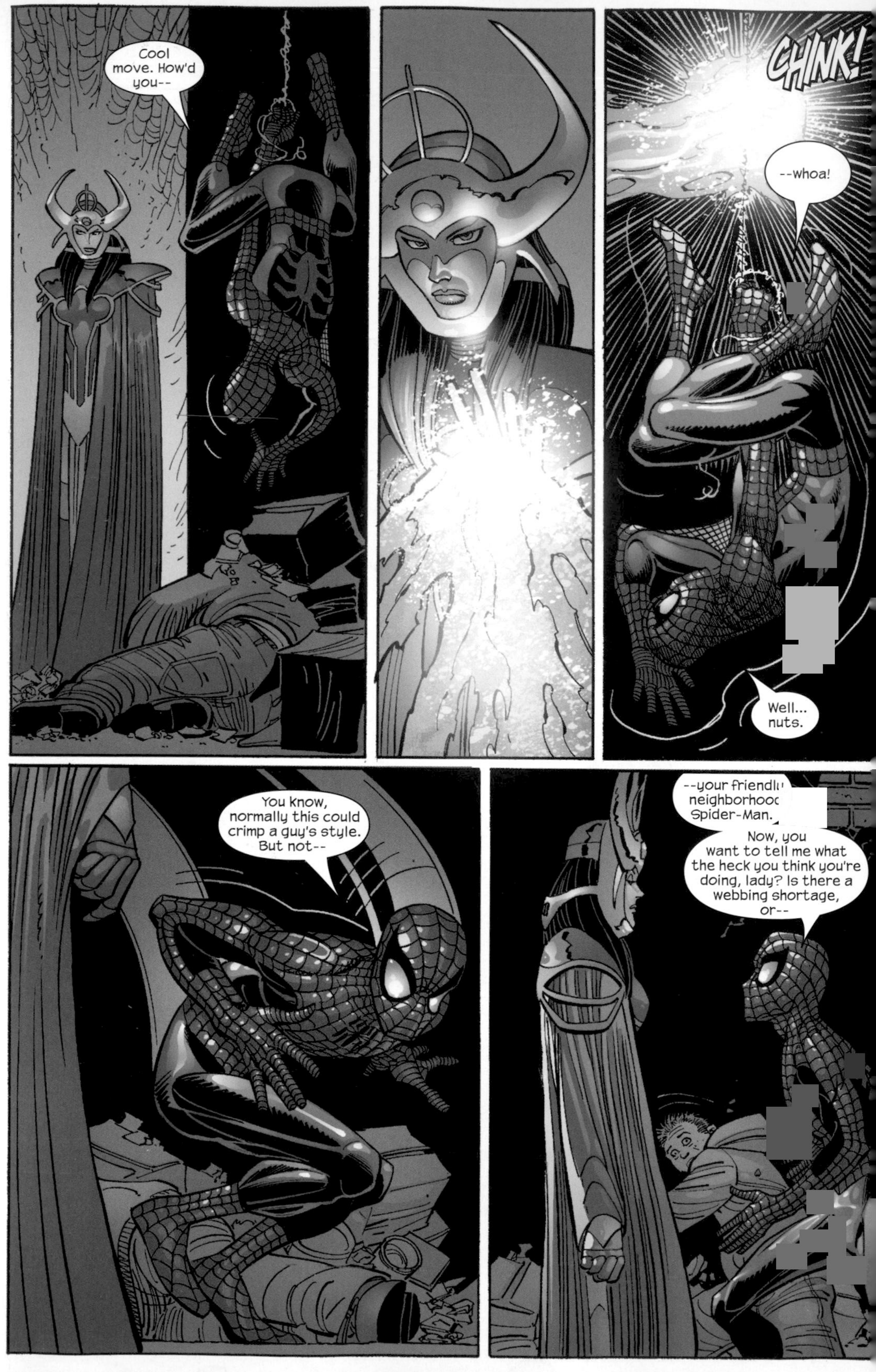
Cool move. How'd you--
CHINK!
--whoa!
Well... nuts.
You know, normally this could crimp a guy's style. But not--
--your friendly neighborhoo
Spider-Man.
Now, you want to tell me what the heck you think you're doing, lady? Is there a webbing shortage, or--

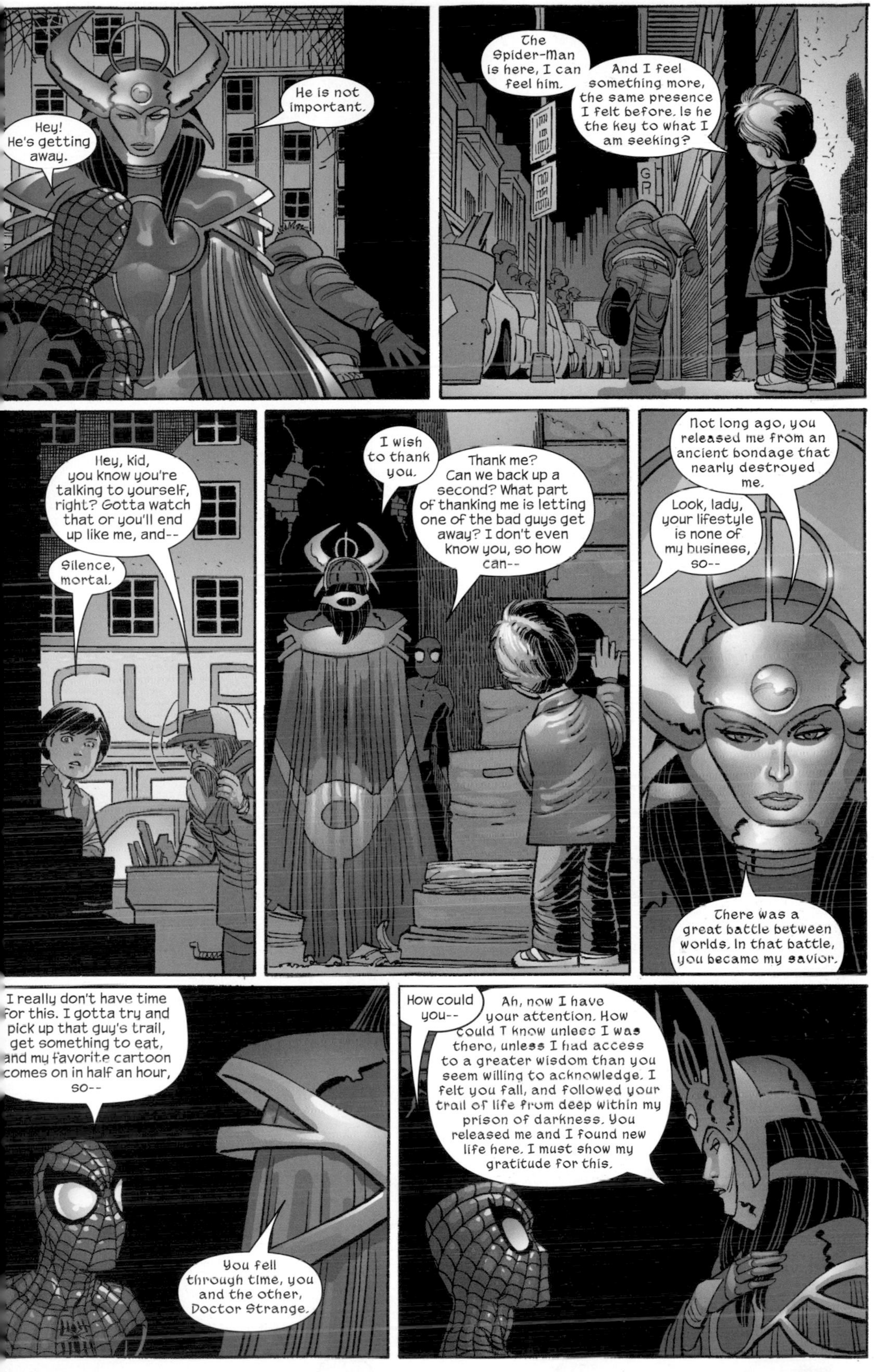
He is not important.
Hey! He's getting away.
The Spider-Man is here, I can feel him.
And I feel something more, the same presence I felt before. Is he the key to what I am seeking?
Hey, kid, you know you're talking to yourself, right? Gotta watch that or you'll end up like me, and--
Silence, mortal.
I wish to thank you.
Thank me? Can we back up a second? What part of thanking me is letting one of the bad guys get away? I don't even know you, so how can--
Not long ago, you released me from an ancient bondage that nearly destroyed me.
Look, lady, your lifestyle is none of my business, so--
There was a great battle between worlds. In that battle, you became my savior.
I really don't have time for this. I gotta try and pick up that guy's trail, get something to eat, and my favorite cartoon comes on in half an hour, so--
You fell through time, you and the other, Doctor Strange.
How could you--
Ah, now I have your attention. How could I know unless I was there, unless I had access to a greater wisdom than you seem willing to acknowledge. I felt you fall, and followed your trail of life from deep within my prison of darkness. You released me and I found new life here. I must show my gratitude for this.

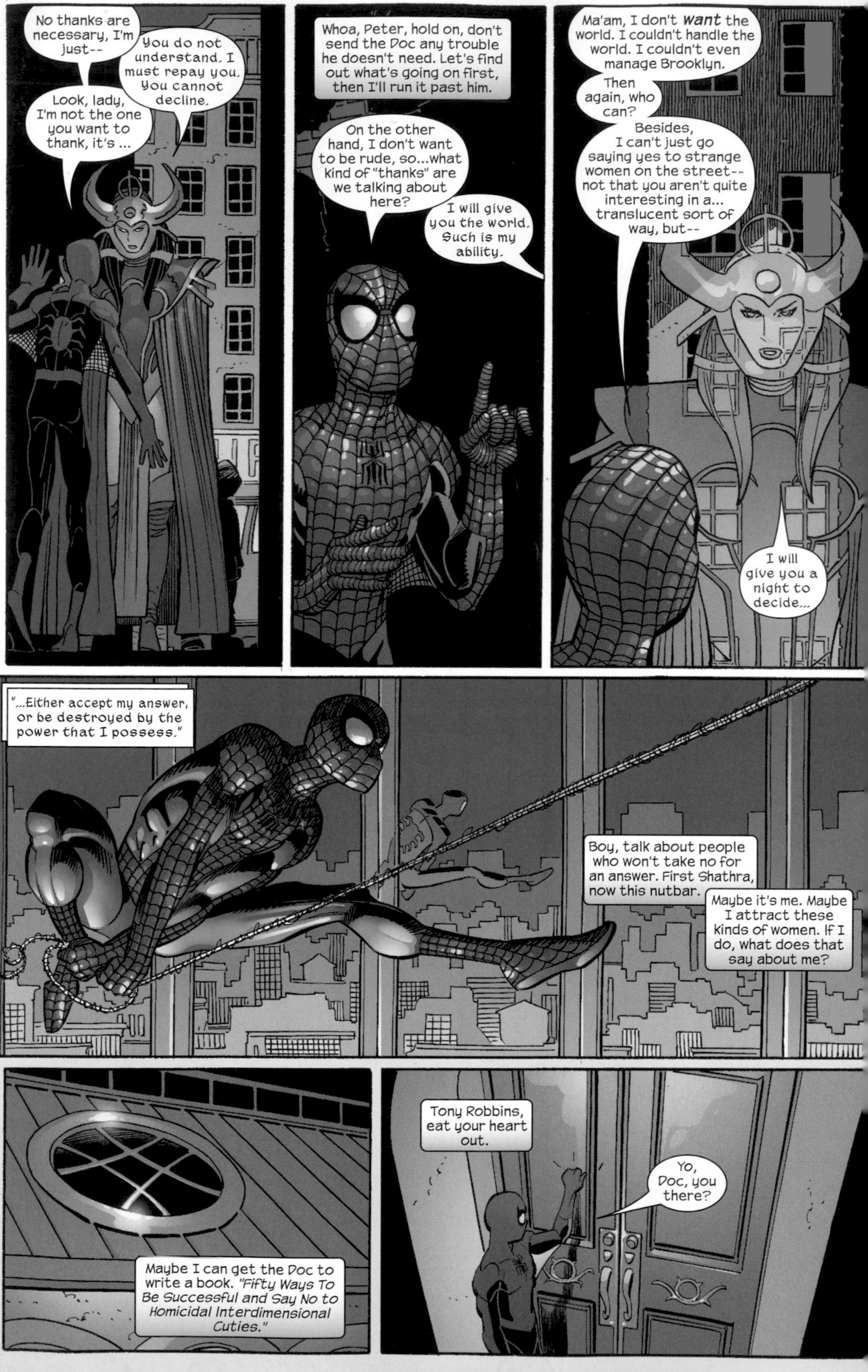

No thanks are necessary, I'm just--
You do not understand. I must repay you. You cannot decline.
Look, lady, I'm not the one you want to thank, it's ...
Whoa, Peter, hold on, don't send the Doc any trouble he doesn't need. Let's find out what's going on first, then I'll run it past him.
On the other hand, I don't want to be rude, so...what kind of "thanks" are we talking about here?
I will give you the world. Such is my ability.
Ma'am, I don't **want** the world. I couldn't handle the world. I couldn't even manage Brooklyn.
Then again, who can?
Besides, I can't just go saying yes to strange women on the street-- not that you aren't quite interesting in a... translucent sort of way, but--
I will give you a night to decide...
"...Either accept my answer, or be destroyed by the power that I possess."
Boy, talk about people who won't take no for an answer. First Shathra, now this nutbar.
Maybe it's me. Maybe I attract these kinds of women. If I do, what does that say about me?
Maybe I can get the Doc to write a book. *"Fifty Ways To Be Successful and Say No to Homicidal Interdimensional Cuties."*
Tony Robbins, eat your heart out.
Yo, Doc, you there?

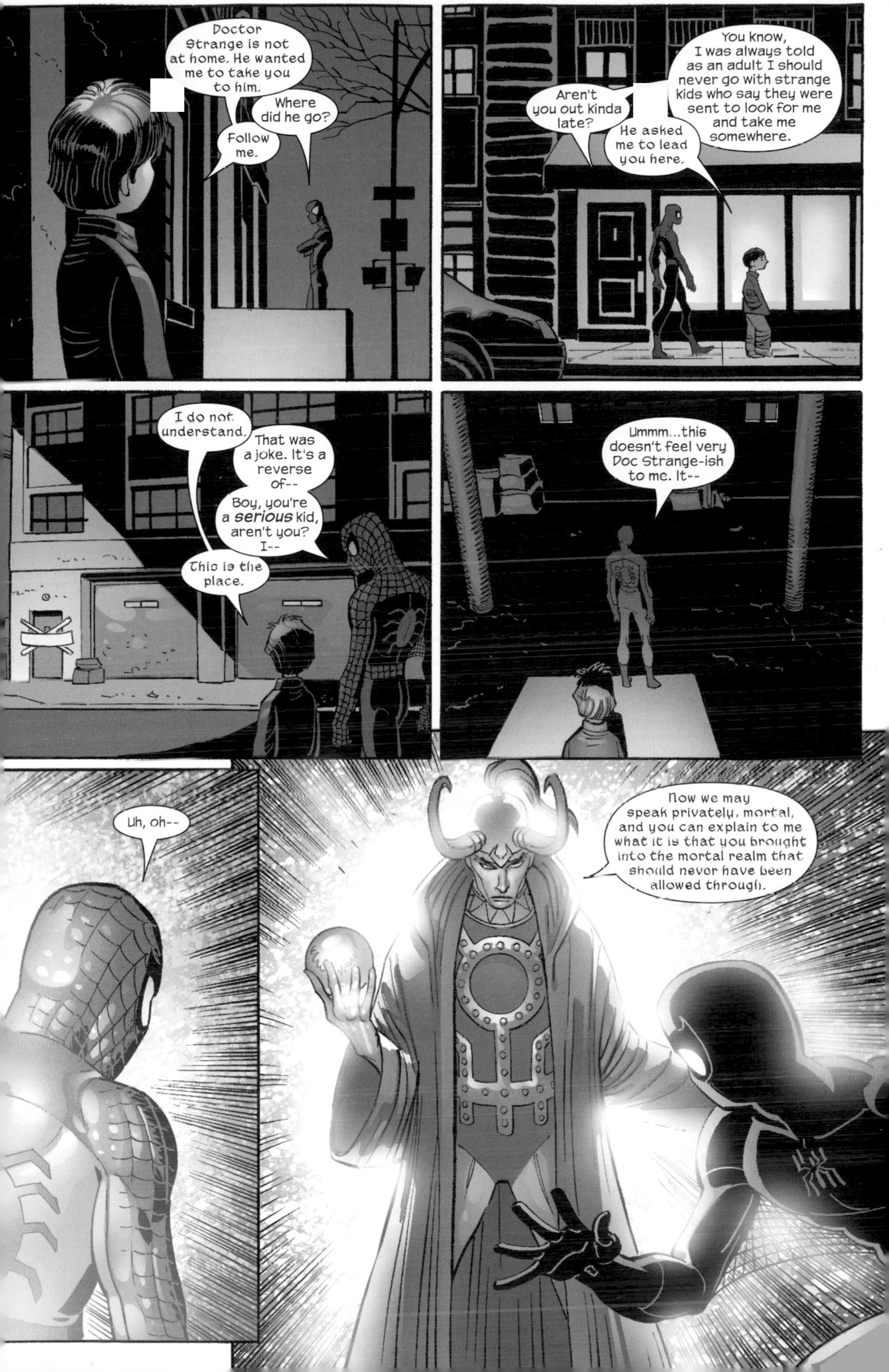
Doctor Strange is not at home. He wanted me to take you to him.
Where did he go?
Follow me.
Aren't you out kinda late?
You know, I was always told as an adult I should never go with strange kids who say they were sent to look for me and take me somewhere.
He asked me to lead you here.
I do not understand.
That was a joke. It's a reverse of--
Boy, you're a *serious* kid, aren't you? I--
This is the place.
Ummm...this doesn't feel very Doc Strange-ish to me. It--
Uh, oh--
Now we may speak privately, mortal, and you can explain to me what it is that you brought into the mortal realm that should never have been allowed through.

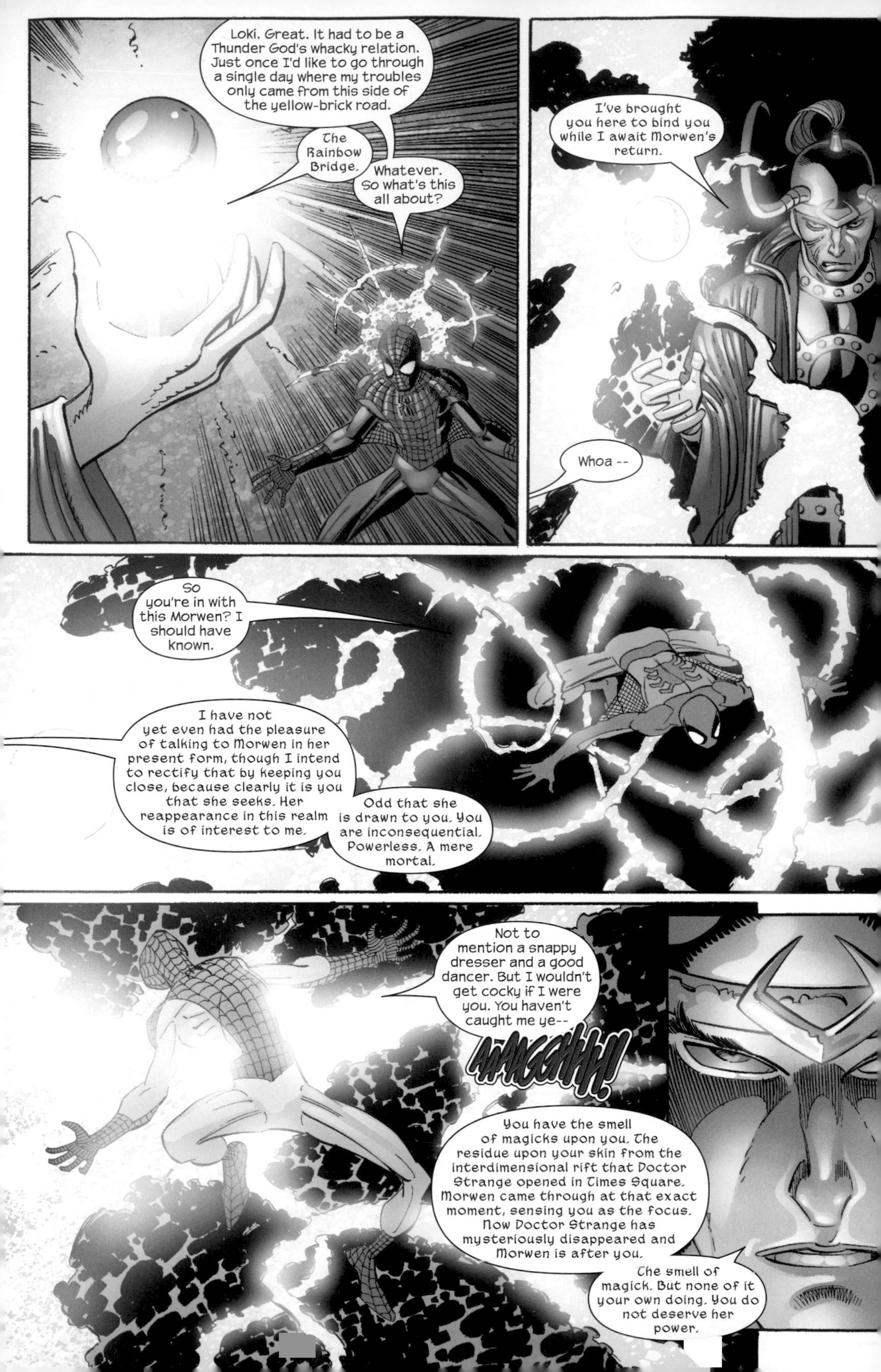
Loki. Great. It had to be a Thunder God's whacky relation. Just once I'd like to go through a single day where my troubles only came from this side of the yellow-brick road.
The Rainbow Bridge.
Whatever. So what's this all about?
I've brought you here to bind you while I await Morwen's return.
Whoa --
So you're in with this Morwen? I should have known.
I have not yet even had the pleasure of talking to Morwen in her present form, though I intend to rectify that by keeping you close, because clearly it is you that she seeks. Her reappearance in this realm is of interest to me.
Odd that she is drawn to you. You are inconsequential. Powerless. A mere mortal.
Not to mention a snappy dresser and a good dancer. But I wouldn't get cocky if I were you. You haven't caught me ye--
AAAAGGHHH!
You have the smell of magicks upon you. The residue upon your skin from the interdimensional rift that Doctor Strange opened in Times Square. Morwen came through at that exact moment, sensing you as the focus. Now Doctor Strange has mysteriously disappeared and Morwen is after you.
The smell of magick. But none of it your own doing. You do not deserve her power.

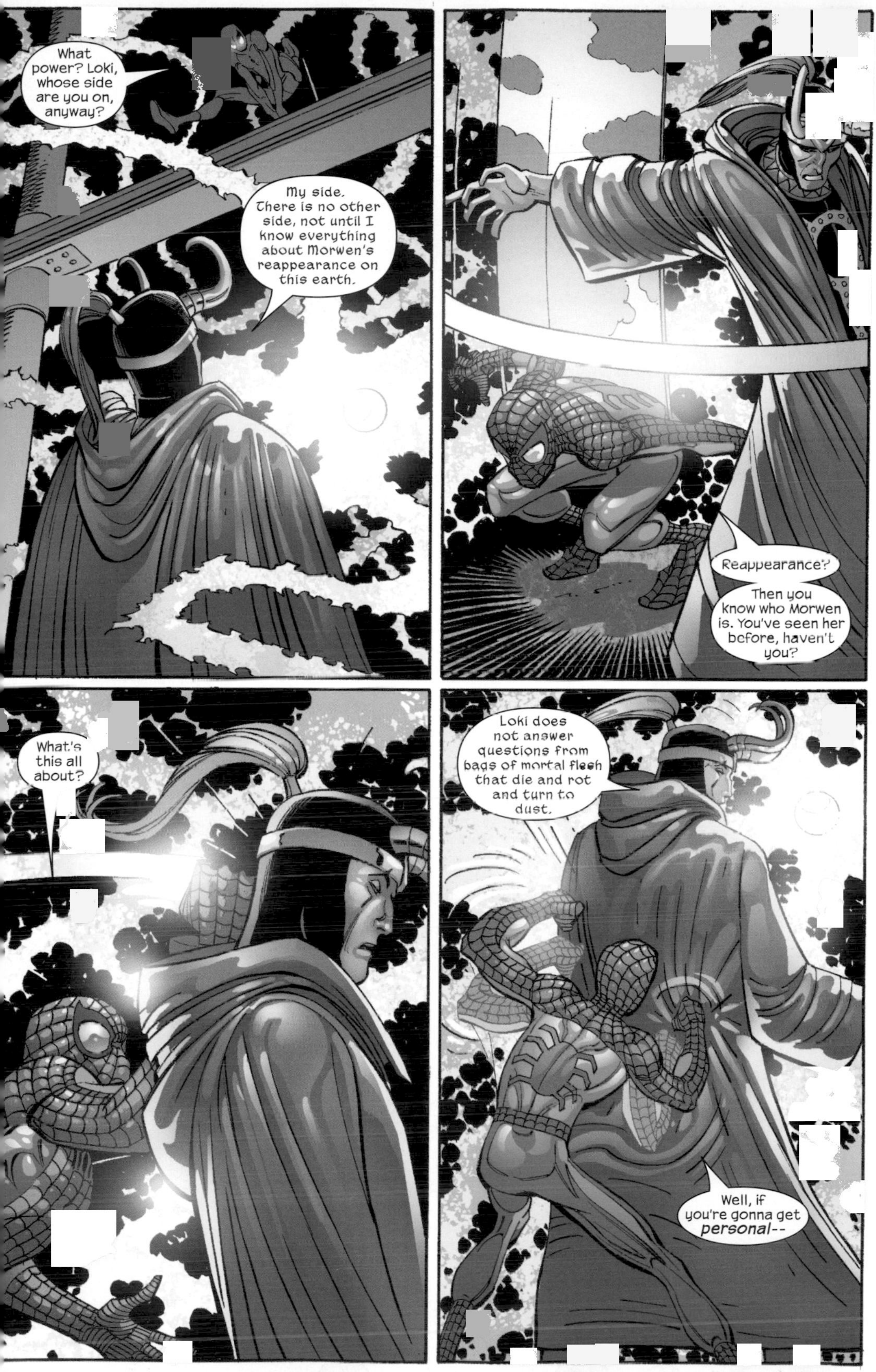
What power? Loki, whose side are you on, anyway?
My side. There is no other side, not until I know everything about Morwen's reappearance on this earth.
Reappearance?
Then you know who Morwen is. You've seen her before, haven't you?
What's this all about?
Loki does not answer questions from bags of mortal flesh that die and rot and turn to dust.
Well, if you're gonna get *personal*--

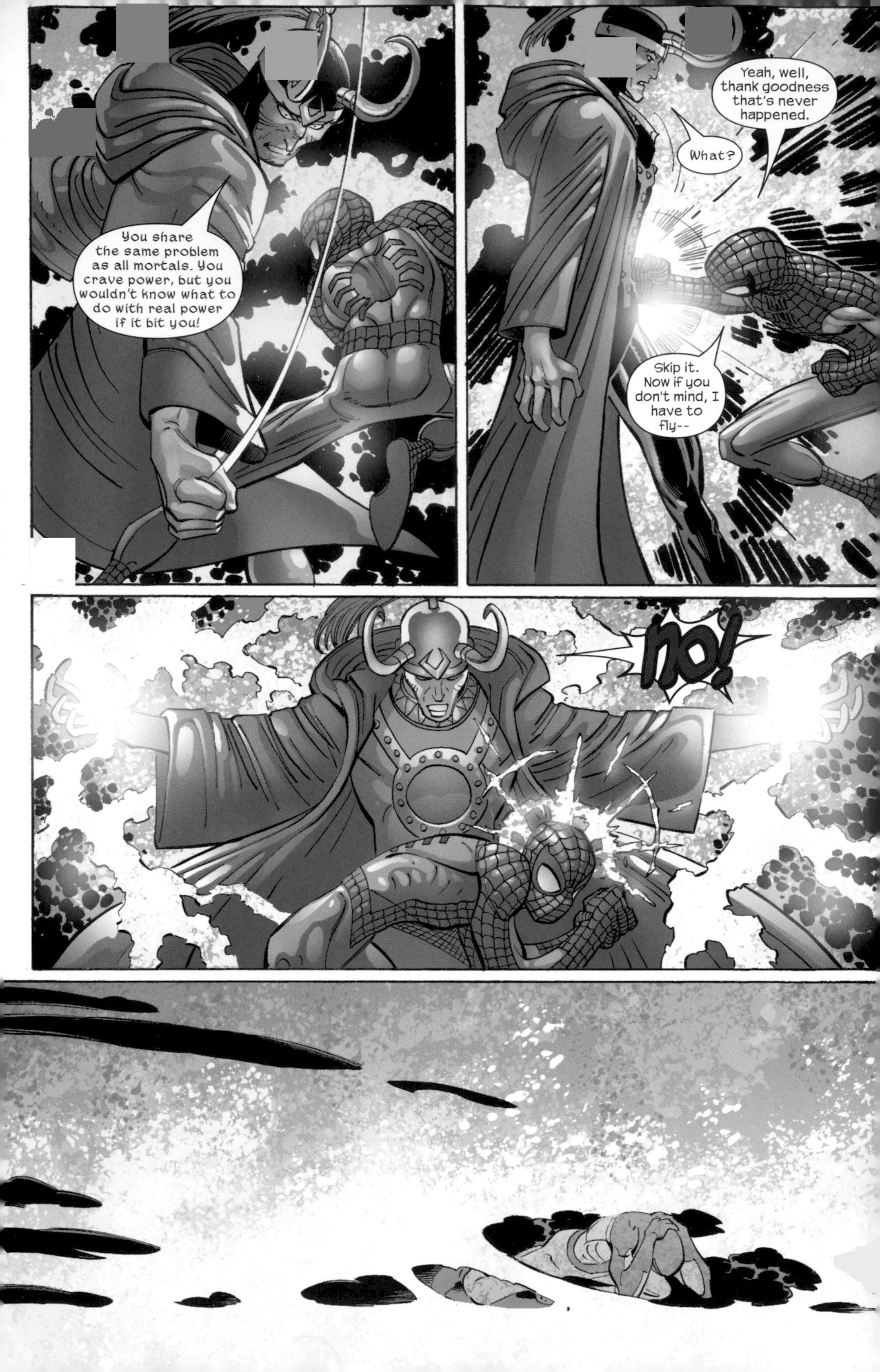
You share the same problem as all mortals. You crave power, but you wouldn't know what to do with real power if it bit you!
Yeah, well, thank goodness that's never happened.
What?
Skip it. Now if you don't mind, I have to fly--
no!

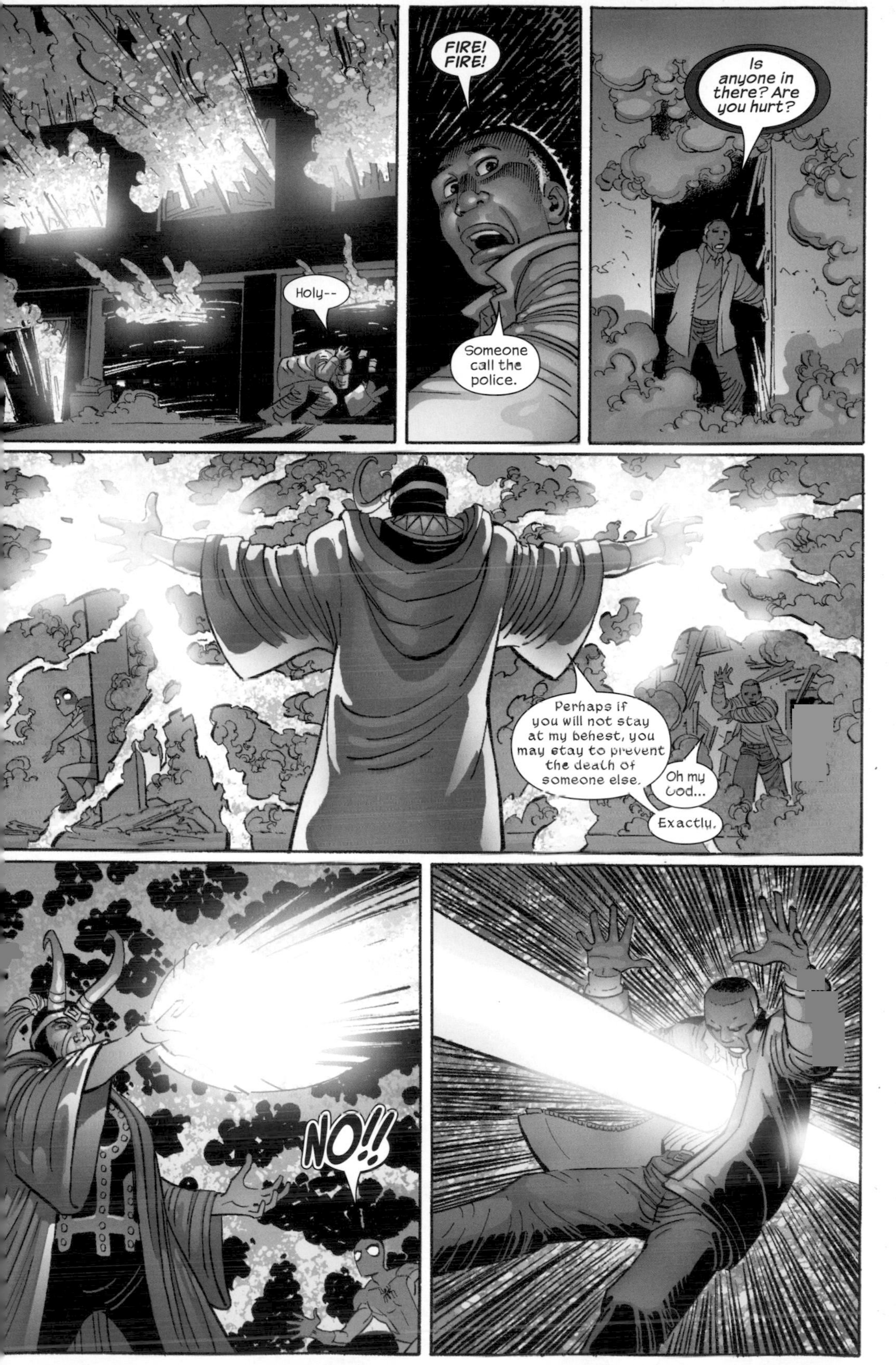

Holy--
FIRE! FIRE!
Someone call the police.
Is anyone in there? Are you hurt?
Perhaps if you will not stay at my behest, you may stay to prevent the death of someone else.
Oh my God...
Exactly.
NO!!

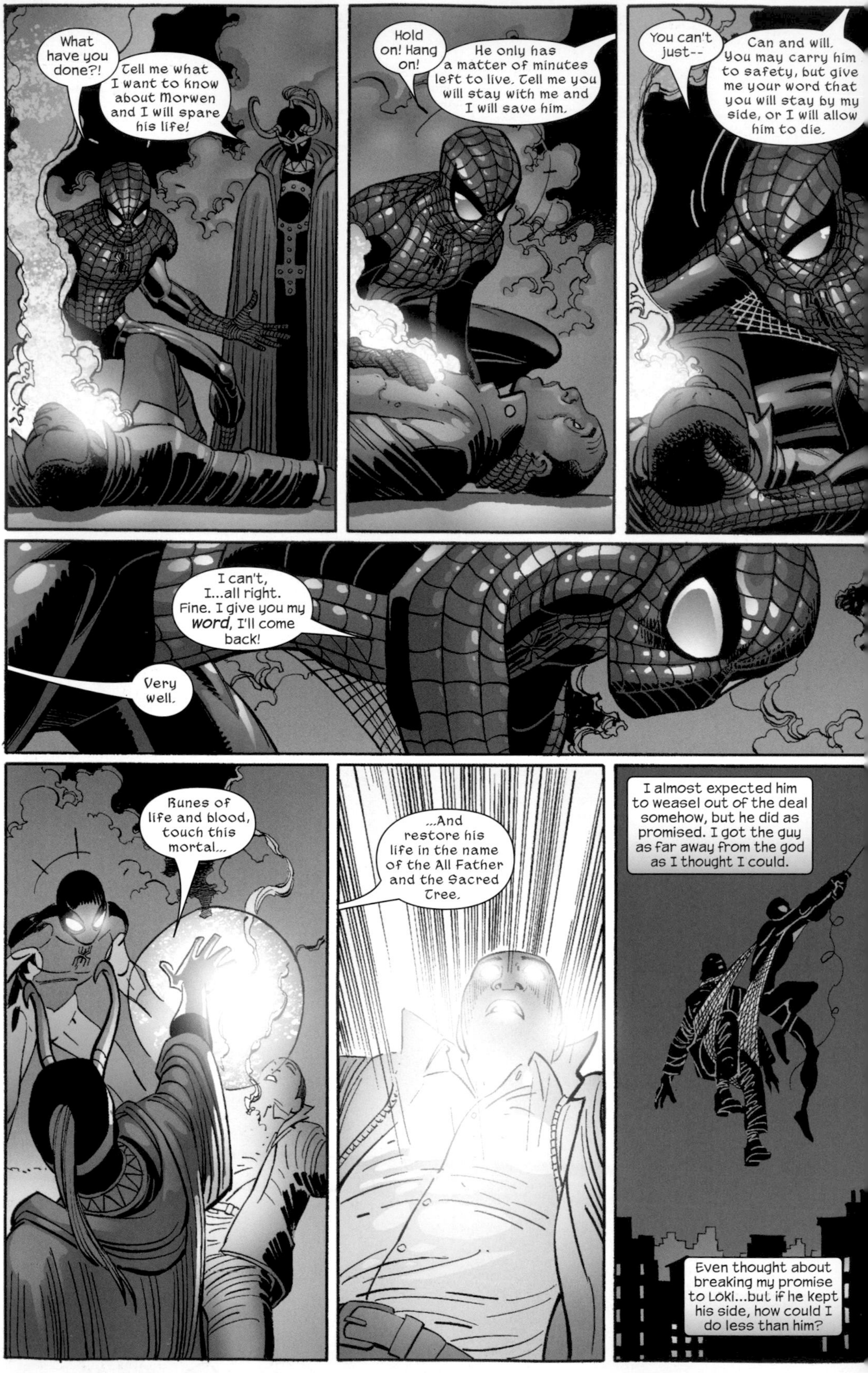
What have you done?!
Tell me what I want to know about Morwen and I will spare his life!
Hold on! Hang on!
He only has a matter of minutes left to live. Tell me you will stay with me and I will save him.
You can't just--
Can and will. You may carry him to safety, but give me your word that you will stay by my side, or I will allow him to die.
I can't, I...all right. Fine. I give you my *word*, I'll come back!
Very well.
Runes of life and blood, touch this mortal...
...And restore his life in the name of the All Father and the Sacred Tree.
I almost expected him to weasel out of the deal somehow, but he did as promised. I got the guy as far away from the god as I thought I could.
Even thought about breaking my promise to Loki...but if he kept his side, how could I do less than him?

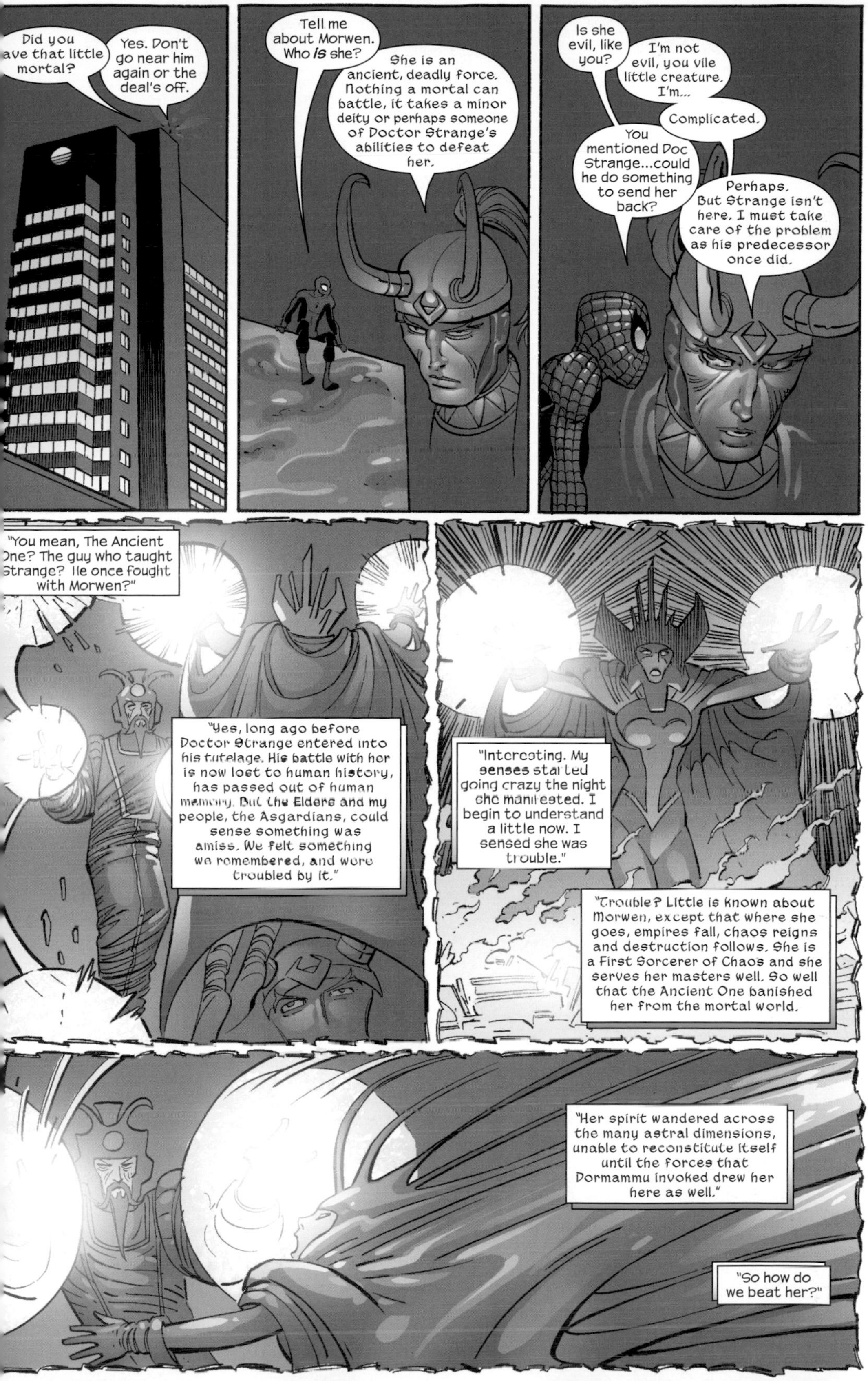
Did you ave that little mortal?
Yes. Don't go near him again or the deal's off.
Tell me about Morwen. Who *is* she?
She is an ancient, deadly force. Nothing a mortal can battle, it takes a minor deity or perhaps someone of Doctor Strange's abilities to defeat her.
Is she evil, like you?
I'm not evil, you vile little creature. I'm...
Complicated.
You mentioned Doc Strange...could he do something to send her back?
Perhaps. But Strange isn't here. I must take care of the problem as his predecessor once did.
"You mean, The Ancient One? The guy who taught Strange? He once fought with Morwen?"
"Yes, long ago before Doctor Strange entered into his tutelage. His battle with her is now lost to human history, has passed out of human memory. But the Elders and my people, the Asgardians, could sense something was amiss. We felt something we remembered, and were troubled by it."
"Interesting. My senses started going crazy the night she manifested. I begin to understand a little now. I sensed she was trouble."
"Trouble? Little is known about Morwen, except that where she goes, empires fall, chaos reigns and destruction follows. She is a First Sorcerer of Chaos and she serves her masters well. So well that the Ancient One banished her from the mortal world.
"Her spirit wandered across the many astral dimensions, unable to reconstitute itself until the forces that Dormammu invoked drew her here as well."
"So how do we beat her?"

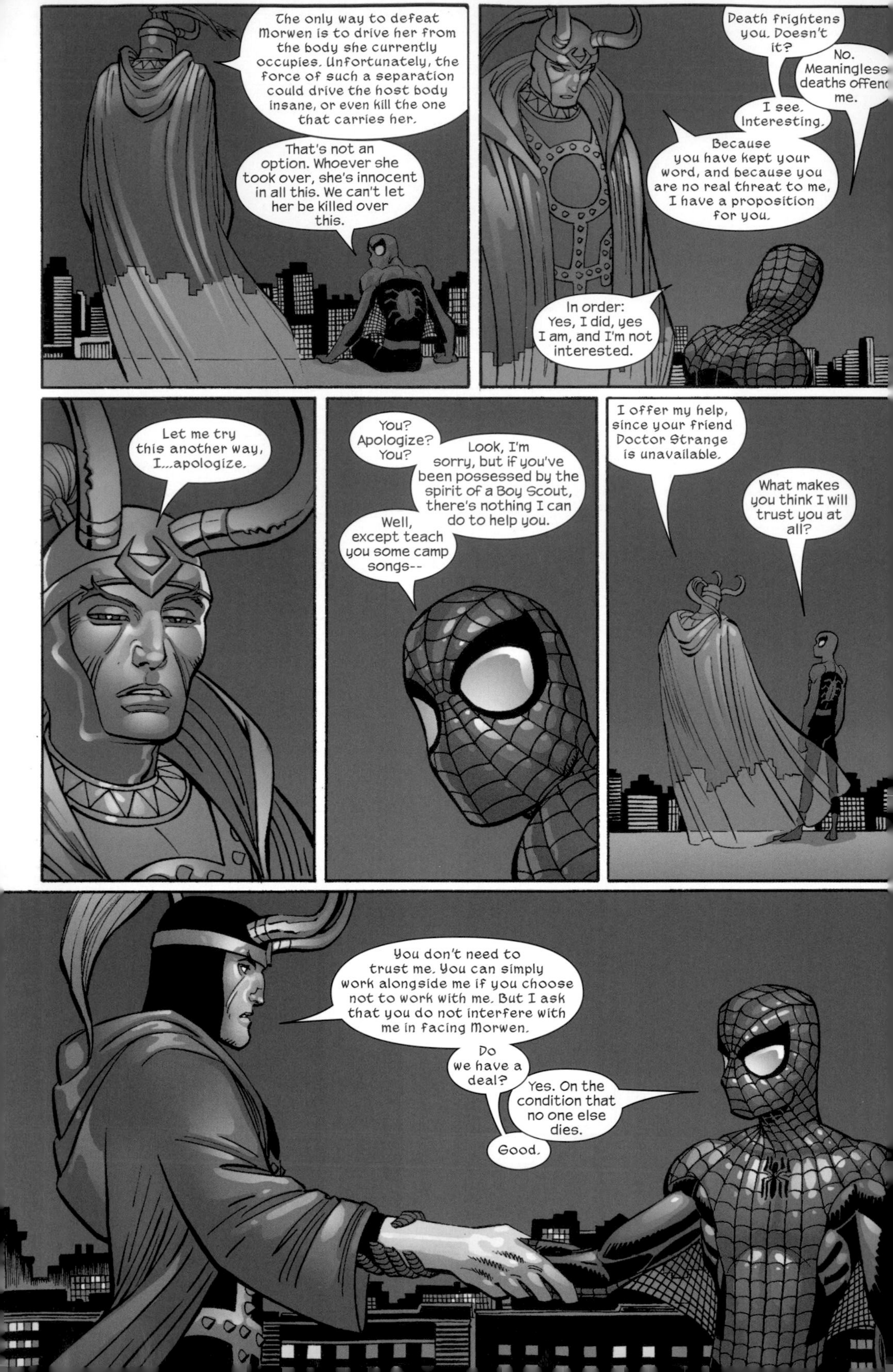
The only way to defeat Morwen is to drive her from the body she currently occupies. Unfortunately, the force of such a separation could drive the host body insane, or even kill the one that carries her.
That's not an option. Whoever she took over, she's innocent in all this. We can't let her be killed over this.
Death frightens you. Doesn't it?
No. Meaningless deaths offend me.
I see. Interesting.
Because you have kept your word, and because you are no real threat to me, I have a proposition for you.
In order: Yes, I did, yes I am, and I'm not interested.
Let me try this another way, I...apologize.
You? Apologize? You?
Look, I'm sorry, but if you've been possessed by the spirit of a Boy Scout, there's nothing I can do to help you.
Well, except teach you some camp songs--
I offer my help, since your friend Doctor Strange is unavailable.
What makes you think I will trust you at all?
You don't need to trust me. You can simply work alongside me if you choose not to work with me. But I ask that you do not interfere with me in facing Morwen.
Do we have a deal?
Yes. On the condition that no one else dies.
Good.

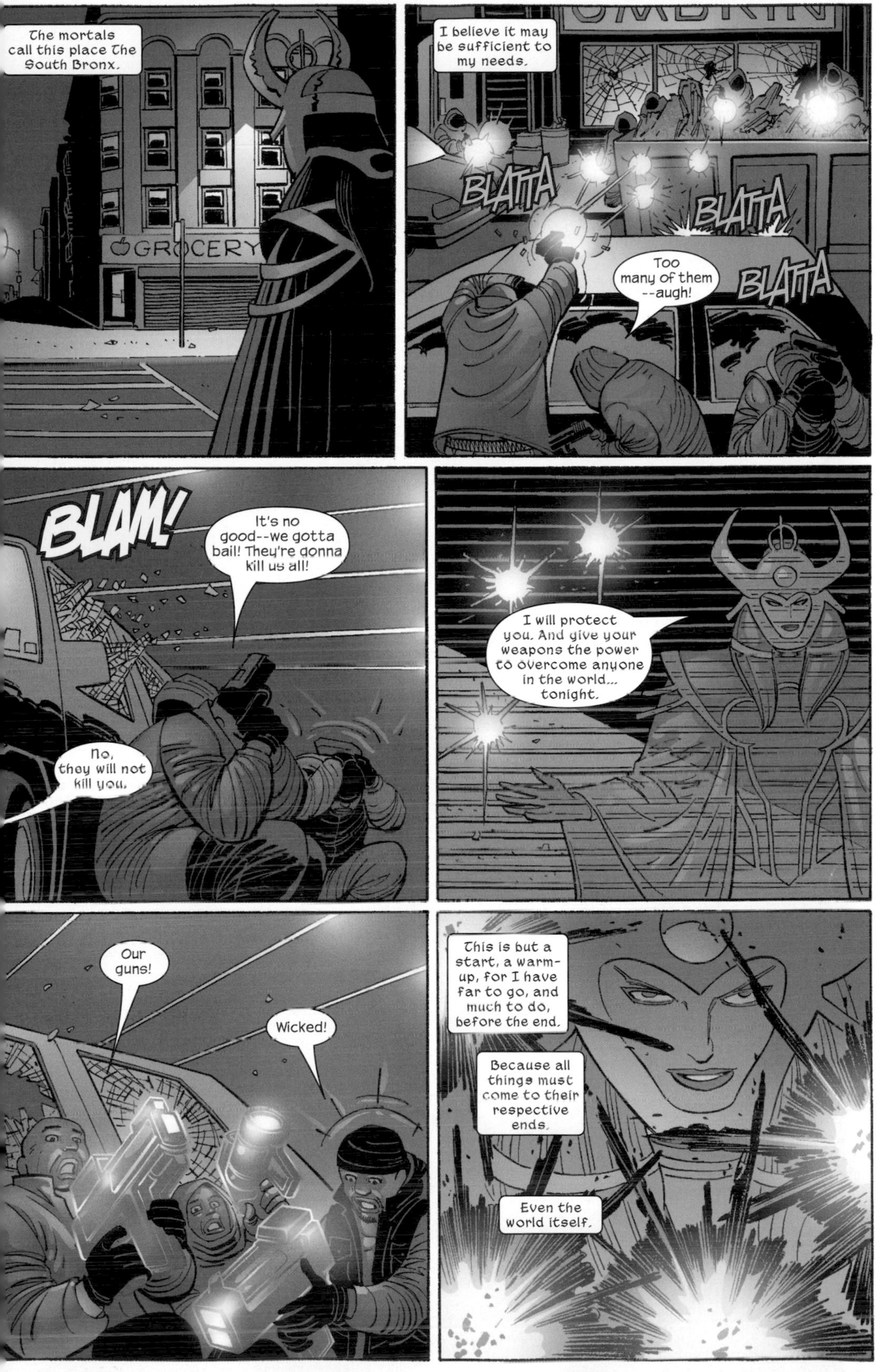
The mortals call this place The South Bronx.
I believe it may be sufficient to my needs.
BLATTA
BLATTA
Too many of them --augh!
BLATTA
BLAM!
It's no good--we gotta bail! They're gonna kill us all!
No, they will not kill you.
I will protect you. And give your weapons the power to overcome anyone in the world... tonight.
Our guns!
Wicked!
This is but a start, a warm-up, for I have far to go, and much to do, before the end.
Because all things must come to their respective ends.
Even the world itself.

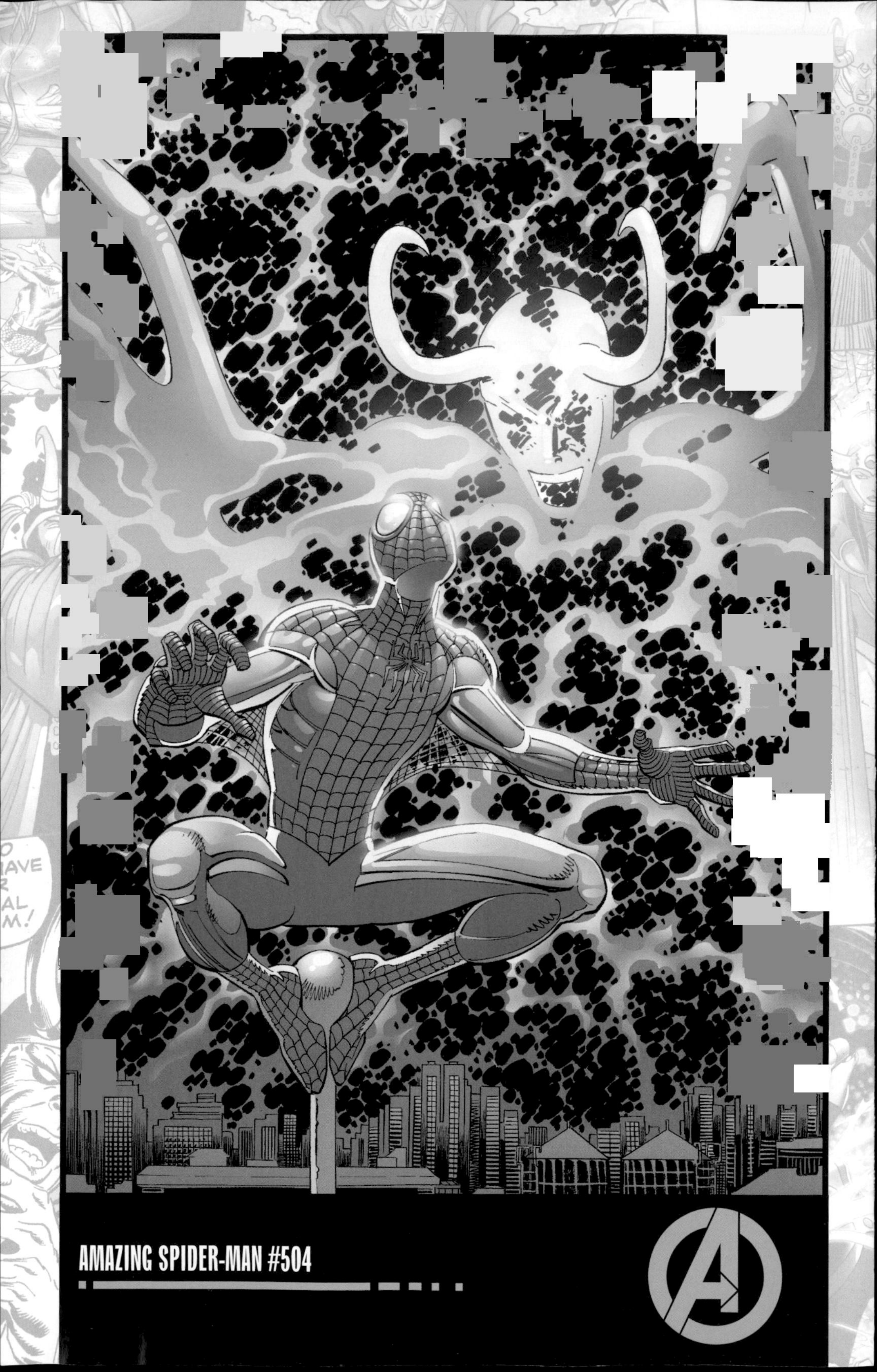
AMAZING SPIDER-MAN #504

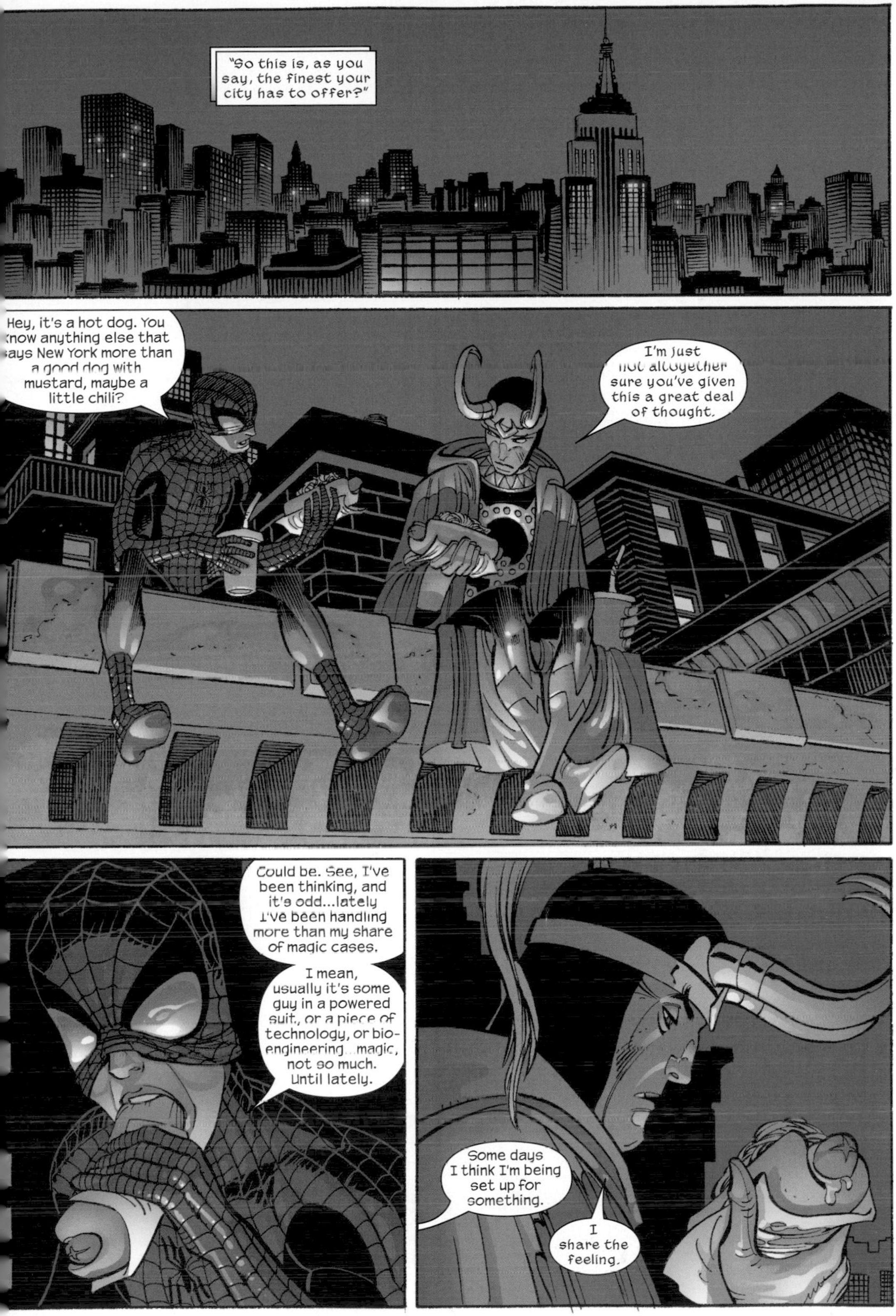
"So this is, as you say, the finest your city has to offer?"
Hey, it's a hot dog. You know anything else that says New York more than a good dog with mustard, maybe a little chili?
I'm just not altogether sure you've given this a great deal of thought.
Could be. See, I've been thinking, and it's odd...lately I've been handling more than my share of magic cases.
I mean, usually it's some guy in a powered suit, or a piece of technology, or bio-engineering...magic, not so much. Until lately.
Some days I think I'm being set up for something.
I share the feeling.

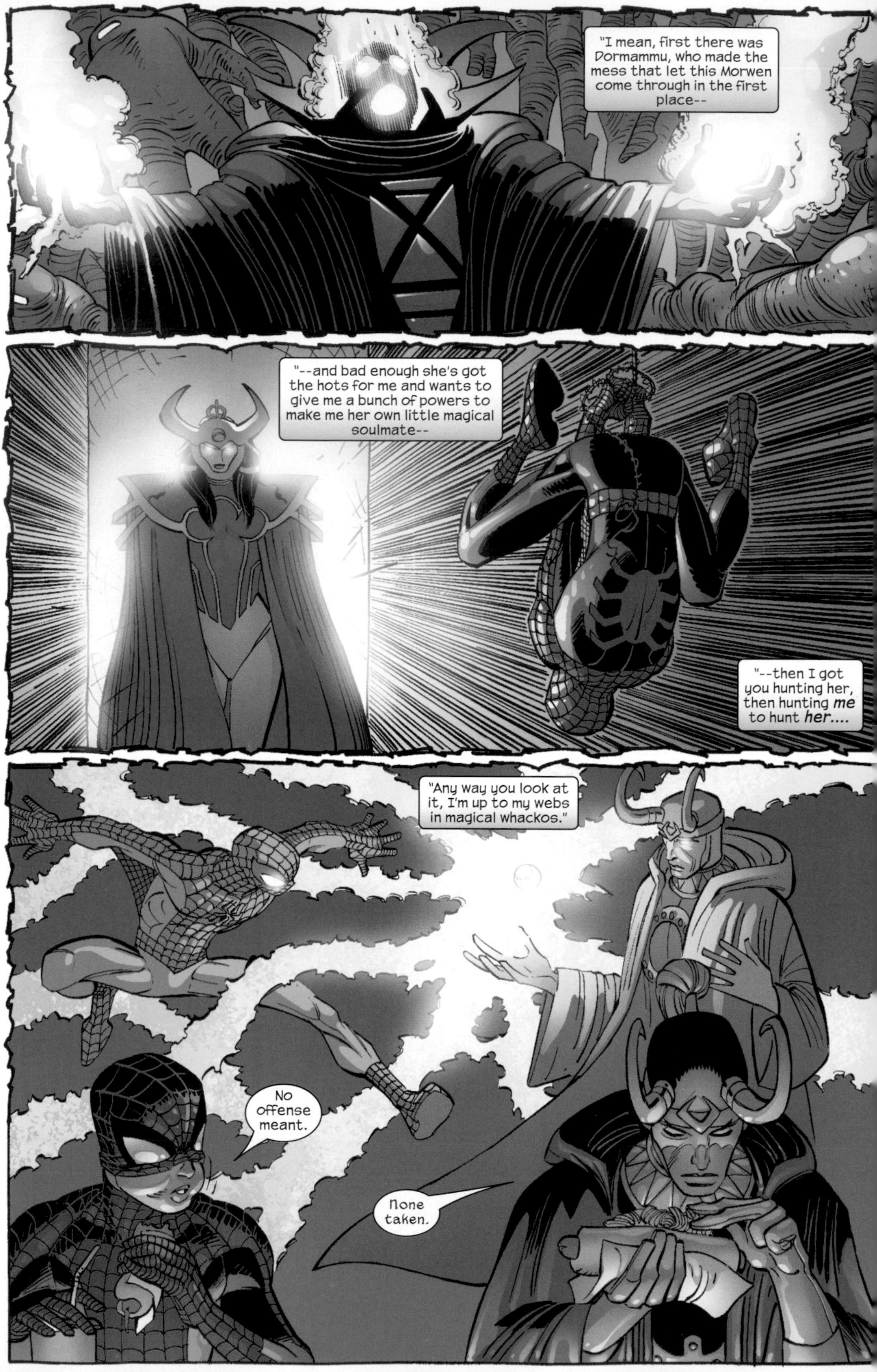
"I mean, first there was Dormammu, who made the mess that let this Morwen come through in the first place--
"--and bad enough she's got the hots for me and wants to give me a bunch of powers to make me her own little magical soulmate--
"--then I got you hunting her, then hunting *me* to hunt *her....*
"Any way you look at it, I'm up to my webs in magical whackos."
No offense meant.
None taken.

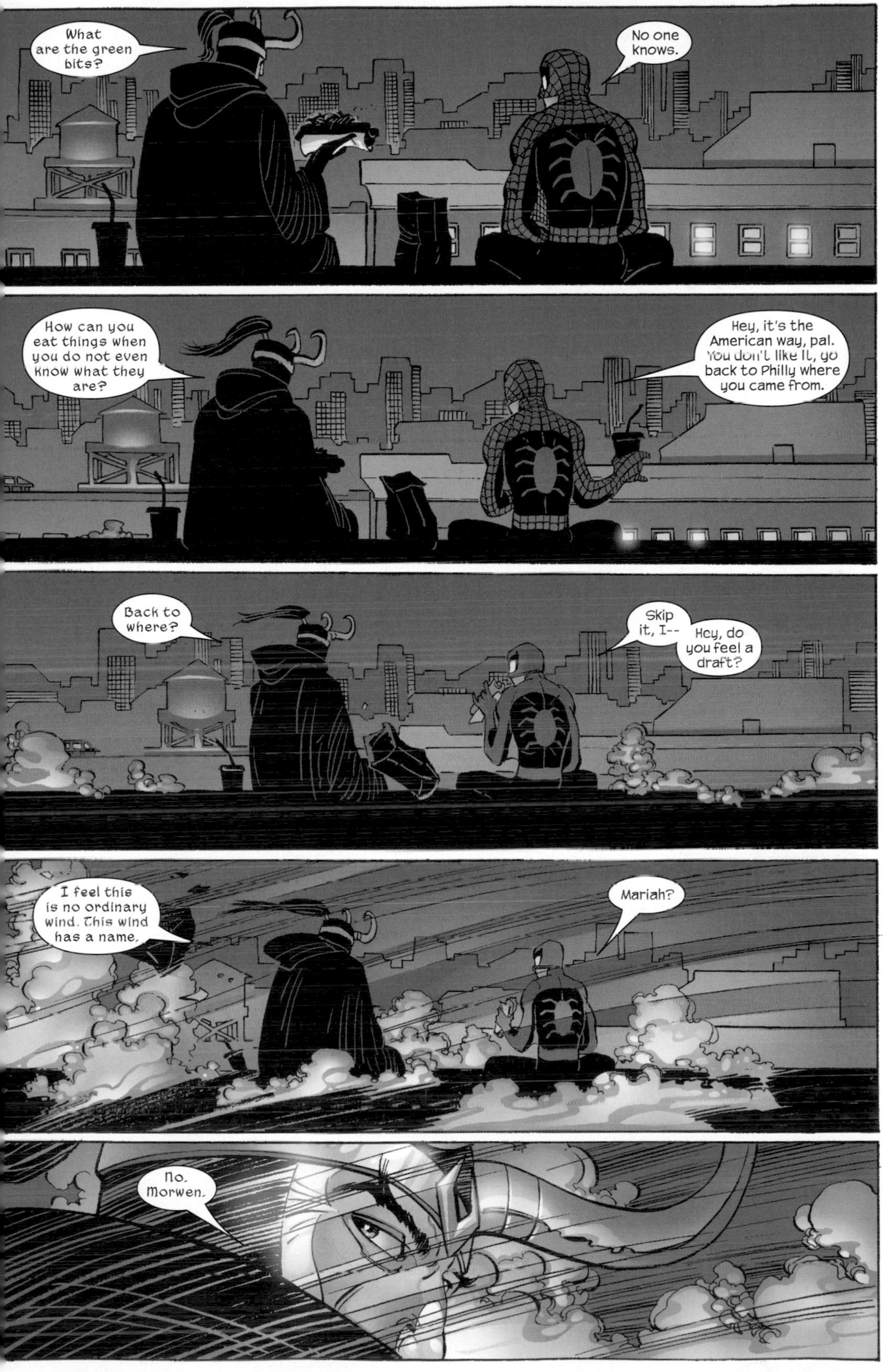
What are the green bits?
No one knows.
How can you eat things when you do not even know what they are?
Hey, it's the American way, pal. You don't like it, go back to Philly where you came from.
Back to where?
Skip it, I--
Hey, do you feel a draft?
I feel this is no ordinary wind. This wind has a name.
Mariah?
No. Morwen.

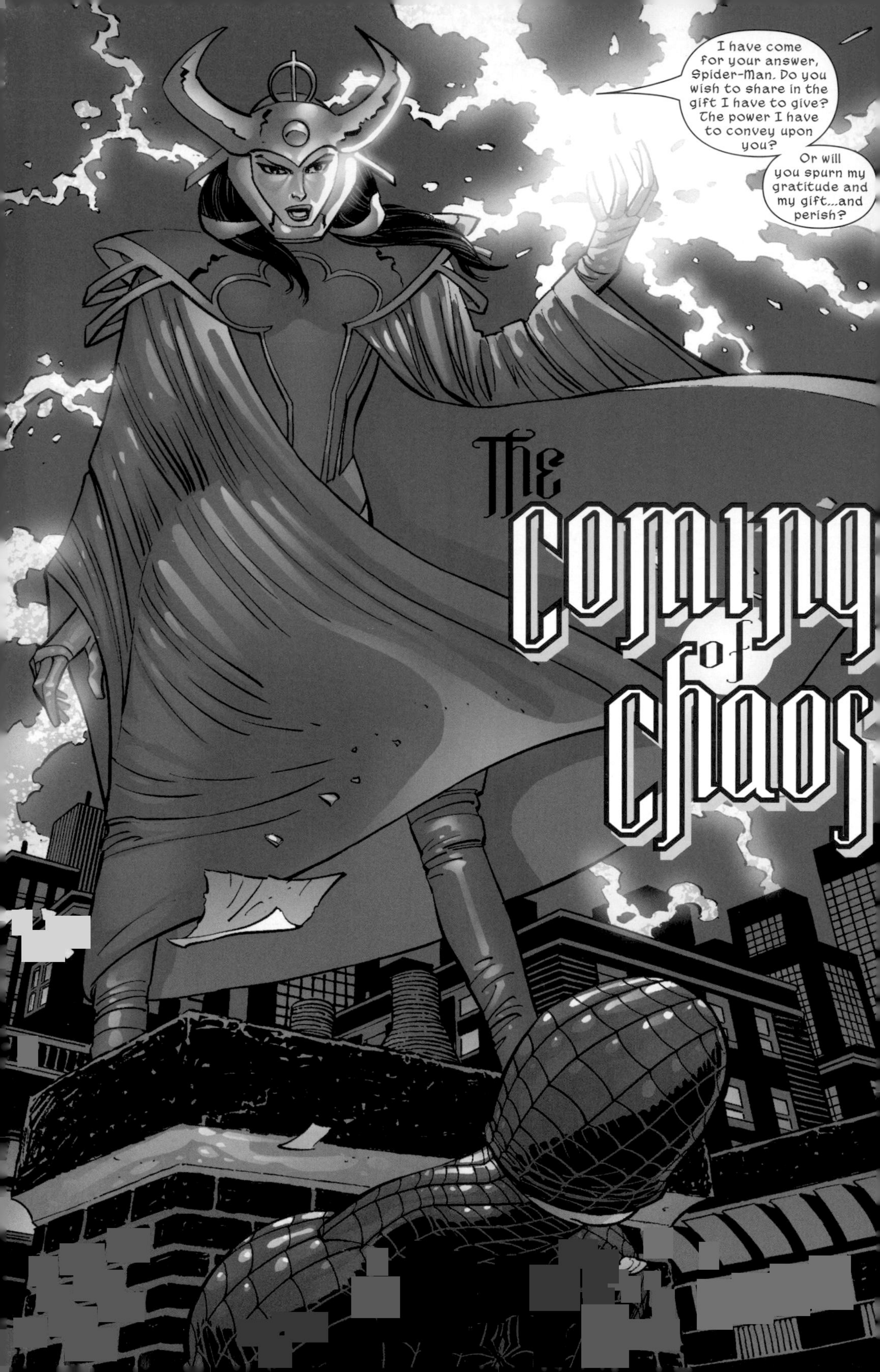
I have come for your answer, Spider-Man. Do you wish to share in the gift I have to give? The power I have to convey upon you?
Or will you spurn my gratitude and my gift...and perish?
The Coming of Chaos

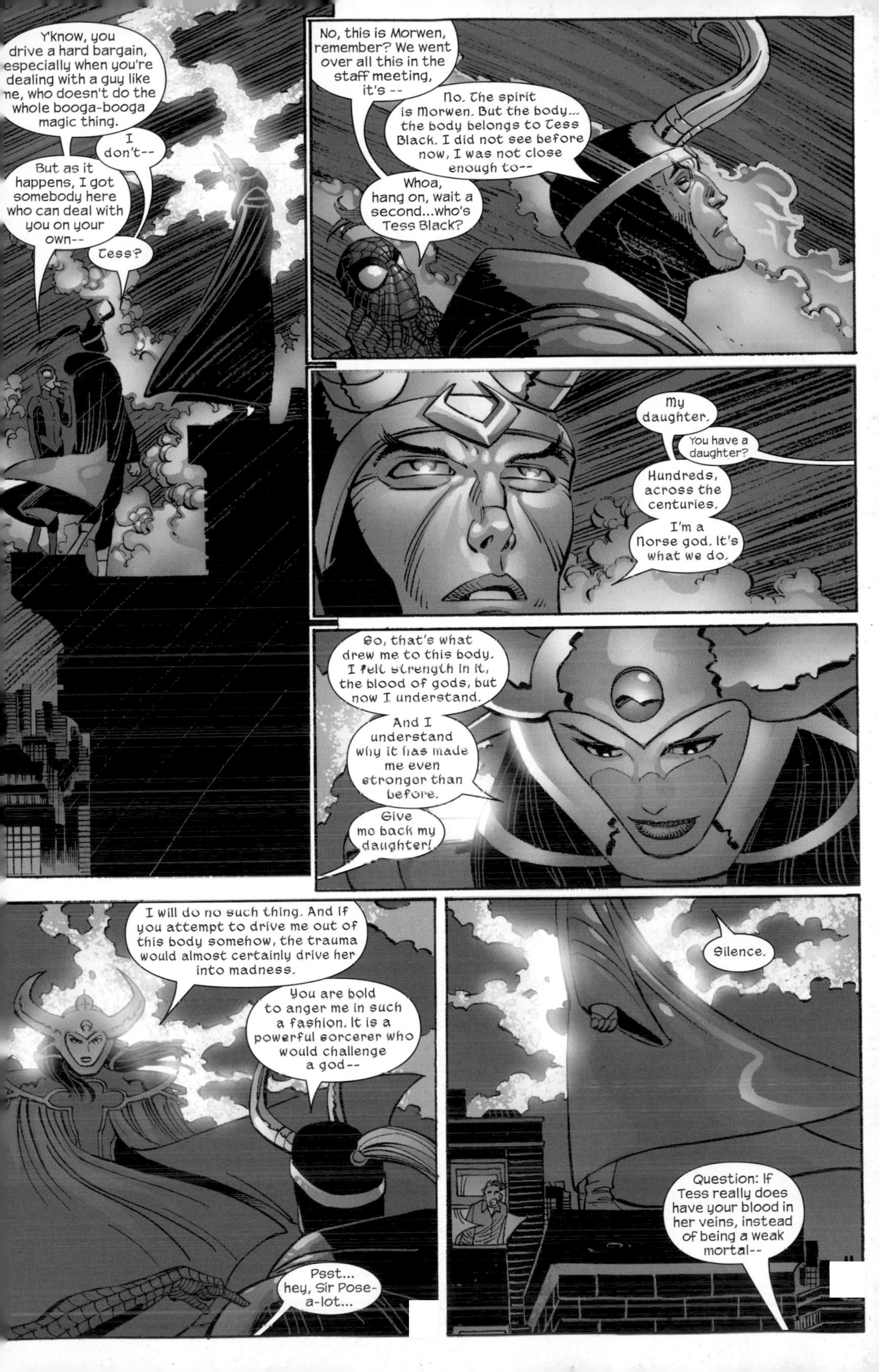

Y'know, you drive a hard bargain, especially when you're dealing with a guy like me, who doesn't do the whole booga-booga magic thing.
I don't--
But as it happens, I got somebody here who can deal with you on your own--
Tess?
No, this is Morwen, remember? We went over all this in the staff meeting, it's --
No. The spirit is Morwen. But the body... the body belongs to Tess Black. I did not see before now, I was not close enough to--
Whoa, hang on, wait a second...who's Tess Black?
My daughter.
You have a daughter?
Hundreds, across the centuries.
I'm a Norse god. It's what we do.
So, that's what drew me to this body. I felt strength in it, the blood of gods, but now I understand.
And I understand why it has made me even stronger than before.
Give me back my daughter!
I will do no such thing. And if you attempt to drive me out of this body somehow, the trauma would almost certainly drive her into madness.
You are bold to anger me in such a fashion. It is a powerful sorcerer who would challenge a god--
Psst... hey, Sir Pose-a-lot...
Silence.
Question: If Tess really does have your blood in her veins, instead of being a weak mortal--

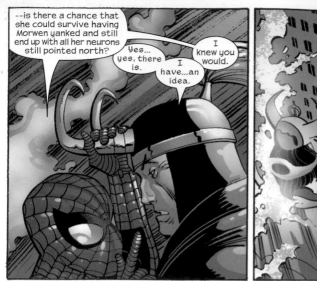

--is there a chance that she could survive having Morwen yanked and still end up with all her neurons still pointed north?

Yes... yes, there is.

I knew you would.

I have...an idea.

How about this?

If the Spider-Man doesn't want the power you're offering, I will happily take it and work with you. If it's all about gratitude, surely the assistance of a god is superior to that of a mere mortal.

This by you is an idea?

Being of assistance is not the reason I want this man. My role as sorceress is to serve the forces of chaos. Only through chaos does a race grow stronger.

The Spider-Man is a born agent of Chaos.

Yeah, I get that all the time.

Long have my masters watched him. There is much of the trickster in him, much of chaos...much of the spider.

But I'm the GOD of trickery, how much more chaotic can you get?

At what point, exactly, did this conversation turn into the supernatural version of American Idol?

Just asking.

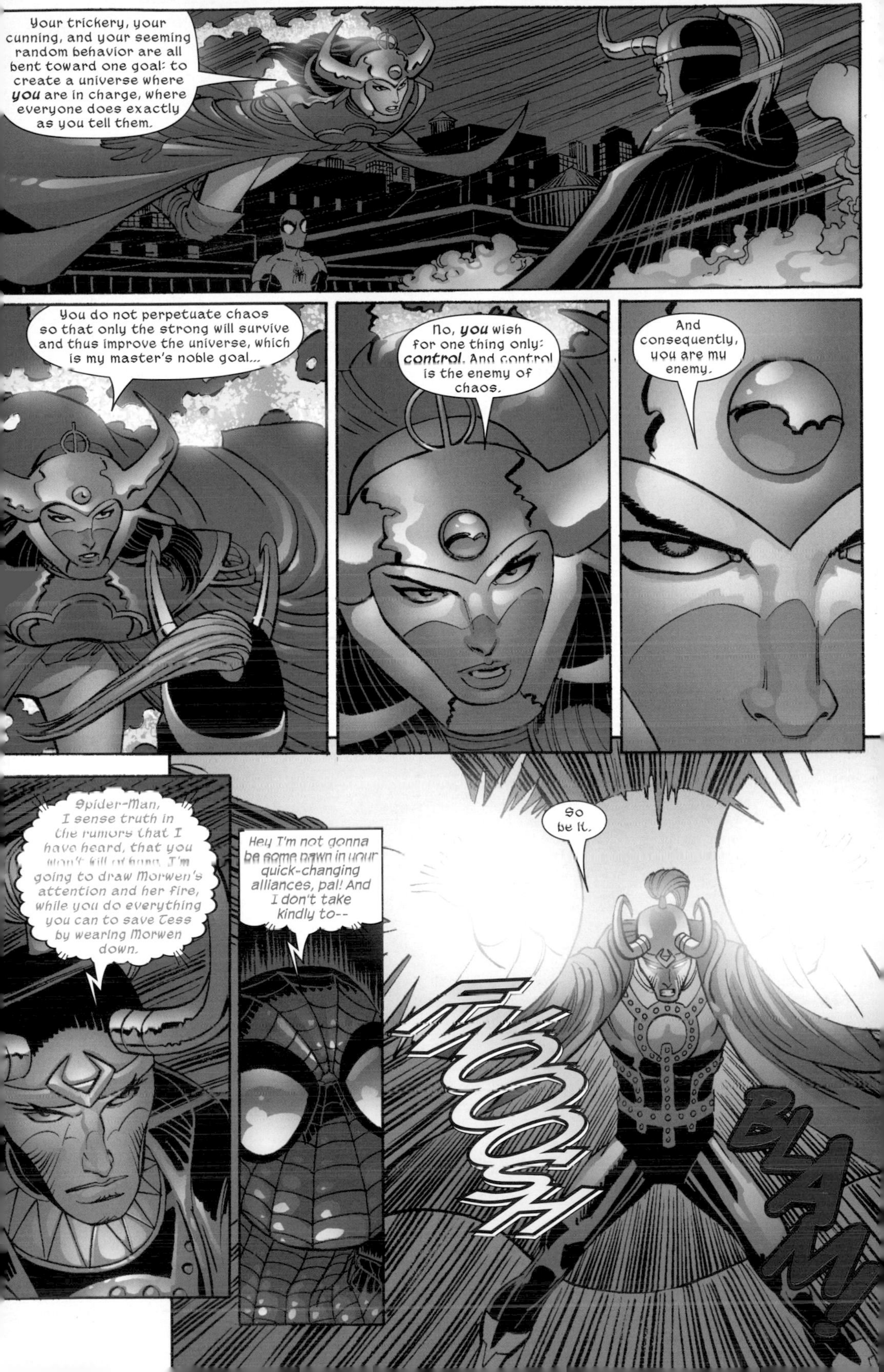
Your trickery, your cunning, and your seeming random behavior are all bent toward one goal: to create a universe where **you** are in charge, where everyone does exactly as you tell them.
You do not perpetuate chaos so that only the strong will survive and thus improve the universe, which is my master's noble goal...
No, **you** wish for one thing only: **control**. And control is the enemy of chaos.
And consequently, you are my enemy.
Spider-Man, I sense truth in the rumors that I have heard, that you I'm going to draw Morwen's attention and her fire, while you do everything you can to save Tess by wearing Morwen down.
Hey I'm not gonna be some pawn in your quick-changing alliances, pal! And I don't take kindly to--
So be it.
FWOOOSH
BLAM!

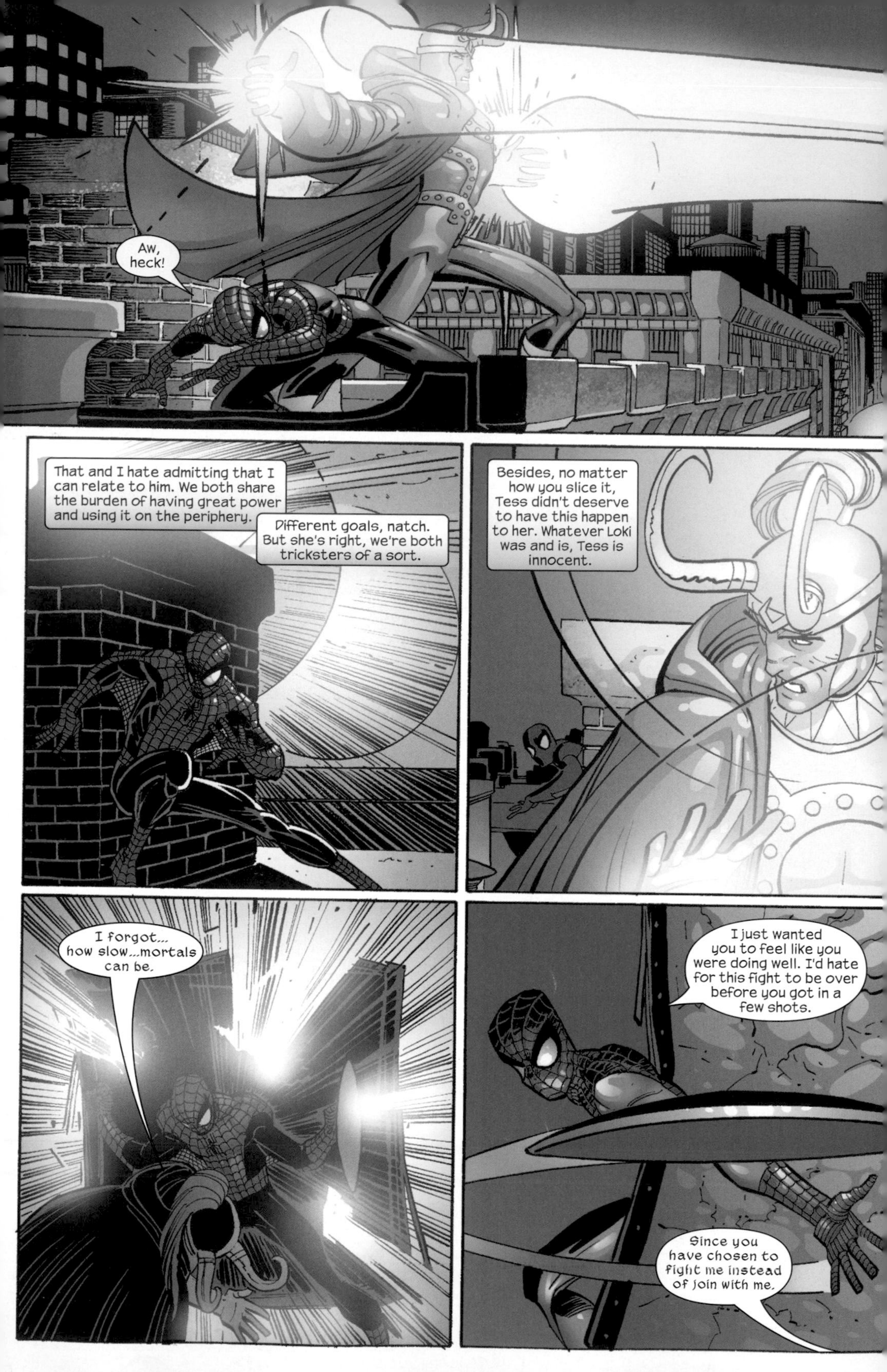
Aw, heck!
That and I hate admitting that I can relate to him. We both share the burden of having great power and using it on the periphery.
Different goals, natch. But she's right, we're both tricksters of a sort.
Besides, no matter how you slice it, Tess didn't deserve to have this happen to her. Whatever Loki was and is, Tess is innocent.
I forgot... how slow...mortals can be.
I just wanted you to feel like you were doing well. I'd hate for this fight to be over before you got in a few shots.
Since you have chosen to fight me instead of join with me.

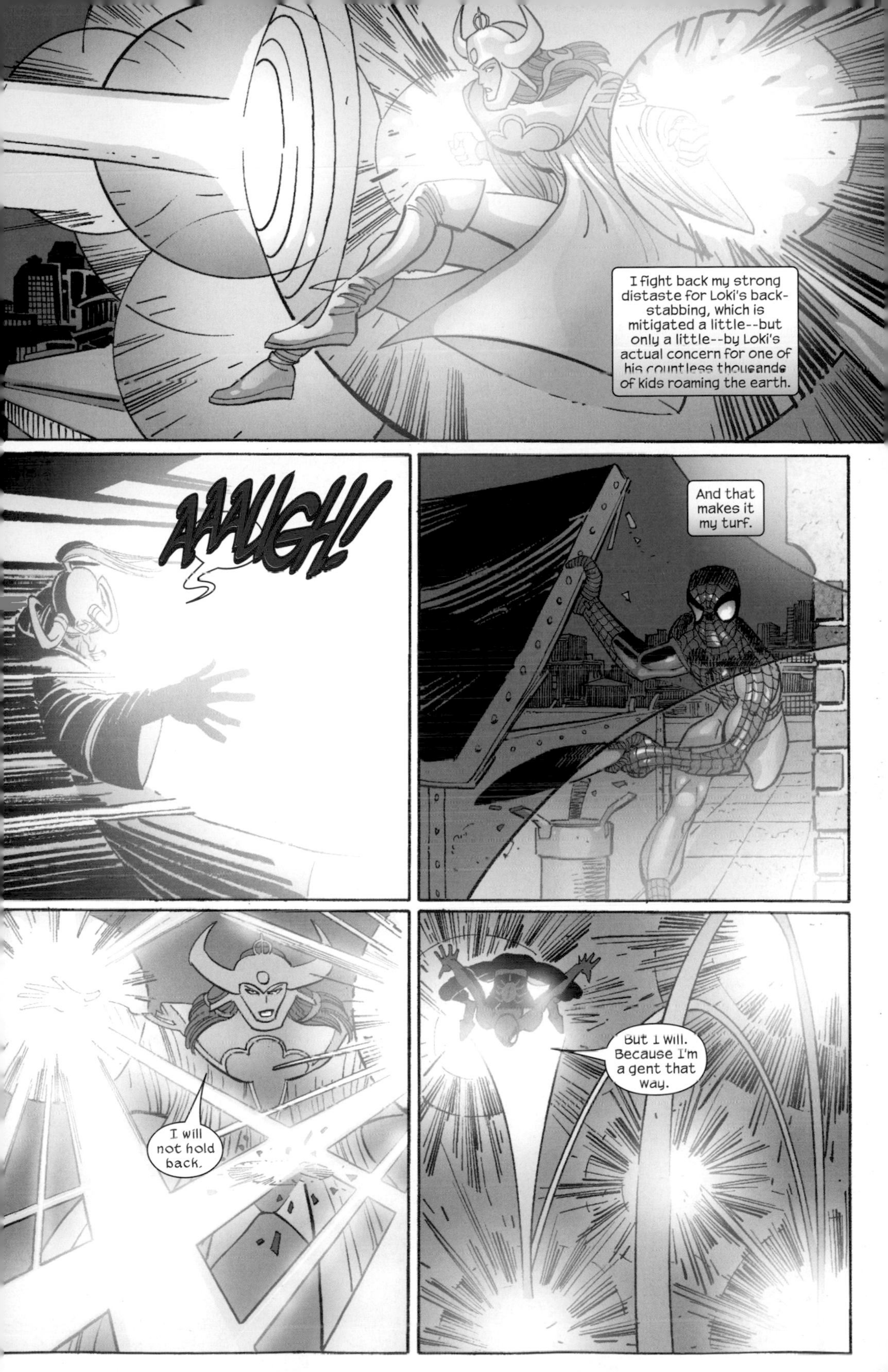
I fight back my strong distaste for Loki's back-stabbing, which is mitigated a little--but only a little--by Loki's actual concern for one of his countless thousands of kids roaming the earth.
AAAUGH!
And that makes it my turf.
I will not hold back.
But I will. Because I'm a gent that way.

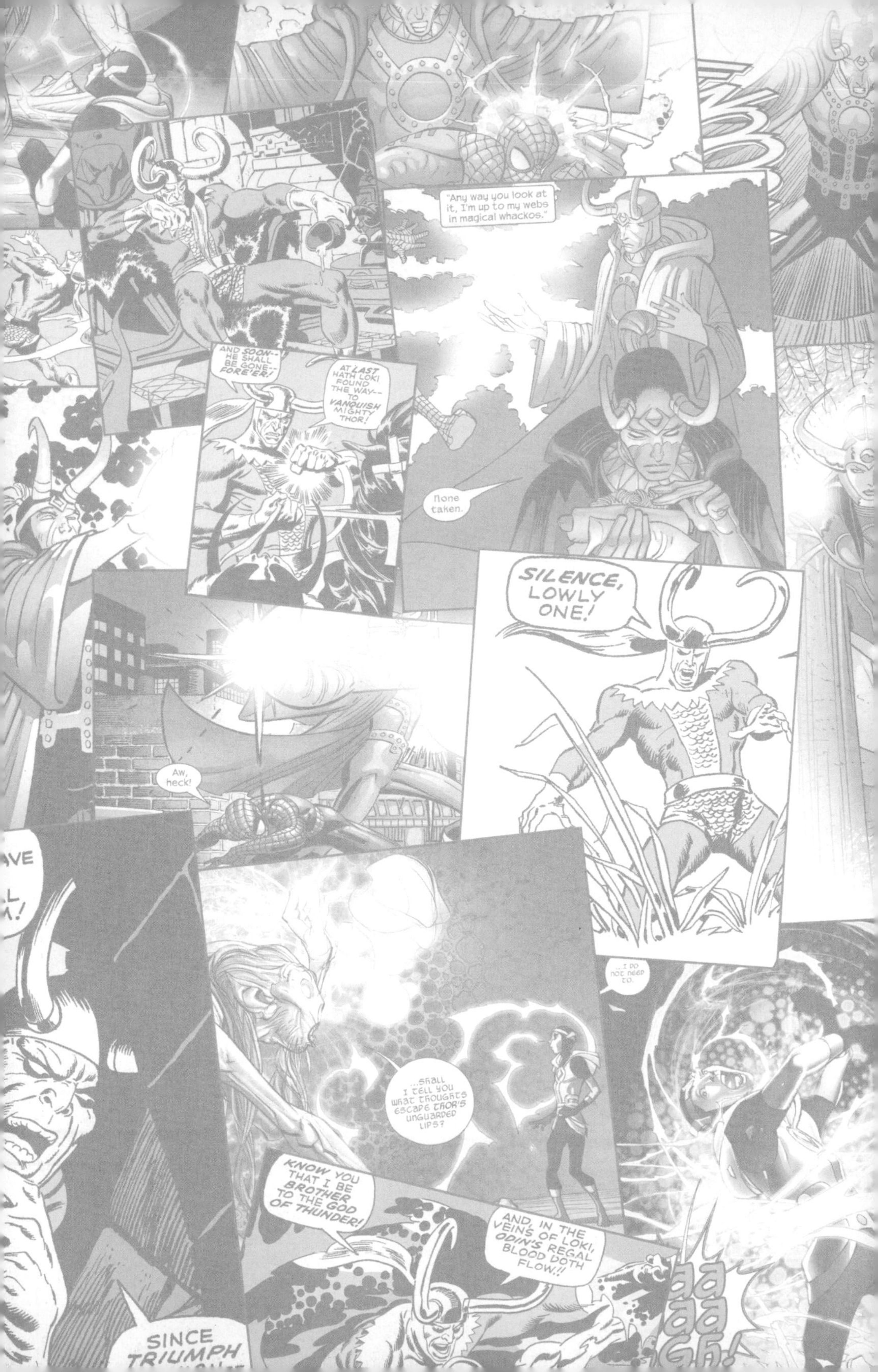
"Any way you look at it, I'm up to my webs in magical whackos."
AND SOON-- HE SHALL BE GONE-- FORE'ER!
AT LAST HATH LOKI FOUND THE WAY-- TO VANQUISH MIGHTY THOR!
None taken.
SILENCE, LOWLY ONE!
Aw, heck!
...I DO NOT NEED TO.
...SHALL I TELL YOU WHAT THOUGHTS ESCAPE THOR'S UNGUARDED LIPS?
KNOW YOU THAT I BE BROTHER TO THE GOD OF THUNDER!
AND, IN THE VEINS OF LOKI, ODIN'S REGAL BLOOD DOTH FLOW!!
SINCE TRIUMPH

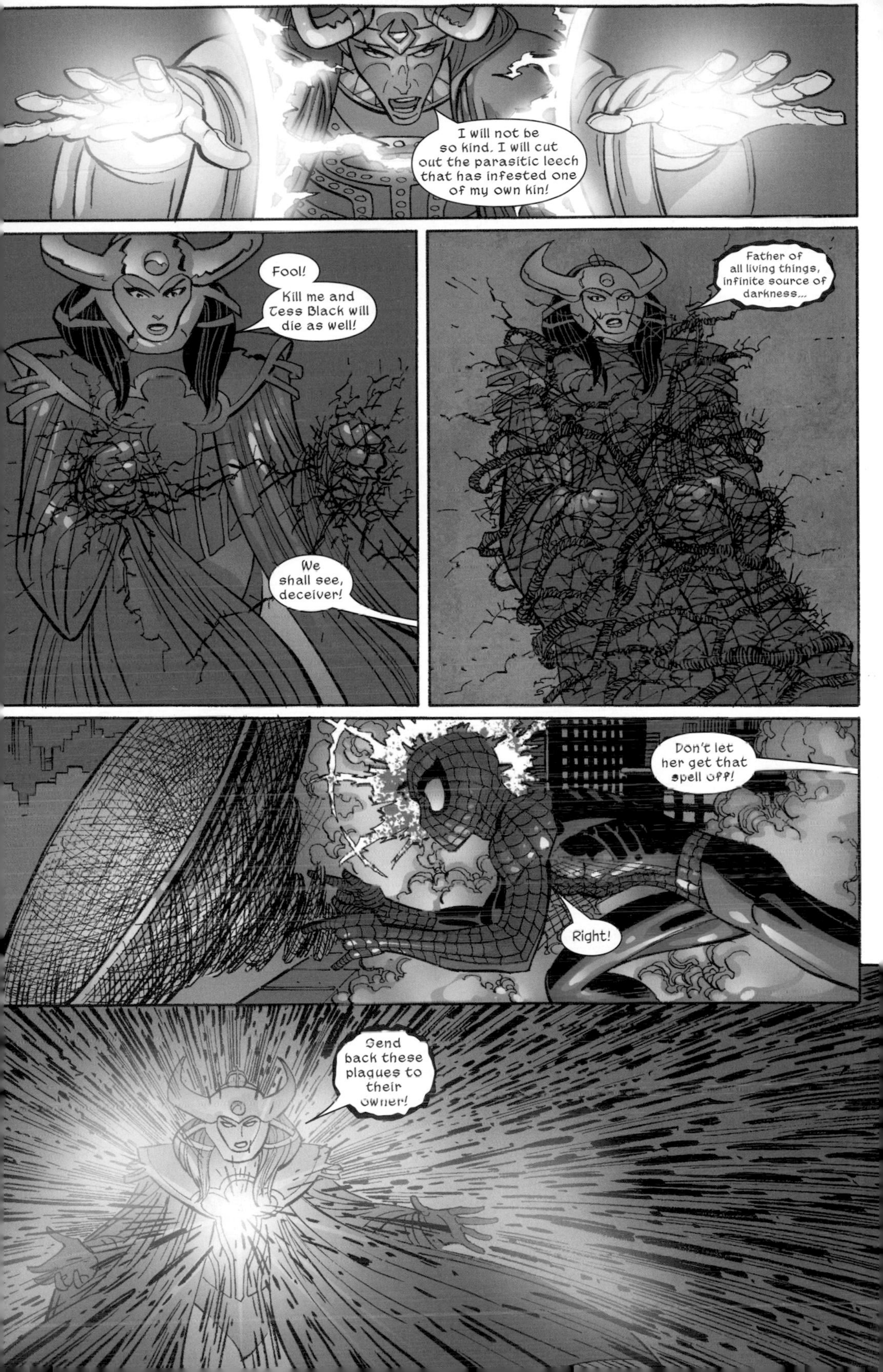
I will not be so kind. I will cut out the parasitic leech that has infested one of my own kin!
Fool!
Kill me and Tess Black will die as well!
We shall see, deceiver!
Father of all living things, infinite source of darkness...
Don't let her get that spell off!
Right!
Send back these plagues to their owner!

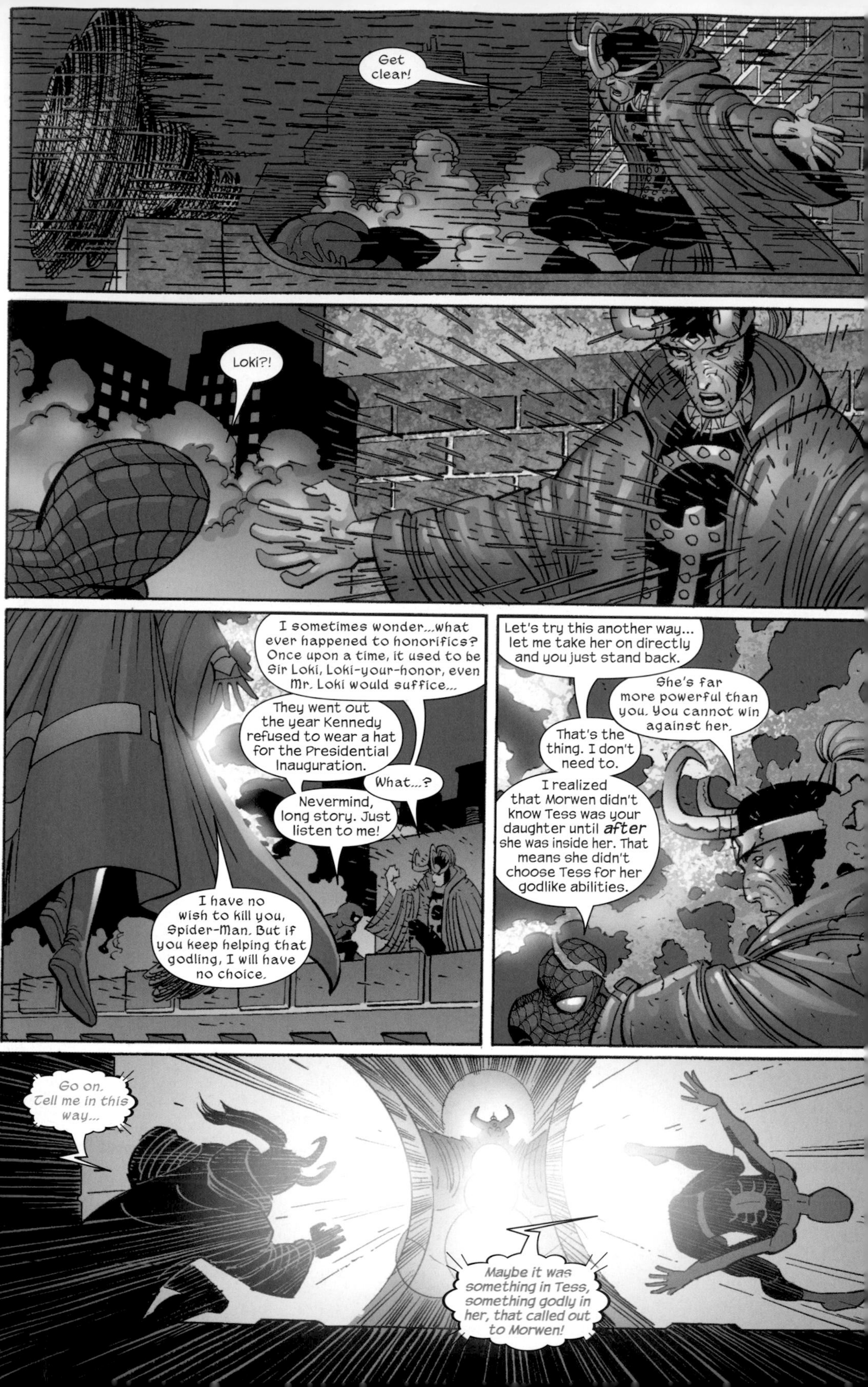
Get clear!
Loki?!
I sometimes wonder...what ever happened to honorifics? Once upon a time, it used to be Sir Loki, Loki-your-honor, even Mr. Loki would suffice...
They went out the year Kennedy refused to wear a hat for the Presidential Inauguration.
What...?
Nevermind, long story. Just listen to me!
I have no wish to kill you, Spider-Man. But if you keep helping that godling, I will have no choice.
Let's try this another way... let me take her on directly and you just stand back.
She's far more powerful than you. You cannot win against her.
That's the thing. I don't need to.
I realized that Morwen didn't know Tess was your daughter until *after* she was inside her. That means she didn't choose Tess for her godlike abilities.
Go on. Tell me in this way...
Maybe it was something in Tess, something godly in her, that called out to Morwen!

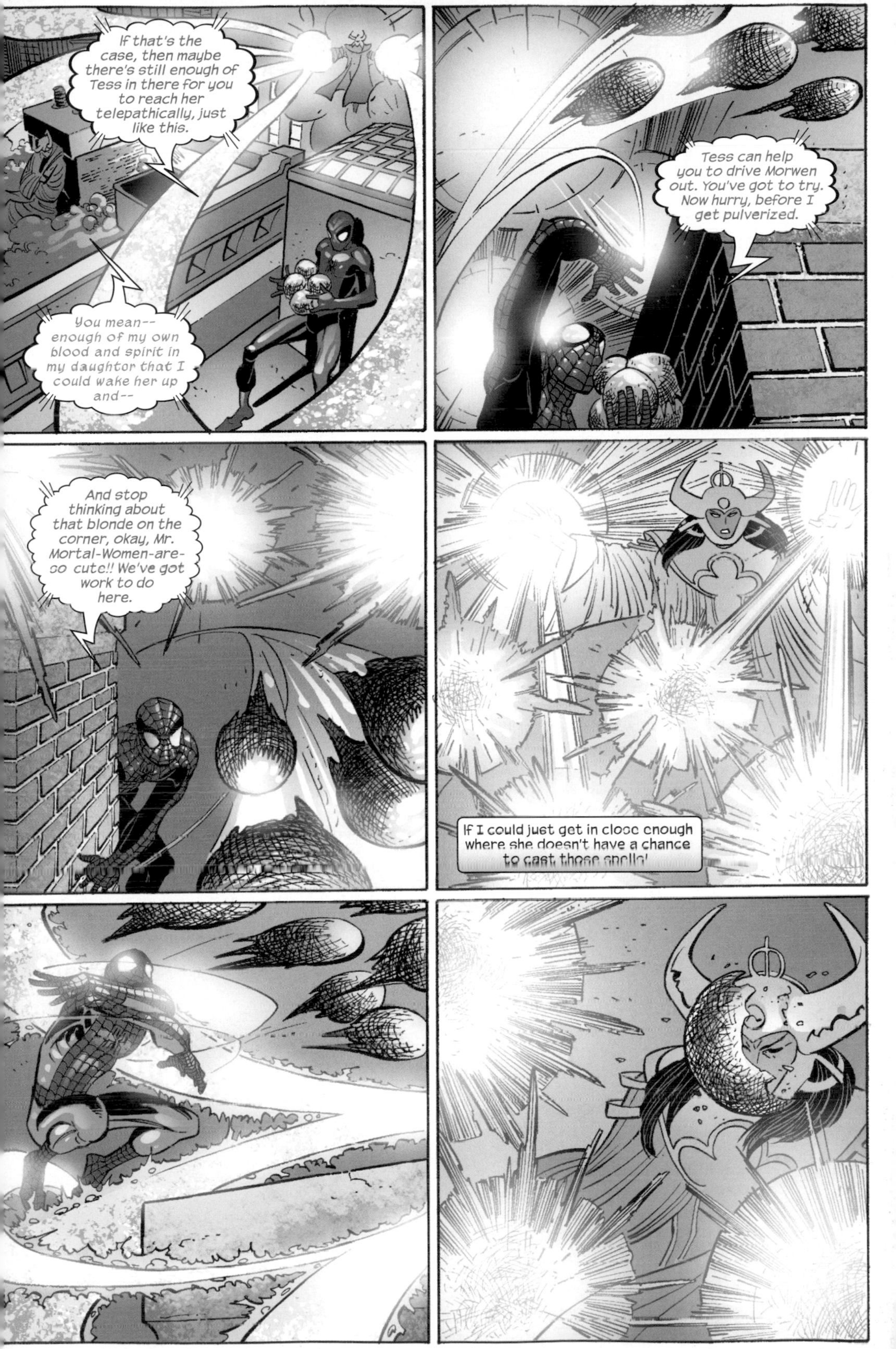
If that's the case, then maybe there's still enough of Tess in there for you to reach her telepathically, just like this.
You mean-- enough of my own blood and spirit in my daughter that I could wake her up and--
Tess can help you to drive Morwen out. You've got to try. Now hurry, before I get pulverized.
And stop thinking about that blonde on the corner, okay, Mr. Mortal-Women-are-so cute!! We've got work to do here.
If I could just get in close enough where she doesn't have a chance to cast those spells!

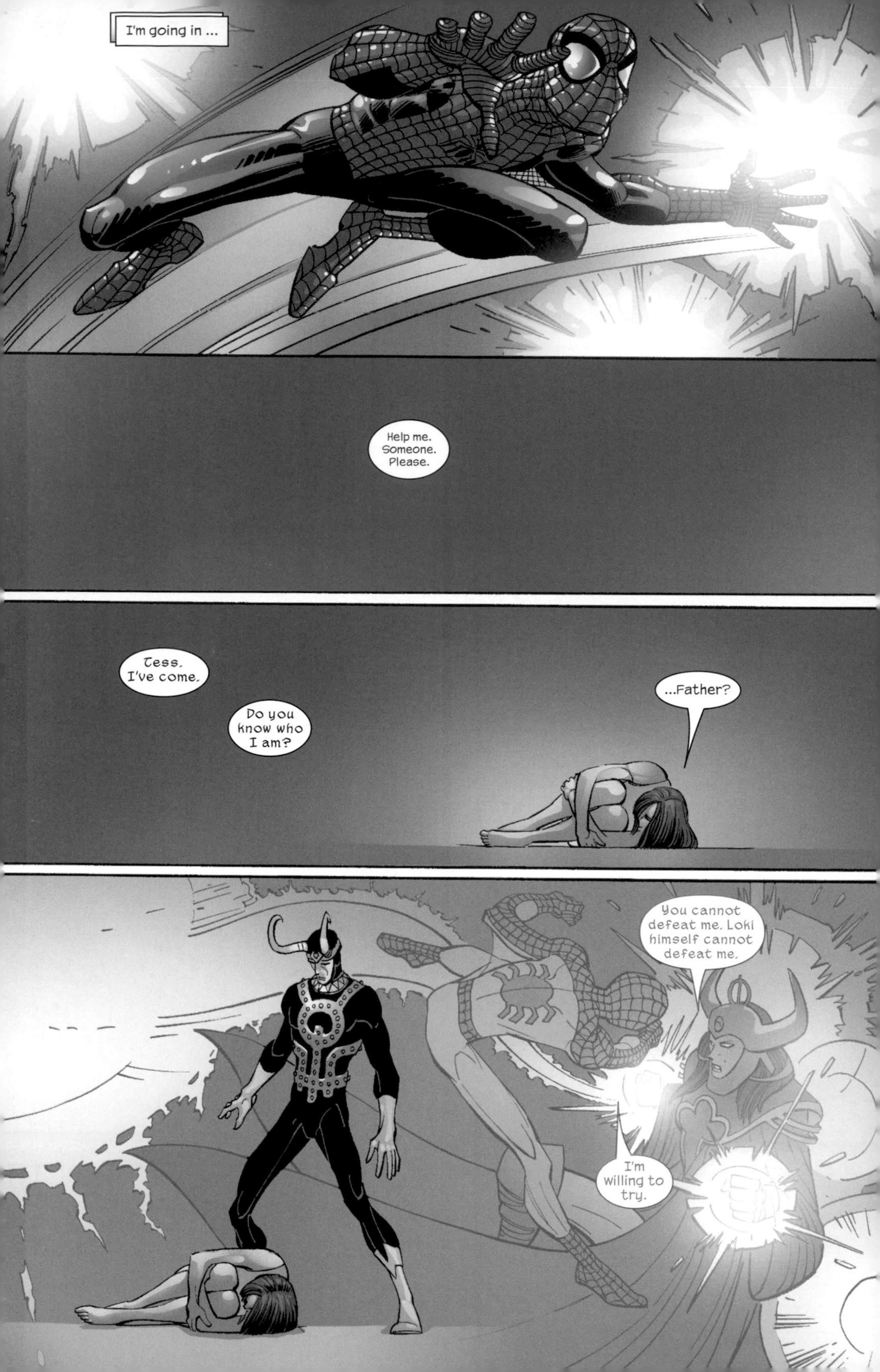

I'm going in ...
Help me. Someone. Please.
Tess. I've come.
Do you know who I am?
...Father?
You cannot defeat me. Loki himself cannot defeat me.
I'm willing to try.

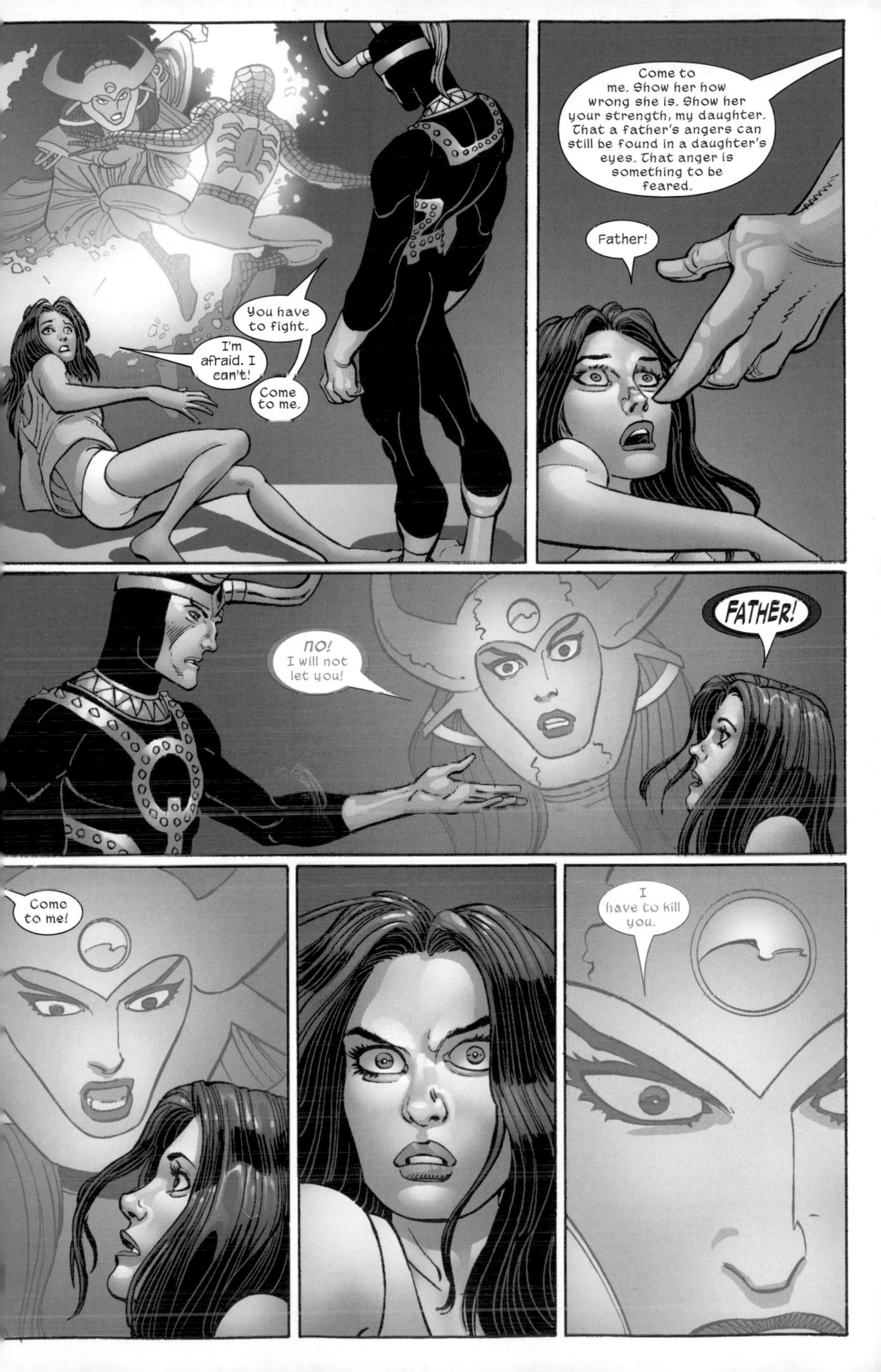

I'm afraid. I can't!
You have to fight.
Come to me.
Come to me. Show her how wrong she is. Show her your strength, my daughter. That a father's angers can still be found in a daughter's eyes. That anger is something to be feared.
Father!
NO! I will not let you!
FATHER!
Come to me!
I have to kill you.

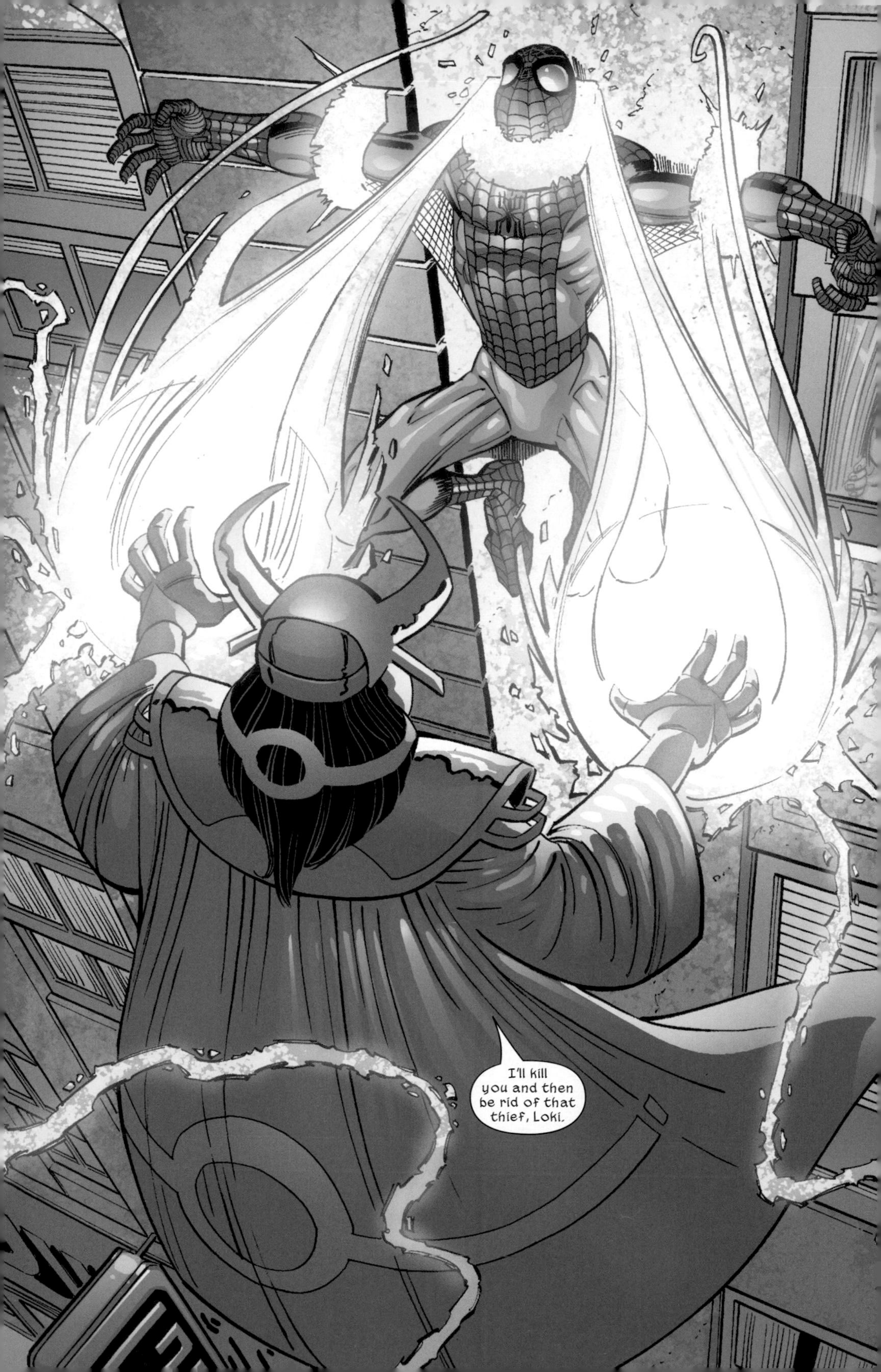
I'll kill you and then be rid of that thief, Loki.

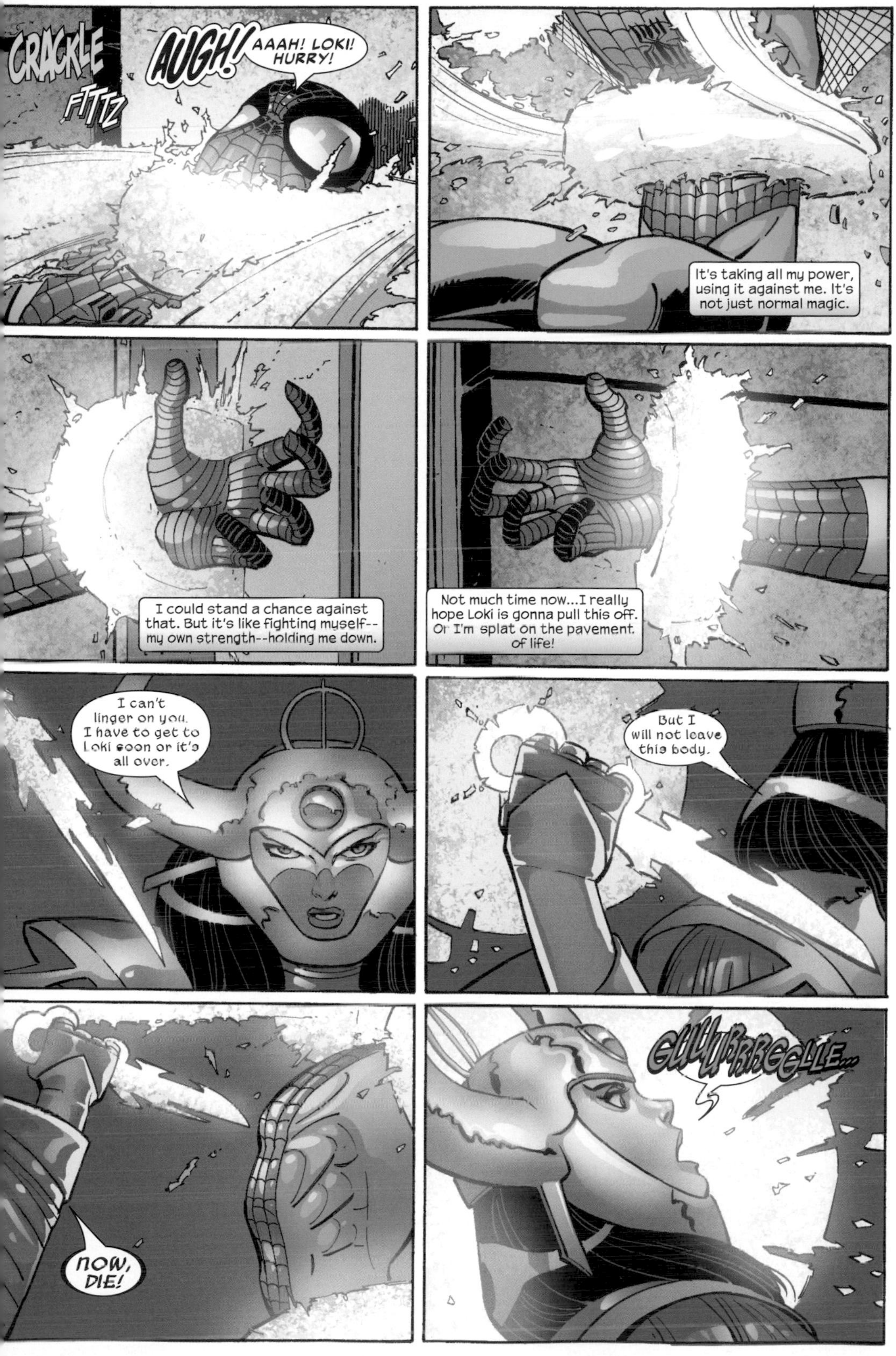
CRACKLE
FTTTZ
AUGH!
AAAH! LOKI! HURRY!
It's taking all my power, using it against me. It's not just normal magic.
I could stand a chance against that. But it's like fighting myself--my own strength--holding me down.
Not much time now...I really hope Loki is gonna pull this off. Or I'm splat on the pavement of life!
I can't linger on you. I have to get to Loki soon or it's all over.
But I will not leave this body.
Now, DIE!
GLUURRRGGLLE...

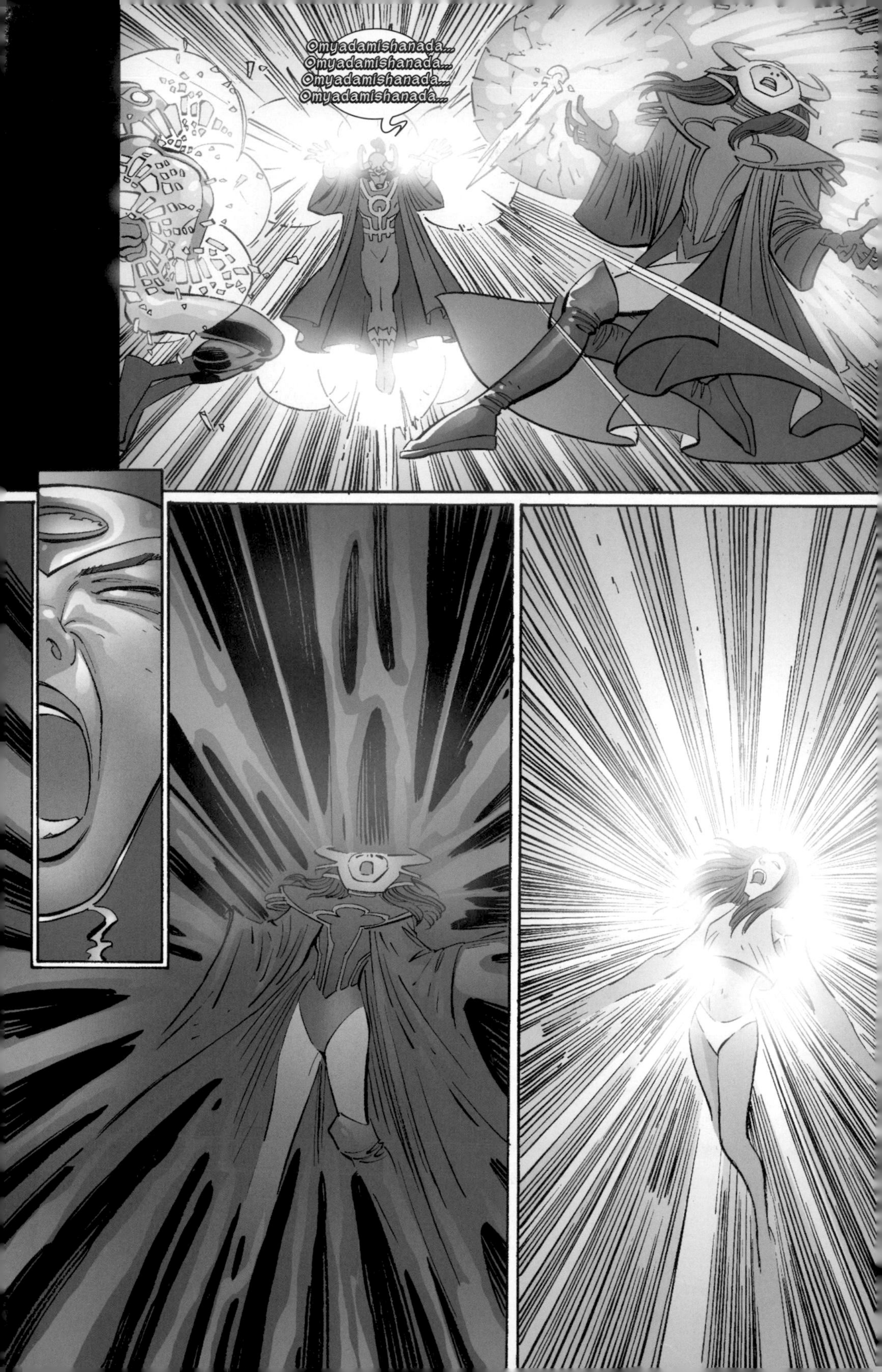
Omyadamishanada... Omyadamishanada... Omyadamishanada... Omyadamishanada...

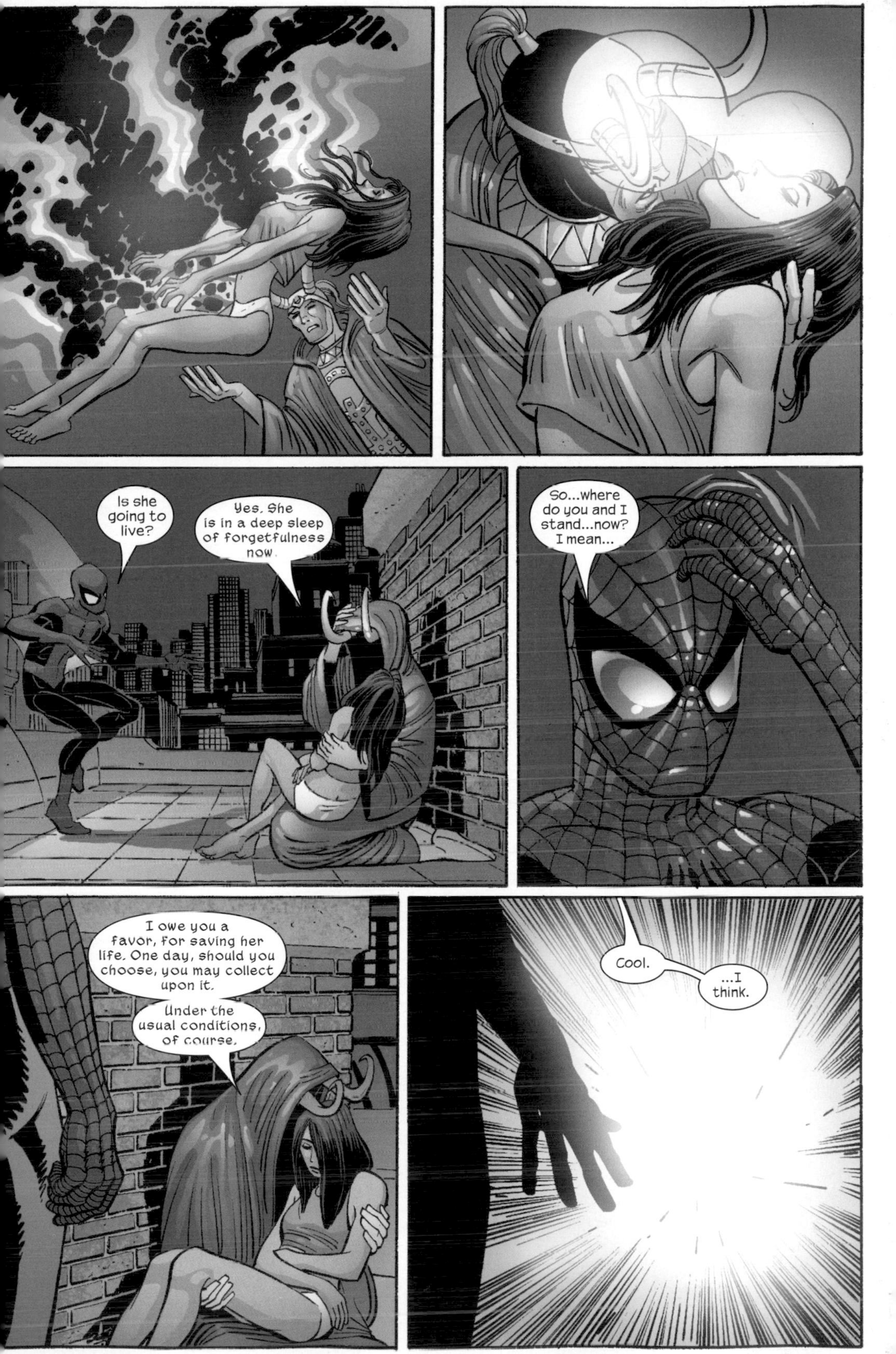
Is she going to live?
Yes. She is in a deep sleep of forgetfulness now.
So...where do you and I stand...now? I mean...
I owe you a favor, for saving her life. One day, should you choose, you may collect upon it.
Under the usual conditions, of course.
Cool.
...I think.

Doc Strange still wasn't in town, so I did a little investigating of my own at the public library.

There was nothing on microfiche or any literature on Morwen, First Sorcerer of Chaos.

I looked her up online too. All I got were X-rated sites. Thankfully the public library has a block on that stuff. Talk about embarrassing!

Shopping | Money | People & Chat

Search ▷ Morwen + Sorcerer of Chaos

Then I did some checking on Tess Black.

Doesn't seem like Loki's kid. For starters, she's respectable, even made the paper a few times. She's a stock trader an' pretty well-off.

I put her home phone number into the new feature online and got a map of her address. I think the service is stupid--stalkers could have a field day--but it's handy for a guardian angel like myself.

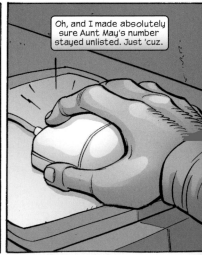

Oh, and I made absolutely sure Aunt May's number stayed unlisted. Just 'cuz.

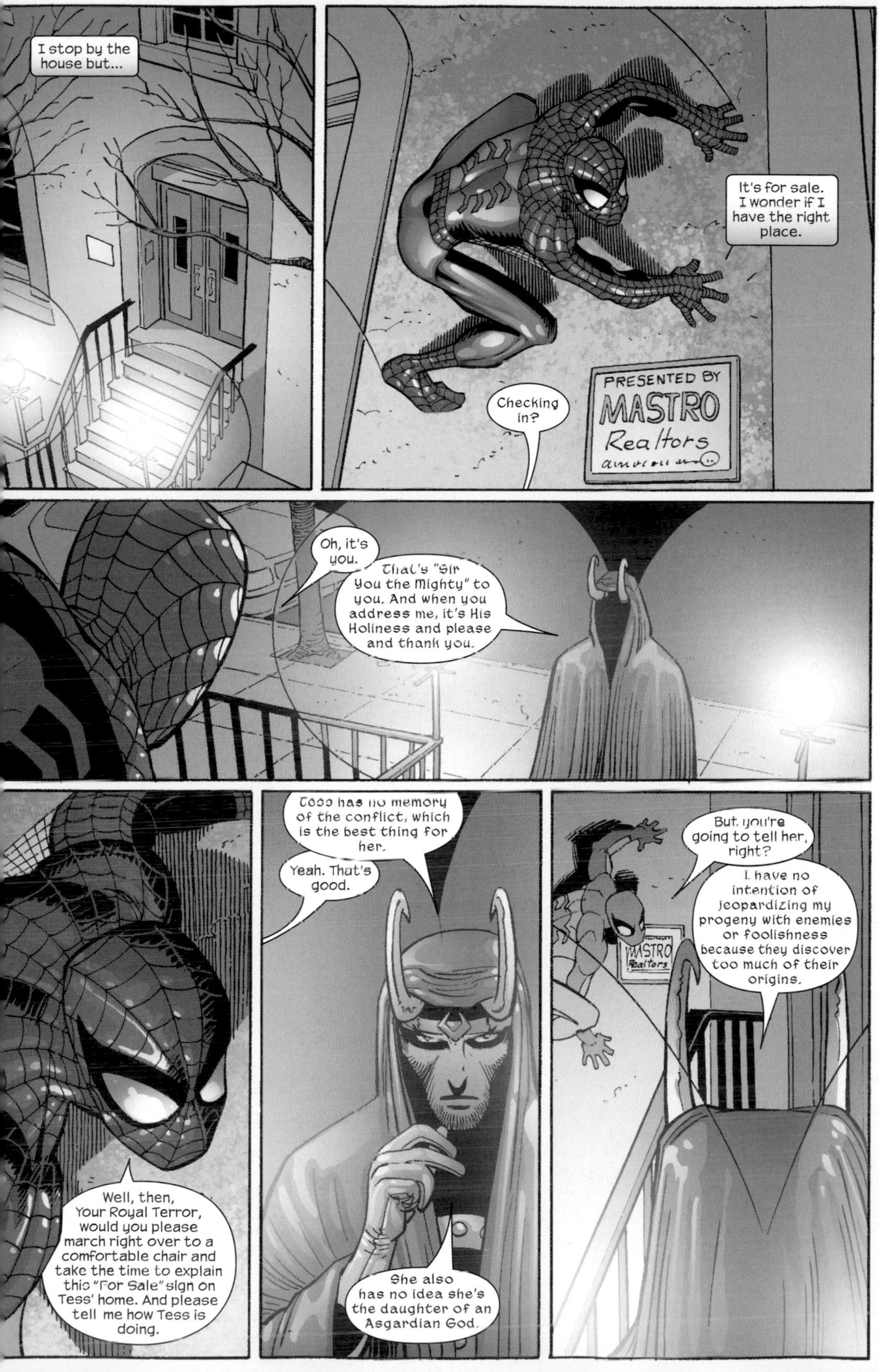
I stop by the house but...
It's for sale. I wonder if I have the right place.
PRESENTED BY MASTRO Realtors
Checking in?
Oh, it's you.
That's "Sir You the Mighty" to you. And when you address me, it's His Holiness and please and thank you.
Well, then, Your Royal Terror, would you please march right over to a comfortable chair and take the time to explain this "For Sale" sign on Tess' home. And please tell me how Tess is doing.
Tess has no memory of the conflict, which is the best thing for her.
Yeah. That's good.
She also has no idea she's the daughter of an Asgardian God.
But, you're going to tell her, right?
I have no intention of jeopardizing my progeny with enemies or foolishness because they discover too much of their origins.
MASTRO Realtors

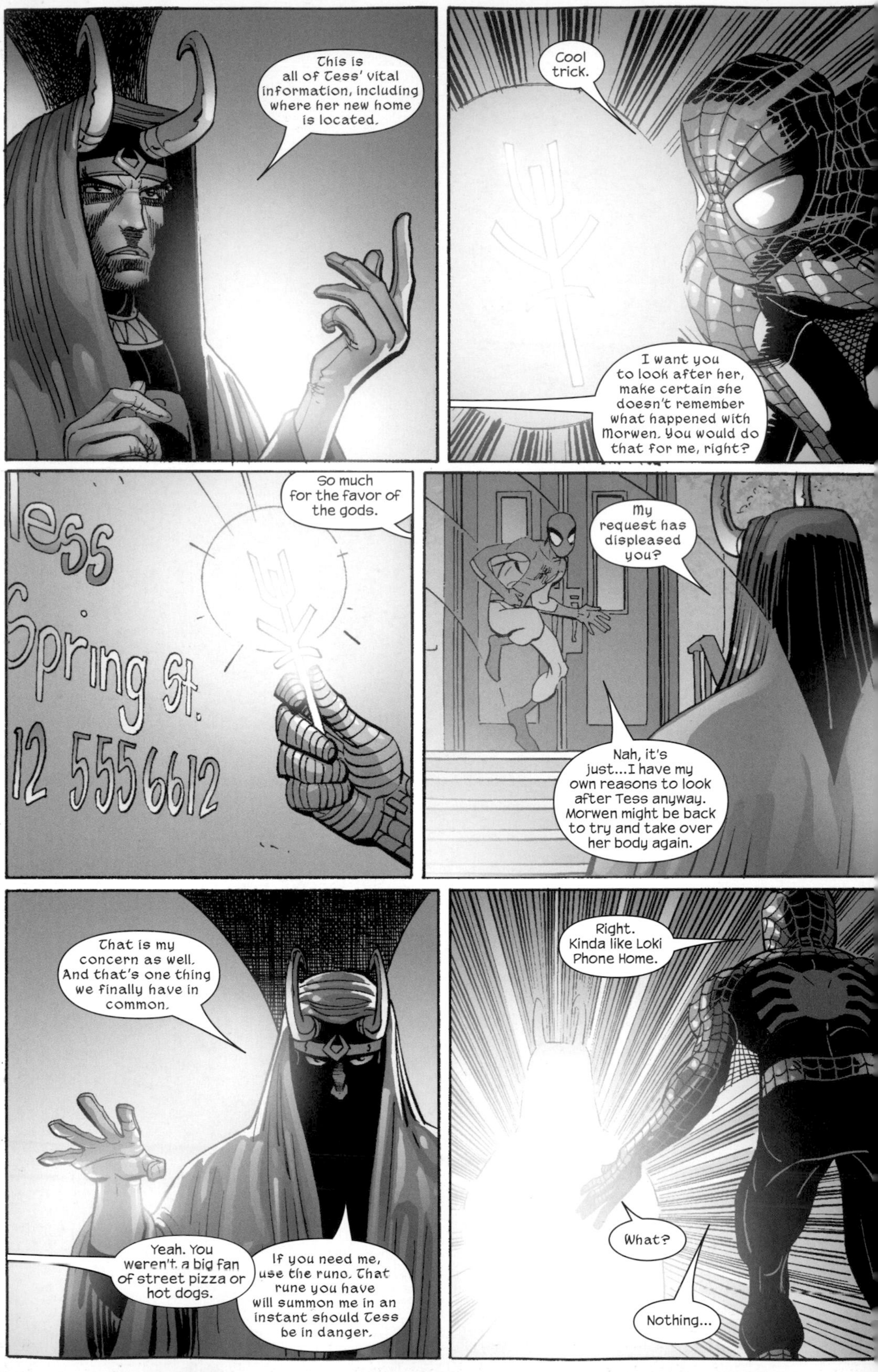
This is all of Tess' vital information, including where her new home is located.
Cool trick.
I want you to look after her, make certain she doesn't remember what happened with Morwen. You would do that for me, right?
Tess
Spring St.
12 555 6612
So much for the favor of the gods.
My request has displeased you?
Nah, it's just...I have my own reasons to look after Tess anyway. Morwen might be back to try and take over her body again.
That is my concern as well. And that's one thing we finally have in common.
Yeah. You weren't a big fan of street pizza or hot dogs.
If you need me, use the rune. That rune you have will summon me in an instant should Tess be in danger.
Right. Kinda like Loki Phone Home.
What?
Nothing...

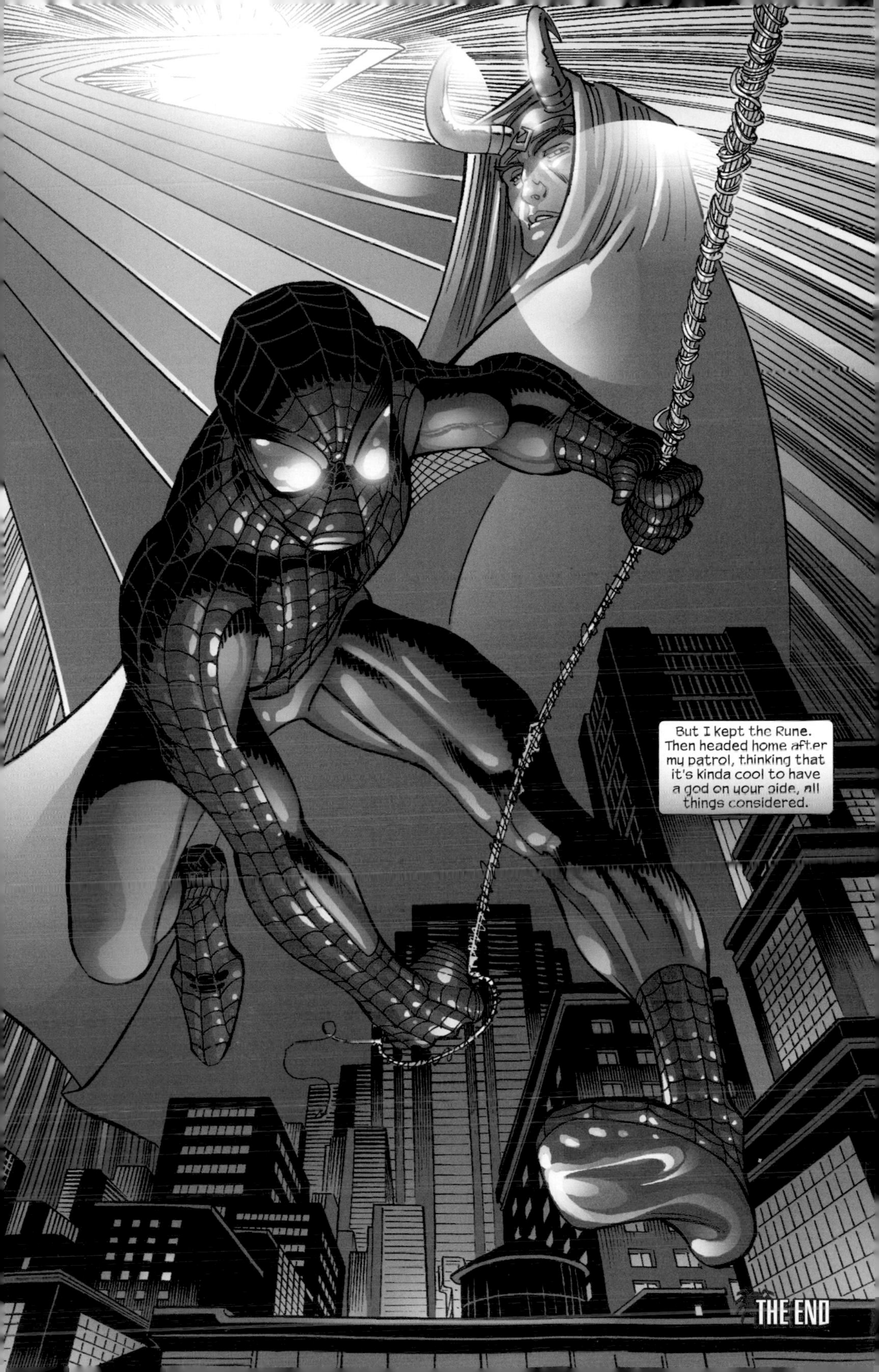
But I kept the Rune. Then headed home after my patrol, thinking that it's kinda cool to have a god on your side, all things considered.
THE END

JOURNEY INTO MYSTERY #626.1

THE GOD OF MISCHIEF IS REBORN AS KID LOKI! WHILE HE TRIES TO BE
BETTER THAN HIS PREVIOUS LIFE, EVERYONE IN ASGARD REMEMBERS
HIS PAST SINISTER DEEDS.

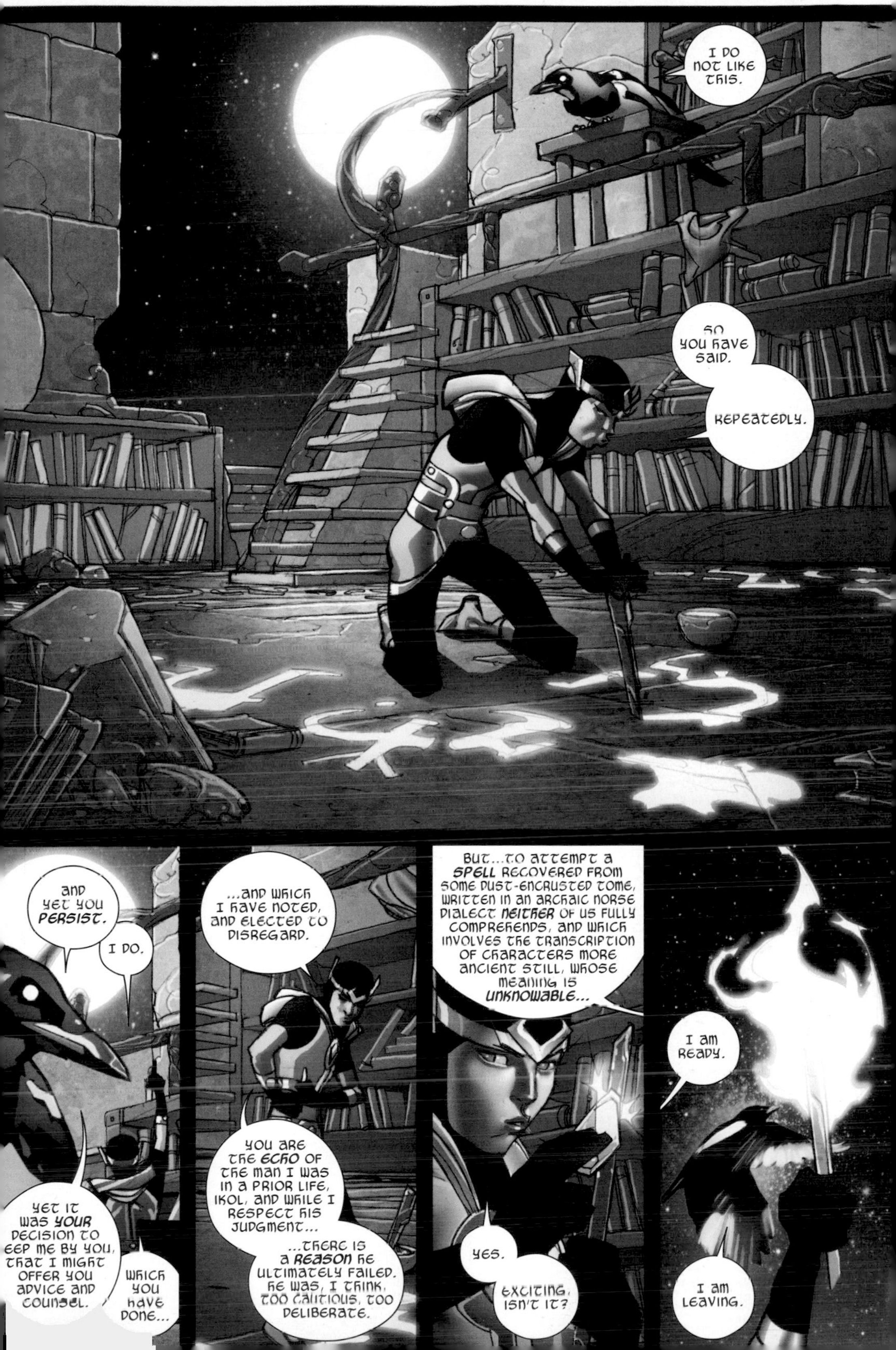
I DO NOT LIKE THIS.
SO YOU HAVE SAID.
REPEATEDLY.
AND YET YOU PERSIST.
I DO.
YET IT WAS YOUR DECISION TO EEP ME BY YOU, THAT I MIGHT OFFER YOU ADVICE AND COUNSEL.
WHICH YOU HAVE DONE...
...AND WHICH I HAVE NOTED, AND ELECTED TO DISREGARD.
YOU ARE THE ECHO OF THE MAN I WAS IN A PRIOR LIFE, IKOL, AND WHILE I RESPECT HIS JUDGMENT...
...THERE IS A REASON HE ULTIMATELY FAILED. HE WAS, I THINK, TOO CAUTIOUS, TOO DELIBERATE.
BUT...TO ATTEMPT A SPELL RECOVERED FROM SOME DUST-ENCRUSTED TOME, WRITTEN IN AN ARCHAIC NORSE DIALECT NEITHER OF US FULLY COMPREHENDS, AND WHICH INVOLVES THE TRANSCRIPTION OF CHARACTERS MORE ANCIENT STILL, WHOSE MEANING IS UNKNOWABLE...
YES.
EXCITING, ISN'T IT?
I AM READY.
I AM LEAVING.

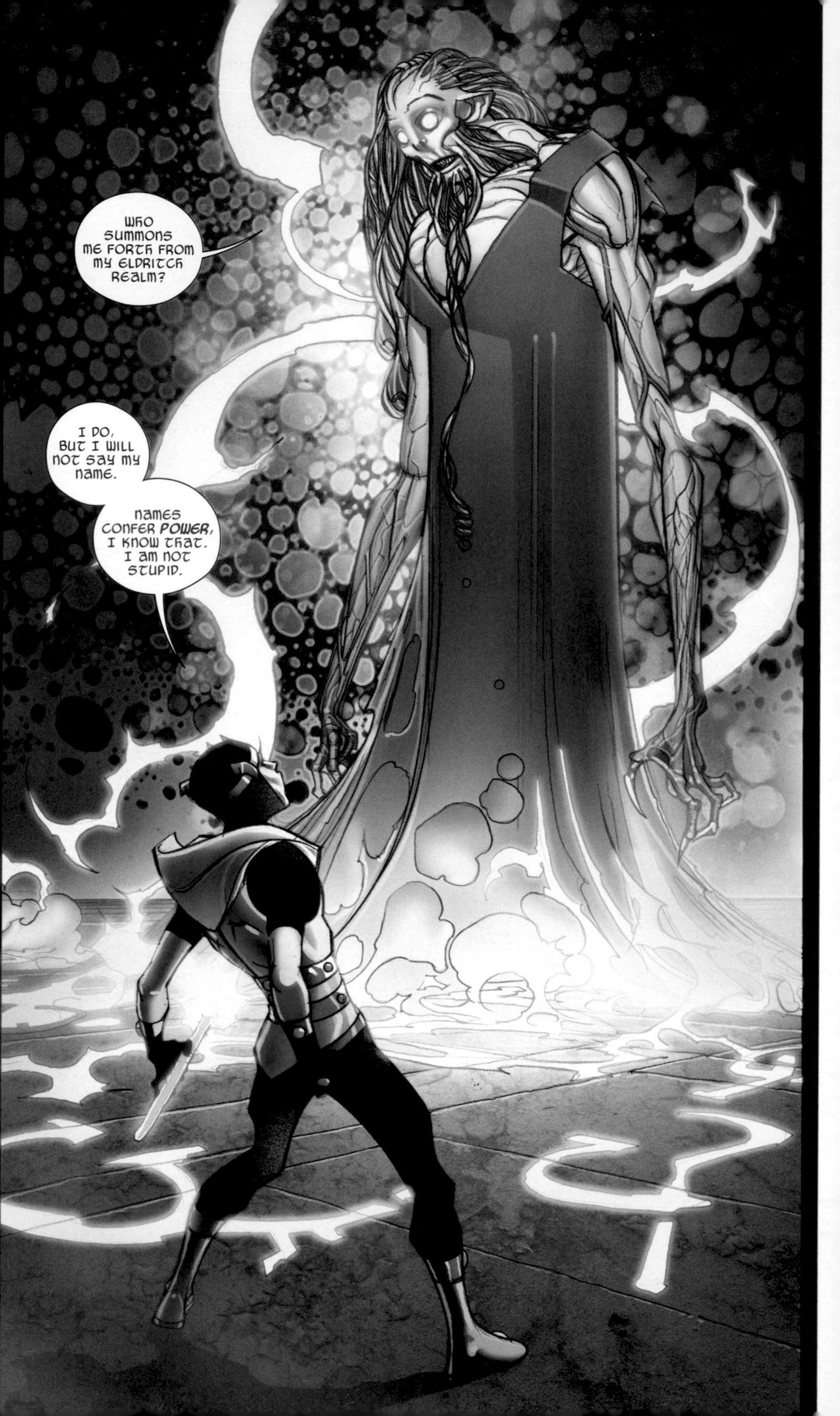
WHO SUMMONS ME FORTH FROM MY ELDRITCH REALM?
I DO, BUT I WILL NOT SAY MY NAME.
NAMES CONFER POWER, I KNOW THAT. I AM NOT STUPID.

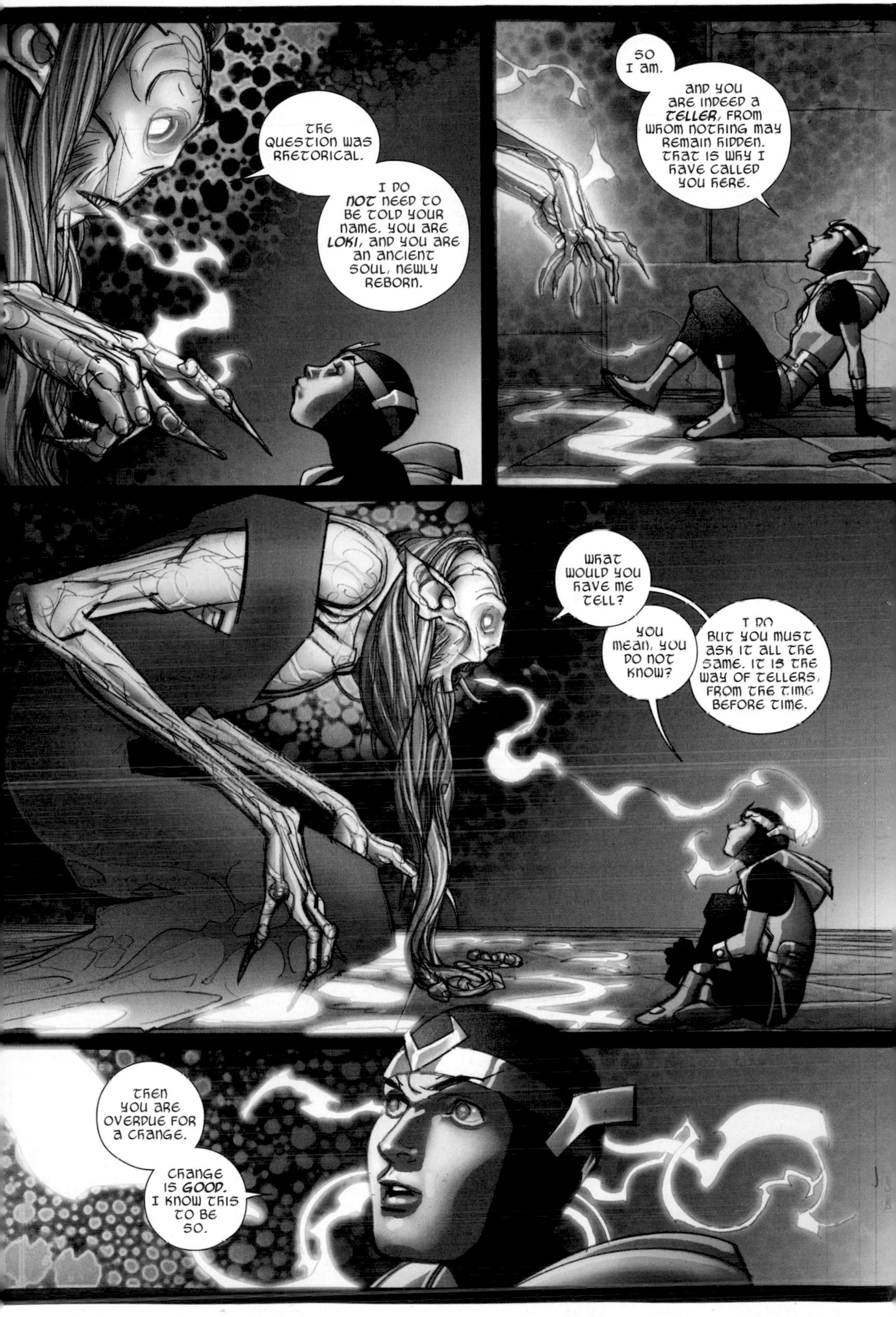
THE QUESTION WAS RHETORICAL.
I DO NOT NEED TO BE TOLD YOUR NAME. YOU ARE LOKI, AND YOU ARE AN ANCIENT SOUL, NEWLY REBORN.
SO I AM.
AND YOU ARE INDEED A TELLER, FROM WHOM NOTHING MAY REMAIN HIDDEN. THAT IS WHY I HAVE CALLED YOU HERE.
WHAT WOULD YOU HAVE ME TELL?
YOU MEAN, YOU DO NOT KNOW?
I DO BUT YOU MUST ASK IT ALL THE SAME. IT IS THE WAY OF TELLERS, FROM THE TIME BEFORE TIME.
THEN YOU ARE OVERDUE FOR A CHANGE.
CHANGE IS GOOD. I KNOW THIS TO BE SO.

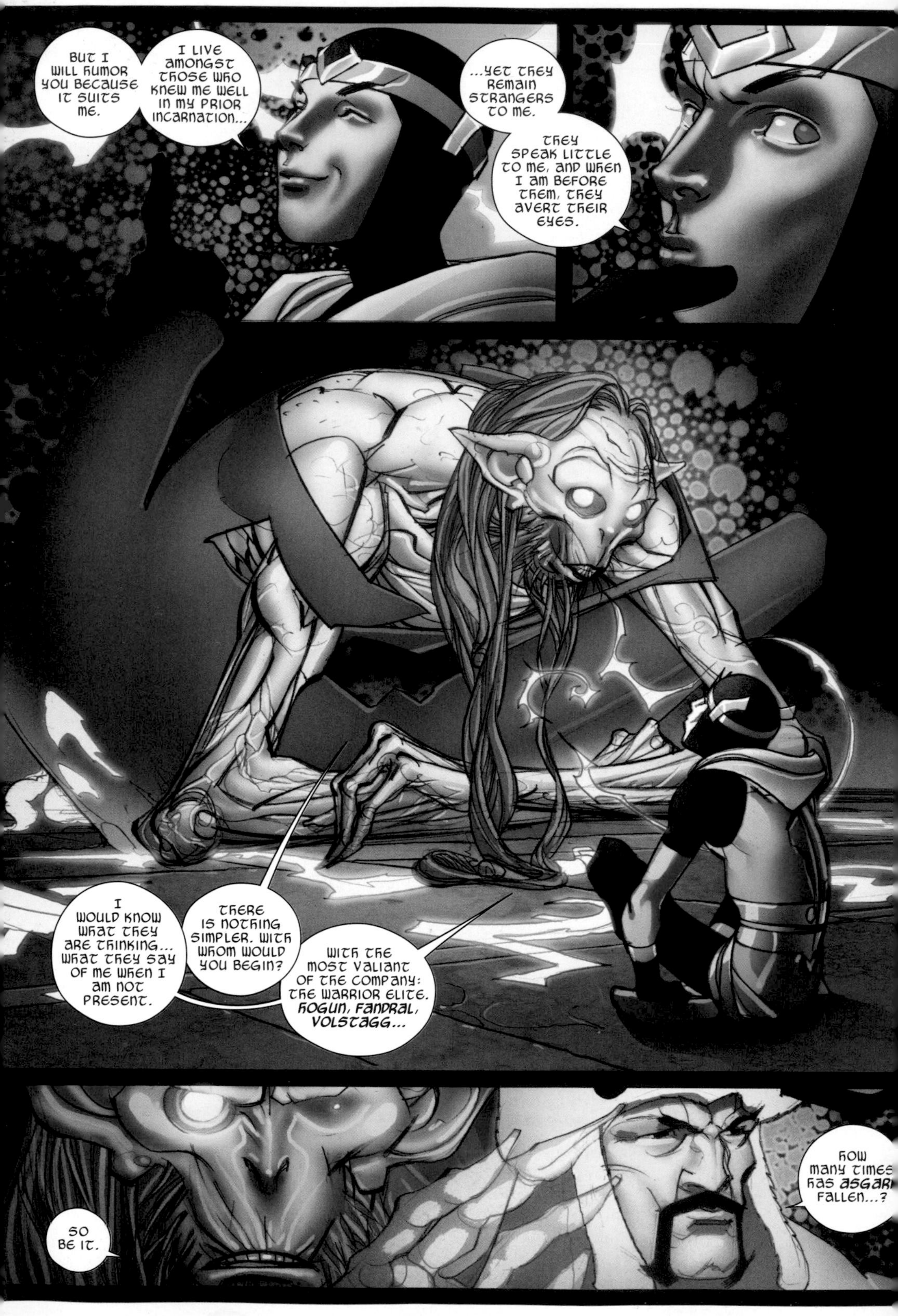
BUT I WILL HUMOR YOU BECAUSE IT SUITS ME.
I LIVE AMONGST THOSE WHO KNEW ME WELL IN MY PRIOR INCARNATION...
...YET THEY REMAIN STRANGERS TO ME.
THEY SPEAK LITTLE TO ME, AND WHEN I AM BEFORE THEM, THEY AVERT THEIR EYES.
I WOULD KNOW WHAT THEY ARE THINKING... WHAT THEY SAY OF ME WHEN I AM NOT PRESENT.
THERE IS NOTHING SIMPLER. WITH WHOM WOULD YOU BEGIN?
WITH THE MOST VALIANT OF THE COMPANY: THE WARRIOR ELITE. HOGUN, FANDRAL, VOLSTAGG...
SO BE IT.
HOW MANY TIMES HAS ASGARD FALLEN...?

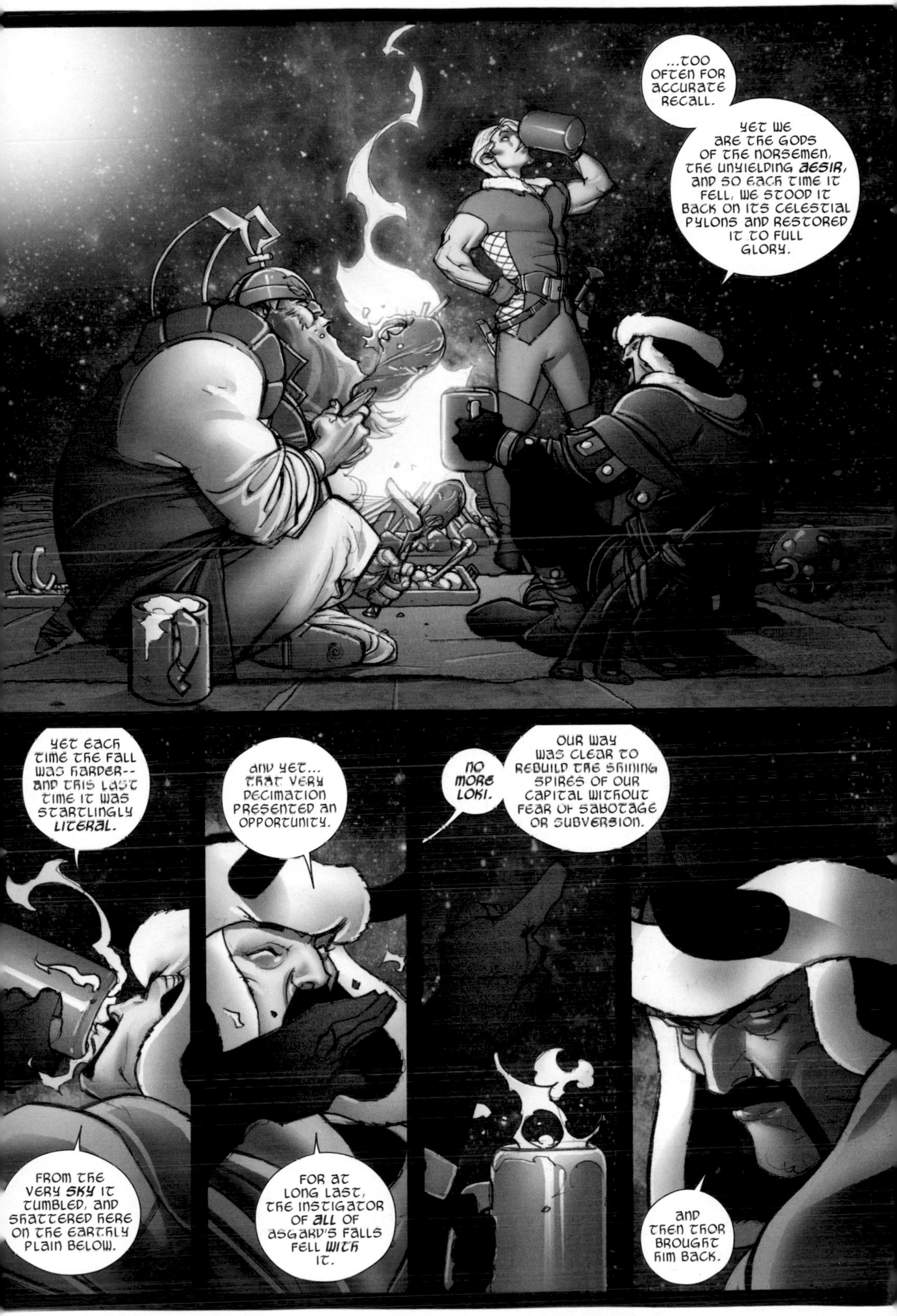
...TOO OFTEN FOR ACCURATE RECALL.
YET WE ARE THE GODS OF THE NORSEMEN, THE UNYIELDING AESIR, AND SO EACH TIME IT FELL, WE STOOD IT BACK ON ITS CELESTIAL PYLONS AND RESTORED IT TO FULL GLORY.
YET EACH TIME THE FALL WAS HARDER-- AND THIS LAST TIME IT WAS STARTLINGLY LITERAL.
FROM THE VERY SKY IT TUMBLED, AND SHATTERED HERE ON THE EARTHLY PLAIN BELOW.
AND YET... THAT VERY DECIMATION PRESENTED AN OPPORTUNITY.
FOR AT LONG LAST, THE INSTIGATOR OF ALL OF ASGARD'S FALLS FELL WITH IT.
NO MORE LOKI.
OUR WAY WAS CLEAR TO REBUILD THE SHINING SPIRES OF OUR CAPITAL WITHOUT FEAR OF SABOTAGE OR SUBVERSION.
AND THEN THOR BROUGHT HIM BACK.

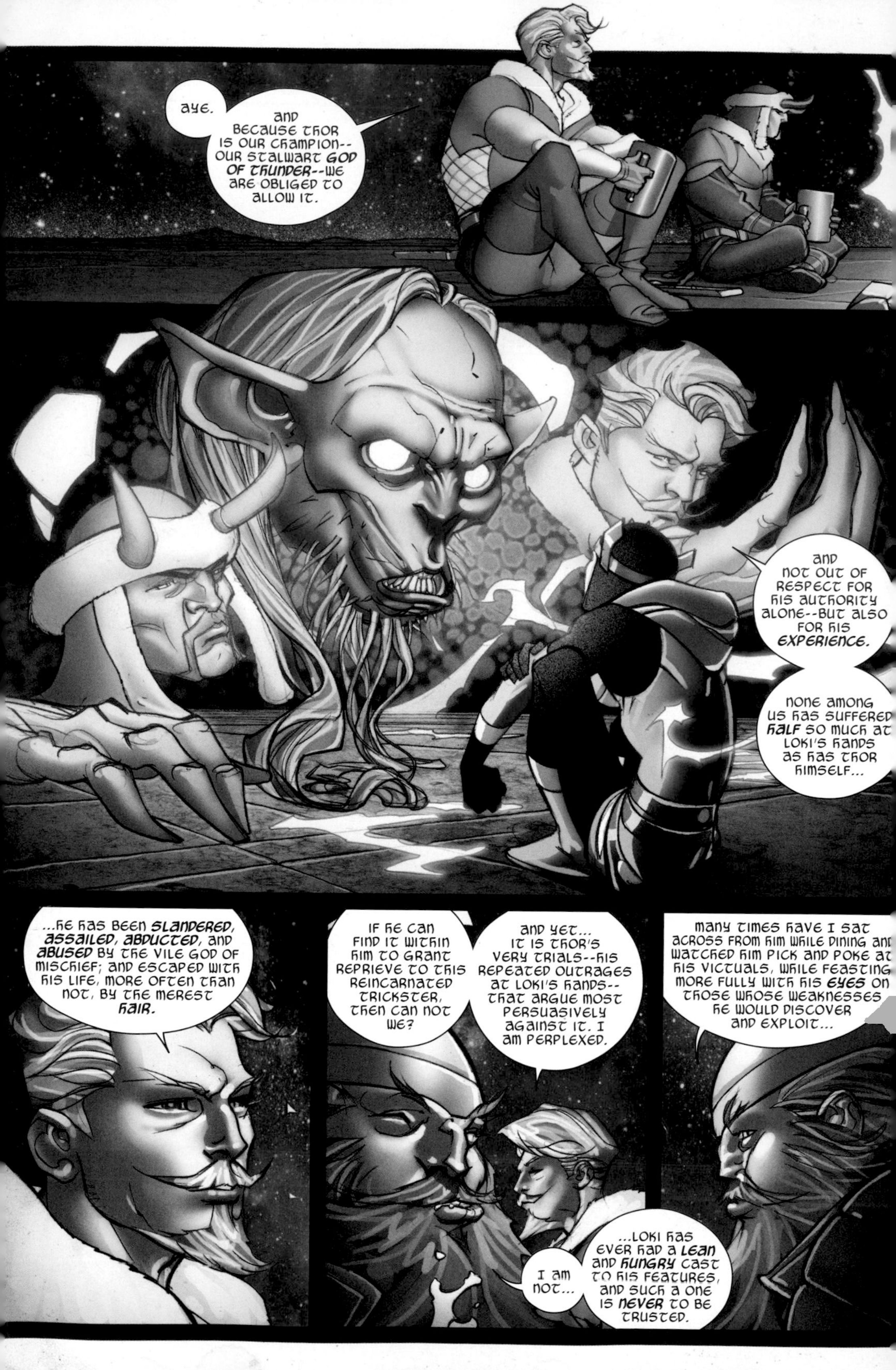
AYE.
AND BECAUSE THOR IS OUR CHAMPION-- OUR STALWART GOD OF THUNDER--WE ARE OBLIGED TO ALLOW IT.
AND NOT OUT OF RESPECT FOR HIS AUTHORITY ALONE--BUT ALSO FOR HIS EXPERIENCE.
NONE AMONG US HAS SUFFERED HALF SO MUCH AT LOKI'S HANDS AS HAS THOR HIMSELF...
...HE HAS BEEN SLANDERED, ASSAILED, ABDUCTED, AND ABUSED BY THE VILE GOD OF MISCHIEF; AND ESCAPED WITH HIS LIFE, MORE OFTEN THAN NOT, BY THE MEREST HAIR.
IF HE CAN FIND IT WITHIN HIM TO GRANT REPRIEVE TO THIS REINCARNATED TRICKSTER, THEN CAN NOT WE?
AND YET... IT IS THOR'S VERY TRIALS--HIS REPEATED OUTRAGES AT LOKI'S HANDS-- THAT ARGUE MOST PERSUASIVELY AGAINST IT. I AM PERPLEXED.
I AM NOT...
MANY TIMES HAVE I SAT ACROSS FROM HIM WHILE DINING AND WATCHED HIM PICK AND POKE AT HIS VICTUALS, WHILE FEASTING MORE FULLY WITH HIS EYES ON THOSE WHOSE WEAKNESSES HE WOULD DISCOVER AND EXPLOIT...
...LOKI HAS EVER HAD A LEAN AND HUNGRY CAST TO HIS FEATURES, AND SUCH A ONE IS NEVER TO BE TRUSTED.

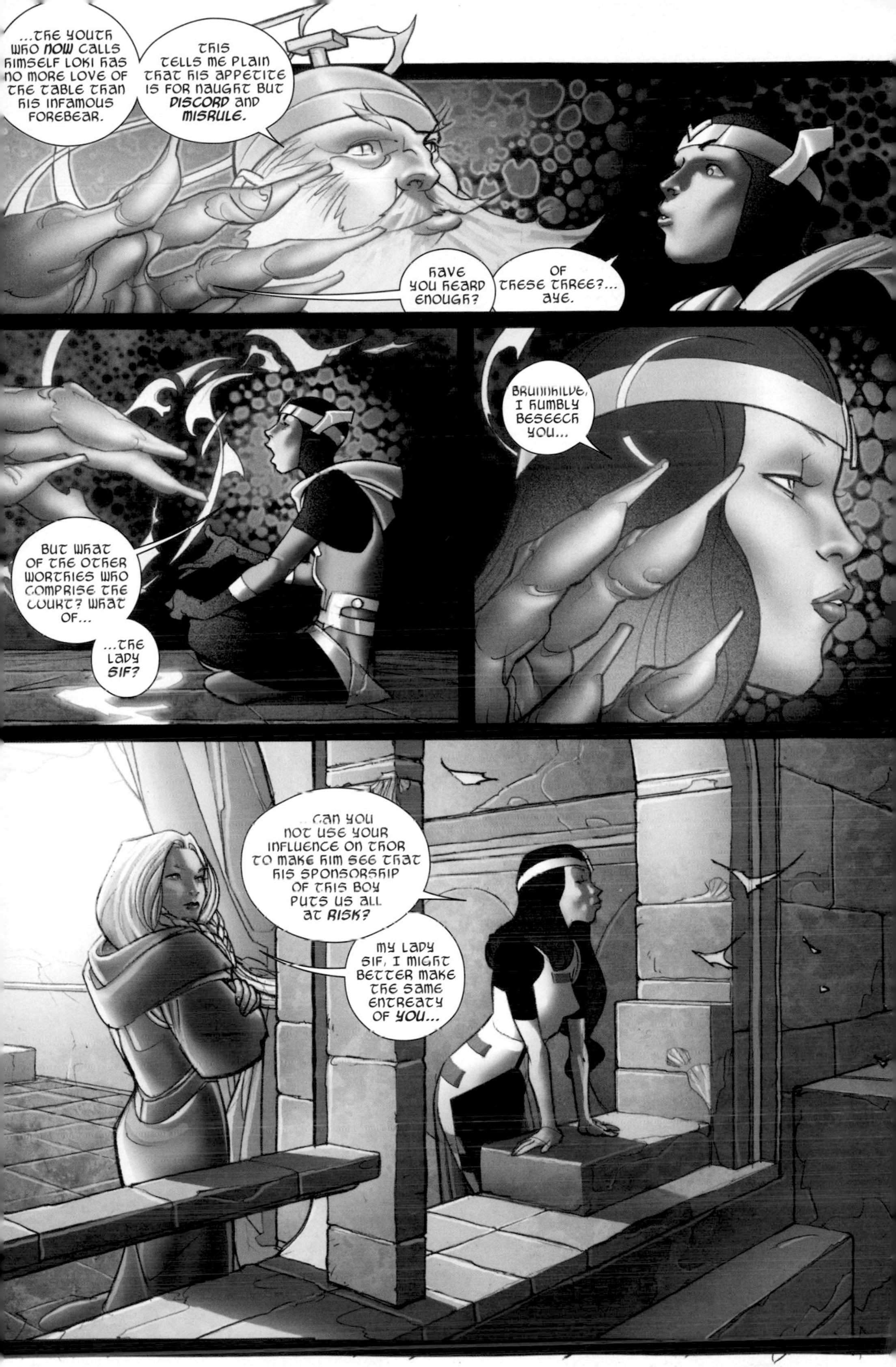
...THE YOUTH WHO NOW CALLS HIMSELF LOKI HAS NO MORE LOVE OF THE TABLE THAN HIS INFAMOUS FOREBEAR.
THIS TELLS ME PLAIN THAT HIS APPETITE IS FOR NAUGHT BUT DISCORD AND MISRULE.
HAVE YOU HEARD ENOUGH?
OF THESE THREE?... AYE.
BUT WHAT OF THE OTHER WORTHIES WHO COMPRISE THE COURT? WHAT OF...
...THE LADY SIF?
BRUNNHILDE, I HUMBLY BESEECH YOU...
...CAN YOU NOT USE YOUR INFLUENCE ON THOR TO MAKE HIM SEE THAT HIS SPONSORSHIP OF THIS BOY PUTS US ALL AT RISK?
MY LADY SIF, I MIGHT BETTER MAKE THE SAME ENTREATY OF YOU...

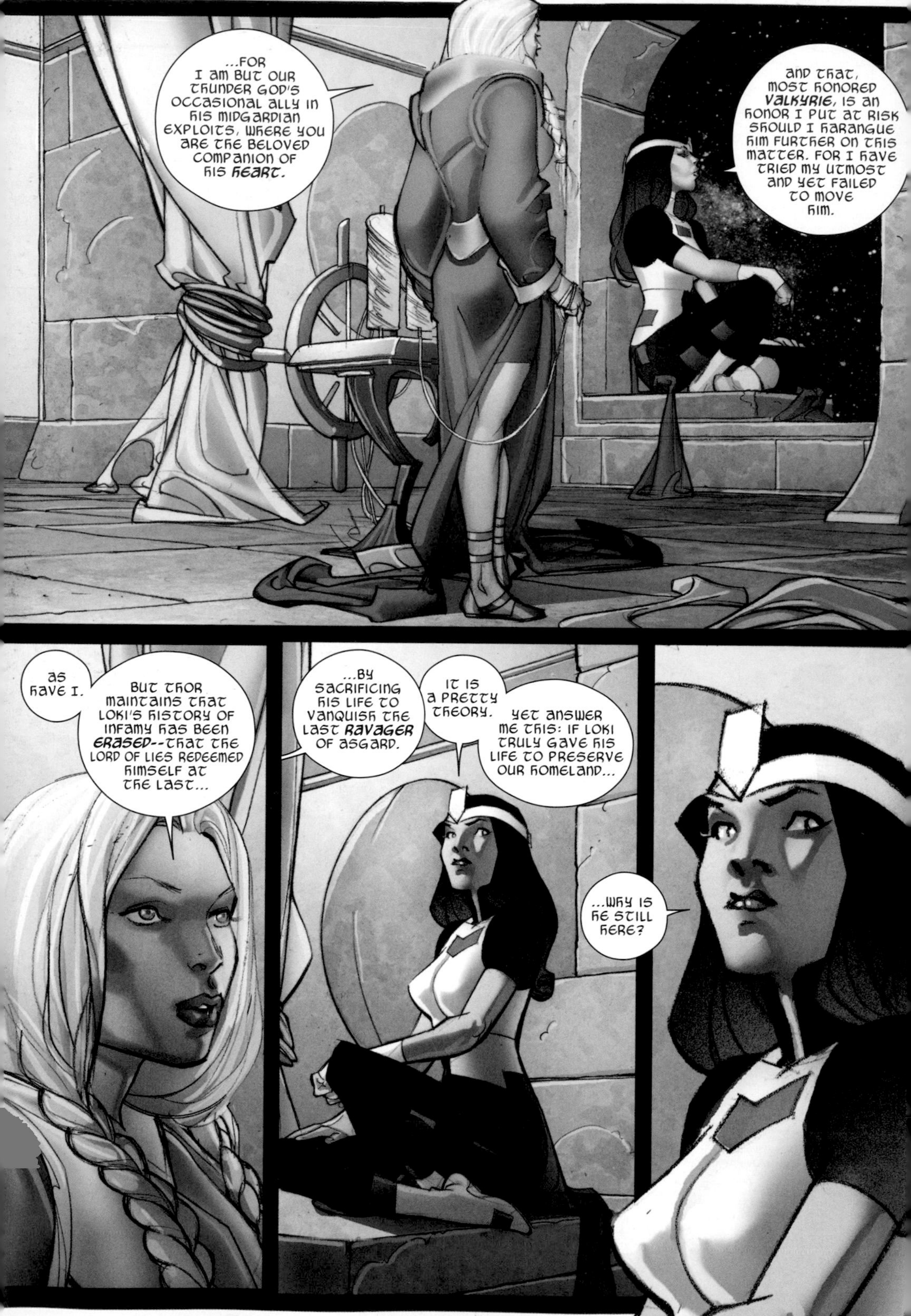
...FOR I AM BUT OUR THUNDER GOD'S OCCASIONAL ALLY IN HIS MIDGARDIAN EXPLOITS, WHERE YOU ARE THE BELOVED COMPANION OF HIS HEART.
AND THAT, MOST HONORED VALKYRIE, IS AN HONOR I PUT AT RISK SHOULD I HARANGUE HIM FURTHER ON THIS MATTER. FOR I HAVE TRIED MY UTMOST AND YET FAILED TO MOVE HIM.
AS HAVE I.
BUT THOR MAINTAINS THAT LOKI'S HISTORY OF INFAMY HAS BEEN ERASED--THAT THE LORD OF LIES REDEEMED HIMSELF AT THE LAST...
...BY SACRIFICING HIS LIFE TO VANQUISH THE LAST RAVAGER OF ASGARD.
IT IS A PRETTY THEORY.
YET ANSWER ME THIS: IF LOKI TRULY GAVE HIS LIFE TO PRESERVE OUR HOMELAND...
...WHY IS HE STILL HERE?

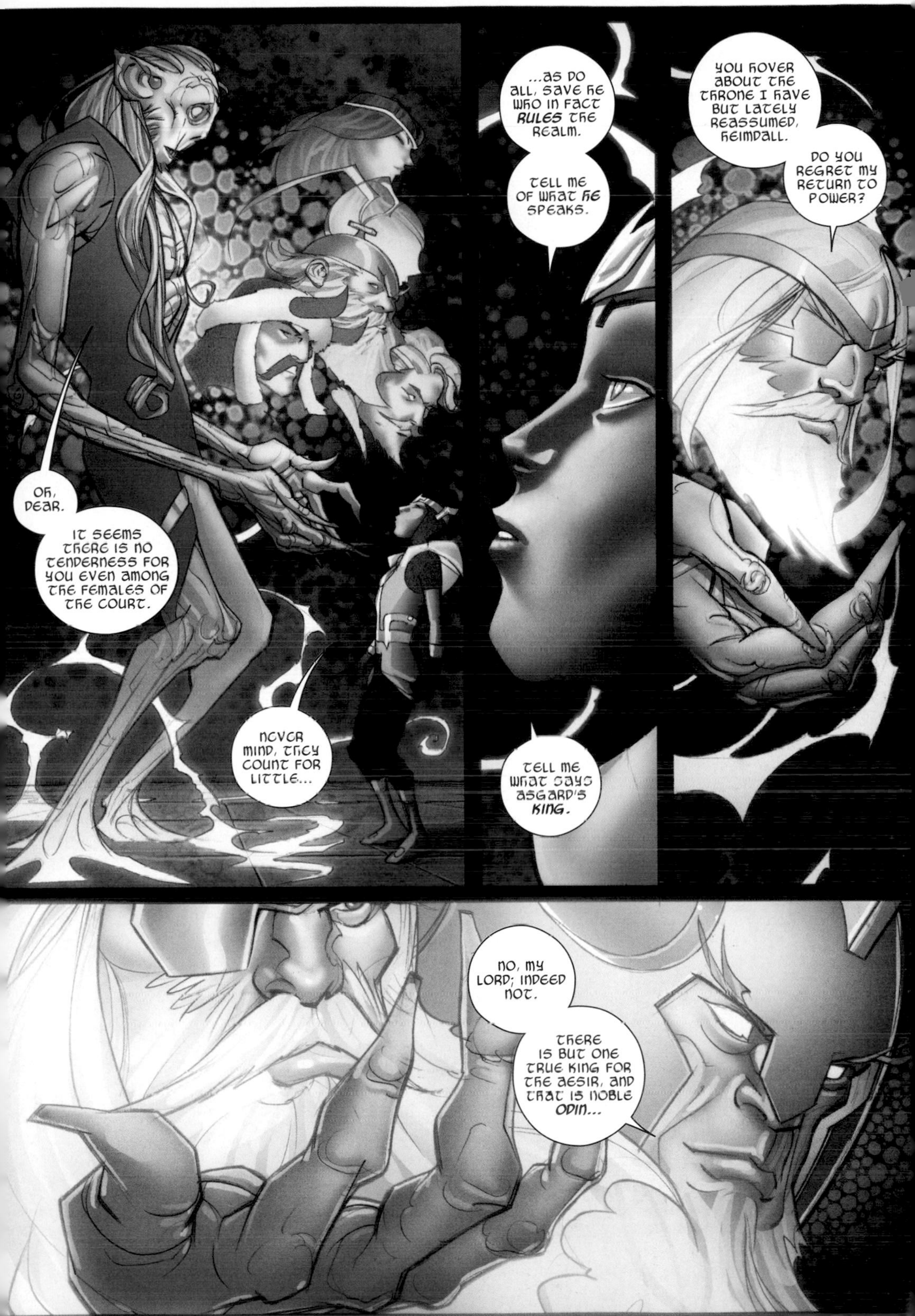

OH, DEAR.
IT SEEMS THERE IS NO TENDERNESS FOR YOU EVEN AMONG THE FEMALES OF THE COURT.
NEVER MIND, THEY COUNT FOR LITTLE...
...AS DO ALL, SAVE HE WHO IN FACT RULES THE REALM.
TELL ME OF WHAT HE SPEAKS.
TELL ME WHAT SAYS ASGARD'S KING.
YOU HOVER ABOUT THE THRONE I HAVE BUT LATELY REASSUMED, HEIMDALL.
DO YOU REGRET MY RETURN TO POWER?
NO, MY LORD; INDEED NOT.
THERE IS BUT ONE TRUE KING FOR THE AESIR, AND THAT IS NOBLE ODIN...

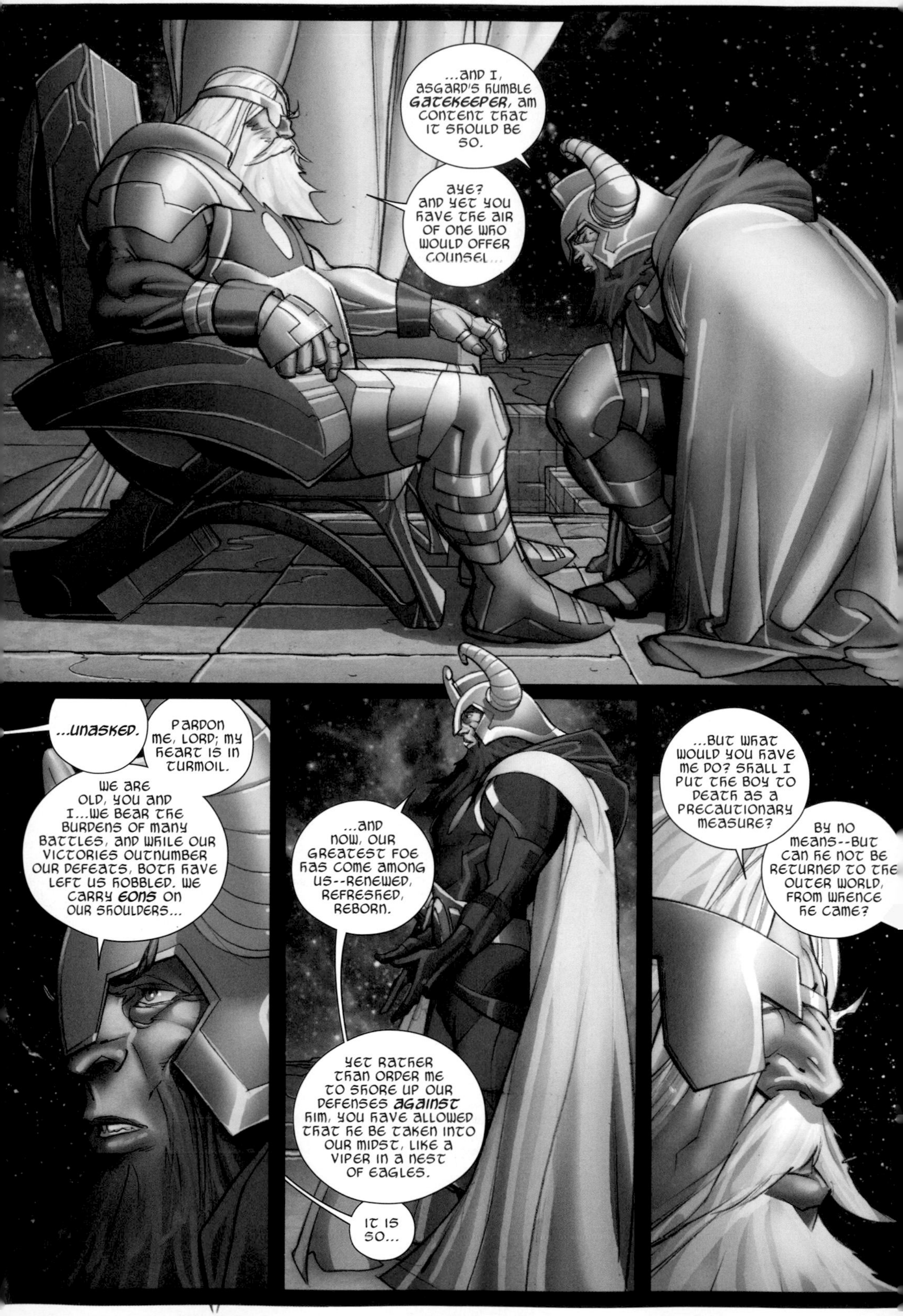
...AND I, ASGARD'S HUMBLE GATEKEEPER, AM CONTENT THAT IT SHOULD BE SO.
AYE? AND YET YOU HAVE THE AIR OF ONE WHO WOULD OFFER COUNSEL...
...UNASKED.
PARDON ME, LORD; MY HEART IS IN TURMOIL.
WE ARE OLD, YOU AND I...WE BEAR THE BURDENS OF MANY BATTLES, AND WHILE OUR VICTORIES OUTNUMBER OUR DEFEATS, BOTH HAVE LEFT US HOBBLED. WE CARRY EONS ON OUR SHOULDERS...
...AND NOW, OUR GREATEST FOE HAS COME AMONG US--RENEWED, REFRESHED, REBORN.
YET RATHER THAN ORDER ME TO SHORE UP OUR DEFENSES AGAINST HIM, YOU HAVE ALLOWED THAT HE BE TAKEN INTO OUR MIDST, LIKE A VIPER IN A NEST OF EAGLES.
IT IS SO...
...BUT WHAT WOULD YOU HAVE ME DO? SHALL I PUT THE BOY TO DEATH AS A PRECAUTIONARY MEASURE?
BY NO MEANS--BUT CAN HE NOT BE RETURNED TO THE OUTER WORLD, FROM WHENCE HE CAME?

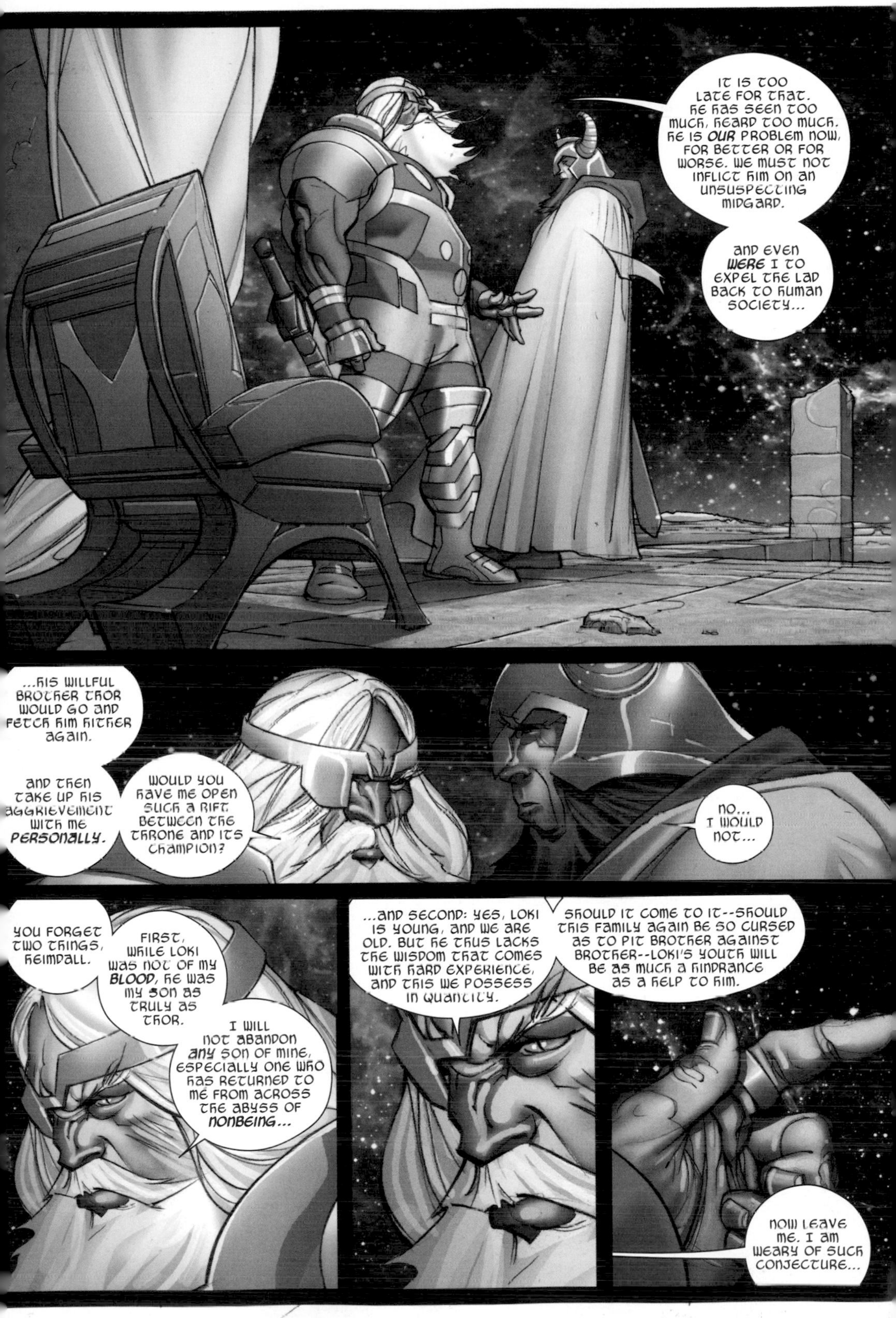
IT IS TOO LATE FOR THAT. HE HAS SEEN TOO MUCH, HEARD TOO MUCH. HE IS **OUR** PROBLEM NOW, FOR BETTER OR FOR WORSE. WE MUST NOT INFLICT HIM ON AN UNSUSPECTING MIDGARD.
AND EVEN **WERE** I TO EXPEL THE LAD BACK TO HUMAN SOCIETY...
...HIS WILLFUL BROTHER THOR WOULD GO AND FETCH HIM HITHER AGAIN.
AND THEN TAKE UP HIS AGGRIEVEMENT WITH ME ***PERSONALLY.***
WOULD YOU HAVE ME OPEN SUCH A RIFT BETWEEN THE THRONE AND ITS CHAMPION?
NO... I WOULD NOT...
YOU FORGET TWO THINGS, HEIMDALL.
FIRST, WHILE LOKI WAS NOT OF MY ***BLOOD,*** HE WAS MY SON AS TRULY AS THOR.
I WILL NOT ABANDON ***ANY*** SON OF MINE, ESPECIALLY ONE WHO HAS RETURNED TO ME FROM ACROSS THE ABYSS OF ***NONBEING...***
...AND SECOND: YES, LOKI IS YOUNG, AND WE ARE OLD. BUT HE THUS LACKS THE WISDOM THAT COMES WITH HARD EXPERIENCE, AND THIS WE POSSESS IN QUANTITY.
SHOULD IT COME TO IT--SHOULD THIS FAMILY AGAIN BE SO CURSED AS TO PIT BROTHER AGAINST BROTHER--LOKI'S YOUTH WILL BE AS MUCH A HINDRANCE AS A HELP TO HIM.
NOW LEAVE ME. I AM WEARY OF SUCH CONJECTURE...

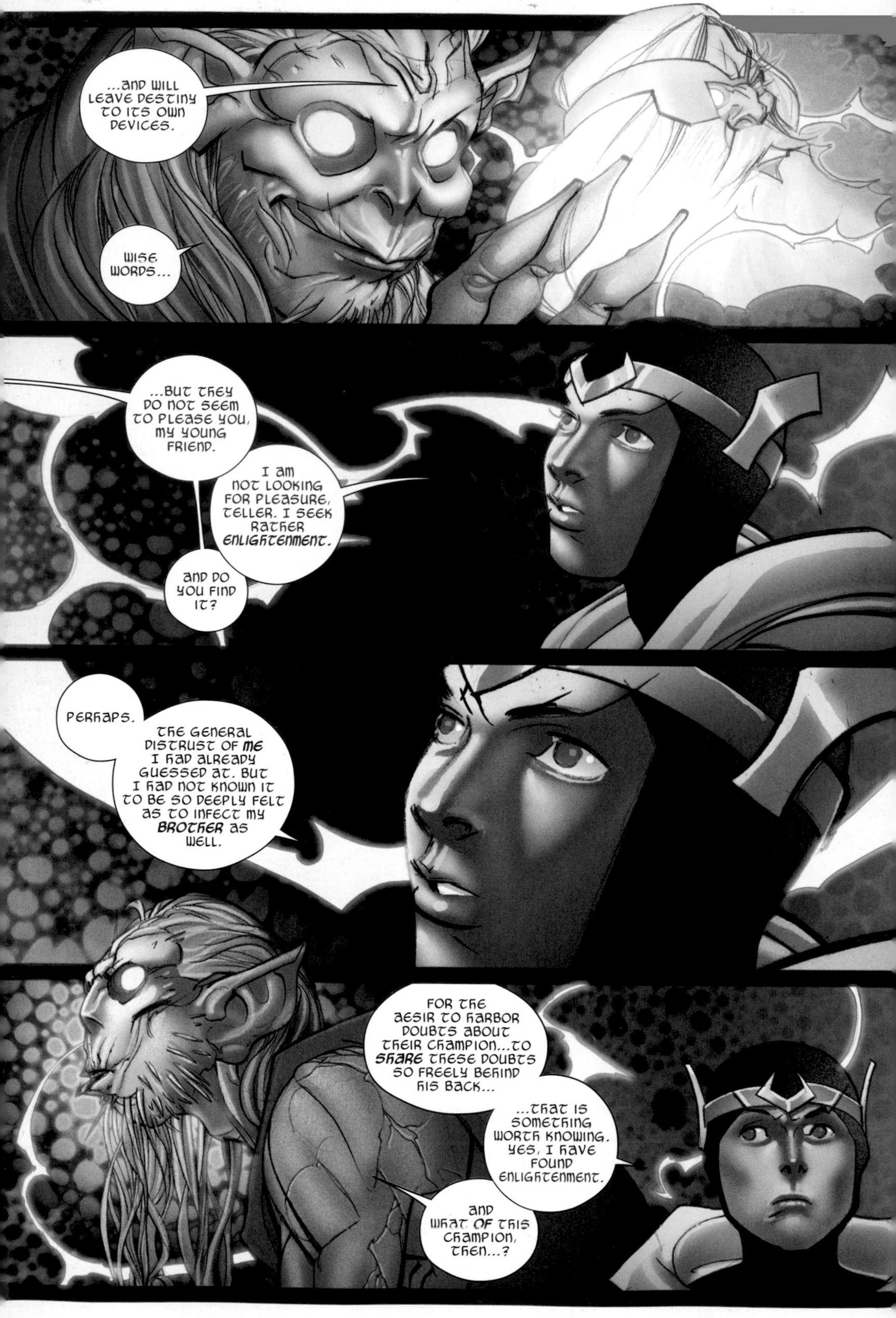
...AND WILL LEAVE DESTINY TO ITS OWN DEVICES.
WISE WORDS...
...BUT THEY DO NOT SEEM TO PLEASE YOU, MY YOUNG FRIEND.
I AM NOT LOOKING FOR PLEASURE, TELLER. I SEEK RATHER ENLIGHTENMENT.
AND DO YOU FIND IT?
PERHAPS.
THE GENERAL DISTRUST OF ME I HAD ALREADY GUESSED AT. BUT I HAD NOT KNOWN IT TO BE SO DEEPLY FELT AS TO INFECT MY BROTHER AS WELL.
FOR THE AESIR TO HARBOR DOUBTS ABOUT THEIR CHAMPION...TO SHARE THESE DOUBTS SO FREELY BEHIND HIS BACK...
...THAT IS SOMETHING WORTH KNOWING. YES, I HAVE FOUND ENLIGHTENMENT.
AND WHAT OF THIS CHAMPION, THEN...?

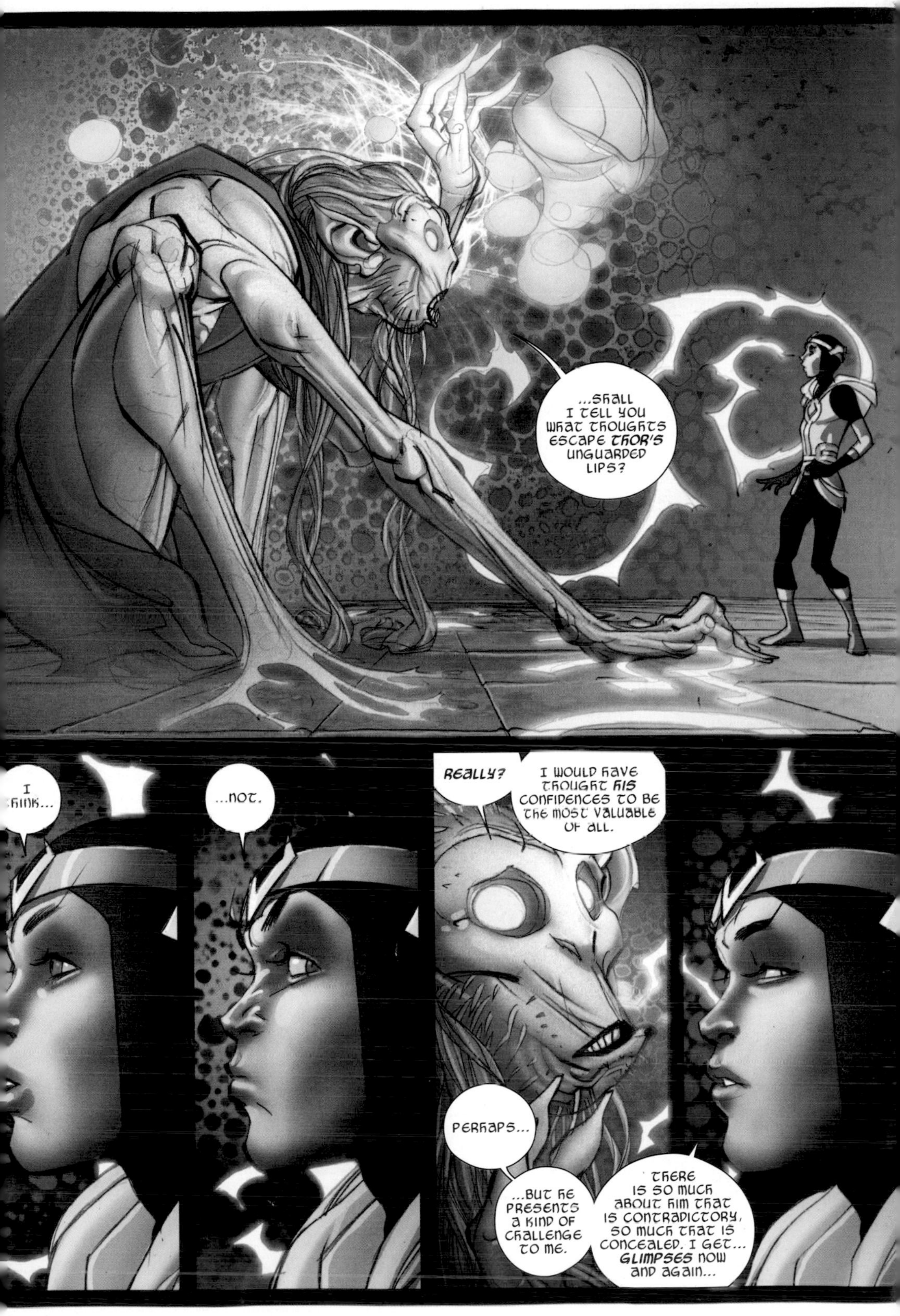
...SHALL I TELL YOU WHAT THOUGHTS ESCAPE THOR'S UNGUARDED LIPS?
I THINK...
...NOT.
REALLY?
I WOULD HAVE THOUGHT HIS CONFIDENCES TO BE THE MOST VALUABLE OF ALL.
PERHAPS...
...BUT HE PRESENTS A KIND OF CHALLENGE TO ME.
THERE IS SO MUCH ABOUT HIM THAT IS CONTRADICTORY, SO MUCH THAT IS CONCEALED. I GET... GLIMPSES NOW AND AGAIN...

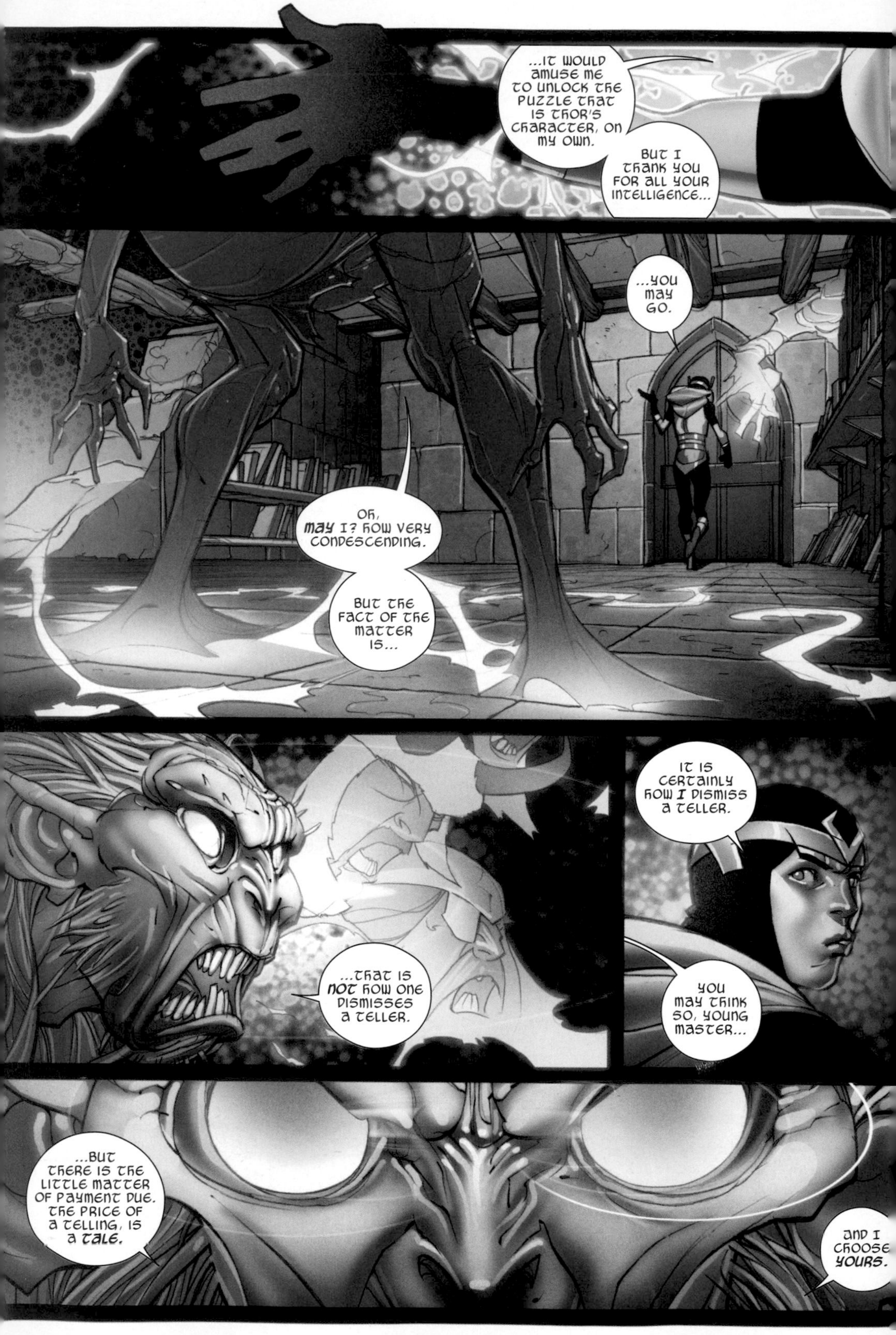

...IT WOULD AMUSE ME TO UNLOCK THE PUZZLE THAT IS THOR'S CHARACTER, ON MY OWN.
BUT I THANK YOU FOR ALL YOUR INTELLIGENCE...
...YOU MAY GO.
OH, MAY I? HOW VERY CONDESCENDING.
BUT THE FACT OF THE MATTER IS...
...THAT IS NOT HOW ONE DISMISSES A TELLER.
IT IS CERTAINLY HOW I DISMISS A TELLER.
YOU MAY THINK SO, YOUNG MASTER...
...BUT THERE IS THE LITTLE MATTER OF PAYMENT DUE. THE PRICE OF A TELLING, IS A TALE.
AND I CHOOSE YOURS.

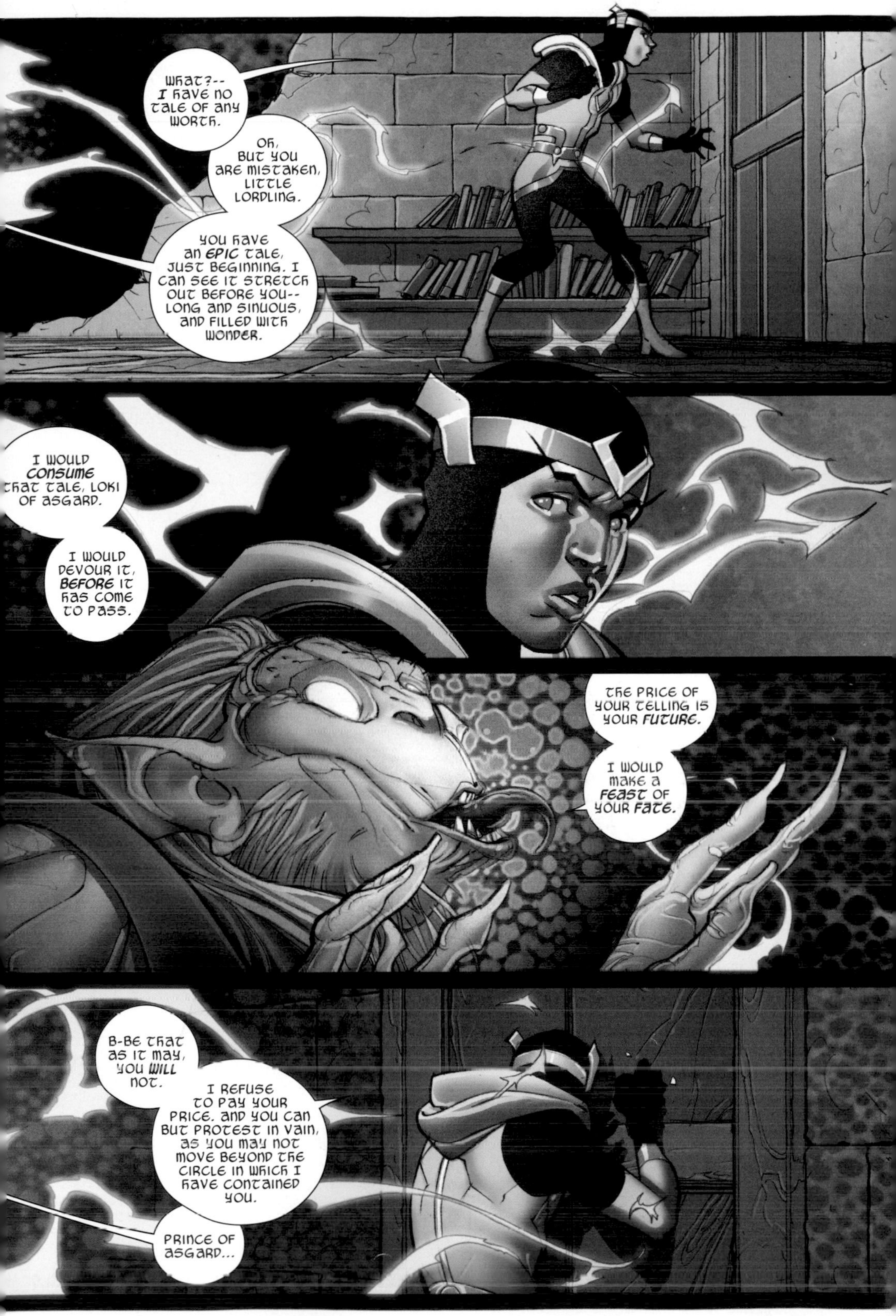
WHAT?--
I HAVE NO TALE OF ANY WORTH.
OH, BUT YOU ARE MISTAKEN, LITTLE LORDLING.
YOU HAVE AN EPIC TALE, JUST BEGINNING. I CAN SEE IT STRETCH OUT BEFORE YOU-- LONG AND SINUOUS, AND FILLED WITH WONDER.
I WOULD CONSUME THAT TALE, LOKI OF ASGARD.
I WOULD DEVOUR IT, BEFORE IT HAS COME TO PASS.
THE PRICE OF YOUR TELLING IS YOUR FUTURE.
I WOULD MAKE A FEAST OF YOUR FATE.
B-BE THAT AS IT MAY, YOU WILL NOT.
I REFUSE TO PAY YOUR PRICE. AND YOU CAN BUT PROTEST IN VAIN, AS YOU MAY NOT MOVE BEYOND THE CIRCLE IN WHICH I HAVE CONTAINED YOU.
PRINCE OF ASGARD...

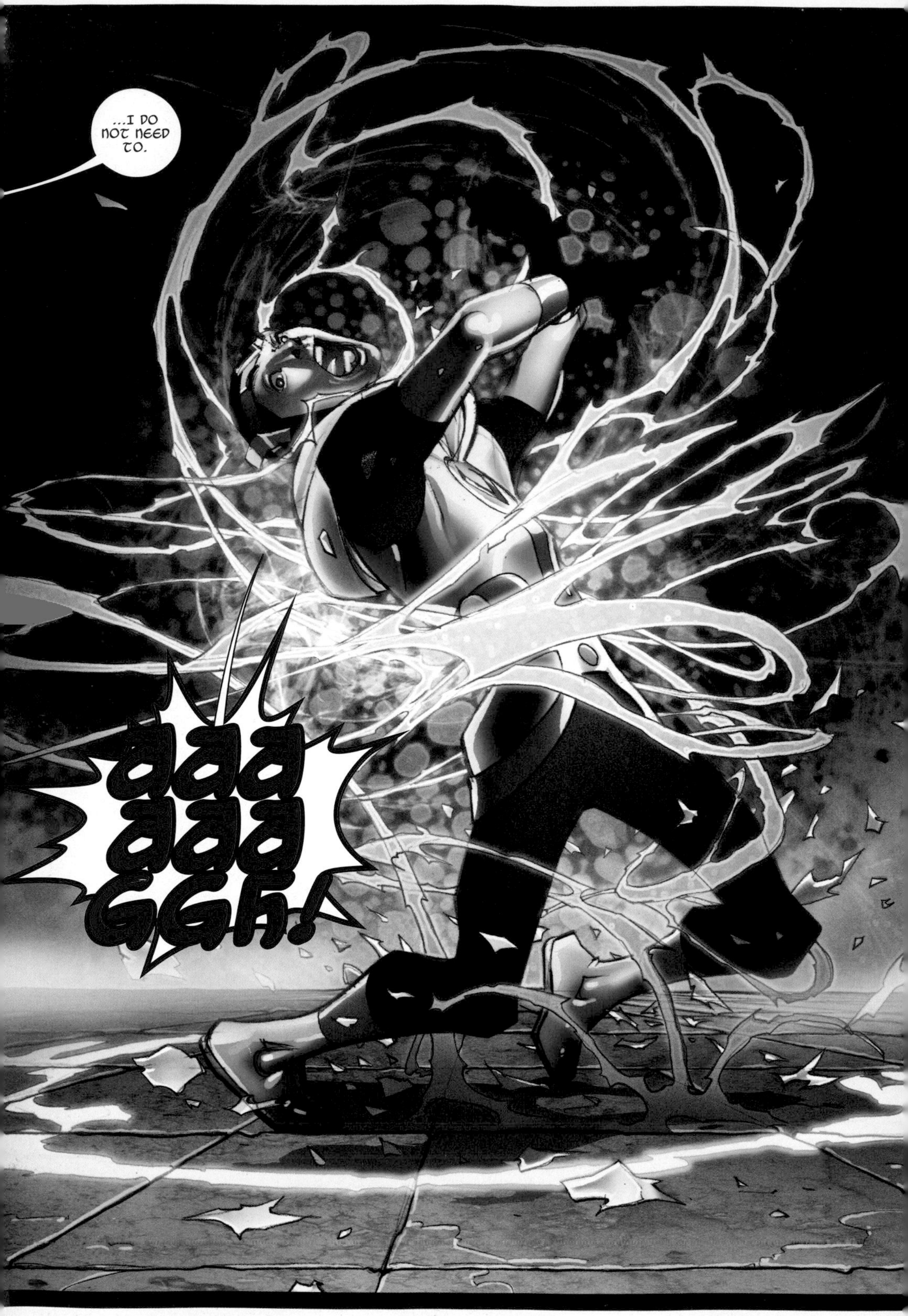
...I DO NOT NEED TO.
AAAAAAGGH!

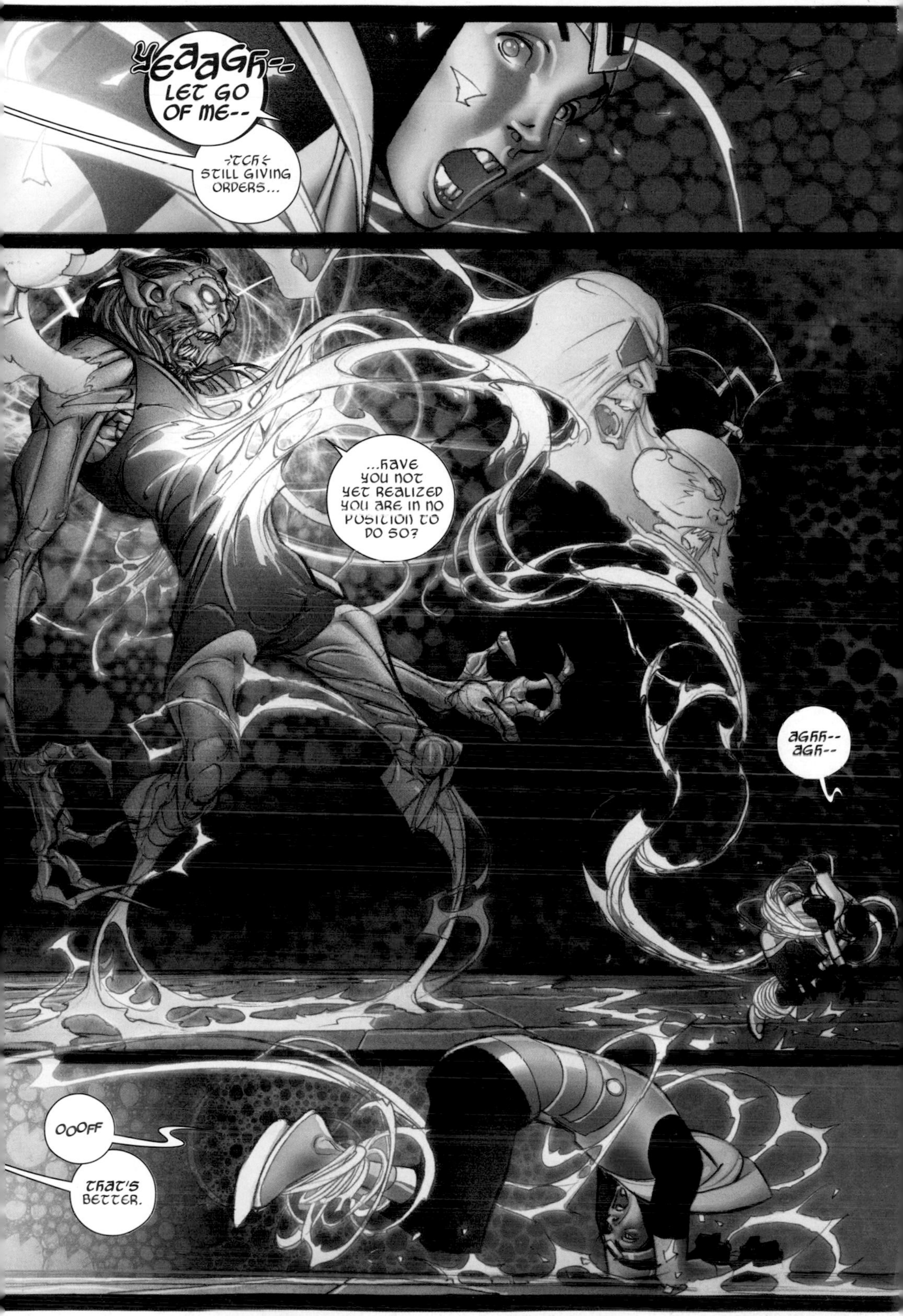
YEAAGH--
LET GO OF ME--
-TCH- STILL GIVING ORDERS...
...HAVE YOU NOT YET REALIZED YOU ARE IN NO POSITION TO DO SO?
AGHH-- AGH--
OOOFF
THAT'S BETTER.

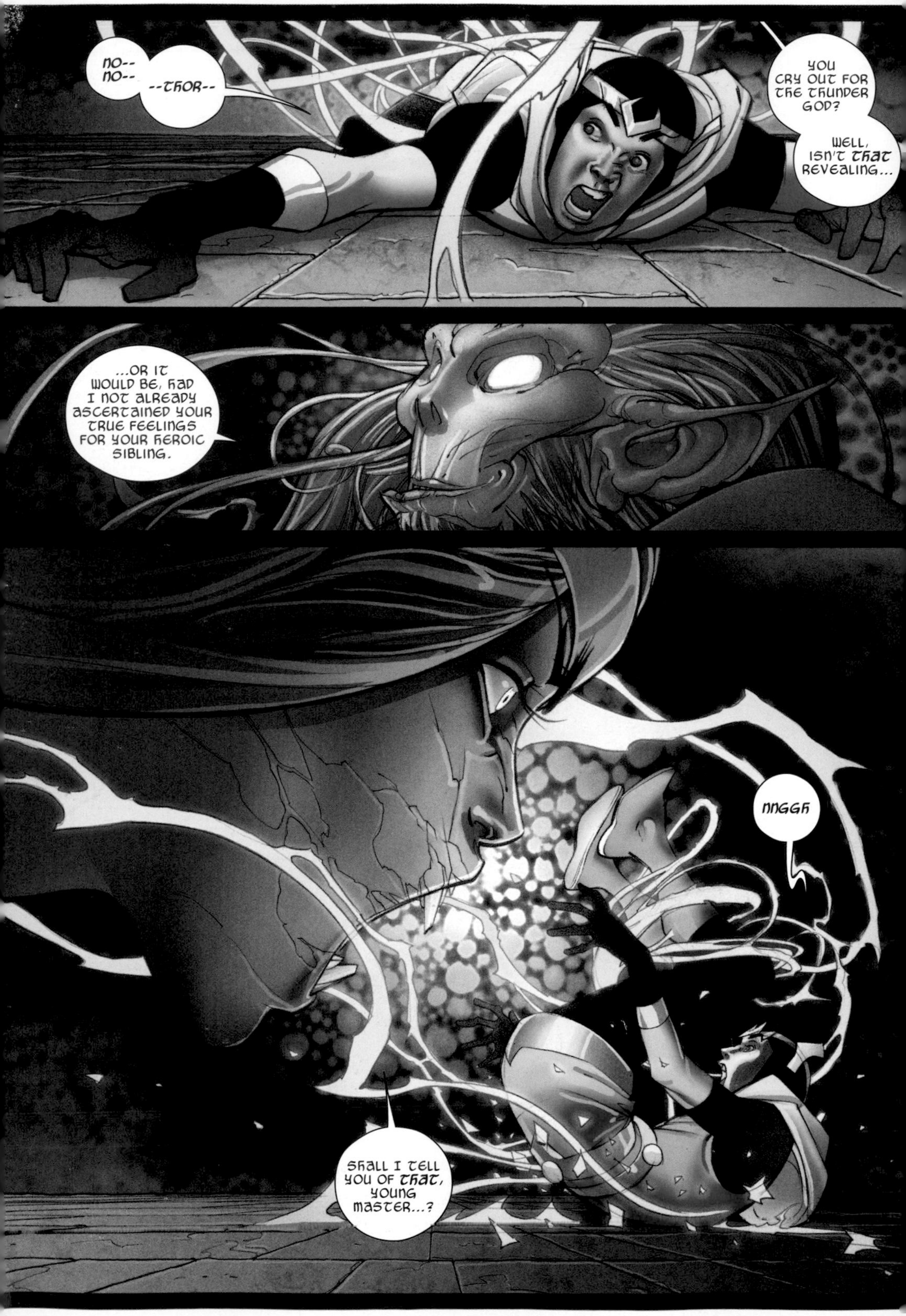
NO-- NO--
--THOR--
YOU CRY OUT FOR THE THUNDER GOD?
WELL, ISN'T THAT REVEALING...
...OR IT WOULD BE, HAD I NOT ALREADY ASCERTAINED YOUR TRUE FEELINGS FOR YOUR HEROIC SIBLING.
NNGGH
SHALL I TELL YOU OF THAT, YOUNG MASTER...?

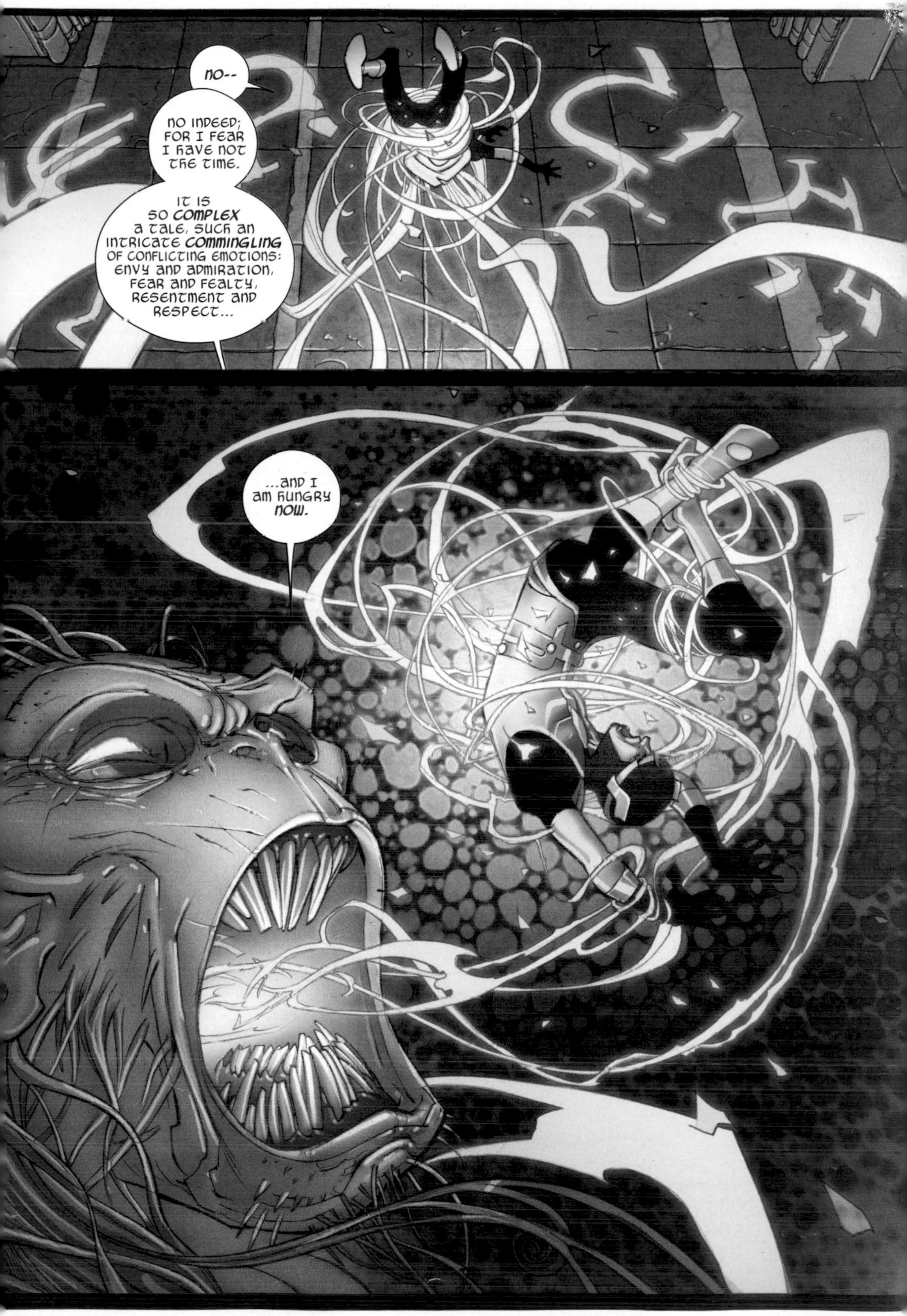
NO--
NO INDEED; FOR I FEAR I HAVE NOT THE TIME.
IT IS SO **COMPLEX** A TALE, SUCH AN INTRICATE **COMMINGLING** OF CONFLICTING EMOTIONS: ENVY AND ADMIRATION, FEAR AND FEALTY, RESENTMENT AND RESPECT...
...AND I AM HUNGRY **NOW.**

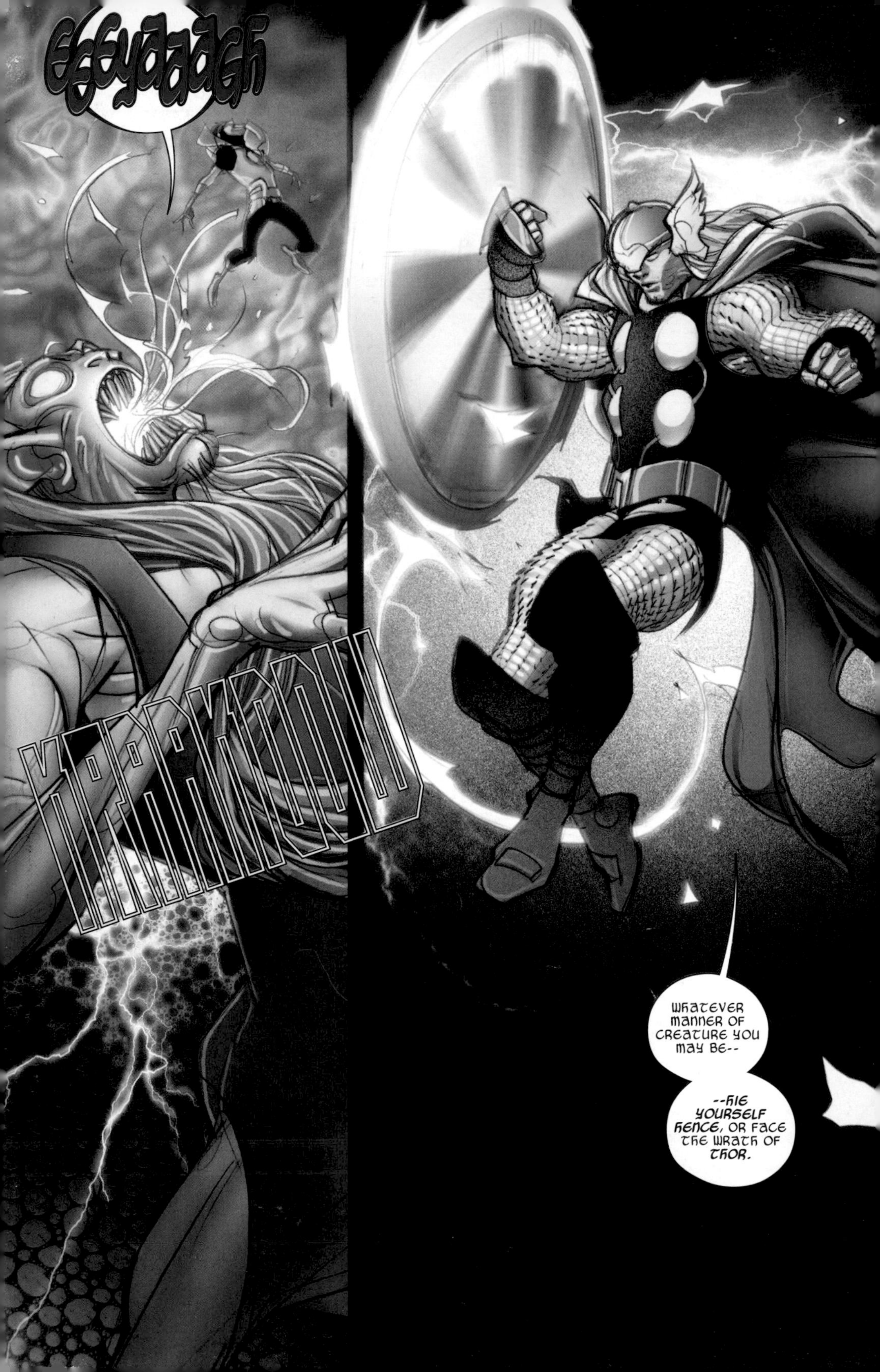
EEEYAAAAGH
KRRAKOOOM
WHATEVER MANNER OF CREATURE YOU MAY BE--
--HIE YOURSELF HENCE, OR FACE THE WRATH OF THOR.

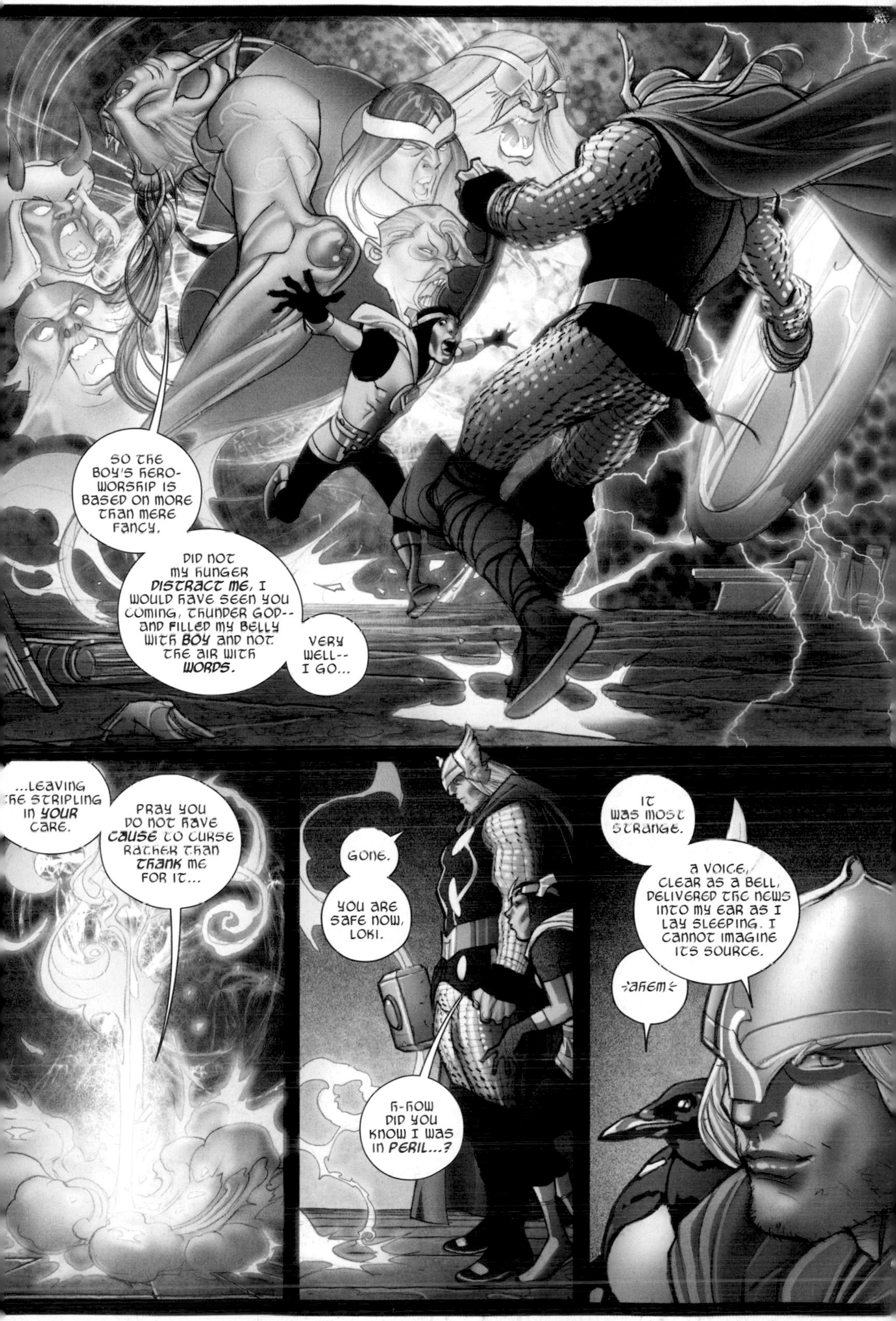
SO THE BOY'S HERO-WORSHIP IS BASED ON MORE THAN MERE FANCY.
DID NOT MY HUNGER DISTRACT ME, I WOULD HAVE SEEN YOU COMING, THUNDER GOD--AND FILLED MY BELLY WITH BOY AND NOT THE AIR WITH WORDS.
VERY WELL--I GO...
...LEAVING THE STRIPLING IN YOUR CARE.
PRAY YOU DO NOT HAVE CAUSE TO CURSE RATHER THAN THANK ME FOR IT...
GONE.
YOU ARE SAFE NOW, LOKI.
H-HOW DID YOU KNOW I WAS IN PERIL...?
IT WAS MOST STRANGE.
A VOICE, CLEAR AS A BELL, DELIVERED THE NEWS INTO MY EAR AS I LAY SLEEPING. I CANNOT IMAGINE ITS SOURCE.
AHEM

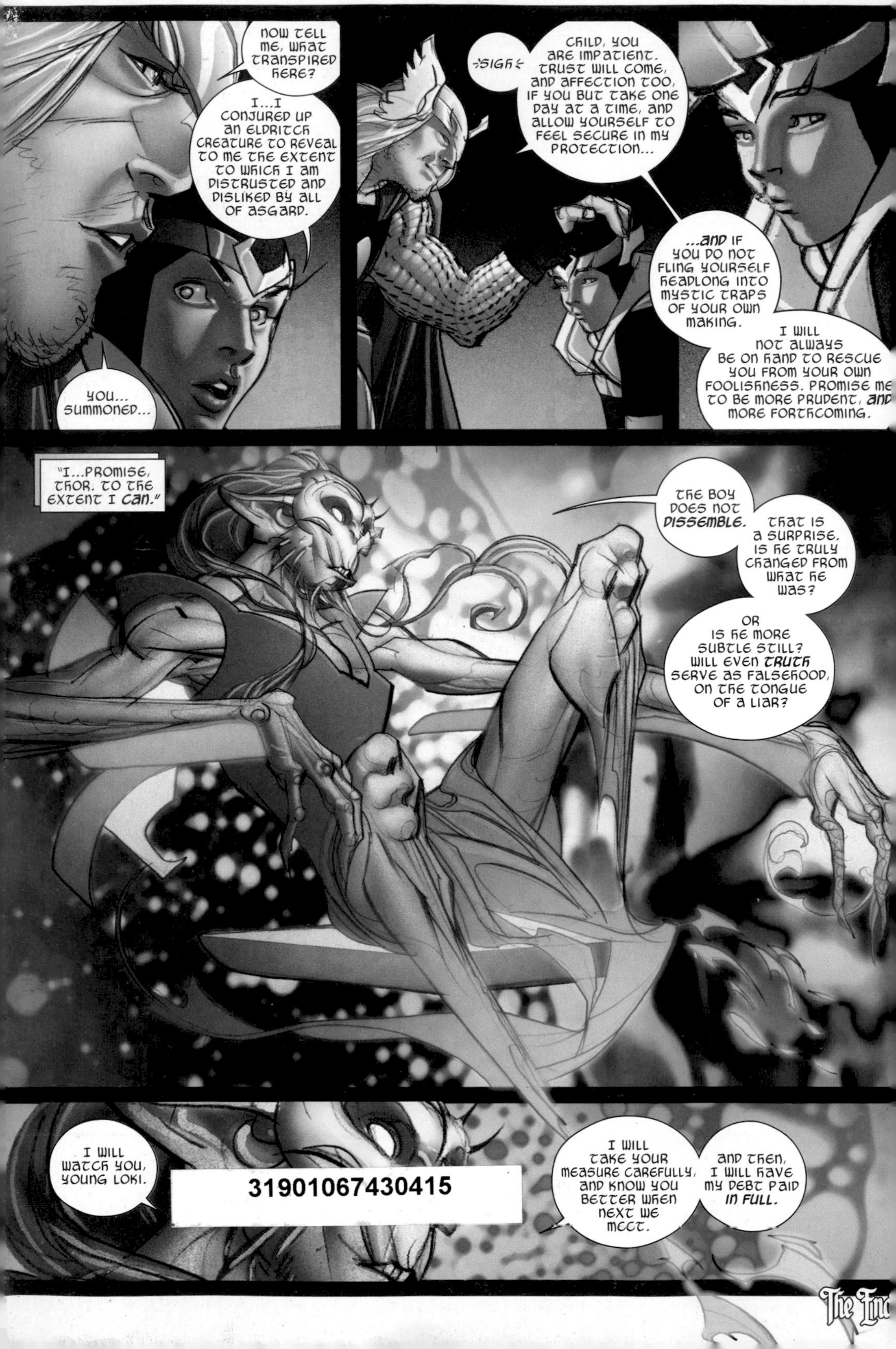
NOW TELL ME, WHAT TRANSPIRED HERE?
I...I CONJURED UP AN ELDRITCH CREATURE TO REVEAL TO ME THE EXTENT TO WHICH I AM DISTRUSTED AND DISLIKED BY ALL OF ASGARD.
YOU... SUMMONED...
=SIGH=
CHILD, YOU ARE IMPATIENT. TRUST WILL COME, AND AFFECTION TOO, IF YOU BUT TAKE ONE DAY AT A TIME, AND ALLOW YOURSELF TO FEEL SECURE IN MY PROTECTION...
...AND IF YOU DO NOT FLING YOURSELF HEADLONG INTO MYSTIC TRAPS OF YOUR OWN MAKING.
I WILL NOT ALWAYS BE ON HAND TO RESCUE YOU FROM YOUR OWN FOOLISHNESS. PROMISE ME TO BE MORE PRUDENT, AND MORE FORTHCOMING.
"I...PROMISE, THOR. TO THE EXTENT I CAN."
THE BOY DOES NOT DISSEMBLE.
THAT IS A SURPRISE. IS HE TRULY CHANGED FROM WHAT HE WAS?
OR IS HE MORE SUBTLE STILL? WILL EVEN TRUTH SERVE AS FALSEHOOD, ON THE TONGUE OF A LIAR?
I WILL WATCH YOU, YOUNG LOKI.
I WILL TAKE YOUR MEASURE CAREFULLY, AND KNOW YOU BETTER WHEN NEXT WE MEET.
AND THEN, I WILL HAVE MY DEBT PAID IN FULL.
The End